TRUST REVEALED

DIANA CASTILLEJA

Purple Sword Publications
Tucson, Arizona

TRUST REVEALED
Copyright © 2014 DIANA CASTILLEJA
ISBN 978-1-61292-123-5
ISBN 10: 161292 123x

Cover Art Designed by Anastasia Rabiyah
Edited by Shoshana Hurwitz and Traci Markou

Published by Purple Sword Publications, LLC
Tucson, Arizona, USA
www.PurpleSword.com

Dedication

I have to acknowledge (or they'll hunt me down and eat my cookies) the Texas Renaissance Festival in Magnolia, Texas as well as the Northern California Renaissance Faire in Hollister, California for the majority of inspiration for this particular book. One was for experience; the other was for the beautiful location. I also want to acknowledge the SCA (Society for Creative Anachronism) for their dedication and wonderful detail of swords, blacksmithing, and the art involved in armory, weaponry, and sword fighting.

Prologue

It was the dream, the merciless attack on his sleep that Morgan couldn't avoid. Unconscious, he craved it, though he silently decried it and its meaning when awake in the light of day. The nameless goddess had plagued Morgan for over a month. A woman of uncommon beauty with eyes the color of the darkest green, like the dew-kissed nettles of a mountain fir tree. Helpless in his sleep, he tossed restlessly as the image of the woman enthralled him, made his blood sing, creating sparks of flaring desire that never really faded.

Within the hidden secrets of his dream, the silken sweep of her lustrous hair seared his thighs. The long, ebony tresses defied their own darkness, glinting a red and gold fire in the full moonlight that sliced into his room, as though there were flames hidden within the heavy fall of midnight. A wild, untamable fire flowed through her, moved with her. Even in a dream, the surging heat lingered under his skin everywhere she caressed and teased him. He tasted it on the air. When she moved, her hair swayed with a scalloped motion, a natural wave that called out to him to touch, to worship. He followed it hungrily, feasting on all of her like a starving man.

This woman had become an enticement, a temptress of unfulfilled desire as he slept. She beckoned to him, calling to him not by name but by a word: *mine*. The one word was all she ever said, a seductive whisper winding over his ear, a sultry sound that made him ache.

His goddess would appear slowly, only her eyes, as if his vision were panning out, opening wider to enjoy her completely. Her features would become more focused until he could see her entire face, smooth, fair skin crowned with the full, rich midnight and fire of her hair. Delicate features, high cheekbones forming to a lush mouth, parted with the promises of passion. She glided over him with a graceful presence as he hungered for the next moments of the dream. After so long, he knew what to expect, and she didn't fail him.

Her body was long and lean, supple, hot flesh, arching and writhing beneath his fingers. She brought the same burning hunger he carried when she invaded his dreams. Long, red nails, sharp but purposely teasing, brought him to a fever pitch, stroking, holding, tempting. The sensations were electric, tightening his skin until it was almost painful to breathe. He never questioned her weight as she rose over him, taking him deep inside of her heat, like a velvet caress. It was a dream, but it was so good. She would cry out, and he would moan in pleasure as they met, the length of her hair singeing the heated skin of his thighs with her rocking movements. He quivered when she raked his stomach with her nails, the green depths of her eyes blazing with possessive ecstasy, daring him, challenging him, demanding he fulfill her every wish.

Morgan would exist in his dream, fall into the in-between world of real and make-believe willingly. Regrets would be for later, when he lacked sleep and the cold stab of deception mocked him. Right now, he imagined every word, every caress, every desire he knew he wanted, desires she wanted from him, that together they wanted to share. Her cries filled his ears, her spine bowed tight, moonlight streaking over luscious breasts like a beautiful offering to the gods. As she rocked over him, he would revel in the fire burning between them. Smooth skin would flow like heaven beneath his fingers, heat roaring up his arms to settle in his chest with every caress.

Until he couldn't take any more. Until he was thrusting his hips, dying to feel her rapture, needing to bury himself inside her silken sheath, wrapped intimately by her. It was an ecstasy in itself.

Morgan awoke, snapping straight up in bed, the images crystal clear in his mind as his body finished what had started in the dream. He groaned thickly as a fierce orgasm ripped over him, his hips clenching in release, unable to stop the result of her nightly visit. Clutching cool sheets in shaking fists, snarling his frustration with a loud echo into the dark room, his head reared back at the cruel misleading vision of passion.

Because he was alone.

The green-eyed vixen who had tortured him for over a month was not there, and she never had been.

He tore the twisted, sweat-soaked sheets away from heated, naked skin, the keen disappointment like a scorching, stabbing knife. It was a heated blade he was familiar with and wished he weren't. Rising, he stalked to the open window of his bedroom, glaring out into the unforgiving Oregon sky.

His heart pounded behind his ribs. If he breathed deeply enough, Morgan could find the scent of her skin, of her heat surrounding him, on him. He gripped the window mercilessly, wanting to throw his head back and howl with rage.

None of this made sense to him. Morgan had never met the woman of his dream. There was no name for the goddess of seduction who came to him with an unerring nightly appearance, a woman who tortured him with an unbelievable body and a voice that spoke of promise and pleasure. With one word, she invited him. With only one word, she seduced him. Every night.

He breathed deeply of the late summer air flowing over him, the cooling breezes of the night's darkness soothing his stressed sex. Gradually, his reaction to the dream faded. His tensed muscles relaxed until he could stand at his full height without animalistic need clawing through him, without the desire to be sated spearing him with a viciousness never experienced in his lifetime. The breeze entering his home through the window danced over cooling skin, teasing shoulder-length, black hair, raising a ghost of the sparking touch he had yet to experience, yet knew too damned well regardless.

Morgan was the last of the four. Roman, Selene, and Brooke were all either married or bonded. He was the lone wolf, remaining single by choice. His head sank forward a fraction, his gaze unfocused as adrenaline continued to resonate through his blood with the hunger of his unsatisfied sexual dreams. He wasn't disappointed that of the women he'd shared an occasional interlude with, none had met his long-term expectations or his deepest desires. What did bother him was this unknown vision who tempted him, drawing him into a world of seduction and sex every night.

Since her initial invasion of his dreams, no other woman had raised even a whisper of attraction or appeal to him. Even the thought of slackening the lust with another woman was impossible. Any woman other than his dream-induced siren left him cold and disinterested.

His seductress was mystery, desire, hunger, and maybe something more he couldn't put a finger on.

Something that called to him almost as strongly as her voice and scent, a hidden element that he knew he recognized but couldn't place. And with just a dream, she could make him experience things he'd never felt wide awake and in bed with a flesh and blood woman.

Needing to escape the torment of his dream, Morgan stepped away from the wide window and called the heat of the change. He craved the rush of blood, the changed tempo of his heart pounding in his ears. He needed the change like a dying man needed forgiveness. The lupine form standing within his room a moment later was as well-known to him as his own human one. Anyone in his family would have recognized him.

He leaped through the window with a fluid movement, sprinting into the starry night. His long, harried gait carried him miles into the woods where he slid to a stop in the complete stillness, breathing heavily, trying to leave his misery behind but knowing he had failed. He let out a long, piercing song, hearing the reverberation of his voice combined with the echo of nature. Gradually, peace calmed his erratic pulse, though he knew it was only temporary, until he slept again.

For nearly thirty-two years, he'd lived a contented life, living and sharing with his family and pack, having never really sought out his own mate, never compelled to be proactive for the one woman who would be his.

Evidently, she was tired of waiting.

Chapter One

Morgan glanced up from his plate to find both his sisters waiting expectantly. "I'm sorry. Did you say something?" he managed to mumble around the mouthful of food that he was chewing. He swallowed the chunk of meat, wincing as it slid to weigh heavily in his ungrateful stomach, and waited for the coming storm.

Selene waved an impatient hand at him. "See? That's what I'm talking about. He's oblivious to the entire world." Facing her brother, she placed a hand across her growing abdomen. "Morgan, you've been in a serious funk for weeks. What's going on?"

He shrugged, setting his fork beside his plate, avoiding his sisters' contemplative gazes, glancing at his dinner with longing instead. Somehow he didn't think he'd get to eat more anytime soon. "I don't know. Nothing I can think of," he replied innocently. Too bad Bram and Mitch had stepped outside for some brotherly bonding when they'd finished dinner. Morgan felt outnumbered two to one.

Selene's gray eyes flashed at him with irritation, her brow taut with her frustration at his answer. Morgan knew that stare. He had the exact same storm-gray eyes, which were just as capable of slicing a person in two. She'd learned it from him. Maybe too well.

"You're lying. You never used to," Selene scolded coolly.

"Maybe he needs a change of scenery," Brooke suggested with a teasing pitch in her voice.

Morgan didn't think so, but he knew her exuberance usually meant something he wasn't going to enjoy. He waited to be proven right.

"Hey, I know! Mitch and I are going south for a couple of weeks. There's a Faire we wanted to wander through before he starts with the fire department here."

"A Faire?" Morgan echoed with a sour burn. Yep, just as he suspected. It might have been his dinner making that ache in his stomach, but he doubted it. "Why a Faire?"

Brooke's whole face lit up with the idea of a new adventure. "Something different. Malls are boring. It's near Sacramento, I think. Autumn is right around the corner. It'll be beautiful with all the trees. Summer days and cooling nights," she told him.

"Call Roman," Morgan suggested with a firm '*no, thank you*' tone.

"Oh, come on," Brooke cajoled with a winsome smile. "It could be fun."

"It could also be the most nauseating time of my life," he muttered. "I don't want to go."

"Morgan," Selene said with a sharp undertone. "You need to do something. You've been haunting the woods like a damned ghost for weeks. You're restless."

"So? Since when has it ever mattered?" He didn't restrain the cold chill in his tone. He didn't need his sisters needling him over this.

Selene drummed her fingers over the table in a rapid rhythm. Morgan knew she was aggravated with him, and he wasn't making it any easier on her. She was seven months pregnant with Bram's child. Except for the annoyed frown she wore between her brows, she glowed with the pregnancy. Both his sisters did. Brooke was barely six weeks pregnant herself.

Brooke and Mitch had returned from Belgium a few days before after a stay with Aunt Jerry. Except for the absence of Roman and Delilah, the quadruplets were at Selene's for dinner. It was a regular gathering, and silently he wished he could have missed this one.

Selene's voice lowered with anxiety for her brother. "You may be the oldest, but we do have the right to worry about you." Her face smoothed, her hidden concerns out in the open. "And right now, I'm worried."

He controlled the black thunder pulsing under the surface of his skin, raking over sensitive nerves, the urge to snap painfully close from too many restless nights spent first enjoying, then suffering, his dream seductress. His sisters weren't the meddling type, but being family, both were more than capable of getting under his skin. He tempered the impulse to a simmer with deliberate effort. His lack of sleep wasn't their problem.

Brooke leaned toward him, pulling his attention in her direction. "I know we're going," she said, her brow twisted with her own worry. "We put a bid on the old Victorian on the outside of town. Mitch wanted to be closer to town than this for his shift duty. We've got a lot of work ahead of us if we get it, and I'm looking into the vacant corner shop off Main to open an apothecary. So this is probably going to be the extent of our travels for at least a year." She rose from her seat at the table and settled a comforting hand on his shoulder, her warmth flowing over his soul. "If you want to go, you're welcome to come with us." She started to leave but peeked at him with a devilish grin. "And before you ask, we're driving." She gave him a telling wink and left them sitting at the table, vanishing through the front door to go outside to join Bram and Mitch.

He snorted. "Well, I would hope she wouldn't transport." Selene didn't twitch a ghost of a smile. He grabbed his napkin from his lap and tossed it on the table, completely giving up on eating more of his steak. "All right, Selene. It's just you and me. Say it."

Selene's fingers stopped tapping on the tabletop abruptly. He wasn't surprised when she didn't hedge her feelings any either.

"Our birthday is right around the corner. You're the last of the pack without a mate. Don't you think you should at least think about it?" she prodded.

"Why?" he objected, though he was able to force his tone to a disinterested level. He planted his elbows on the table, kicking his plate forward from the edge, ignoring the gnaw of hunger in his gut for the moment. Aside from sleep, he hadn't been eating enough either. "First of all, it isn't exactly a requirement. Second, I don't need one." This really wasn't something he wanted to talk about.

She uttered a discouraged sound, stretched, then sat taller on her chair to get comfortable. "If you honestly think that, then you haven't been paying attention. I'll be the first to admit, having to share all of me with someone never appealed to me either. It terrified me, and you know it. None of us knew how to react when we met our mates, but each of us has found theirs. Except you." She paused, narrowing accusing eyes at him. "I would go so far as to say you've avoided it."

Cupping his hands above the table, he wanted to shout *prove it*, but knowing any of his family, they probably could. It was no secret he liked his single status, his privacy. "I haven't thought about it," he said, evading the topic instead. He tossed his head, wanting his sister to leave it alone. He wasn't going to find, nor did he want, a mate. The last thing he needed was a wife, a woman to interrupt his life. He had enough responsibilities without that being added to the long list. "Look, I know you and Brooke are completely happy, and you should be. Roman was lucky."

Her fingers started drumming again, her tone musing. "Ah, so you don't think she's out there, do you?"

His chest tightened, remembered ecstasy striking him blindly. He swallowed, hiding it behind a menacing scowl. No, he knew she was. That was the problem. He didn't want to have anything to do with her. What kind of a woman would torment and torture him nightly the way his unnamed goddess did? What kind of a woman could infiltrate his deepest sleep and awaken him with a craving that left him roaring into the night, every night, with unfulfilled desire and need? Not any woman he wanted to know.

He managed to produce a bored expression instead of letting his frustration leak through. "Selene, whether she is or isn't, the matter isn't relevant. I am perfectly capable of managing myself and my life without the interference. I don't need a wife or a mate. "

"No, I imagine you, of all of us, don't," she conceded. She tried a different tack, weaving sisterly caring through her voice. "Morgan, we all love you, but lately you've become withdrawn. You need to find the source of this problem and face it. If you never find your mate, if that is what is causing your restlessness, then that is an arrangement made by fate, but your black looks and pissy attitude need an adjustment." Her gray eyes flashed at him as her impatience got the better of her. "And if I wasn't pregnant, I'd give it to you!"

He smacked his hands to the table's edge, gripping it, answering her challenge with bared teeth. He shoved the rising snarl down his throat, his jaw burning with the ache of restraint. Selene was pregnant and not up to a brawl, which, though he hated to admit it, was exactly what he wanted, from any of them. A release, any kind.

"Don't pull any punches! Why don't you tell me how you really feel," he almost shouted. A fight would definitely help take the edge off, but not with his sister.

She didn't so much as flinch, merely continued to study him with an imperious stare, one he knew came straight from their mother. He blinked and slouched, the depth of his sigh sounding throughout the small cabin as the fight in him evaporated.

"Aw, hell," he said, rubbing his tired eyeballs with the heels of his palms. "You're right. Damn it! Why do you always have to be the right one?"

"Annoying, isn't it?" she purred with a little gloat thrown in, but in the next instant her voice wrapped around him, filled with a sister's concern for her older brother, soothing as it filled his ears.

In this, some things never changed. The four stood as a pack, supporting each other no matter the need. He knew he loved his brother and sisters, and times like this reminded him why.

Reaching, Selene curled a hand over one of his, giving him anything he needed. "Morgan, whatever this is that's driving you, you can't avoid it. Roman was first with Delilah, and he survived. This last year alone, both Brooke and I have found mates." She lifted her hand from his to stop his popped mouth. "It doesn't count that they're brothers. Brooke was still in Belgium when I first met Mitch through Bram when he came to fly over the fires. That was nothing but chance and coincidence for them, and you know it." She folded her hands lovingly across her abdomen, a thoughtful pause falling between them. "I think Brooke is right. You do need a change of pace, something away from here. You need to go with them."

"I don't want to," he repeated. "It's not my thing. A Faire?" He punctuated his declination with a disinterested flip of his hands. At least he hadn't left finger marks in the wood where he'd gripped it a moment before. His frustration was getting to him. Not a good thing.

"Something new and different. That's what it means to make a change." She rose carefully from her chair, albeit with a little waddle. "Now, finish if you want. I'm going outside." She took two steps and changed direction. "After I pee," she muttered.

His lips twitched at her groused tone. Pregnancy was difficult in different ways, but Selene was holding up. He was honestly thrilled for the lives and loves both his sisters had found. He couldn't fault her for wanting the same for him. Morgan knew Selene had never been happier, married to Bram. He was the perfect complement to his logical, steadfast sister. Morgan was thankful both his sisters had found mates who appreciated their specialness as much as Morgan and Roman did. And that didn't take into account the family secret they now protected with their very lives. Both men, and even Delilah, Roman's wife, were spectacular beings in Morgan's book.

When the door clicked around the corner, he let his head sink to the top of his chair to stare aimlessly upward. Selene was right. Whatever was going on, he was going to have to face it. Whether it had something to do with the green-eyed vixen of his dreams he couldn't say, but he'd bet his entire house on it.

The ethereal beauty still visited him nightly, with the same arousing sensations, the same carnal incompletion when he awoke. Could insanity be induced by subliminal sexual torture? He sighed, the wall of frustration swelling and crashing over him with an overwhelming punch that reverberated through his chest until it settled below his waist with a known ache he couldn't cure. Morgan had tried, with zero pleasurable results.

"Who are you?" he whispered to no one as he blocked out the world, piercing the cloud of desire fogging him with a determined shock of reality. "I don't need you." He lifted his arms and cupped behind his head with his palms. "I don't need anyone."

When he heard the bathroom door open a moment later, he stood to clear the table. No sense in being caught talking to himself. He smiled at Selene and saw affection in her return smile as she passed to join the others on the front porch. She wouldn't stay mad with him. None of them could, not with another sibling. They were too close. They had survived so much together, all of them. They were all connected, standing as one. He placed the plates on the counter, bracing his hands on the edge, collecting himself before joining the others.

So he didn't have any choice. Whatever waited for him wasn't here. It was out there, somewhere. He doubted anything would come of this trip with his sister and brother-in-law, but it would get him away from everything else for a while, and Selene would quit breathing down his neck. Maybe if he simply left home, the dreams wouldn't follow him. He doubted that too, but he could hope.

Morgan cut off a chunk of his uneaten steak before he walked out to join the others in the cool night. Two happy couples and himself. It never bothered him personally that his brother and sisters had found their mates. He was the oldest, even if by only minutes. The gap of time didn't matter to him. Morgan wouldn't turn his back on the pack for anything or anyone. He wouldn't call himself alpha — it wasn't realistic considering their birth, but he wouldn't ignore his responsibility either, especially now that they all were mated and with child. Delilah and Roman were the first with his nephew, Adrian, and now his sisters were expecting. Family was all the Aiza's had. There were no other shifters they knew of, except for their eccentric aunt, but she was a wolf of a different color. Aunt Jerry was also perfectly capable of handling anything short of Hell on her own. His vow to protect them all would never waver regardless.

He tore off a bite with his sharp teeth and chewed as Brooke tossed colored bubbles of glowing light into the air with a flick of her hand. About the size of large oranges, they bounced and swung over the porch.

"Those are beautiful," Selene said with wonder as the spheres spread colored light over everything.

"Wait, I've been working on this one," Brooke told her with a grin, then waved her hand through the air.

"Oh my God! Is that...polka dots?" Selene cried through a childish laugh at the impromptu show.

"Yep," Brooke said with a satisfied smile. "Took me over a week to get it right."

"That's really good," Bram said, admiration rumbling in his deeper voice.

"Hey, honey, show them the other one," Mitch urged with a nudge.

Brooke ducked her head. "Oh, I couldn't. It's not perfect." Mitch tenderly coaxed and prodded her until she blushed.

"Oh, all right. Just remember, it's not quite right," she warned. Mitch gave her room and winked at Morgan. Mitch was a horrible influence on his sister, but in a good way. He was always pushing her to improve her casting and spell ability.

When the bubble formed and began to develop indents and points, Morgan paused for the beauty of the creation. "You can make shapes?" he asked in quiet surprise. He couldn't recall anyone in the family with that talent.

"I'm learning them as I go along," she answered him as she moved her hands with delicate, concentrated motions, like a sculptor, as she cut and patted the air.

"Wow." Morgan took in a sharp breath. "That's gorgeous."

"I know," Mitch agreed. "I'm so proud of her." He followed his wife's hands as she finished the shape.

Brooke stretched her arms, sliding her palms over the shape that was now near its full size, making the last motions midair. "That's it. I got the idea from Mitch's carvings." She leaned into her mate's chest, her grip clasped around her bent knees as she tucked into his embrace.

"That is truly remarkable," Selene whispered, as awestruck as the rest of the group.

Morgan gaped for a silent moment at the black-hued wolf head hovering above the ground. A chill snaked around his spine. "Is it one of us?" he asked, swallowing once when he sounded rough. He almost prayed it was. Studying it closer, there was something about it...something that he should know, should recognize. The unwelcome chill on his spine refused to go away.

"No, not really. Why? Do you think it looks like one of us?" Brooke shifted to study him from her seat.

Morgan rolled his head on his neck, an odd sensation settling over him staring at the floating image. He had seen that wolf...in his dreams...maybe.

"No. But it seems familiar somehow." He shook himself free of the recognition notion and released a small grunt of dismissal. "Probably nothing." Catching his sister's attention, he told the couple, "By the way, I'll go. If you still want a grumpy older brother along for a wet blanket." He didn't miss Selene's satisfied smile before she managed to tuck her face away from him against Bram's supporting arm. Inside, he saluted her for a battle well fought and well won.

Mitch smiled. "Cool! We asked Selene and Bram too, but she's too far along for a long road trip now." Mitch kissed Brooke's temple. "We've got a few months before this one gets that way."

For the first time, a pain hit Morgan close to his heart. His day had been long and his nights too exhausting to want to think about it, or why. He attempted a smile in answer, ignoring the twinge instead. It was probably closer to a grimace, but it was dark outside now. "And Roman?"

"When we called, he said they were flying to Japan for a week to visit," Brooke said.

"Oh, I completely forgot," Selene murmured. She offered an apologetic shrug to the group. "Pregnancy amnesia." Bram chuckled, holding her closer.

"Well, time to kill the lights," Brooke joked, snapping her fingers. The floating balls popped with little bursts, like cascading fireworks.

"You're such a kid," Morgan teased her.

"Yeah, so sue me," she said, her lilting laugh filling the air.

Morgan popped the last of his dinner into his mouth, grinning easily at her antics. "Well, I'm heading home. Thanks for the food." He stopped on the steps and glanced back at them. "When are you guys heading out?"

"Saturday morning, early," Brooke said. "It's a good drive, but we can be there by the opening of the gates."

"I'll be here." He crossed the gap to his truck, waving to them when he turned it around and headed for the bridge out of the cabin's clearing. His last passing thought as he left his sisters behind was that maybe tonight, he would sleep. He wasn't holding his breath to find out.

* * * *

They arrived at the Faire grounds not long after the gates opened and joined the milling crowds as they perused the booths and activities. There were strolling minstrels, town criers, jugglers and jesters, and of course, Faire-attending guests in costume — all kinds. Morgan could only shake his head when a Jedi passed him going the other way. Scents and sounds swarmed over him — smoked meat, perfumes, herbs, shrieks of laughter, the sound of metal being pounded. The entire grounds were in constant motion as they ambled through them.

Morgan resisted the urge to roll his eyes when a woman with the thrusting bosom of the era tried to grab his attention and body parts a scarce ten minutes inside the grounds. She spoke with an old English accent as fake as her red hair, but she was enjoying herself. She eventually left for better game when he proved too difficult.

"See? I told you," he grumbled into Brooke's ear. "Nonsense." He was not in the mood to play along. He'd spent another restless night with his nighttime seductress, and sleep wasn't kind to him. Unable to fight it, he'd slept on the drive. The continued interruption of his nights was making him more and more irritable.

Brooke glowered at him in exasperation. "Try to have some fun. You don't have to jump in feet first, but Selene is right. You need to shake it up."

Morgan ranted under his breath and kept pace with the other two who were obviously enjoying the frivolity of the activity a hell of a lot more than he was, pointing and exclaiming over every little detail.

"Hear ye! Hear ye! Lord Duncan is in need o' a swordsman o' uncommon ability." The shout came from ahead of them as the crier marched the road winding through the specialty booths, reading from a long scroll spread between his hands as he paced his words. "A swordsman o' uncommon valor and strength. Ist there a man 'ere today who can provide 'is Lordship with fair entertainment?"

With a sinking feeling, Morgan knew what was coming and dug in his heels. Hard.

"Right here!" Brooke shouted. "He'll do it!"

Morgan glared over his shoulder and cursed plainly enough for her to hear him, discovering her arm raised and a devilish gleam dancing in her dark eyes.

"Brooke! Behave yourself! I don't know a thing about a broadsword." He bared his teeth at her when she refused to acknowledge his reticence. For a bare second, he hated his sister.

"How hard can it be? You're a guest. They'll be gentle with you, I'm sure," she informed him. She stood on her toes, waving to get the crier's attention. "Over here!"

"Brooke!" He ground out her name through clenched teeth. She continued to ignore him. Running wasn't an option. They'd drawn a crowd.

"I say, sir, are ye willing to agree to Lord Duncan's challenge?" The crier and about a dozen people closed in to listen.

"I'll do it if you will," Mitch egged him. Morgan groaned.

"I'm going to kill the both of you," he threatened for their ears only. He was too damned tired to play knight. Brooke fluttered her lashes up at him in all feigned innocence, and Mitch laughed. Morgan stopped arguing and made a shallow nod, wishing he was anywhere else.

The crier faced the crowd and announced with lifted hands, "Lord Duncan's search is completed! We 'ave not one, but two worthy opponents for 'is Lordship's battle training for this afternoon."

The crowd cheered, and Morgan wanted to snarl at all of them.

"Great! An entire day down the drain," Morgan growled.

"Quit your bitching," Brooke said. "How much more different can you get than this?"

He didn't bother to grace her with an answer as he fell into step behind the crier with his brother-in-law. They followed the man in dark green tights and an emblazoned red tunic to the roped-off areas of the Faire grounds. The oversized feather in his gold trimmed velvet hat flounced with his movements.

"We will first make thy introduction to Lord Duncan, the Master of Swords, for this grand tournament and then begin thy training."

"Training? Can't he just beat me up and get it over with?"

The man in costume gave Morgan an amused smirk and kept walking. A few minutes later they stood outside a large blue canvas tent with a pennant of a broadsword held in a bird's claw waving from a pole raised from the supports of the tent.

Morgan's exasperation hit a new level as they announced him and Mitch, but he managed to not say it out loud. The crier in the green L'eggs let him pass through as he held the opening wide.

"My pleasure," boomed the bass voice from the corner of the tent. "Gentlemen, I thank thee for thy eager," he drawled with a rolling chuckle, "participation in our fun and games."

"Pressed into service," Morgan muttered. "But I'm here."

Lord Duncan's brow lifted. "Was he pressed into service?" He stepped before them, clasping his hands behind his back. He was a large man, almost as tall as Roman and as big across as Mitch.

"By his sister," Mitch said, biting off a laughing grin and failing. Morgan wanted to run a fist into him *and* his grin.

"Ah, for the honor of a lady," Lord Duncan mused.

"No. She is my wife," Mitch said instantly, standing taller, his attention pinned on the man before them.

Lord Duncan summed them up, humor making his body shake with suppressed laughter. "Impressive, the pair of ye. Honor and loyalty roll from ye both. Ye shall be worthy in the ring this afternoon. Have either of thou ever fought with steel?" They both shook their heads. "Good, I will not have to correct stupidly learned skills." He stepped to the side and shouted. "Cale! Find armor and two swords. Give them a run. Let us see how ye fare." Duncan did a once-over on Mitch. "I want to see thee first at arms." Then he turned his focus to Morgan. "Thee," he said on a dragged-out breath. "Thee have a fire. I can see it in thine gaze. Thee have an anger. This is not a blood match."

Morgan's lip lifted at the assessment, making the leap to guess at what the man meant. "It won't be." But he could dream. Now, *that* kind of fight he was more than willing to jump into.

Both Mitch and Morgan complied when Cale called for them. The pair were helped out of their shirts, replaced with soft undershirts and padding, which was then topped with leather chest armor and buckles, while gauntlets covered their hands and wrists.

"Is all of this necessary?" Morgan said.

"Morgan, I swear you are whiny today," Mitch told him. "Go with it for once. You're fine; no one is going to get hurt, and the last time I checked, no one is after us."

Morgan pictured his hands around Brooke's throat as a buckle on his shoulder was tugged tight. He glared at Mitch, who simply offered his back to ignore him. "Not yet." He cursed as another buckle was yanked and locked. He didn't pay attention to their new squire's confusion.

Morgan followed Mitch and Cale to the plain, dirt, baled-off area set apart with ropes and stakes, waiting as Mitch got a run-down on broadsword fighting.

"Thine friend has strength," Lord Duncan said casually, leaning on the hilt of a long sword with a foot propped on a hay bale to hold his weight. He followed the fighting pair closely.

"He's a firefighter. He has to be strong." A strong clash of steel screamed through the air. The ring of steel vibrated through him. It held a savory echo. It felt almost...familiar. He stood a little straighter, watching more attentively as the pair circled each other in front of him. Mitch's swings were untutored but more than sufficient to make a person ache under the power of the blow.

"What are you?"

"I'm with the forestry division of the North Pacific Rim Environmental Protection Agency. A Ranger." The silence stretched between them. Morgan assumed it was because Mitch was kicking Cale's ass, but it wasn't.

"Just remember, this is for the crowd's entertainment, and yours, hopefully. We don't fight to the death." Duncan's lowered voice held no remnants of his lord's accented character.

Morgan wanted to laugh at the assumption. "I've never killed." *Not on two feet.*

Lord Duncan twitched his dark blond, bearded head as if in answer to his words, and Morgan saw a flickering shadow of doubt in the other man. "I don't believe you." Duncan returned his attention to the fighting pair. "Halt!"

Mitch was drenched in sweat and wore a huge grin. "Damn, that's fun!" he crowed, tugging and lifting the helmet they had loaned him for the practice run. He jogged up to the bales and slipped under the rope divider, clapping Morgan soundly. "You are so going to love this."

"Kiss my ass," he muttered as he stepped forward, sliding on an identical helmet, a black steel face guard that covered his face to his neck.

Morgan took the first position Cale showed him and copied the fluid motions, rising and falling with the weighty blade. The ear-splitting clash of steel reverberated through his palms, and his heart jumped like a defibrillator had jolted him clear through.

"Again," Cale instructed. Morgan steadied his hands and prepared for the next swing.

Five minutes later, halt was called, except when Cale jumped to leave the ring, Morgan faced Lord Duncan. "I want to test thee myself. I may take thee into the knights as well as you fight!"

"Hey, I'm only here for the weekend," he interjected, taken by surprise as the larger man attacked.

"Rise and defend, sir!" came Lord Duncan's war cry and suddenly, Morgan was rushed by the steeled edge of Duncan's long sword.

* * * *

N'Réa heard the grunts and the sting of steel through the buzz of the grounds when she neared Duncan's World and wondered who Duncan had cornered. She needed to return to her tent. The longer she was out of her tent investigating the grounds, the more money she lost, but the sound of clashing steel and the loud, rumbled curses captured her attention.

"Foul smelling beast of Hell!" Duncan roared before another crash jangled like a vicious ringing gong ahead.

Disbelieving eyes snapped open in surprise. Oh, she had to know who he was fighting! Duncan never swore outside of the tourneys!

"Beast of Hell!" The voice was enraged. "They wouldn't spare you a glance!"

A cheer rose from the crowd as steel colliding against steel shrieked through the midmorning air. Wedging herself a spot between bodies in the gawking crowd, she glimpsed a peek of a thick black mane from beneath the collar of a steel combat helmet and a solid body as the two met and sparred in the center of the practice ring.

"Who is that? He's not from Duncan's camp," she wondered aloud.

A man in training leathers holding a petite blonde in his arms made room as she neared. "No, he's my brother," she said with a vivacious grin. "And he's giving Lord Duncan a run for his money."

"I'll say," she said with a wince as steel rapped and vibrated. "Duncan never swears in practice."

"Swine son!" Duncan shouted in a brusque roar, drawing his full height over his opponent.

"At least I had a mother!" the man in the training leathers shouted without a second's hesitation. The crowd gasped, then cheered as they met and their swords slid together.

They were magnificent, the pair sparring and blocking, the clash and ring of steel reverberating with a depth of real effort. He was in leathers, but he wasn't fighting to train. He fought with a heat she'd never seen in training. N'Réa winced as Duncan cursed vividly. She'd seen a lot of his duels over the years and knew his vocabulary was well rounded. Calling his opponent a puny, ill-breeding foot-licker only enraged the man in leathers more. Duncan met his swing with an oath and pushed with straining effort until N'Réa was sure a sword would snap.

In craned fascination, she followed as they circled. N'Réa didn't recognize his opponent with the wall of bodies in front of her and the safety of the armor, but a few seconds later, it ceased to matter. It was over when Duncan literally yanked the sword out of the other man's grip. The crowd erupted and surged forward. N'Réa managed to inch toward the outer edge of the crowd, not wanting to get trapped in the congratulatory mass.

Lord Duncan's harsh-breathing voice overrode the crowd's excitement. "Here I test the opponent of the day and have found the most worthy Sir Morgan! Arise, honorary knight, and welcome to the Kingdom!"

Her mouth fell open. He knighted him on the spot! Good Lord, he must be incredible.

The crowd swarmed the pair as they moved to congratulate them on a good duel. Oh, crap! How long had she been standing there listening and trying to see? She needed to get to her tent. She picked up her skirts and fled to the aisles of booths and tents.

When she finally sat in her chair and fluffed her skirts, her hands were shaking, and she couldn't place why.

Chapter Two

Morgan's lungs heaved like a bellows, sweat pouring from every cell. He collapsed to his knees when the sword was ripped from his grasp. He tore off the helmet, desperate to breathe. "A knight?" He shook his head in a daze, opening his mouth to protest when he snapped up, the entire world vanishing in an instant.

She was there! His heart began to race erratically for a completely different reason. It couldn't be, but he knew it was her, instantly. He wasn't mistaken. Her scent floated to him, infiltrated his senses, as his eyes closed and his mind cleared of everything else. Summer rain. It was the only thing he could compare her to. Humid days cooled beneath the thunderous onslaught of a summer storm. Morgan imagined the thin mist of the water hanging in the air, feeling it moisten his skin, no matter how dry the air surrounding him actually was. That was her, completely. After so many excruciating nights tortured by her beauty, by her desire, he couldn't mistake it.

For a span of seconds, nothing mattered, not the crowd, the noise, the man before him, nothing except the faint trail of her on the wind. He took another breath and could taste her on his tongue. The scent was real. This was not a dream. She was flesh and blood. Somewhere in the last few minutes, his dream goddess had stood less than ten feet away. Morgan searched the crowd but couldn't distinguish one face from another. He vaguely recognized the tip of a sword as it tapped his shoulders.

A meaty hand thrust in front of his face disrupted his efforts to find the elusive source of summer rain. "Arise, Sir Knight."

He mumbled something unintelligible, fighting to breathe while hefting himself up.

"Take a bow. Thee earned it," Duncan suggested with a relaxed motion toward the crowd.

Morgan focused on the faces around him. Hell! All these people were watching him? He gave a stiff waist bow, unsure how to respond to their applause. More cheers and whistles erupted.

"Cale! Relieve Morgan of his armor and give refreshments."

"Wow!" Brooke cried from Mitch's side when they reached him. "That was incredible."

"He's a natural," Mitch said. He clapped Morgan on the back. "I told you, you would enjoy this." He was still grinning from ear to ear with his newfound enthusiasm.

Morgan flexed. He was tired, sweaty, and thirsty, and his arms and shoulders weren't quite starting to scream at the abuse, but... "You know what, I did enjoy it," he said with a half-cocked grin himself.

"Need to work on thine accent and give thee some good swearing lines, and the women shall be throwing underwear and car keys for thy attention," Lord Duncan said with a hearty wink. He offered his hand. "The name is Patrick Duncan, and I really am a Master of Swords, but you're impressive."

"Morgan Aiza, and this is Mitch Benedetti," he replied along with a firm handshake.

"Would this be the fair maiden who thee so cursed for being pressed into service?" he asked with a purred chuckle as he bowed over her hand next.

"Brooke," she replied, giggling in enjoyment at Duncan's gallant antics.

"I'll be right back, honey," Mitch said, leaning to speak into her ear to be heard. "Need to give them the cow." He pulled at the bottom of the leather chest gear.

Patrick led them all from the practice ring. "If thee are interested, thee can join the camp for the tournament. Thee can be an alternate in the case one becomes injured."

"Like with real chain armor and stuff?" Morgan asked, baffled at the ease that Duncan switched in and out of his lord's character. The battle had knocked the surly right out of his attitude. He felt almost light-headed. He definitely wasn't feeling the lack of sleep. Not now, not by a long shot.

Patrick laughed, humor glinting easily in his gaze. "And stuff, yes."

"What do knights do?" he asked as another young squire rushed up and began to unbuckle him. Morgan lifted his arms to cooperate, far more than he had while putting it on, at least.

"We protect the King, walk around and look pompous and generally make a ruckus. We parade in the afternoon and draw attention for the duels. It's the tournaments the people like to watch." He stopped walking, informing him with a degree of seriousness, "We don't allow drugs, and any alcohol has to be shared. Other than that, it's pretty easy."

"Never done the first, and I don't drink to excess." He ran a hand over his sweat-soaked head. "I don't even remember the last beer I did have."

"We can remedy that." Patrick slapped him in camaraderie, his meaty hand thwacking against Morgan's shoulder. "If you are interested, you can meet with the council after the exhibitions. You will be fighting as a guest under the conditions we set to keep people from being injured, but if they approve and you're interested, I'd be happy to have you in my camp." He made a snorting noise. "Better here than in an opponent's, anyway."

"I guess that's a fair compliment," Morgan said, feeling a little better about being pressed into service. "When is the afternoon show?"

"At three. Be here a half hour early for dress, and don't worry about the clothes. We'll have a costume for you and Mitch."

He groaned. "Not tights." *Please, not tights.*

"No. You'll have period trousers." But something about his devil-edged tone worried Morgan just the same.

"I was only supposed to be here for the weekend," Morgan explained as an afterthought. He shook his head, sweat flying. "I don't know how much I can fight if I'm not around."

Brooke placed a hand on his arm. "Morgan, if you want to do this, we can stay. We were planning to stay for at least a week at some point. Go to the wharf and sightsee."

"Are you sure?"

He met her penetrating gaze, knowing she was searching, wondering. It didn't bother him because she'd find no more than he already knew himself, which was next to nothing.

Gently, she asked him, "Morgan, do you want to do this?"

He lifted his head and sniffed, as if testing his new territory. Her scent was gone, but it didn't matter. He knew he wasn't wrong. This was the first time he'd ever found even a hint of her presence outside of his dreams. It wasn't coincidence that he was there. Morgan knew how Fate loved to play with his family.

"Yeah, I think I do," he said with a distracted inflection, reeling from the shock of finding his dream seductress in the crowd.

He bent at the waist at a request a moment later and gave a sigh of relief when the leather armor was hefted free. The late morning breeze cooled his soaked skin, the wisp of air not yet fully heated by the sun overhead. His helmet and gauntlets disappeared into a tent, and he wondered, not for the first time, what he was doing.

"Come on, I'll take you to where you can clean up. You and your family have free admission for the remainder of the tournament."

Morgan followed Patrick. "It's just the three of us." Mitch joined them as they neared the water.

"I know it's not a shower but until you actually join, if you decide to, those are sectioned off," Duncan said, motioning toward the spigot.

Morgan didn't care. Water was water, he thought as he grabbed the hanging bucket and sluiced it over his head. He gave another hard shake, water going everywhere.

"Well, well, well," purred a feminine voice as the commotion settled around them. "Is this the meat for today?"

Morgan stood straight and met the owner of the voice. She was dressed in wench's garb and wasn't at all shy about thrusting herself or her cleavage forward. Lush red lips matched the fullness of her bustline. Brick-red hair hung in thick spirals under a flowered ring and ribbons. Promises to be had were an obvious offer. Morgan's first impulse was to take a step in the other direction, and he did.

"This is Leslie," Patrick said with a curt frown. Morgan didn't need to be told much else. The invitation was all over her face.

"Hello," he said, accepting a towel from Cale. He dried off and tugged his waiting shirt on. He wasn't comfortable letting her ogle him like a cheese danish at six in the morning. Leslie cast a flickering glance in Mitch's direction, and her face lit up more with appreciation.

"Not married. Even better," she mused, lust filling the sigh. "Two of you."

"They're married, in a way you'll never understand," he told her under his breath.

"No ring, he's fair game," she remarked stiffly.

"Tell that to Brooke, and she'll turn you into a snail," he purred as he inched closer, invading her space, a malicious glee filling him when she herself took a step at his veiled threat. He faced Patrick, seeing hidden amusement in his expression. "See you at two thirty." He left the camp with a wave.

"I look forward to it, Morgan," Duncan called as they left the camp.

Morgan shook his head. "Watch out for the wench. She's trouble," he told Mitch.

"Who? I didn't see anyone." Mitch gave him a blank stare.

"Be thankful," he retorted on a chuckle. "Be very thankful."

"Man, I'm starving," Mitch said a minute later, rubbing his stomach. "That's a hard workout."

"Me too," Morgan said as his stomach agreed loudly. "Let's eat."

After thirty minutes of silent feasting, Brooke decided to browse the stalls. She wanted to find blown glass and artwork to decorate with so they began walking, strolling, and window shopping. Morgan didn't mind, following the meandering crowd, answering his sister's questions, and otherwise enjoying the morning, something he had been sure wouldn't happen when his day started.

Morgan reached for his sunglasses as the noonday sun became stronger the more they strolled. A raucous sound reached his ears as laughter, then curses and more laughter. Now he knew from personal experience that the entire village was one big stage, and any passerby was a participant or a victim. So he waited for the show, stepping clear as the sound of running feet and squeals wafted over him.

"Stop ye heathen witch!" a loud, masculine voice shouted.

His breath froze in his chest as the green-eyed goddess of his dreams sped right past him laughing in enjoyment and amusement with her black hair flying behind her, a rich, sun-streaked banner of onyx. She stopped a few feet beyond him, whirled, and cried, "Never!"

"Take your stoning like a good witch," one voice cackled, and others in the mob roared their agreement.

She fell to her knees in supplication, clasping her hands. "No, I beg of thee! I am not the witch you seek!" Yet she was chortling in theatrical horror as the fake stones began to rain on her, tossed from several in the chasing mob. They bounced like little Nerf balls, and she wailed in misery.

She sat up on her haunches, her hands pushed forward. "I plead thy mercy!" Another volley came from overhead, and she covered herself. She yelped once and popped out from under her arm, her eyes flashing in pain and anger as she rubbed her elbow. One of the rocks wasn't a fake.

She finished the act, crying her innocence, making the finale grand by disappearing in a puff of smoke. The onlookers cheered for the show, and the mob began to pick up the Nerf-like rocks for their next victim. There were about a half dozen costumed participants in the mob; others were followers of the group, cheering and heckling as they passed.

"Hey, who is the witch?" Morgan asked, leaning close to one of the girls in wench's garb.

"N'Réa? She's a Tarot reader two aisles over. She's a good sport when we pick her out." The girl scooped up the lemon-sized rocks into a sagging pocket of her dress. "Need to find someone else," she said with a cheery giggle.

He watched the departing mob until they and the excitement of their little show had disappeared.

"Brooke, I'll find you later," Morgan called to his sister. She was in deep conversation with a booth owner and waved a distracted hand at him in answer.

He walked to the end of the aisle and strode in the direction the girl had mentioned. He couldn't believe it. She *was* here! She was a participant in the Faire. He shook his head. Morgan thought he might have imagined it after the exertions of being beaten with a long sword for almost twenty minutes, but he couldn't argue with what he'd witnessed. He couldn't rationalize away his surprise from earlier with seeing her in the flesh now.

Her jet hair flashed with the fire he'd dreamed of, her sparkling eyes green as spring grass. Her costume had swirled and swayed with her running and movements, a flashy gypsy skirt and blouse of red and blue which molded to her with every fluid movement, showcasing her like the real-life dream she was.

His steps dragged to a stop, and he wet his dry lips when the scent of summer rain curled around him in the aisle. She was close. He examined the signs waving in the breeze over tent openings and found hers. She was a palm and Tarot reader. He immediately labeled her a fake.

There were a lot of people who could read the cards and did it well, but he knew real magic. Brooke was immortality short of being a sorceress. His own family, all of them, held a magic secret of their own.

So why had she been tempting him, torturing him for so long? Who was she to have invaded his dreams? Who was this green-eyed vixen who demanded his attention?

"N'Réa." He whispered her name. It rolled off his tongue, a sensual caress on his lips that made him think of passion-filled nights. Many nights. His dreams were perfect teasing examples. He clenched his fists. He didn't need this!

A black surge of frustration filled his veins as he neared the tent. He'd spent too many nights with this woman's face and body tormenting him to not know why.

"Ah-ha! There you are!"

He whipped around sharply when a possessive hand clasped his arm less than a handful of steps from his goal. He frowned at the redhead. "Sorry, Leslie. I have someone to see," he replied coolly.

She rubbed against his arm suggestively, tossing her crimson-red hair behind her with what he was sure was supposed to be a provocative move. It did nothing for him. No woman had since the first night of his dreams.

"I'm sure you have a few minutes for a new friend." She pouted up at him.

"When I make one, I'll let you know."

Her rising lust chilled at the block. "You know, most would be pleased I have chosen them," she retorted, offended he didn't leap at the chance she was offering.

He removed her hand with two fingers, releasing her with a tight smile. "I am not most. Excuse me," he said and retreated, not caring if she left or not.

Morgan reached N'Réa's tent in a few quick steps, the other woman's advances already forgotten so close to his goal.

"She is tenacious," a sultry voice said from the dim interior. It slid over him like a lover's caress. Like his dreams. It made his blood sizzle immediately. "She won't give up."

His vision adjusted to find her sitting calmly behind a colorfully draped table. A single black square about one third the size of the table covered the middle. Her hands stretched flat before her as she regarded him. The edge of the tent walls from the front to behind her were draped with long, shimmery sheets of silk and materials of different colors — reds, blues, purples, and vibrant greens and yellows. There was a large Persian carpet on the ground and pillows thrown around the dim space.

"I see," Morgan replied. It was the most his brain was supplying at the moment, standing in front of her.

"Leslie is a poor example of what we try to promote," she said by way of apology. Her tempting mouth curved into a welcoming smile as she waved a hand for him to take a seat. "Don't let her color your judgment."

The tent was cool, shaded, yet he could see her easily from behind his sunglasses. Her midnight hair hung in the long wave he knew if not intimately, it was close, like a silken curtain to her waist. Green eyes flashed with secrets as he neared. The sunlight behind him brightened the tent when he strode forward.

"How can I help you?"

He wanted to demand why she had been tormenting him in his sleep, but he didn't, couldn't, ask. Not yet. Morgan had to find out what her game was. Weeks of her nightly visits had brought them to this. No point in rushing it now. Surely, it was almost over. For now, he would go with the flow.

"You read?"

"Since the first grade," she answered. The playfulness of her tone stroked his spine, and he fought to suppress the shiver of excitement. Long arms and delicate wrists were covered with gold and silver bangles and stone bracelets. Slim fingers ended in the long red nails he knew she would have. She wore a silver pendant, which drew his gaze to her throat. The creamy, flawless texture of her skin was the incarnation of his most sensual desires. He ached. There was no other way to phrase it. He wanted.

Morgan forced the raging desire for this woman out of his mind with a steel-clad effort. Determined to face this, Morgan strode in.

He took the chair in front of her table and reversing the seat, sat astride. "What can you tell me...?" he began to ask her reluctantly, his eyes narrowing behind the lenses of his sunglasses when he couldn't finish the thought with something profound, a request she hadn't heard a thousand times already.

Her scent filled his head, making it impossible to think clearly in the small space of her gypsy tent. It reminded him of riding on a seesaw. One direction craving her scent, her voice, needing to know her touch, her taste and her kiss. The other, refuting it as no more than a tempting dream. A dream that he wasn't sure she hadn't created herself. He focused on the many nights she'd disturbed, the wall her image placed in front of him, and managed to cool his hungers down to a low ember instead of the rising inferno trying to surge to life inside his chest.

"About? Your future? Your love life?" Her sultry voice was resonant and beautiful.

He blinked. What the hell was going on? She was just a woman! He commandeered his control with an iron fist. He frowned. "Who are you?" He could ask that without seeming suspicious. Maybe. The dreams, he reminded himself. He had to find out about the dreams. And make them stop.

"N'Réa." Her red-tinted lips lifted with a knowing curl. Not the first time she'd been asked, he was sure.

"Just N'Réa? No last name?" he taunted her.

One regally arched eyebrow lifted. "I don't need one." Her gaze flowed over his face. "You seem familiar," she said, the husky timbre blasting heat through his blood as though he were a living furnace.

His hands gripped the chair where they lay crossed in front of his chest, his arms holding his weight. "I doubt it. We've never met." It was with a supreme effort that he managed to keep his voice cool, unattached.

A sensual reaction roamed along his entire length at her leisurely assessment of him, at once remembered and known, the scorching heat traveling with the same speed over his skin as those green eyes of hers. He bit the retort off at his tongue. He had started this.

"I agree. We've never met," she said, calm indifference remaining on her face. "How can I be of service today?"

He almost called her on it, wanting her to admit it was a lie, but her expression told him it wasn't. She didn't know him any more than he knew her. Was she the one behind the dreams? He crowbarred another dose of calm patience into his lungs, breathing steadily, if not deeply. Her scent was driving him insane. The images of her body, supple and flush with passion, continued to make him ache.

"Can you really read the cards?" He asked the question with as much genuine curiosity as he could gather. It sounded more like disbelief to his ears. It wasn't intentional. N'Réa was *something*. As for her abilities, that remained to be seen.

"As much as you will believe in them," she replied, voicing his thoughts, the fire in her eyes speaking her mind, knowing he was challenging her. She lifted a slim hand bearing several stoned rings, and a Tarot deck appeared in her palm. "But you," she said, those fire-lit, green eyes narrowing, "You don't need the reading."

"I want the reading," he said. To prove it, he pulled his wallet from a pocket and laid a twenty on the table between them. She didn't glance at the money once, never losing his gaze.

"Very well." She spread the deck on the table to show him the cards. "Seventy-eight cards, they're all here." She flipped them like a line of dominoes and ran them into a perfect pile. "Ask a question, your heart's desire, financial inquiry. Perhaps a job," she offered as she deftly split a large portion of the cards with card-shark precision in one hand.

"I want to know about my dream," he said evenly. She nodded. There was no sign the question meant anything to her. He waited.

"On one condition," she intoned as she palmed the cards together. "The sunglasses."

He took them off with an unhurried motion. No reaction, no spark of recognition. He breathed a little more easily. He could *control this*. "Satisfied?" He focused to bring his heart rate to a respectable rate, squelching the thunder it had maintained for the last ten minutes.

"For now," she replied, dropping her mysterious gaze to the cards in her hands. A few seconds later, she set them before him. "Shuffle them as long as you want. Think of your question, your deepest desire, and let your energy flow into the cards. When you feel it is time to stop, cut three stacks, anywhere, any order, your choice."

He shuffled and cut the deck, then resumed his position a few silent moments later. His heart picked up an erratic beat as she moved with grace and purpose in front of him. He controlled his body with an iron will, her scent enveloping him like a heady cloud, slamming the memory of his dreams forcefully into his mind, clear as day, as sharp and specific as the woman who sat across from him right now. She was indefinable beauty, her thick hair cascading around her shoulders in a coal-black cloud. He fought the pull of her, battled the driving need as it ripped through him. He took slow, measured breaths, demanding that his body obey. He would control this!

He swore to himself following the enticing curve of her lips, moistened by a delicate movement of her pink tongue. The clawing grew and rose until he thought he would explode with her so close, yet untouchable.

N'Réa lifted the first card from the stack to his right with a steady hand, her voice intensifying his reactions, filling him. "Interesting, the chariot. Shows challenges ahead, struggles and conflict, physical and mental, but they will be well worth the effort." Her voice flowed like warm silk encircling him as she spoke, then she lifted the second card from the center. "The king of cups. Very fortuitous. Masculine in nature, you have decided to seek your heart's love." He wasn't so sure about that, but he was willing to wait out the reading. She slid the third card free and showed the face of the card, or rather, the faces.

She fell silent for a long heartbeat, the heaviness in the air between them prickling his skin. Even Morgan could guess at the meaning, the depiction of a naked couple entwined.

"The lovers," she said on a rasped whisper, stroking heated nerves into a frenzy.

"I take it that means I will find her?" he asked, then cleared his throat when he sounded dry.

"Yes, but there is no time frame involved, and decisions and changes will be part of the meeting," she warned. Her hand rested on the tabletop, a single red-tipped finger pinning the corner of the last card. "Does this help decipher your dream?" She didn't lift her face to look at him, her expressive eyes hidden by the veil of hair swinging before her face.

"Yes." He rose and replaced the chair. "Thank you for your time, N'Réa."

She bowed her head in answer. "You're very welcome." Her words coursed around his spine like a living vibration, and he stiffened, spinning on an escaping heel.

He stepped outside and took a deep breath. He needed one. Several. Her scent was addictive, filling his head, urging his needs and hungers like he'd never experienced. He put his sunglasses on, then with a single-minded purpose, went to find Brooke and Mitch. He needed to think about this new development.

Not only was the torturing dream there, but the very woman he hungered for informed him it was all true and going to happen. There was no reason to believe any of it, but he did know when something was real. N'Réa was real. He released the clenched fists he hadn't realized he'd made. He swore violently. He did not need this, a woman or a mate!

Who was she? What was she? A fire raged inside her, something ancient and elemental glowed around her, visible to him within the dim interior of her little tent. It was all around her, filling the void of the tent, sparkling on the air practically, which meant it was completely possible that she was behind the dreams. She held enough power to manage it; whether she knew it or not, or was responsible, he didn't know. Whatever she was, he had no use for it or for her.

He shook his head, refusing to be used or played. Morgan was the last of the four and remained so by his choice. He refused to let some woman change it now. He'd been solitary and fine with it for so long, he didn't want to make the change. Fate couldn't force him to accept this. He marched past a corner with strides churning over the distance, leaving her farther behind while he made his decision. When they were done for the day, he would not return to the Faire. There was no reason to. He'd offered to fight that afternoon and was anticipating it with the renewed edge of his frustrations beating at him, but afterward he had not one reason to return. Brooke and Mitch were on their own.

* * * *

N'Réa let out a savage snarl when he was gone. "The lovers?" she fumed. "I don't think so!" It had taken every ounce of her acting ability to keep herself impersonal and professional with him in there.

It was him!

She had thought it was, but he'd seemed so...unaffected. It wasn't until he took off the sunglasses when she knew without a doubt. It was a wonder she hadn't jumped clear out of her seat! She gathered the cards to store them in their case.

She missed twice because her hands shook uncontrollably.

"Damn it!" She swept up his twenty out of spite and jammed it into her bag under the table. She didn't charge half that, but for him, she should have charged forty! She shivered as the memory of his voice wove over her, stronger now that she'd met the real thing. "Just who the hell does he think he is?" she yelled to herself. "Coming in here like he owned the damn place!" She refused to admit she'd invited him.

She threw things around in disturbed anger, her vision clouded with fear. The dream had been steadily growing, but it was always his eyes, nothing else. Storm gray and unforgettable. She never remembered much, but she always woke up knowing her life was about to change when they met. Even she was smart enough to recognize a damned portent!

"Lovers!" She spat the one word with a vicious breath. "No fucking way!" There was no way she was hooking up with a damned guest! Or anyone. No way in hell!

She lurched from her seat to her feet. She needed to breathe! N'Réa threw open the hanging side of her canvas tent and released the tied side. She knotted them together, knowing she would miss the money being out of her tent so much today, but she needed to walk, or she was going to bite someone's head off!

She took off in a random direction, oblivious to the activity of the grounds swarming around her. What was he doing there anyway? He wasn't dressed to play a part. He looked like a guest. Her step stumbled as her brain caught on to that fact like a life preserver. He was a guest! He wouldn't be staying! Today, maybe for tomorrow, but the chance of him hanging around were nil.

N'Réa slackened as if several rods had been yanked free of her frame, a grateful sigh escaping, releasing weeks of pent-up frustration culminating in today's meeting.

So what if she'd dreamed of him, of his voice, of his gaze for what seemed like ages? He was just a person. As in a visiting person, and the chance of her running into him again were even smaller than nil. He wouldn't be back, not to see her.

She brushed her hands together, thankfully dismissing the whole situation.

Chapter Three

"Hey, N'Réa, let's go watch the knights." A burly, male head appeared around her tent opening, sporting a huge smile of invitation. "Everyone who's heard is already over there." N'Réa focused from where she'd been casually playing with the cards on the table.

"Hi, Bailey." She peeked beyond her neighbor into the aisle. There wasn't a soul out there. "Sure, it's been dead today." It didn't help playing hooky from her tent so much. Now the day was mostly gone. She vowed to do better on Sunday. She stood up and walked out to join him, then tied her tent together with swift hands. "I wonder where everyone is."

"Didn't you hear?" Bailey asked. "Duncan is going to fight a guest, and there's a bet Duncan may not win."

"You're kidding?" She grabbed her skirts and scurried to keep pace with his longer stride. He and his wife, Marie, sold knives, swords, and scabbards in the booth slot next to her, and she'd run into them at a lot of events over the years.

"No, the word that made it out of Duncan's camp is that if he does defeat Duncan, he's going to be sponsored to alternate for the tourney," Bailey said as he shouldered his way into the crowd, anticipating the coming duels. He was impressive in size, a bulky guy, at least six feet, and he had a deep voice with a glaring look if he needed it. Trailing him, they made their way to the open dirt arena where they were able to squeeze viewable room near the edge.

She let her skirts fall, dusting them with her palms. "I wasn't able to see much earlier, but he got a good row from someone. Duncan made him a knight on the spot."

Bailey shook his head quickly with a broad smile. "That's him! Even Dirk was impressed."

"Dirk?" She frowned. "As in, the world is my toy, Lord Dirk Brassballs?"

Bailey guffawed in his deep bass at the well-known moniker. "Yeah." He leaned on his elbows on the corner of the railing. "He's already said that if this guy is willing and Duncan doesn't take him, Lord De Brasse will snatch him up."

"But what about the trials, and squiring, and all the penance you have to go through to make knighthood?" She squinted up at him as the afternoon sun beat on them. A thin haze of dust rose from the arena, making the air dry and gritty.

Bailey shrugged, unconcerned. "This guy isn't a Reni, he doesn't know the rules, but from what I've heard he's a bloody killing machine with a sword. It's a good thing they use armor."

"I wonder who he is?" she said, only half aware that she'd spoken. It was really unusual for Duncan to take so much interest in a guest. No one was that good. It took years to gain a respectable fighting knowledge and skill with a sword. The King's guard always opened the Faire with an exhibition fight and a willing victim, taking it easy on him to not hurt their volunteer, but for some reason she couldn't guess, this fight was anticipated by everyone.

Bailey cut into her thoughts. "I don't know, but I know he's fighting. Word spread quickly when he made it to camp to dress. A lot of us assumed that after the training, he'd walk away. It's grueling what those guys do, and it's all fun for them."

She chuckled with Bailey. "Don't you fight? To test your blades?"

"Well, yeah, sure, but I fight a friend who isn't intent on decapitating me." He changed his weight to not lean into his neighbor on the other side, tossing his chin to the arena. "These guys don't go blood match, but they fight like they could."

Her attention switched to the arena when the announcer called for the fighters to prep for the duels. There would be a total of five battles. Afterward, the jousters would do targeting games. At least an hour, she estimated. Since the fighters wouldn't be out for points or blood, the duels would likely last a little longer than the average fight to put on a good show and build enthusiasm. A lot of time to not be in her tent. She stretched her head around Bailey. There were people as far as she could see. N'Réa reached over the rail at her waist, bending the other way, finding spectators even under the lower steps of the grandstands watching through feet.

No one was going to be needing her for a while.

"All right, Bailey, but I can't stay for the jousters."

"Me neither," he admitted. "But I wanted to see this guy. Don't worry, I left Marie in charge. She'll keep an eye on things." N'Réa nodded, feeling better with that news. Marie was a sharp woman. Nothing would happen while she was around.

Ten bodies in armor and helmets marched out from behind the king's podium at the call of the horns, saluted, then filed proudly into the shaded prep space behind the royal court.

The first match was between one of Lord De Brasse's men and a knight N'Réa recognized from Duncan's camp. They were dressed in chain mail shirts with breastplates over colorful tunics of their realms and protective helmets. Sir William from Lord

Duncan's camp put up a good fight, but he was defeated to the collective boos of the crowd.

Lord De Brasse and his camp were the evil knights of the realm, and they played it up to the hilt. Arrogant, generally rude, and known for womanizing, theirs was a reputation many Ren Faire folk knew. Faire guests only knew the reputation they were meant to know. Some members of Dirk's camp were exactly the worst any person could find to play the evil nemesis of the King's guard. Lord De Brasse played dirty for the enjoyment of the crowd but never with intended malice. That couldn't be said of all of his knights. Dirk's leadership and control were the only things that kept his crew from going full-tilt insane. Musing, watching the fight, she did admit it helped keep the tourneys lively.

The voice announced the winner as he slid off his helmet, bowed to the court, and left the arena.

The next announced match was between Mitchell Benedetti, an invited guest, and one of Lord Duncan's trained knights, Sir Beuchard. She knew the knight was good from catching the team's fights over the years. He was also trained well enough to know not to decapitate a guest.

She waited until the crier called them on, then held her breath. This Mitch guy fought well, but she could tell he wasn't comfortable in chain mail and plate armor. His moves were strong, but broad and sluggish. "Is that him?" she yelled to be heard over the crowd cheering all around her.

He shook his head. "You'll know," he answered as a cry went up and Mitch lost his sword and his footing.

As the crowd cheered for the next fighters, it wasn't too hard to guess that Duncan was saving his fight for last. He was the kingdom favorite and as the fourth fight ended, she could almost feel as the crowd collectively held their breaths, anticipation undulating through the masses of spectators following on a wave of whispers and calls. *What hadn't she heard about this fight?*

The announcer's voice called out loudly, "To the arena we call Lord Duncan of the King's personal guard. Today his challenger is a guest to our Kingdom of unquestionable ability! His fame has spread far and wide for being an unheard swordsman of such skilled hands on steel!"

N'Réa rolled her eyes. They were milking it, that was for sure. He was just a guy, for heaven's sake!

"Today, Lord Duncan's challenge was answered by Morgan Aiza!" The crowd let out a roaring cheer as the announcer's voice rose and urged their responses. The two combatants entered the ring from opposite sides, as all the opponents had, wearing chain shirts and helmets. He was a magnificent spectacle in the armor and carrying the large sword in both hands at the ready. Even as a guest he was in period garb, which brought him up in her estimation. So many people don't let loose and be silly every now and then. It helped to keep the world sane. She studied Duncan's opponent and realized something was different about him.

He wasn't wearing any plate! Only chain and no shield. Her eyes widened as he took his stance. Whoever this man was, he knew his way around the battlefield. His stance was fierce and bold. It was hard to look away.

She shook her long hair out as a tingle of anticipation slithered down her neck, her eyes glued on the magnificent form in the arena. Long legs, broad shoulders, a trim waist. The finer details were hidden beneath his protective chain and clothing, though it wouldn't take much to imagine it. The roar of the crowd subsided and she waited, her hands tight on the rail.

"Lay on!" Suddenly the crowd erupted as Lord Duncan made the first swing, an overhand chop his opponent blocked, then slid out from under. With a fluid twist of his solid length, Duncan fell forward like a gushed wind had pushed him over, it was so smooth and surprising. His opponent slammed Duncan with the hilt of the sword dead center in the back of his mail, and he went sprawling into the dirt.

The duels were a three fall or unarming declaration. With his unexpected show of ability, the guest was up one to nothing on Duncan. The crowd roared to cheer him on when Duncan rose to his feet and raised his sword for the next attack. She couldn't hear it, but N'Réa was sure he was cursing the other man backward and forward.

When the swords crashed together she whooped out a cheer, diving into the excitement with the rest of the onlookers. Even Bailey winced and jumped when Duncan forced his opponent to spin away or take a knee.

The clash of steel rang with an incredible echo, singing through the air like screaming gunfire, as the two met and slashed and paced each other.

"This guy is just a guest?" She had to shout to be heard.

Bailey nodded, intent on the fight. The two men met in the middle, pushing and shoving with obvious effort, when Duncan managed to get his challenger off balance and knocked him over like a felled tree. The crowd leaped to their feet, waiting to see if he would get up.

She actually sagged in relief when he hefted himself to his feet, watching with as much breathless anticipation as every other set of eyes present. The challenger was a ferocious fighter, persistent and unrelenting as he hacked and cut across Duncan's swing path. Duncan began to windmill off-balance and two steps later was in the recent position of his challenger, flat on his back in the dirt. The crowd gasped and cheered.

The volume became deafening when Duncan rose to his feet with a surly tension. The score was two to one in favor of the challenger, and he was putting everything into it now. As the tension escalated and the two circled looking for that critical opening, she knew Duncan didn't have a chance.

The sound of sliding steel reached her a heartbeat before Duncan lost his sword. It spiraled in a shallow arc and landed in the dirt a few feet away.

Her jaw dropped. "He unarmed him." She clutched Bailey's jerkin, gaping in disbelief. "He unarmed Duncan!" she shouted. "I can't believe it!"

The crowd flew into a full roar as the challenger walked to Duncan and helped him to his feet. She couldn't believe it! She had never seen anyone unarm Duncan. He was the best!

The sound of horns eventually pierced the crowd's noise, signaling the end of the duels. Duncan leaned over and shouted something to the other man who stepped away to stand before the King and his entourage and knelt on a knee.

It was standard procedure to pay the King honor when a combatant won. What she hadn't expected to see when he swept the visor helmet clear was a thick black mane of hair. Her eyes bulged in shock as she caught his profile, numb as the combatant joined Duncan under the awning.

It couldn't be! It couldn't have been him!

"Well, if he says yes, he'll be on someone's team by morning," Bailey said as they joined the line out of the arena area.

"What? That was him?" she said in a squeak. "That was the guy he knighted?"

"Yes, do you know him?" he asked, with a nod toward the crowd, careful to not knock anyone out of their way now that they were all in the flow.

She schooled her features, determined to keep her heart in her chest and her shock off her face. She shook her head. "No, not really. He visited me for a reading this morning." And in her dreams every night! *If he joins...* She couldn't finish the thought. Her mouth went dry with fear. "He won't join," she said in an airy voice, desperately wanting to dismiss the emotions watching him produced. "He's a guest. Probably here just for the weekend, and then he'll be gone."

Bailey only shrugged. "I'm sure it will be known within the hour," he responded as they filed out with the others who were going to bypass the jousting. She would love to stay and watch, but she needed to make money. Plus, she needed to figure out what she would do if Morgan stayed.

* * * *

"Bloody hell!" Duncan thundered, sounding like a wounded bull as the men walked away from the arena. "You lied to me!"

Morgan staggered under the weight of the chain suit, surprised at the man's rage. Duncan glared at Morgan with a fierce growl, then spun away.

"About what?"

Duncan stomped away, then stalked back. "You're too damn good! You are trained!" He shook a finger at Morgan as though he were a young boy needing to be chastised.

Adamant, Morgan shook his sweaty head, his chest tight as he fought for air. "No! Never." Morgan called Mitch over. "Tell him," he said, gesturing for him to do it, and now, before Duncan decided to use his sword on Morgan without his helmet on.

"No, Duncan. He's never fought. Neither of us have."

Duncan threw Mitch a disgusted look. "You, I believe. You're good, but you lack finesse. This one!" His voice boomed beneath the tent coverings. "Do you realize it has been three years since even a trained fighter has unarmed me? I have never been beaten by a guest!" He slashed the air with a hand for emphasis, others clearing a wide path to avoid his raging fury.

"Do you want me to apologize?" Morgan honestly didn't know what he was supposed to do. He tucked his helmet under one arm, keeping a hand on the hilt of his sword, tip down as they'd been instructed before the duels. The whole afternoon had gone from weird to weirder. His heart at least had stopped trying to claw its way through his ribcage, and he was going to be sore in the morning. Duncan knew how to land a blow with his sword!

Duncan ran a stiff hand over his blond head. "Hell, no, of course not! I invited you to do this! But bloody hell and ground scum!" He fumed a while longer, glaring and stalking away to glare again.

If he hadn't lost to anyone in years, it was no wonder how much losing to Morgan stung. The last thing he wanted to do was rub it in.

"If he doth not wish to join your band of losers, he can camp with us." A smooth voice came from the cool shadows behind them. "He is an excellent arm, and I do not care if he trained with the Templars themselves, I will take him."

"Dirk!" Duncan spat, whirling with a savage warning for the intruder on his expression. "He is a guest, not a damn chalice!"

Morgan sized up the other large, blond man. He carried a stiff arrogance, which literally trailed him as he walked up.

"That is Lord De Brasse, dog whelp," he taunted as his dark brown gaze flashed with dry humor at Duncan.

"You do not have to decide this now," Duncan said as he blatantly dismissed the other man, forcefully putting a cooler on his temper. "If you want to join, you still have to be presented to the council. Usually there is a long wait to be at knight status. It takes years of training and service."

"Look, I told you," Morgan said, explaining when Duncan seemed to misunderstand. Morgan wasn't interested in being a knight or a pin cushion for their enjoyment. "I only planned to be here for the weekend."

"Well, that settles it, then doth it not, Lord Dung Heap?" Dirk lifted an insolent eyebrow, far too pleased to know Morgan wouldn't be staying. "Thee shall still lose to the best in the Kingdom," he offered with a mocking bow. Morgan decided he really just didn't like the other lord, Dirk or Dick, he missed that part.

"Morgan, you can if you want to," Mitch interjected. "This is the first day. We can set up and stay. We can camp. Brooke would love it."

Morgan rolled his eyes. Was everyone out to see him be annihilated by sword? "What about supplies?"

"Not a problem," Duncan offered, his voice evening out. "There are plenty of ways to get you what you need, and there are two blacksmiths here for the tournament anyway."

Morgan bit out a low curse, then a reluctant sigh. "I'll think about it." He sliced a glare at Mitch. "But it's my choice!" He knew he was half done in already. Mitch was grinning like a kid on Christmas morning. Ignoring him, Morgan faced Duncan. "How long do I have to think on this before I have to meet your council?"

"They meet after hours to discuss the events and outcomes. You have at least until then," Duncan said. He started to lead the way to his camp, and he and Mitch followed with the other knights who had fought, along with supporters of the camp.

Mitch leaned over. "Whatever you need, Brooke will be happy to fill in the blanks."

"Gee, that makes it oh so tempting," he scoffed. "Why are you so gung-ho about this, Mitch? What about the house? This thing goes on for weeks."

Mitch shrugged. "The house is fine. I know we got it. We can drive up when the bids are opened and sign the paperwork. We'll be gone a day at most." He presented Morgan a brotherly smile. "As for the rest, I'm saying this because I know as well as everyone else does that you need to blow steam. You've been going nuts at home, and you knocked the snot out of the King's protector." He finished the sentence on a lowered whisper.

"I heard that," Duncan muttered.

"No offense," Morgan told him.

"None taken," Duncan replied on a groused huff.

"Well?" Mitch asked. "It could be fun. Get to stretch. Sleep under the stars," he said, trying to persuade Morgan.

"I can do that at home," Morgan reminded him with a flat tone and far less enthusiasm than his brother-in-law.

Mitch straightened, walking alongside him. "Fine. You want to be a sour apple, go ahead. Brooke and I will be here until next weekend, at least. You want to go home, we'll take you. You want to mope in a hotel room, we'll let you. I did my duty. I got you away from Selene before she snapped both our heads off."

"She's pregnant," he retorted. "That's all she does."

"Your wife?" Duncan asked as they entered camp, winding their way through tents and cords from the few RV's in attendance. "Cale!"

"Sister," Morgan corrected. "Seven months pregnant." Cale appeared with two others and started to help Mitch and Morgan out of the borrowed chain mail

"It isn't all fighting," Duncan continued to explain. "There's carousing, and a lot of us stay on during the week. You can come and go as you please. You don't have to stay all week, but we practice and work on mail and outfits while we have the time."

"You travel to these events all the time?" Mitch asked, intrigued.

Duncan nodded, heaving a sigh of relief as the last of his armor came off. "Yes, we do several throughout the year." He took a deep drink from a cup someone handed him before going on. He wiped his mouth on the sleeve of his shirt, saying, "Those of us who don't camp stay at a local lodge and do our own thing. Jobs, family. If they live close to the Faire, it isn't bad at all. I own my own welding business, and my manager covers for me when I do these. Couldn't do it without him."

"You do this for fun?" Morgan asked with skepticism as he received a cup for himself. He sniffed and drank. It was cold and wet. Exactly what he wanted.

"The tournaments pay money." Duncan let out a long belch and laughed. "Damn, I needed that!"

"That makes sense," Mitch said. "It wouldn't make any financial sense to do this for nothing considering the investment you put into it." He waved a meaningful hand at the racks of armor and chain ready to be repaired and polished. Several swords aside from the ones they used were lined up, tied securely to hanging racks.

"Then there's the clothing, food, mad money," Duncan said, shaking his head. "No, it wouldn't be fun at all."

"How many teams are there?" Morgan asked as they strolled to the camp spigot to wash up from their exertions for the second time that day.

"At this event, for the tournament, there are twelve teams with eight jousting teams. It makes for a full house. People come from all over to watch us beat each other up," he said, a gleam for the fight in his eyes. "We don't fight every day, but all of us will fight in the tournament."

"So, like tomorrow, you won't be exhibition fighting?" Morgan dropped the cold water over his head and shook, wiping his face and chest with a fresh towel.

"No. We got first choice for being the King's knights, but we all watch, size up the competition."

Morgan made room and toweled off as Mitch did the same with the water. "I can see that." Studying those around him, there were the men and women of the camp, the other knights in the party, and their own entourages. All in all there were probably thirty people in his camp, if not more. "How will they feel with an interloper? I'm not familiar with the Faire rules." Mitch grabbed a towel, gave Morgan a grin, and followed Cale to get his clothes and dress.

Duncan focused beyond Morgan's shoulders. "William, Beuchard!" he shouted, waving them over. "Tell me, how do you see our friend here? Would you be against having him as an alternate?" he asked when they were close.

William spoke up first, a thick-muscled redhead with a braid. "No, hell no!" A broad grin split his face. "I wish it was me putting you on your arse for once!"

"Will it be temporary?" Beuchard asked, in a surprisingly cultured New England accent.

"Definitely. I don't even live in the area."

"Oh, that's a shame," Beuchard said, amicably, but disappointed. "You would make a fine addition." His voice held a nasal sound because his nose had been broken. He didn't talk tough, but he looked it. He'd fooled Morgan. He was willing to bet it worked on his opponents too.

"You're free to talk to the other teams and see if one is better suited to your likes, of course," Duncan proposed.

"No, I think if I do this, I'll be fine here." He raked a hand through his saturated hair. Becoming resigned to the inevitable, he asked, "How long do I have?"

"Time!" Duncan bellowed. "We don't wear watches usually, it kills the effect of our costumes," he pointed out in an aside to Morgan.

"Almost five thirty!" shouted a feminine voice from a few tents away.

"Just over an hour. Let us know before the close of the gates at seven," Duncan told him.

"I can do that. I want to talk to the other two, but I think I already know how they'll answer," he said with a groan, picturing their exuberance and excitement. He should have said no right then. A smarter man would have. Duncan slapped him on the back with a thick hand.

"We have a place for you if you do decide to join, Morgan." He started to leave, then returned. "I guess I better put it all on the table," he said with a shadowed pain filling his expression. "If you do join, watch out for Leslie."

"I've already come to that conclusion," he replied. "Who is she?"

"My ex-wife," Duncan bitterly revealed.

Chapter Four

N'Réa was running late from the vendor campground the next morning, gingerly cradling her right arm to her side. It throbbed like a bitch now and had swollen like a waterlogged sponge under her bracelets. If it didn't stop hurting, she would go to the med tent and get them to examine it. If it was broken, she would have no choice but to shut her tent for another day to go to the local emergency room and have a cast put on it. This was the worst start to any show she'd ever had.

She bit her lip to lock the yelp inside when she accidentally bumped her arm, blinking hard to keep the tears at bay. She managed to tie one side of her tent opening without too much cursing. Yesterday had been a total waste. She'd earned hardly any money. Usually she made her Faire costs on the first day and her mad money on the second. The way things were going for her, it would take at least the next weekend to cover those alone!

Of course, being out of her tent so much didn't help any. Her little foray to see who was in attendance, her distraction by the training fight, then the tournament. She sighed, disgruntled. Everyone had been at the arena for the exhibitions. No one conducted any business in the afternoon from what she'd gathered at the dinner hour last night.

It was the oddest thing, someone said, that everyone attended the exhibitions on opening day, and now, this morning, she was holding an injured hand.

She was doomed, she silently wailed. She didn't sleep well because of that...man, and now this! She fumed at her arm, agony slicing into her elbow with every motion of her hand. She tried to hide it under the excess of bangles and bracelets she wore, but it was going to be difficult if she couldn't use it. Thank God she knew how to work one-handed. She could always switch her readings to the minor arcana, and no one would know it wasn't how she always worked. That she knew she could do one-handed.

She didn't want to think about how her arm had been injured. She was still shaken, unable to process the attack. She would have to be more careful. Be more aware. The fact that it happened at all was unusual. She'd never been injured like this at a Faire. Most of the Ren folk were a gregarious group, but they held honor and friendship high.

After placing her things under the table, she grabbed her small clutch. No big purse or cash box today. She didn't want anyone to think she was loaded with cash. With her small clutch in hand, she headed out to get something hot to drink. Maybe it would help calm her. She hoped so. At this point, she'd take anything she could get to soothe her frayed nerves.

* * * *

Morgan arrived at the Faire grounds with the other two early in the morning to dress and hear a description on how things were done at Duncan's camp. Sir William showed them samples of his period clothing, and Brooke said she would return after lunch with a respectable wardrobe for all of them.

Morgan was afraid of what she intended. She and Mitch were enjoying this way too much. He flinched when he heard how much the mail, breast plates with gauntlets, and helmet cost, but Brooke smiled in a '*don't worry, I got this*' way that made him wince harder inside.

"We'll have a tent and set up gear after hours tonight," she informed him as she walked away, already creating lists and Lord only knew what else with Mitch. They were going to talk to the blacksmith, Morgan was sure of it.

He cursed silently, hiding his angst from the others as he sat on a camp chair with Beuchard and William having coffee. It wasn't their fault his sister was diving headfirst into this. He prayed she didn't spend a fortune.

"You don't have to get it all," William was saying, distracting him from his worries. "We have a good supply of armor because as a team, we chip in and buy odds and ends of pieces we find so we have the extra for the training, to give guests an opportunity like you two did yesterday."

"I appreciate you loaning me so much." Morgan was trying to figure out how he'd been roped into this, but as Mitch pointed out the day before, maybe he did need to blow steam with a change from everything going on at home, which included his lack of sleep.

Morgan wore loose, saddle-brown trousers, leather boots, and a linen shirt that Brooke provided for him first thing this morning. He wasn't going to ask how or from where she procured the clothing on such short notice. If she'd bought it or waved her hand, either indebted him to his sister. It wasn't a sore point, but he didn't want her to do it all. She was also dressed in character this morning, but as a comely lady of honor, as she pointed out with mock sternness that she couldn't quite hide behind her laughter, and Mitch was her lord. Mitch even wore the damn tights! God, he would do anything for Brooke. All Morgan could do was roll his eyes at the first sight of his brother-in-law this morning. Mitch had spread his arms, studying himself, trying to see what it was that Morgan was shaking his head at. Mitch didn't get it, and Morgan wasn't going to wear it. He was fine with that.

He listened with half an ear as the others through the camp woke and joined them. Morgan didn't sleep well considering the level of physical torture from the day before, and it was taking time for his brain to hit full gear. He should have been exhausted from two intense duels. His shoulders ached and his back wasn't sure if it was going on strike, but even after a hot shower his sleep, at best, had been torturously nonexistent.

The dream from the night before wouldn't leave him.

Last night's disruption hadn't been the least sexual in nature. Nothing like the meetings they'd shared up to this point. No, this was a dream he'd never experienced during all the restless nights of insignificant sleep. His green-eyed vixen had been scared, screaming in silent fear and pain, and he'd awakened in his hotel room with a sharp start. His reaction was to throw the blankets from the bed in a rush, wanting to attack the person behind that fear, but between one heartbeat and the next, Morgan realized he was too far away to be of any help. There was nothing he could do, and it bothered him now in the light of day that he'd wanted to. He didn't want to have anything to do with the woman, yet he felt compelled to protect her. It made his disgruntled, fatigued mood multiply quickly.

"Here, Morgan," Duncan greeted, holding out a sword and ringed belt as he neared the growing group. "A knight is never defenseless. This was one of my favorite light swords. You have to keep it peace tied."

Duncan pointed to the leather strip snugly wrapped around his own hilt.

He stood and buckled the scabbard with a few jests of the others. The weight rested well on his hips. "Thank you," he offered as the blade settled against his waist like it had always been there.

"He almost looks like a man," William jested in a good Old English accent. "And it's 'I thank thee, your Lordship.' Need to get you up on the way it's done. Some Faire folk are more fastidious about the language, but a lot of us have been at this for so long that when we step away from camp, it kicks in."

"Like being on stage?" Morgan asked, resuming his seat. He moved automatically to accommodate the length of the sword. Somehow, it felt natural, complete. The way the broadsword had in his hands yesterday. He shook his head, dispersing the notion as sheer fantasy. Lack of sleep could make almost anything seem realistic.

"Exactly," one woman said as she neared with another gentleman. "Hi, I'm May, and this is my lord, Hugh. Welcome to Duncan's World."

A smiling woman of roughly forty, she wore a long gown similar to Brooke's but reddish-brown, with a draping braid of blonde hair. Hugh was tall, like Duncan in height and coloring. "Brothers?" Morgan wondered aloud.

"Cousins. We've lived close to each other most of our lives. He started doing this, and I had to follow. Stupid me," Hugh explained with a roll of his eyes. Most everyone laughed at what must have been an old joke between the men.

Morgan was beginning to relax with the new group when Duncan walked away from a young man in period garb, frowning. "That was the King's messenger. He's advising any woman to be escorted after hours. Someone was attacked last night."

"What?" May cried in fear-filled astonishment. "Who? Have they been caught?"

"The Tarot reader. She was moving about early. Someone heard the scuffle and chased off whoever was bothering her." Duncan crossed his arms, scanning the group, a tautness shadowing his face.

The minute Duncan voiced the warning, Morgan went stock still, his focus shifting inward, the memory of his dream reborn. In detail. "N'Réa? She was attacked?" The dream hadn't been a dream at all. Tension grew along his spine, and he had to force his fist to relax. The images from the night before were very real.

"Yes. You know her?" Duncan sank into an empty camp chair next to his cousin and May. He held his chin in his hand, saying, "She's a good person. Usually keeps to herself, but she is as known as most of us for doing the Faires." He shook his massive head, confusion weighing heavily on his thoughts. "I don't know why someone would hurt her."

Morgan forced his voice to remain level as the intensity of the dream resurfaced. It made him relive the anger of her attack all over again. His instinct to protect pulsed through him. "I know her, in a sense. Was she hurt?" She had been injured in his dream. Was it only a warning of what happened, or the real vision of her attack?

"I don't know," Duncan replied with concern. "The messenger is spreading the word to the camps. No one saw who her attacker was, only that it was a larger male. They walked her to her tent, and no one else saw anything. The young squire who helped is the one who actually reported the fracas." His hand to his chin, a finger pressed over his mouth, indicated that was the entirety of what he knew.

The thick silence of the group was telling. Several worried faces circled the little camp space where the evidence of last night's fire remained.

"This doesn't happen often, I take it?"

May said with a trembling hand pressed to her chest, "No! I've never heard of someone being attacked!" She leaned into Hugh, who wrapped an arm around her.

Morgan stood, anger making his movements jerky. "I'm going to go find Brooke and make sure she knows. She likes to walk at night." Which was true, but she almost always went with Mitch, or as a wolf, but that wasn't something he was about to share. He heard the camp call their farewells as Morgan headed to the interior of the grounds.

N'Réa had been attacked. A seething rage filled him that someone would dare put their hands on her. It didn't occur to him to question if he was enraged because it was her or whether if any woman had been the victim, if he would react the same. He hastened along the booth corridor to her tent with a stiff, impatient stride. He wouldn't relax until he knew for certain she was all right.

Relief loosened some of his strain when he noted her tent flaps hung half open, which seemed to be what she preferred, leaving her tent in half shadows through the day. She'd made it to her tent that morning. Knowing that much helped ease his concern, but not enough. Who would hurt her? Why? Where had she been?

He paused outside her tent and questioned what he was doing. What could he do? What was he doing there to begin with? Nothing about this trip, about this woman, made sense. He argued silently for a few minutes with himself about the purpose of seeing her again. Only to make sure she wasn't hurt. That was his argument. This visit had nothing to do with his haunting dreams, or the one from the night before, which had awakened him from a sound sleep. No. This was only to ease his conscience that she hadn't been hurt. Maybe tonight he'd get to sleep for doing this good deed. Morgan could hope.

Firming his resolve, he gripped the edge of the tent opening. He slipped inside before he could make himself leave. His sight adjusted quickly away from the brighter morning light. She sat at the same table as the day before with one arm resting close to herself, her hand clutched, partially hidden beneath her clothing.

"N'Réa?" He swallowed, resisting the impact of seeing her, of being bathed in her sweet scent. He'd given up for the moment of ignoring it completely. Not happening. He'd do his duty and leave.

"You're still here." It was an accusation, not a question. Her emerald gaze flashed at him in the bands of light sneaking into the tent. He caught the confusion flitting over her features, but he could also see the shadow of pain as clearly. Something was wrong.

"It seems that way." He made his legs move, taking him to the table. "Are you all right?"

Her expression cooled like a sheet of ice water was splashed over her, the fiery depths vanishing as though drowned. "I'm fine. Why?"

"I heard you were attacked." He frowned as her scent invaded his thoughts, winding through his senses, slicing into his system anew. It was like a drug pumping into his blood, and he craved more. It only added fuel to his anger. He did not want this woman! "Why?"

She flinched at the flung word. "Hell if I know!" she snapped. "I went to the privies in the early hours. What concern is it of yours, anyway?"

Morgan didn't miss her wince when her arm slid across the table with her movements. "Stand up," he ordered.

Cradling her arm, she rose in front of him, the green of her eyes sparking in defiance like the reflection of the sun striking rolling waves on the sea. The green glistened as bright as diamonds and was just as breathtaking. He swallowed, falling headfirst into those depths. "Hell," he whispered, breaking the spell with effort. "Let me see your arm."

"Why? You can't do anything. I was going to the med tent later."

He took a breath, seeking even a thread of control. It was super fine and stretching to its limit. "Please," he asked in a calmer tone. "Let me see your arm."

He sucked air between his teeth when he steadied her bracelets and discovered the gaudy green and purple bruise encompassing her fragile wrist. "They hit you with something, didn't they?" he asked as he ran a finger carefully over the swollen, mottled skin.

Her swallowed whimper escaped no matter how tender his stroke. "Yes." She shivered in his hold. "I had a small pouch. I guess whoever it was thought I had money."

"I'll be right back," he said, carefully letting her arm settle naturally against her body, trying to be as gentle as possible with her in his hands. "Don't go anywhere, and don't try to use it. It's broken." He sought her expression, finding confusion and wariness.

"You're sure?" she asked on a cautious note, wavering on her feet.

Why did he feel so protective of this woman? The reactions annoyed and confused him more. Inside, he wanted to strangle the growing cauldron, but had no idea how. Instead, he focused on her injury.

"Yes, but I can take care of it." He spun on a heel but stopped at the tent opening, speaking over his shoulder. "N'Réa, we need to talk after this is taken care of." He left before she could answer him, not sure what else he could say the way his insides were coiling with emotion, lust, and a burning hunger for the woman he couldn't explain. Morgan marched into the grounds, the crowds growing along with the rise in volume of activity as he hunted for Mitch and Brooke.

He found them, as he had feared, talking to the blacksmith about armor. His sister tensed when he pulled her aside, but she didn't say a word about his expression.

"I need you," he said simply.

She turned to the vendor. "I'll be right back." He nodded as he continued to pound out a dent in a breastplate. Mitch followed as Morgan explained what had happened and the King's warning for all the women.

"She'll be with me," Mitch stated immediately.

"I'm not worried about her," Morgan said with a loving smile for his sister. "It's everyone else that's here." They reached N'Réa's tent, and Morgan gave Mitch a commanding motion. He untied the separated panels behind them when Morgan and Brooke entered the tent, then crossed his arms, standing guard. No one would get past him to interrupt.

Morgan's attention narrowed once more to the woman behind the table. "N'Réa," he said, tipping toward his side in introduction. "This is my sister, Brooke. Can she see your arm?"

The raven-haired beauty focused on Brooke. "I saw you yesterday, at the training match."

Brooke nodded. "Yes, I remember," she replied in a comforting voice. "Morgan says you've been injured." She held out a hand. "Can I see it?"

"I don't know what you can do. He says it's broken."

"Don't worry," she informed her soothingly. "I've done this before." Brooke whipped up, staring briefly with a wondering expression, when N'Réa cautiously placed her arm in Brooke's care. A scant moment later, her face went blank and she began to examine N'Réa's arm in earnest.

Brooke eased the bangles out of her way as she cradled N'Réa's injured arm but the bracelets slid forward too easily, blocking the worst area. "I'm taking these off so I can see what I'm doing."

N'Réa shook her head. "My hand is swollen. They won't go over. I've already tried."

Brooke gave a calming smile to the other woman, then ran a finger over the line of bangles and bracelets, and one by one, they appeared in a pile on the table. N'Réa shuddered in astonishment, her eyes widening as the pile grew. "What are you?"

"The real thing," Brooke answered simply. "Now, relax. It won't hurt, but wrist bones are difficult. I don't want to miss my mark." Brooke grew silent as her featherlight touch traveled up N'Réa's arm to glide with delicate grace downward.

N'Réa's mouth gaped in silent shock, frozen as her arm healed while Brooke spoke in a language Morgan didn't know, but had heard. First the bruise faded before her moving fingers, then when Brooke reached the wrist, she pressed into the skin and murmured a phrase.

"Flex your fingers. Does anything hurt?" Brooke asked, concentrating as the remainder of the bruise disappeared leaving her arm and wrist a flushed pink, which faded as well.

N'Réa did as told, a wary, stunned expression flitting over her face. "No, it's fine. How... Why did you do that?" N'Réa gawked at Brooke, her face pale in the morning brightness.

Brooke shrugged with little concern. "Morgan trusts you. Otherwise you would be at the hospital and still in pain."

"But why?" N'Réa repeated. "How?"

"Because I asked her to," Morgan told her, unable to give her a better answer either. He gave Brooke a kiss on the forehead. "Thank you, sister." He straightened with a humoring lift to his mouth. "Don't go crazy with the armorer. This is only one event, and I'm an alternate, all right?"

Brooke laughed, a pleasant sound, completely amused by what he said. "Sure it is." She patted him on the sleeve and gliding out, she placed her hand on Mitch's lifted arm, leaving the two of them alone in thickening silence as the canvas fell together, blanking out the world beyond.

Morgan paced a few seconds, dragging a hand over his head. N'Réa hadn't moved. Not that he could blame her. He waited for the coming storm. He'd been impulsive, but it had been the right thing to do. Now he had to wait for the fallout.

"My God!" She finally choked out the words. "I need to sit down." She plopped onto her chair with a boneless whoosh and a whimper. "What just happened? Why are you still here?" Her hand shook as she reached for the pile of bangles in disbelief, her expression a stunned blankness. "And for the twenty thousand-dollar question: why the hell are you in my dreams?"

He jerked to a stop, whirling to face her. "Your dreams?"

She leveled a glare at him that would melt the icecaps. "Yes, damn it! My dreams. I have my own, you know. You've been there! Why?" She dropped her head into her hands, her breathing harsh and ragged, the bracelets forgotten.

"I wish I knew," he replied softly, but with that news, Morgan feared he did.

* * * *

N'Réa forced her attention to rise, taking in the man who filled a large portion of her tent interior. Ominous and brooding, expressive. Lethal. She stopped her rambling brain right there.

"Why are you still here? You were a guest yesterday." Her hopes that he would be leaving came to a grinding halt as a shiver flew across her skin at the sound of his voice. *This could not be happening!*

"I was knighted last night in council. I'm an alternate for Duncan's camp."

"But you have to squire! Take the trials!" she cried as fears overrode her common sense. She shouldn't be yelling at a man whose sister was a damned witch! *The real thing,* she thought with a flash of fear. Brooke made N'Réa look like a carnival freak.

She thought he shrugged. "They made a concession for Duncan. I impressed them. How, I don't know. I've never held a sword." He started pacing the caged confines of her tent, but he walked like he'd always carried a sword, with a natural fluidity. The sword hung with ease on his hip, an extension of the man and his step.

Her assessments of him continued to grow as his measured steps carried him from side to side, reaching the walls of her tent only to have to spin and do it again. He prowled, a strength and grace she had never seen in a man, a lithe movement. His stride reminded her of a pacing predator. A stealthy, dangerous animal, barely controlled. She shivered as the thought formed and refused to be dislodged.

"So you will be staying on then?" she asked, morose and unwelcoming of the idea.

His coal-black brows flew up. "You sound as happy as I am about this situation. That's a relief."

"A relief!" she shouted, leaping to her feet to not have him above her. "You have no idea. I don't fuck Renis or guests." *Damn the lover's card!*

The thoughtfully silent expression on his face vanished, and his chiseled mouth thinned into a brutal line. "That's good to know," he retorted as he marched forward and planted his palms on the table, his face a breath from hers. The mercurial gray of his eyes flashed with an inner lightning, and her skin tingled, popping with the electricity arcing between them. "Because I have never *fucked* a woman in my life!" Her lungs quivered when his voice dropped, hinting at something she knew she didn't want to touch. Not from this man. "I make love to them."

His breath whispered against her lips. The shock of him so close rifled heedlessly down her spine, turning her insides into something living and hot. He shoved away from her with a snarl on his lip. "Something you will never know," he vowed with a thunderous snarl.

"Praise be!" she mocked, raising her hands upward.

He whirled and stalked to the canvas overlap. He pitched it open and tied the one side with practiced ease. She thought he was done, that he would leave, but he surprised her. As if he hadn't done so already.

"N'Réa," he said, once more cool and distant as a stranger as he paused in the opening. "Don't go anywhere at night alone. Your attacker wasn't caught."

Dropping her fists to her hips, her jaw clenched at his directives. "Who should I call? Superman?"

He gave her another smoldering glance. "Just say my name," he told her, a demand that she obey in the way he said it. "I will find you." And before she could tell him and his offer where to go, he vanished outside.

"Oh God!" N'Réa collapsed onto her chair a second time, her legs giving out on her, her skirt billowing out in protest. Her bracelets clinked on the table, scattering into a loose bunch from the semi-straight stack Brooke created. She reached for them automatically, then stared at her arm. Her healed arm. She dropped the bracelet from between numb fingers to the table, touching her right arm.

Feeling braver, she poked it gingerly, then poked the bones. Nothing. Not a twinge, or an ache. Even the bruise, the whole ugly blue-green-purple thing was gone. "How did she do that?" she asked the open space of her tent.

She swallowed when Brooke's voice, light as a spring breeze, easy and caring returned. "Hell, she's a real witch!" She heaved for air. N'Réa swept the opening. And he's related to her! At least for the moment, neither Brooke nor Morgan were anywhere she could see. How do you deal with meeting an honest-to-goodness *real* witch?

"N'Réa! Are you all right? I just heard." Marie, Bailey's wife, rushed her way inside the tent just then amid a bundle of fabric and worried frowns.

N'Réa took a deep breath and plastered on a smile. She'd have to work it all out later. "Yeah, I'm fine. A tussle. Nothing happened." *At least no one else knew about her arm,* she thought with a swell of relief.

Marie swept her up in a hug, nearly cutting off her air supply in her worry. "Oh, good grief! I don't understand. You don't know who it was?"

N'Réa shook her head when Marie loosened her strangling hold. "Clueless. It was dark, around five this morning, I guess."

Marie pulled up the other chair to sit and visit. She was a robust woman, and like Bailey, easy to smile. Yet, right then, her smile was nowhere to be seen, a mama hen's worry there instead after N'Réa's attack. She clasped N'Réa's smaller hands tightly within her own. "Well, if you would feel safer, we can pal up. You're here alone, aren't you?"

"Yeah, but I'll be fine." Without meaning to, her attention crawled to the opening of the booth. Her head whipped to Marie with a snap when she realized what she was doing, who she was searching for. She firmed her smile into place once more. "Really, I'm sure it was a single occurrence." She swallowed, not letting *that man* penetrate her thoughts for another second.

Marie pressed her cheek to N'Réa's. "All right, if you're sure?"

She nodded, warmed by Marie's concern long after she left for her own business.

The rest of the morning provided ample traffic to draw her thoughts away from the worry of the attack as well as from her disturbing reaction to Morgan. Alternately cool and unattached to gentle and tender while he held her injured arm. There was no larger example of a man of contradictions.

He left her too unsettled, too breathless. Way too confused. As business continued to flow, she was able to dismiss him completely out of her thoughts.

It wasn't until late in the afternoon when she heard a known voice. "N'Réa? How are you feeling?"

Her head snapped up from her quiet musings as the petite blonde strolled into her tent.

"Brooke," she said in a squeak. N'Réa wet her lips, her heart tripping over itself.

Brooke smiled, as if to ease her fears. "Don't be afraid. That was why I wanted to see you. I was concerned this morning might have overwhelmed you, since you don't know any of us." She palmed her vibrant blue skirts out of the way and took the chair sitting close to the table, her slim hands resting clasped on her lap. Brooke's hair was a single twist to her shoulders with ribbons threaded through it. She looked the part of an honored lady. Her genteel voice and mannerisms were exact, and somehow N'Réa knew they weren't faked. She didn't dare push her thoughts to find out.

N'Réa met her unbelievable, coffee-brown gaze and could see nothing but genuine kindness. "Know of you? I've never met any of you."

Brooke nodded once. "I know. This is our first Faire, and I think Mitch and I are hooked. Morgan..." She waved a hand through the air. "No one ever knows with that one."

N'Réa kept her hands clasped on the table to keep them from shaking uncontrollably "Your brother?" she asked hesitantly.

"One of two, and a sister," Brooke offered with a glowing smile. "But I came to see if you were experiencing any problems." Brooke's concern homed in on the arm in question.

N'Réa sharply shook her head. "None. I've never..." She licked dry lips, her nerves telling her to shut up, but sensing she was safe with this woman, somehow. "I've never experienced true magic," she whispered, her pulse ticking with the admittance and the acknowledgment of what had happened earlier.

N'Réa could read the cards, sometimes getting stronger feelings if she tried. That had happened when she'd been a child, but she'd never pushed herself since to see what she could do, how far she could reach. She kept her entire life locked up like a safe. No one in and no one out. She had nowhere near Brooke's ability, either. Brooke actually frightened her a little.

"And you shouldn't fear it," Brooke said with a straight face, her tone soothing, comforting. "I'm an herbalist first, a witch second."

N'Réa swallowed a gasp. Brooke's straightforward approach was making N'Réa's head spin. The blonde didn't bat an eyelash talking about magic and healing broken bones. Years of caution wouldn't let her relax that much, though she did sense a kindred spirit in Brooke. Releasing a little of the tension, she poorly blurted the first thing that came to mind.

"How does your husband...?" N'Réa ducked her head. "Sorry. That was rude."

Brooke laughed with sincere mirth. "Not even. Mitch had to swallow facts the size of an ostrich egg when it came to me." She leaned into the chair, unperturbed with her questions as they talked like old girlfriends. "But he came around. I love him with a depth I never thought to find."

N'Réa smiled as the warmth of her honesty flowed from Brooke. "You can see it. It's in his gaze when he looks at you. He didn't even notice Leslie from what I heard yesterday, and she makes sure every man with equipment sees her." N'Réa knew she'd already propositioned Morgan. Duncan's ex had the brass to do it right outside her tent.

"I trust Mitch to the ends of the earth. He is my soulmate, my protector, my heart, my mate."

N'Réa tucked her hands under her chin. Brooke's words sent a wistful wave through her. "I doubt I'll ever find that."

"You're welcome to stay with us in Duncan's camp. Everyone is on alert until we figure out who attacked you. I noticed there isn't much security after hours." Brooke's brow furrowed.

N'Réa shook her head. "No, people are expected to act with dignity and honor. Someone doesn't want to, I guess."

Brooke rose from her chair, straightening her lengthy satin skirts. "Well, I better go find Mitch. I left him next door with Bailey. He had an interest in a particular sword." She started to walk away, but said over her shoulder, "I meant the invitation. I have no fear, but too many women are here alone."

"I'll think about it," she conceded. Brooke nodded in acceptance, gratefully not pushing. "Brooke?" The woman paused with a hand on the tent edge. "Morgan? Is he dangerous?"

Sunlight glowed over the blonde where she stood swathed in an arch of golden light. "Only when someone he cares about is threatened. He's very controlled usually." There was speculation in her voice as she spoke to N'Réa. "I was a little surprised he came to me this morning, but I feel better now that we've talked. You're well protected now." Then with a final nod, she ducked outside to find her husband.

N'Réa slumped in her chair. Morgan? Controlled? She couldn't picture it. He was walking energy. He pulsed and vibrated with it. And care for her? She was more positive he didn't like her at all, which was fine with her. She didn't want to become involved with anyone, and she knew Morgan was definitely not a smart choice to start with.

She could picture the strength of him as he'd paced, for some reason concerned for an absolute stranger to have come to her, to offer his help and Brooke's.

Brooke was gentle, kind, completely different from the fierce aura Morgan exuded. She'd offered without question, without demanding to know one thing about N'Réa or questioning Morgan's reasons. The least N'Réa could do was take her a gift to say thank you for her unselfish act. She snapped her fingers as she remembered seeing the perfect thing during her morning walk. She grabbed her money and tied her tent closed, hoping it was still there.

Chapter Five

It was not quite fully dark by the time N'Réa reached the edge of Duncan's camp and heard, "Halt!" She didn't argue, letting the guard do his bit. The more they practiced, the better they sounded.

"Who dares to enter his Lordship's domain?" a young man bearing a red tunic of Duncan's knights called in accent.

"N'Réa. I bear a gift for Lady Brooke."

There was a squeal from the faceless group around the firepit. "Oh, get out of the way, Turner!" Brooke appeared under his arm and grasped her hands. "She's welcome, you clod."

"Have you been drinking?" N'Réa asked immediately, taken aback at the exuberant woman standing before her in colorful shorts and a T-shirt now. This was the woman she'd met today?

"No, I'm not in character now," she replied, laughter dancing in her coffee eyes. "How did I do?"

N'Réa put her weight on a hip, laughing in genuine surprise. "Excellent! You have the grace of a queen in your voice when you play the lady."

A pink blush rose on Brooke's cheeks. "Thank you. I still need to work on lines and my accent, but I assumed it would happen. I needed to find the person I wanted to be first."

N'Réa let Brooke drag her forward to the group. "That's true." She leaned over and whispered, "So Mitch is the strong, silent type?"

Brooke stopped walking and slapped a hand over her mouth, giggling. "Oh, I'm going to like you!" she cried. "Hey, look who's come to join us!"

N'Réa hit the brakes. "No! I mean I brought you this to say thank you for this morning. For my aches from last night," she clarified, clearing her throat, trying to hide her embarrassment of almost saying too much. Brooke gave her an understanding pat on her arm. There was no fretfulness to be found that N'Réa would say anything about the *kind* of help she'd received. Brooke was trusting her with much more than N'Réa had ever shared with anyone. It continued to leave her confused and cautious.

"Why? What did you do?" William asked as he rotated spitted chickens over the firepit. N'Réa swallowed at the sight. She was starving. Her waiting noodle soup mix lost its thrill as the aroma of spice and juices hit her empty stomach. It was as bad as standing in front of a buffet after not eating for three days. She had to get out of there.

"She gave me a tea blend. She's a talented herbalist," she improvised, recalling the conversation earlier in the afternoon as a quick coverup. She pushed the folded gift in her hands toward Brooke. "Please, Brooke. I saw this earlier today and thought you might like it."

As though sensing her need to turn tail and run to her own tent, Brooke didn't look at what N'Réa held at all.

"You have to stay. There's plenty to eat. Are you hungry?" Brooke avoided the gift until she got an answer. N'Réa would have argued, but she didn't get the chance.

"Her stomach is!" cried Beuchard. Several around the circle burst into laughter. N'Réa glanced around the group, embarrassed only to find several welcoming smiles, and began to relax. She relaxed more when she realized Morgan wasn't part of the group waiting on dinner.

"All right, for a while." She stepped forward, all but shoving the gift at Brooke. "Oh, here, for heaven's sakes! Here."

Brooke took the cloth and deliberately unfolded it. She let out a delighted gasp. "This is beautiful."

"I thought it would match your gown, and it's reversible. Especially if you stay or do other events. The chill can get strong in the mornings."

Brooke handled the cloak with appreciative hands. "This is wonderful! I'll have to pass out more tea if I get this for it." She shared a secretive wink with N'Réa, then Brooke swung the cloak over her shoulders, clasping it around her throat. It draped like a luxurious curtain of deep blue down her body. "How do I look?"

"Charming!"

"Beautiful!" they all cried.

"How fare thee, good mistress?" Duncan asked with a concerned note, arriving from behind them dressed as usual in his lord's garb with a towel over his arm, shower kit in hand, and hair wet.

"I fare well, Lord Duncan," she greeted him with an easy curtsy, pleasantly warmed by his greeting. "Thee have made good friends for thine efforts." Her gaze rose over his shoulder and found Mitch, and *oh no*! Morgan was bringing up the rear.

"Aye, welcome for the e'en meal, good mistress."

She barely heard the parting as Morgan walked up with finger-combed hair, his shirt clinging to him in damp spots. She swallowed as her heart picked up speed without doing anything to make it happen. When he stood close enough, she discovered that he smelled of hot, damp skin and soap, and male. Very, very male.

"How are you feeling?" His voice lowered to a private timbre between them, vibrating the air with energy. Controlled. She could understand that word now. His eyes burned her as he studied her, the energy he exuded in the gray depths. Their intensity was no less unsettling when the sun was down than when it was up.

Trying to hide her need for it, she minced a step to put a bigger gap between them. "Better." She peeked behind her, motioning with a weak hand. "I brought Brooke a gift."

His lips lost their firmness as he followed his sister, amazed to see his expression turn almost tender as Brooke paraded the cloak for the camp. "She'll wear it until if falls off, I'm sure." His expression became a blank canvas when he faced her. "Excuse me?" She let him pass without a single breathed protest. The more space between them, the better.

"N'Réa? Come sit with us," Brooke called, patting a chair next to her and Mitch.

It wasn't easy, but she resisted the urge to run, convincing her feet to carry her to join them. She could get through one stinking meal! She was careful to not touch anyone accidentally, to not let the walls down as the conversation flowed around her. Eventually, someone placed a plate with chicken, bean salad, and a roll in her hands.

"To drink?" Brooke asked.

"Water is fine," she replied, and a bottled water appeared next to her. "This is good." N'Réa pointed to the chicken on her plate, half eaten before she realized it.

"I guessed it was the least I could do, since they are loaning Morgan equipment and swords," Brooke said. "I chipped in on the food and cooking." Brooke's cheeks were rosy, and her eyes sparkled in the reaching flames of the firepit.

"You're really enjoying this, aren't you?"

Brooke practically bounced. "Incredibly! Aunt Jerry would love it too, but I'd have to tell her to meet us here."

"Does she live nearby?" N'Réa finished her plate without a thought to manners, she was so hungry. Dry soup couldn't compare to fresh, hot food.

"No, unfortunately." Brooke noted the empty dish. "More? I bought dessert earlier from the bakery." She leaned over to whisper, "I hid it so we'd have dessert!"

"Hey, I heard that!" William piped up.

"I didn't point fingers, but the cinnamon rolls lasted a total of eight seconds. I counted!" she retorted with a hand on her hip, grinning widely, everyone laughing as William's face reddened. N'Réa hadn't laughed so much in ages. Brooke fit in like a true Reni. Mitch rested against one of the oversized coolers, stretched out with one arm propped over a knee as he ate. He was smiling and laughing too at the camp antics. They both fit in.

Morgan was a silent observer, watchful, guarded as he ate and participated. He fit in, but in a different way. She imagined the walls around her mind, just to be safe, fortifying her barriers. His attention touched everywhere, constantly roving, the intense weight and curiosity hesitating on her on more than one occasion. The intense vibration of his interest seemed to slow in his visual travels when he reached her.

She couldn't help herself from peeking in his direction, admiring the shape of his thighs molded into camel-brown trousers. His now dried shirt rested on wide shoulders, a smooth chest hinted at underneath through the gap at the throat, opened in a deep untied V. Studying him now obliterated the image she experienced every night in her dreams. The real-life man was a hundred times more potent.

When they put dessert on her plate, she remembered where she was. "What is it?" she asked.

"It's a custard pastry I tried and melted for," Brooke admitted. "I bought four dozen. I hope it's enough."

"You're going to spoil us, fair Brooke," Hugh cried as he stuffed the whole thing into his mouth with a total disregard to tact. May ate hers a little more delicately, but it didn't last long.

"My pleasure," she said. "I have three credit cards I've never used. This seemed like a good time to break them in." She raised her hands when a cheer went up from the crowd. "All right, behave yourselves. I'm not bottomless."

N'Réa ate her pastry with easy enjoyment, finishing her water until nothing remained and she was pleasantly full. One of the other ladies stepped up to help with the cleaning detail. "Thank you," she told her, enjoying the inclusiveness they offered.

She noted movement to her side. A woman's hands floated all over Morgan's chest from behind him, but she was sure she knew who stood hidden by his larger frame. N'Réa yanked away, not wanting to see or know.

"I need to get back," she told Brooke, ready to escape, no longer at ease, her fears and cautions striking to get out while she could, not sure she wanted to investigate why they were tormenting her now. "I have to go shopping in the morning and run some errands." *Lame, N'Réa.* But no one else seemed to notice her anxiousness.

"You stay in camp?" Brooke asked as they stood.

Clasping her hands together, she rolled them, trying to think of how to answer and what would be the quickest one to let her leave. "Um, yes. I was thinking I might do some sightseeing later on." She didn't look behind her again. Getting away was all she wanted.

Brooke clapped happily. "Go with us! We're going to the wharf and who knows where else."

"I couldn't!" N'Réa protested. "I mean..." But she got no further as Morgan's voice wound over her ear like a sensuous caress, smooth and decadent.

"She'll drag you if you don't say yes."

A shiver struck her at the purred words. Her body responded no matter how much she hated the reaction, her skin growing tight and her lungs dragging, seeking oxygen. The spark bloomed and couldn't be ignored because of any animosity this time. *I don't like him!* she reminded herself, the growing need deep inside impossible to ignore anymore. Every time he spoke to her, his voice or a glimpse of his darkened storm eyes negated her argument. Liking had absolutely nothing to do with wanting.

Brooke glowered with mock dismay at her brother. "Stop it, Morgan! I will not," she remarked.

N'Réa stomped her pulse into place. "I'm sorry. I can't," she said, wanting to escape.

"Well, we weren't until probably Wednesday. Maybe by then?" Brooke asked hopefully.

N'Réa relented again. "I'll see. That'll probably work." She waved to the group as they hollered their farewells. She didn't clear two paces before she heard him.

"I'll walk you home," Morgan offered.

"I don't need — " she began, but he cut her off, his expression direct.

"No lady is to walk alone. Period." She saw the determination in his stance and knew it would be nothing less than a knock-down, dragged-out fight to make him change his mind. And even after the effort, it wouldn't make him change his mind.

N'Réa forced a nonchalant stride, not caring if he followed or not, saying, "All right." She offered her goodbyes and aimed for the edge of Duncan's camp. Stuffing her reactions down deep, she shrugged. He did *nothing* for her. Morgan tucked his hands behind his back and kept her pace. She maintained a casual stroll when all she really wanted to do was bolt. The vendor campsite was almost directly across the grounds from where the knights and jousters were camped, allowing the fighters to be closer to the arena. It wasn't a long walk, but the distance seemed interminable to her.

He was silent as he walked beside her. When he broke the silence, the rough sound sliced through the night, catching her off-guard.

"Thank you."

Her head snapped up. "Why?" she asked as her steps slowed to a crawl unintentionally.

"For giving me an excuse to walk away from Leslie. She does not understand no. I feel sorry for her if she tries for Mitch."

"Will Mitch do something?" she asked, but Morgan shook his head.

"No, he's a gentleman, as I am trying to be. Brooke, she's another matter. Those two have been to Hell and back. She might not be as kind."

A chill crawled over her skin, raising goosebumps at the ominous implication of his reply. "She won't, you know..." She couldn't stop the cautionary, speculative tone. If N'Réa had witnessed a fraction of what Brooke could do, Leslie would never survive.

"She might." He stopped and faced her when she gasped. Shaking his head, he clarified. "Brooke wouldn't hurt her. Brooke couldn't hurt a fly, but she will fight for what is hers."

"It's obvious to a blind man that they belong together. I doubt Leslie would try." She tried to sound convincing, except she'd spent several years with Leslie in attendance at different Faires and events, following after Duncan to torment him. The woman deserved what she got after so long.

Morgan seemed indifferent. "I hope you're right." He started walking again. "Thank you for handling things the way you did, by the way."

His voice held a rich, tempting quality. It caused more goosebumps to pile up on her skin. Even her breasts ached. She crossed her arms to hide any outward signs, praying it was dark enough that he wouldn't notice. Why was she reacting like this to him? It made her want to scream. She didn't want to have anything to do with Morgan. Best to get it said and over with. Maybe if this was what cleared out the air between them, he would go away. "You mean about this morning?" She gripped her arms around her middle. The evenings were beginning to chill, with no campfire or crowd to stave off the cooling temperatures. That was the only reason her body had developed aches. It had nothing to do with the man at her side. "I felt it was necessary. She did help me."

"I meant about not broadcasting," he said. "My family has a lot of secrets. I don't share them easily."

"I won't say anything. There's nothing to regret."

"Thank you," he said with distinct relief as they neared her edge of the campgrounds. "Tell me, what does N'Réa mean?"

They stopped not far from the nearest site. She was almost home free. She cleared her throat. "It means mine. It's a variant of a Basque spelling." Slaughtered, as one foster family had pointed out, but it was her name, all hers, and she refused to change its uniqueness.

"Mine," he whispered. His gaze narrowed as though he were delving into her darkest secrets, his irises darkening until there was more black than gray. "Interesting." She stood frozen when his hand lifted and brushed over her skin, sweeping hair from her face to pin behind her ear. He stood so close, she felt the warmth of his skin though inches separated them.

Morgan was a compelling man. She stood there at odds with herself. She drifted over the cut of his jaw until she stopped at his mouth. *Firm lips,* she thought.

She would not let him in, she silently shouted when she realized what she was doing. She tightened her shoulders to reinforce her mind, her thoughts. Whoever this man was, she did not have to let the cards win.

"I meant what I said. If at any time you need me, you only have to call. I will hear you. I will find you," he said with an unaffected tone. Sweeping up, she found his eyes clear and smoky gray. The strength she knew he wielded lay in those eyes, in his voice, no matter how he tried to camouflage it.

She swallowed her heart into place, its rapid-fire beat pounding through her veins. "I'll be fine. Thank you for walking me to my tent."

"Then, good night, N'Réa," he said with a polite tilt of his head. The way her name slid from his tongue sounded like a caress, fading, as he became swallowed up in the darkness. Holding herself tighter, the chill trickled down her spine as her breasts ached. She blew out a breath, fighting to recapture the calm she'd had before arriving at Duncan's encampment. Silently she doubted she'd ever find it again but refused to name Morgan as the cause.

"He's just a man," she sniped. "Just a bloody man." Affirming that, she turned and, a few moments later, crawled into her own tent to get ready for bed.

* * * *

Wednesday she dressed in jeans and a lightweight sweatshirt. The closer she got to Duncan's camp, the harder she dug for a reason to not go with them. She didn't want to go sightseeing, not with Morgan, though going with Brooke would be fun. She'd been torn since Sunday over the differences in the man, from the protector to the passionate man of secrets.

She didn't need a man in her life to help screw it up. She was doing just fine all by herself, thank you! But Morgan was a far cry from the people she'd known, from the life she'd all but left behind for her gypsy lifestyle.

Her fingers were tucked halfway into the front pockets of her jeans, her sneakers making no noise as she walked across the campgrounds, avoiding hazards and saying hi to those who stayed over. Her mind wandered as she crossed the distance.

She'd tried telemarketing and hated it. She'd slaved as a waitress and hated it. She'd tried to go to college but couldn't find a purpose. She'd held numerous odd jobs until she'd decided to live from her tent and car. It was paid for, though it was older than the Rocky Mountains. She made decent money doing the readings and always kept a pocket somewhere with her next fee in it. She did make sure the entrance fees were covered before anything else. Priorities had to be made and kept.

She could stay with people she knew for a few weeks at a time if necessary, but usually during the worst of winter, she headed south and set up shop somewhere for a few weeks, camping. It was enough to pay her bills, the few she couldn't avoid, and living expenses. She'd learned to live frugally and without money.

Orphaned, she'd spent several years with a foster family as a young girl, until her ability to see things and events began to make her different. Try explaining to a Southern Baptist how his foster child knew when the rains would come to help his farm or when his wife became pregnant. When she'd foreseen her foster uncle's death, they'd dismissed it as impossible. Three days later he was hit by a drunk driver. The next day they called Child Services and demanded that N'Réa be placed in a different home.

They'd despised N'Réa, as if she were the cause of the accident, as if at the age of nine she had somehow wished for anyone to die. She had cared for them, wanted to help, to warn, but instead, she was blamed.

She bounced from home to home, never finding that niche family who would fully accept her, finally giving in at sixteen and finding her own way.

She learned to hide her ability after the first mistake. She didn't talk about it, ever. With walls so thick, so hard, very little penetrated, and she never sought outward. Many assumed it was the system that damaged her ability to be open and trusting, and she let them. Only it wasn't the adoption system that had made her impersonal to human emotion, to any kind of affection. She attempted very little to not draw attention to herself, not that anyone paid her much to begin with. She stayed quiet and alone. The status quo had worked for years, and until this show, no one ever noticed her. She couldn't afford to trust anyone. There were a few friends, faces of other Ren Faire folk, who she could count on lightly like Bailey and Marie, but no one who knew the truth, the depths of her secret. She had no idea what she was, secretly terrified of finding out. The only thing she knew for certain, N'Réa could make people fear her, and she didn't want that, ever.

There was only one choice: to keep her secrets hidden. So she was a diviner pretending to be a reader who may or may not be believed. She didn't use her ability, never brought it out in the open. Tarot and palm reading were her only outlets. She kept the blocks up to prevent people seeing into her, and she never let herself open up to anyone else. It wasn't worth the heartache.

She followed the Faire circuit on the West Coast from Salem to Anaheim and little towns in between. How this one caught her interest, she couldn't remember. It was big enough to make good money and well known by other vendors and people who specifically sought the entertainment of the Faires. N'Réa first discovered it two years ago and was grateful for the chance to continue doing what she loved. There was also the fact that she knew a few familiar faces, which helped convince her that it couldn't be a bad event. Well, except for being robbed and attacked. Shaking her head, there was simply no answer and no excuse for that.

Her steps faltered as the clash of steel rang out loud and clear through the air well before she reached the other camp. *They must be practicing.* Setting herself into motion, she hoped to see some of it. They practiced to stay in shape and hone their skills. It was no small feat to win a blades tournament.

Competition was fierce. There were always more fighters than winning slots. The duels were fought with live steel and armor or chain mail, though some used shields. Combat helmets came in a few distinct styles and then there was always the parade armor, flashy and eye-catching, shined to within an inch of blinding.

She wasn't expecting to find Morgan in the ring as she approached, though. He was fighting hard in training leathers and a helmet against Beuchard, a big man who obviously outweighed Morgan by sheer size. Morgan was sinewy and lean, whereas years of fighting and a bit more had left a distinct mark on Beuchard.

She wasn't the only spectator as they circled around the ring. Several of the camp watched, but it seemed quiet as the two continued to slash and clash against each other.

"Halt!" Duncan shouted to be heard when there was a natural lull. "Good show, Beuchard. Where's Turner? He's next."

"Next?" she murmured.

Morgan rested in a corner as one of the others checked his buckles. "You're good," she heard him tell Morgan. The squire patted Morgan on the shoulder and sent him out where Turner, the guard who had stopped her Sunday night, waited in the ring.

"All right, Morgan. Pace him, make him work for it." She caught Morgan's nod. "Lay on!" Duncan shouted.

"Duncan? How many has he fought?" N'Réa asked, curious.

"This is four," he answered, keeping a critical eye on both. "Working on a few fundamentals, but he wears out his opponents. Higher, Turner, you chit! You'll lose an arm like that!" he bellowed as Morgan forced the younger man onto his butt.

He stood and dusted himself off, facing Morgan grimly. He gave a determined huff as they faced off. Turner seemed to be a good fighter, as far as she could tell, just not experienced, not compared to the fluid arcs and leaping attacks Morgan made.

Morgan circled Turner, blade at the ready as Turner tried to sweep across his midsection. The bite of steel on steel sounded with a metallic crunch as Morgan blocked and shoved him off. Turner rose and tried again, and Morgan blocked. His body moved with a feline grace as Turner made swing after swing, unable to penetrate the circle of Morgan's defense. Morgan was lightning fast on his next attack, forcing Turner to block or fall again.

"I swear, if he hasn't fought before, I'd like to know in what lifetime he did," Duncan muttered as Morgan unarmed Turner on the next clash. "Halt! Enough!"

"Where is everyone?" she finally got to ask without all the noise.

"The girls went into town to do something, a movie, I think," he said disinterestedly. "A few of the guys went to get lunch. We're it."

"Where's Brooke and Mitch?" she asked as Morgan, half naked and heavily breathing with fire in his eyes, approached the ropes.

"They went home," he blurted on a rushed gasp. "Oregon. The house..." He leaned over, sucking in air like a vacuum. He took a few deep draughts, then stood straight. "The house bids were opened. They needed to sign. They'll be here by Friday night." He bent over once more, his hands on his well-muscled thighs. Taut shoulders and a solid chest rolled and heaved with each sucked draw of air.

"Oh." N'Réa didn't know if she should be disappointed or not. She hadn't wanted to go sightseeing, not really, but for some reason she felt left alone. "You stayed?" she asked.

Morgan shrugged. "Guessed I could be a better problem here than hanging on them. I don't need anything from home." He stood straight, almost breathing normally with sweat dripping from his chin, his skin slick with the proof of his exertions. The sheen of his chest and the ripple of muscle beneath the soaked shirt kicked her heart into a higher gear.

"Oh," she murmured, tearing herself away. She did not want Morgan! She hoped repeating it would eventually help convince herself.

"I'm going to run under some water," he said as he slipped out of the makeshift arena.

"All right, I'll head back," she said with a weak smile. "See you later." She refused to be disappointed. What was wrong with her? Hadn't she just told herself she didn't *want* to go with them? Her head was trying to ache with all the arguing.

"You can stay for lunch," Duncan offered. "They went for barbecue." Morgan was already halfway to the showers at a jog.

"Sure. I guess my plans have changed without Brooke here." She followed Duncan to the center of camp to help with lunch.

She wondered why Morgan stayed instead of going with Brooke. Giving herself something to do, she helped dish out the plates of ribs and sides to the remaining team members on the grounds, the other girls smiling and laughing at the playful banter, and licked fingers of the guys as they poked into containers. Morgan hadn't needed to stay behind, not for any reason she could think of. So why would he?

Disrupted out of her thoughts, she returned Turner's smile when he said thank you. *Cute for a kid.* Probably twenty. At least he was polite, which was getting rare. It was easy to muse to herself in the general quiet of midweek, letting her thoughts flit from topic to topic.

She startled at a brusque tone when it broke into her musings. "Go sit down, Turner." Morgan didn't wait for her to help him, rather dropping ribs on a plate without any patience.

"You going to eat anything else?" she asked him with a frown, spotting the mound of beef ribs.

He glanced up through thick lashes. "No," he said, then dropped another on top of his stack as if in punctuation.

"Hey, Patrick!" a woman shouted from one of the tents. "William's on my phone."

Morgan took his plate to where several of the other fighters sat and propped his feet up on a cooler to eat.

"Arrogant bastard." She breathed heavily, determined to not let him get to her. Then she put a few bites on a plate for herself and picked a spot a little away from everyone to eat.

A few seconds later, Duncan's shouted curses halted everyone's eating. When it became eerily silent, N'Réa returned to her food, sorry she hadn't declined the offer. She didn't belong here. This wasn't her camp. These weren't her friends. She didn't know any of them and except for the kindness Morgan and his sister had shown her, they probably would have left her alone altogether, which was fine with her. She preferred to be alone. No one could demand answers, no one could question her. No one could care. Being in groups had always made her nervous. Somehow when Morgan was nearby she could forget that, until he noticed her, then all she wanted was to run.

She had to remember to swallow her food at the thunderous expression on Duncan's face when he stomped out of the tent after the phone call. He marched right past the table laden with food and kept going.

"Hell, something's wrong," Beuchard muttered.

"Kind of obvious, don't ya think?" Cale retorted, stuffing another forkful into his mouth.

"We'll have to wait for the end of the fit to find out what," Beuchard said. "He'll be all right in about half an hour, at least to talk."

N'Réa wiped her fingers, following Duncan's agitated form until he vanished around a corner out of sight. "Is it bad?"

Cale hooked his chin in the direction Duncan vanished. "I'd have to say so. He's got a temper, but he rarely lets it out except when he's fighting."

N'Réa found that Beuchard knew Duncan. He reappeared, still breathing heavily but more composed, roughly half an hour later.

"Hugh is off the team for the tourney," he stated curtly without preamble, marching into camp. "He broke his damn foot! William is with him getting it taken care of." He pivoted and faced Morgan, who had finished eating but watched everything through hooded eyes. "Dirk is calling you a ringer, and I'm half willing to agree, but it doesn't matter anymore. You're on the full team. You'll fight in Hugh's place. He's ranked second behind me. Can you take it, Morgan? You'll have some tough fights."

He shrugged with mild unconcern. "I guess I'm here for a reason." His attention slid over N'Réa, and the heat of it lingered until he tore away.

She clenched her plate on her lap, not wanting to react, dying to do something. Why did that keep happening?

Morgan gave a low sweeping bow from his chaired position. "I am at your service."

"Great! Another damn smartass!" Duncan muttered before he grabbed a plate to fill for himself.

When she peered across the camp pit, she caught Morgan's stormy, expressive eyes and couldn't restrain her smile when his lips twitched. "Smartass?" he mouthed with a black, arched brow. She swept up a hand to wipe her mouth to hide her laughter but knew she wasn't fast enough. Those tossed storms of gray told her so.

Chapter Six

After two days and with thick sauce on her beckoning lips, she was still beautiful. He wanted to lick those tempting lips clean and not stop there with devouring her. His green-eyed vixen hadn't lost her allure. In jeans instead of her gypsy skirt, the muted green of her sweatshirt made her glimmering eyes as vibrant as maple leaves. No, in fact, sitting across the common area, her beauty called to him. Just like in his dreams.

He'd stayed aloof, though he'd been aware the very second she'd come into range of the duels. Her scent, her sound. He knew her instantly. He could have gone home, should have if he'd thought about it, but Mitch and Brooke didn't need him along. This was a first for them. Brooke had never had her own den, her own home to call hers. She had always been more the wandering soul of the four. No, they didn't need him along at all. He let his lids slide to half-mast to be able to watch the woman across from him.

Twisting his head to ease the tension in his neck, the fact remained that it bothered him that someone had attacked N'Réa. He'd been walking after hours through the night, listening, testing the air, but he hadn't found any sign of someone lingering or hiding in the murkiest shadows. Whoever it was, it was either a one-shot deal or they worked the weekends. That was the underlying reason he'd stayed behind. *Her*. He needed to be there if she encountered any more problems. If she called for him — he doubted she would

— but he had made an oath to her on Sunday whether she knew it or not. To protect her.

He didn't know why he was compelled to protect her at all. The urge pushed him, and he wanted to push back. He clasped his hands across his stomach to keep them from fisting up under his own thoughts. During his surveillance strolls, he'd noted the simple tent she used and the old car. She was alone, her entire life stored in her vehicle. The rest was set up on the grounds. She was a gypsy in the purest sense of the word. A loner.

He could understand that. What he didn't understand was why she continued to invade his dreams, now with a real voice, a stronger sense of the woman in all her physical glory and sensuous beauty. The dreams had not lessened one bit. They were slowly driving him insane because he knew this was one woman he would not sleep with. Though he had been imagining her for longer than he cared to think about and they were about to spend several weeks within each other's company, there was just one thing he refused to do.

Make this woman his mate.

Morgan curled his lip as the thought circled his mind. He didn't want any woman for a mate. He liked his life the way it was, and if for some reason he was in California playing knight with a large toothpick, it was for only a short block of time. The rest of his life would be normal. He'd return to Oregon before the end of October, preparing to welcome Selene's baby. There was no reason to mess up a good thing now.

N'Réa stood from her chair and tossed her plate, helping close containers and stacking things together. She thanked Duncan for lunch and ambled away for her own camp. Turner leaned over and whispered to Cale, who grinned knowingly in answer, both following her stride with youthful lust as she walked past the pair. Morgan smiled to himself when she flipped them off on her way out of the camp. Something had been said between the two younger men he couldn't hear, but given her answer, he could make a wild guess and probably nail it in one. She was saucy, spunky, and able to hold her own. But his smile dropped like a rock over a cliff when Turner leaped up and jogged after her. That Turner was too young for her was the first disagreeable thought to hit him. Morgan lowered his feet until they rested flat on the ground, ready, but for what he wasn't sure. She was rude and abrasive and didn't want his company, but Morgan would be the first to jump in front of a car if Turner was her preferred choice for company.

Morgan let out a relieved breath when Turner plodded into camp a few minutes later, extremely rejected. A protective anger coiled his shoulders, however, when Morgan heard Turner's disgusted statements as he flung himself into his chair next to Cale. Morgan rose to his feet, already aware he was going to correct him and make sure she was fine. He didn't have to be called on by her to serve as protection. His feet were moving before he thought to question the impulse to do so.

"Turner, that woman is not a bitch," he stated coolly as he strode by. "She knows a sniffing hound when she sees one."

Cale guffawed shamelessly as Morgan kept going, ignoring Turner's pissed snarls.

He found her leaning over the side of her car, cursing in a thick voice, her fists tapping the roof in constrained rage.

"Now, N'Réa, you really shouldn't include his mother in that," he teased her as he leaned on the vehicle next to her, his arms crossed over his chest.

The urge to enfold her into his arms and make her world better continued to grow stronger with every meeting. He didn't like it. He didn't want to feel anything for her. Somehow he didn't think he would be so lucky for it to just stop, so he fought it the only way he knew how.

"What do you want?" She raised an icy glowering stare toward him. "Want to take up where he left off?" she retorted defensively.

He stood erect in a heartbeat. "Did he lay a hand on you?" He closed his own hands before he punched something unable to scream in pain.

She kicked at the dirt under her feet. Morgan saw red when she told him, "No, not hands. Two disgusting lips. Why do guys think I'm easy? I need to buy a damned ring and be done with it."

"He didn't hurt you, did he?" He swallowed the growl, barely, keeping the building rage out of his voice with strangled effort. Turner was a dead squire.

N'Réa rocked her head on her arms where she leaned, fitted to the car door. "No, I'm good at evasion. I'm also good with a right hook, but I didn't need it. This time."

"Don't worry, he'll never touch you again," he informed her stonily. His knuckles popped under the constricted pressure of his self-control. Inside, he snarled long and low, frustrations piling up, winding and knotting tight. Turner had unwittingly made himself a target for all the pent-up pressure Morgan controlled with a paper-thin determination.

She waved a hand. "Thanks, but it won't be just him. I'm a damned challenge. The rude bitchy woman. She doesn't get enough." She mimicked him in a snide, male mocking voice. It sounded like a barb she'd heard more than once. She rolled her head, facing him on her crossed arms, her sorrow-filled eyes bright with tears.

"I wasn't always like this. I have to be now, or I'd be fighting off men constantly. Single, of decent age, doing this," she stated, waving a hand encompassing the grounds, the tents, and the parked RVs. "I must be looking for a free ride."

Immediately, Leslie and all her brash games came to Morgan, but he shook it free. The two women were nothing alike.

She let out a disgusted oath. "I work my own shows, get my ass there and back. I don't need a damned man for that! A mechanic, sure," she said with a hunch of her shoulder. "But not for what guys like Turner think." He became captured by her eyes when she locked on to him, falling into the pain-filled depths of her soul before she began to talk, wrenching him forcefully to the present. "Hell, cards and all, you've been more decent than that rat!"

"Cards?" His tongue was sticking to the roof of his mouth, making coherent conversation difficult.

"Your reading?" She rolled her eyes. "You can't possibly have forgotten?"

He shifted, curling around toward another tent, avoiding her and the impact of that green. Actually he'd been doing his best to block it out, but his best hadn't been successful. "No, I haven't," he admitted. "But they're cards. A chance of what may be." He did know nothing was set in stone when it came to divinity and the Fates.

She narrowed those emerald eyes, thick lashes making them a thousand times more potent. "Then why are you here?" she demanded. "Why have you been haunting me for so long? I don't need a man!" She wailed into the fading day surrounding them. "I don't want one either."

He tried something different. "What makes you think the cards were meant for us?"

"Christ! I'm a woman, not a damned idiot!" She whirled on a heel, but he grabbed her above the elbow and spun her to face him before she could escape.

"All right." He raked a hand through his hair. "I got dragged into this mess because of Brooke. Now I'm committed. The cards were there. You say you've had dreams," he said slowly, silently refusing to mention his dreams. No sense in going there. All Morgan wanted was to find a way to make them stop. "Maybe I'm meant to be protection for you here. I've helped, and I can still help. The cards may not have meant anything at all."

She swallowed and fluttered a hand between them dismissively. "Look, Morgan. I appreciate what you did Sunday. I deeply appreciate Brooke's help. I don't have the money to spend for a cast or the loss it would have cost me to be gone to have it done, but I don't need a protector." She threw herself against her car, crossing her arms to glare at the world at large. "I've been doing these events and shows for nearly eight years, since I was twenty. I know how to stay out of trouble."

With a tender touch, he dried the last tears from her flushed face. "Yeah, but trouble seems to like you."

N'Réa's eyes drifted shut when he made himself stop touching the smoothness of her cheek. The heat of her skin soaked through his fingers with the lightest contact. Her head tilted forward, and he sensed her change, like all the steam had seeped out of her.

"So, what do you do when you're not reading?"

"This is all I do," she told him, rising with a defiant heat, expecting him to challenge her, daring him to. "I make enough to eat and sleep and get me there. I'm happy."

Morgan leaned on the car where he stood. "All year?" She nodded. "Home? Job?"

Her body tightened as though she expected a reaction, but he knew she wouldn't lie. "None and no."

"If you're happy, that's all that matters, isn't it?" Torment filled her expression. The swirling curls of her hair drew him, urging him to sift his hand into her hair, luxuriating in its richness. The heat in his palm electrified him. His mouth dried up as the warmth of her soaked into him. "You are happy with what you want to do, aren't you?" He tugged with a single finger wrapped in her silken hair to make sure he got an answer.

"I love this," she said. "I've adjusted. I've come a long way to be here." She released a melancholy sigh, her chin falling, tipping toward the ground before her. "You should probably go. If I keep talking, I will have to kill you because I'll eventually tell you some dark, ugly secret I don't want to share."

"Hey, you can talk all you want," he said as he inched her toward him. "And you can't kill me." He gave her a broad wink. "I have a secret weapon."

Her smile went limp. "Forgot. Brooke." She shook her head. "That must be something else, having a true witch in the family."

"She's not even the only one. There's an aunt too." He chuckled when her jaw dropped.

"You're kidding? I know you're pulling my leg."

"Nope." He let her hair slide free, missing its curl and richness immediately. "That's where Brooke got her training, and she's very talented." He peered around them, dropping his voice to share. "Maybe some night when we can, I'll ask her to do her little light show. It's fun."

N'Réa's expression was dazed. "If I hadn't seen it for myself," she muttered.

"So, friends?" He made himself ask, to make it clear where he stood, for the both of them. She needed him, even if he didn't necessarily want to have anything to do with her. "I'm here if you need me, seriously. I'm not wanting anything with anyone either, and I'm sorry about the dreams. I had nothing to do with them."

"Sure, friends. I can handle that." Her voice smoothed out, like crushed velvet, an utterly decadent sound, like their first meeting in her tent and every dream she'd ever starred in. There was a lightening in her spirits. The pink of her tongue darted out. The heat he'd been fighting to ignore since she'd walked up that afternoon burst through him. "Is there any way to stop the dreams?" she asked with a tentative nuance.

He wrapped his arms over his chest to keep himself from touching, even if he couldn't avoid the wanting, because with her so close, he found himself really wanting to touch and not stop. "Not that I know of. I don't even know where they're coming from."

"But not from you? Right?"

He shook his head adamantly at her brittle challenge. "No. Not from me." He wished he could stop them!

She heaved a sigh. "I'll figure out something then," she told him. He thought she would object when he brushed his lips across her cheek, but it must have been acceptable for her, and it was done before he could think to not do it. He swore silently at himself. Hadn't he just convinced himself to *stop touching*? N'Réa was tying him into knots.

"Let me know if I can do anything for you," he told her, keeping the wanting out of his voice with effort, taking a purposeful step away from her.

"No, I'm fine. I'm going to the beach until Friday night. I like to walk barefoot in the surf."

He imagined her carefree self playing in the waves, laughter following in her wake, and had to mentally shake himself free of the image's grip. What the hell was going on?

"Be careful," he told her.

"Morgan?"

He started to leave, but her voice stopped him. He turned, and the genuine smile on her lips was almost his undoing against every ounce of his control.

She raised a hand to his face. His heart thudded like a heavy weight behind his ribs at the absolute trust she granted him through that single caress. His heart raced, and his blood burned with a raw heat. Desire made him sway infinitesimally into her palm. It was the first time she'd touched him, completely, willingly. He was losing the battle and knew of no way to stop it.

"Thank you. For being a friend."

He pressed a kiss into her palm without considering the consequences. The petal-fragrant skin of her palm pressed to his lips for a split second of piercing hunger. He let her go, forcing a blank expression. Her scent was embedded into his nerves. The warmth of her skin flowed across his lips as her hand slipped away.

"Save it for when you need it," Morgan told her, then he made himself walk away.

He stalked the long way to camp, trying to get his wants under control. What was it about N'Réa that would not leave him? Long strides ate up the distance, following the winding path to the front of the grounds and then along the opposite barrier, where it would eventually lead him to camp.

He shoved the clawing desire ramming through him every time he was in her company out of his system. Morgan refused to make this woman his mate! He did have a choice in this. His fists curled and unclenched as he covered the distance with a ground-eating pace. It was not his time. He was not ready.

Regardless of what had thrown N'Réa inexplicably into his path, this would be his choice. And he chose no!

He shook his head fiercely, the length of his black hair whipping over his neck in agitation. He could fight this, could fight her. She didn't understand what was going on, of that he was certain. He couldn't explain why she was experiencing dreams, yet because of this...*connection*, he snarled angrily, he was pushed, compelled, to protect her. But she was not his mate! He didn't want a mate! He silently shouted, immoveable against the strength of the Fates, as he glared unseeing at the world around him.

It didn't matter. He would do as he offered. No more. Finding a mate was not necessary for him. His brother and sisters had, and they lived in cohabitation, but he knew he was solitary. He always had been and thrived on it.

As he neared the camp, Morgan set his jaw and his thoughts. He would not let this get out of control. He could handle this. He was the oldest, the pack leader. He had to have the strength to see this through.

He reached for a combat helmet as he stamped toward the ring. If he couldn't run his frustration away the way he'd been craving to, he could fight, and he knew exactly who he was going to take his frustrations out on.

* * * *

By the time Mitch and Brooke returned to Duncan's World at the end of the week, Friday night was brewing a thunderstorm and threatening buckets. Coal-black clouds swirled in the sky. Ferocious winds and bright flashes of lightning raced before the storm. Morgan kept his thoughts away from N'Réa, refusing to bow to the insidious want traveling through his blood, but with each passing hour and the pending storm, the more worried he became. He paced around the camp like a caged cat, swallowing his irritation. Another fifteen minutes ticked past as the storm prowled closer, and there remained no sign of her car.

Confusion and lust battled within. He wasn't her keeper. She was her own woman, as she had so plainly pointed out. She didn't have to report in or tell him anything about when she would be at camp.

There had been no chance to run for the whole week he'd stayed behind in California. For that alone, he knew he would be going home after this weekend. He needed to stretch, to have his home den under his feet.

He was frustrated in more ways than he wanted to openly admit to, worried and anxious with the electricity of the storm screwing him tighter, a spiral that was quickly narrowing under the pressure. He pivoted on a heel and paced in the other direction. Lightning split the sky in raging patterns, slate and coal clouds billowing closer and closer from the coast.

"Morgan, if you can hear me, now would be a good time to be a friend." Her voice reached him, as though from a distance, thick with tears, and it stopped him on a dime.

"Brooke!" He shouted over the sound of the whipping winds, fighting the renewed anxiousness of her distress. Once both were inside, he closed them into their shared tent. "Can you find N'Réa? Something's wrong." Thunder shook the air around them. The storm was closing in and it was a bad one, pushed by the early chill of the northern winds.

"I can try," she offered. She reached for one of his hands. "Picture her for me." Brooke's brow creased, her chin tilting up, searching in a way Morgan could understand but never do. "What color is her car?"

"Gray, I think, maybe old silver."

She nodded, her concentration brief. "I found her. She slid off the road not too far from here. It's pouring where she's at." She squeezed his hand. "She's all right, just scared. Her car is toast."

"How far?" Brooke gave the description of a few landmarks. Morgan's heart pounded like a cannon against his ribs as another blast of thunder rolled over them. "Can I use the Toyota?"

"Of course!" She reached for her keys in her things. "Get all her stuff. She can stay with us." She lowered her voice with warning. "It will be raining by the time you get back. Bring her here, and we'll warm her up."

He kissed his sister and sprinted for the campground parking lot, thunder in his wake, sliding into the vehicle without breaking stride. "Brooke, how about a blanket?" he asked on a quick hunch. One appeared on the seat next to him as he started the engine. "You're an angel," he said, and her loving smile resonated through him as he left to hunt for N'Réa.

He pulled from the grounds and drove the main road leading west toward the coast. Using the landmarks Brooke mentioned he crawled at a snail's pace and after several heart-stopping flashes of lightning and long, stretched moments, he found a wet gleam of metal on the opposite side of the road. Making a U-turn, he parked as close as he dared on the side to move her stuff over.

He slid down the muddy embankment a little at a time and yanked on her door, brushing rain off his face to see. "N'Réa! Are you all right?"

"Yeah, hunky dory," she managed to say through chattering teeth. He lifted her up and carried her to the road, then wrapped her in the blanket. "I'm getting everything wet!"

"Don't worry about it. We'll get it cleaned somewhere. I have to get everything out of your car. Is it unlocked?" He settled her onto the seat, tucking the blanket around and over her with sure hands.

She nodded as he closed the door on her to tackle the muddy incline again. It took him a solid fifteen minutes, getting soaked to the skin, by the time he'd put everything in the back of the SUV. He made sure he grabbed everything valuable before he closed up the car.

He jumped into the Toyota and slammed the door, cranking up the heater on a relieved, gushed exhale. He let his head fall to the seat for a minute as everything warmed up.

"Morgan," she said, the word a quiet, aching sound. He rocked his head toward her. "Thank you." N'Réa was folded into the blanket, warm enough to not be chattering anymore. She was tired, wet, and absolutely beautiful to him.

He lifted a hand to push dripping hair from her face, discovering the blatant surface chill of her skin. His eyebrow arched with concern. "How long were you there?" Tapping the controls, he made sure the heat was going full blast. She was freezing.

"A while," she admitted, dropping away from his searching. "I was furious I fell off the road, furious the car died. I knew the rain was getting worse. It was too much to see through so I tried pulling off the road, and..." She paused and drew a shaky breath. "I went too far. A one-person catastrophe, that's me."

"Never," he told her tenderly. Warmth built in his chest and in places he didn't want to name. He leaned over and cupped her face, holding her in his palms. His thumbs stroked smooth skin, willing the chills to leave her. He moved closer, examining her for any obvious harm for having to sit in the car or for being soaked to the skin, and touched his lips to hers. It was a fleeting caress, less than a heartbeat, but her heat, the softness of her lips, slammed into him with the force of a thousand-foot wave crashing into his chest.

He reared back, stunned at himself. Her gaze was curious, luminous, with a hint of wariness. He hadn't meant to kiss her. It was the last thing he wanted from her. She was tired and cold beneath his palms. She needed something hot to drink and a warm bed...and he wanted to kiss her again. He couldn't deny it, not with her sweet lips so close, with her resting comfortably, complacent in his palms. The desire shocked him more deeply than anything he'd faced since meeting her. And he was powerless to that desire. In spite of everything he'd said, announced, proclaimed, decided, and declared, he needed her kiss. Right now.

He drew her face closer as he leaned. She didn't fight him, though her eyes followed him until they closed with him so near. He brushed her lips, and they trembled gently in response. He held her, supported her as he nibbled his lips over hers. Her sweetness was a rare jewel to his mouth, a touch he had never experienced and never could have imagined on his own.

There was no denying his body's reaction to her softness, her scent. It was immediate and intense as he held her close. It rushed through him, spearing him like the sharp lightning crossing the sky overhead. Every urge to possess, to dominate, he could have ever known ripped through him with the merest of contacts of her skin. Weeks and months of waking and sleeping frustrations surged through him, howling with an intensity that took his breath away.

He pulled away as his body begged for more. This was a mistake! The silently screamed accusation rang like a bell inside his head. He did not want to know this woman. He did not, could not, become involved with her. Yet, when she'd called, when she had needed, he could only answer as he'd promised. A hot jolt seared the pit of his stomach at the simple truth as he moved away from her.

"Jerk," she whispered as he let her head rest on the seat once more. Lowered lashes shut him out with cold-induced fatigue.

"I guess I am," he answered as he put the vehicle in drive and returned to the grounds. Friends don't take advantage of each other. It was a reaction; that was all. She had been stranded for at least an hour, if not longer, in the cold of the rain, her car useless. He was glad she was all right and would soon be yelling and cursing like herself in no time. For now, he let himself think the kiss was harmless.

He carried her bundled, damp form into the tent, where Brooke waited for them. Mitch sat in the corner, keeping Brooke company during the storm. Brooke helped N'Réa strip while he did the same facing the other way, putting on clean sweats while Brooke put N'Réa in a warm robe, settling her on the other side of the sleeping bags with a hot cup of tea.

"Here, drink this. It'll take off the chill." N'Réa did as told, murmuring her thanks.

"How did you get hot water in a rainstorm?" she asked as she sipped gratefully at the tea.

"Family secret," Brooke said with a quick smile. "Just drink. There's some cold sandwiches left if you're hungry."

N'Réa nodded. Morgan sat with Mitch, welcoming a hot cup of tea for himself. "How long before this blows over?"

"A few hours," Brooke replied. "Tomorrow will be beautiful. A cool, clean, crisp day."

"That's good to know. I need the money to get the car towed and fixed," N'Réa said morosely. She let out a huge yawn. "I'm beat!"

"You fall over wherever you're comfortable, N'Réa. You'll be fine here," Brooke instructed her.

Morgan saw her whip around, her brow tightening, taking in the interior of the tent. "But there's not enough bags! Who am I kicking out?" she asked guiltily.

"Me," Morgan said. "I don't mind. Sleep."

"But — "

"No arguments," Morgan stated firmly. He stood and took the few steps between them to sit behind her. "Brush," he commanded. Brooke slapped one into his outstretched hand. "First things first," he said easily. She was frozen solid for several beats. He glided a soothing hand down her arm. "Drink. You're still chilled." He pointed to the steaming tea. "Relax," he told her when she remained stiff and silent. "I have two sisters. I know what I'm doing."

He tested the bottom of the wet tresses in his fingers, wanting to distract her, desperate for the distraction of the activity more for himself. His reaction to the kiss haunted him, though he was keeping it tightly controlled under the surface of his mundane actions. "Towel," he ordered. Mitch tossed him one. He began to rub her hair, working it with light sweeps and tugs until most of the rainwater was gone, then he picked up the brush again and started over. Her head fell forward as he flowed through the waves of heavy onyx. Mitch and Brooke took over a corner and started playing a card game to relax.

"How did you get these highlights?" he wondered aloud as he untangled the ungrateful strands. "They remind me of dragon's fire."

N'Réa chuckled low in her body, a heady sound that infiltrated his deepest corners. His pulse sped up. He cleared his mind of the rising images of her, in his dreams. *Not now.*

"Really? You've seen one?"

Morgan's hand stopped midair, a grin cracking his lips and his thoughts. "Well, no." He picked up another length and began to work through it. "But it's how I would imagine it. Red, gold, heat, hidden inside." He described it, seeing the flames in his mind from past dreams, the same hint of it in her hair, his hands sure and caring through the silken weight.

She murmured in pleasure when he started making long, languid strokes. "You do know what you're doing. That feels wonderful."

And just like that, he was aroused and aching, unable to stop his desires from torturing him more for the woman before him. He cleared his throat, shoving the hunger away and failing miserably. No matter how hard he fought it, he couldn't find any strength left to control it. "Thanks."

What was it about her? Even soaked like a rat, she was beautiful. Now relaxed and pliant as he held her hair in his hands, he was so aroused that all she would have to do was lean into him and his situation would be discovered.

As her scent filled his nostrils, his body hardened painfully. Drawing a breath to clear the fresh rain scent on her skin, the salt air in her hair from her nights on the beach teased him. Morgan groaned low and deep in his chest. Her head tilted to the side beneath the flow of his hand, exposing the cream-colored expanse of her throat in the dim circle of their tent lamp. He swallowed hard when he automatically sought, and found, the beating of her pulse under her skin. He licked his lip, wanting to suckle on that pulse, to taste the salt air on her skin.

Shifting to ease the throbbing ache, he adjusted her position with tender hands, coaxing her to sit straight. "Other side," he said, groaning in pained silence at the hoarse sound of his voice. She didn't react, apparently oblivious to his state of discomfort. Flexing his fingers, he prayed that she remained that way.

"How much do you have in your tent?" he asked, fighting to derail the train he saw a mile away and losing.

"Most of my clothes, some food. My life was in the car." Her voice was slow, drugging. It didn't help the threat of that train bearing down on him at all.

"Well, you get some sleep," he said, setting the brush aside. He ran his fingers through the expanse of her hair and relished the waves in his hold. Her heat flashed through him, the same way he'd burned when he'd curled his fingers through her hair Wednesday night. He dampened a dry mouth, his tongue thick and heavy. His entire body simmered, pulsing, needy. Instead of leaning forward to linger in the aromatics of sea salt and sand, he said, "If you need anything, any of us will help."

He lurched to his feet with an agitated movement, putting space between them before he did follow through on any of the things his body demanded. Mitch followed him with an amused glimmer. Morgan crammed his hands into his sweatpants pockets, pulling the material out to hide his arousal. It didn't hide everything, but it helped. "I'm going for a walk," he stated, then slipped out into a steady drizzle, ignoring the cold of the rain and the curious looks from his tentmates.

He escaped into the depths of the woods. He had to run, even if it was in silence for a few precious minutes. He was going to explode if he didn't.

Morgan walked far into the shadowy woods, ignoring the pattering of the rain, listening, tasting the air, stripping slowly. He would be careful, but the chance of being spotted was slim with the storm keeping everyone inside. Rain spattered his heated flesh, beading to run in rivulets. A minute later, a large grayish-black wolf leaped into the dense cover of trees.

Chapter Seven

N'Réa rolled over, or tried to. Something pinned her leg to the ground. She blinked, trying to place herself. This wasn't her tent. The one overhead was huge, for starters, and beige. Hers was dark blue. She flexed her legs and found the heat of a person next to her.

She was in Brooke and Morgan's tent. She remembered now. The rain, sliding off the embankment. Being rescued. She swallowed the disgusted sound bubbling in her throat. In a moment of weakness, she'd asked for Morgan's help. She didn't need anyone. She did not *need* rescuing, damn it!

She shifted, rolling to the other side, and froze. He was lying *right* there. Her gaze traveled in appreciation over his lean frame. It was his leg holding her prisoner. She drifted up again. He appeared asleep, his naked chest moving with each breath.

She bit her lip while she took him in. He was a buffet of body parts. Midnight-black hair fell to his shoulders, his face carved and strong in the predawn light. His stern mouth was very appealing in his sleep. She could easily remember the pressure of his lips from the kiss. She stopped herself from dwelling on it, studying him further instead. He had a beautiful throat, which fed to strong, wide shoulders. She knew they were strong. He'd carried her from her car, uphill, then to the tent. His chest was nearly hairless, his stomach flat, not quite a six-pack, but more than respectable, with a barely discernible happy trail disappearing beneath his navel. The waist of his sweats hugged him where he lay, one arm thrown over his head, the other flat between them.

She remembered stretching out on the sleeping bag the night before. There was a clean blanket over her that she couldn't remember finding herself. Thankfully, she lay wrapped in the terry robe. She had no clue where the rest of the clothes from her car were.

Propping herself up on an elbow, N'Réa investigated more of the shared space. Mitch and Brooke were already up and gone. How had they woken up and dressed without making any noise? She shook her head in silent wonder.

She lifted a hand, pushing her hair out of her face. She desperately needed a shower. The largest drawback to staying at the beach: sand. Sweeping the interior to the foot of the tent, she discovered her suitcase and her private stock and stash of things. Her clothes! They'd brought them over from her own tent?

"Your tent didn't make it," Morgan said in a sleep-rumpled voice.

Her head jerked around. His eyes remained closed, and he hadn't moved an inch.

"You're awake? How long?"

"Long enough to sense you getting confused and to know you are trying to find a way to get out of here without insulting anyone."

She shook her head. "What happened to my tent?" She pulled the robe together and sat up. Her tent was gone?

"A fight. Two drunks against your tent. Your tent lost."

She slammed a slim fist into the unsuspecting sleeping bag. "Damn it! What else is going to go wrong with this trip?" She raked her fingers through her hair. "I'm attacked, break an arm, make almost no money, wreck my car, lose my tent!" N'Réa knew she was ranting, but she didn't care. She didn't do overwhelmed well. "Great! Now on top of the car, I have to replace my tent. Another shot Saturday! I can't make any money with all of this to do!" She dropped her head into her hands. The weight of tears made her press her palms into her eyeballs. It helped, but only a little.

"Are you finished?" he asked.

She waved a hand. "Give me a minute. I'll think of something else."

He chuckled at her outburst. "Well, I'll talk while you try to think of it." He moved his thrown hand to lay his head on the palm. "Brooke and Mitch have gone to check on the car. If it's worth saving, they'll call a wrecker for you. You have all of your possessions. Everything that could be was saved from the tent last night when we brought your things here for you. I found its demise while I was out walking. Unfortunately, the gorillas who destroyed it had long since vanished. I couldn't find them." Her head shook from side to side at those words. "As for replacing it, you can stay here. Work until you can do something about it."

She lifted her head, her fingers bracing her temples. She'd been awake only a few minutes, and her head was already screaming for aspirin. "Why are you doing this?"

Morgan shrugged. "We take care of our own."

Her gaze narrowed at him. "I don't belong to anyone," she said. Warning bells clamored all over her thoughts.

His head rocked to either side, then his lashes rose up, catching her within the storm-gray depths. "No one person belongs to another. Ever." He lifted a hand and twined her hair through his fingers, roping each finger to let it slide free and curl, doing it over and over. "Friends do take care of one another. We are friends, aren't we?"

N'Réa shivered beneath his caress, the electricity of his voice rendering her speechless for a heartbeat. "Yes," she managed to whisper. The bells fell silent beneath the delicious stroke of his fingers.

His hand slid free, his thumb brushing her cheek as he let her go, then his eyes disappeared beneath thick black lashes once more. "Go take a shower." He motioned his hand toward the foot of the tent. "I think all of your stuff is dry."

"Would Brooke mind if I use the robe?" she asked, clutching it protectively.

He shook his head. "No. But don't take too long. Brooke makes awesome pancakes." She caught a sublime lift to his lips, betting he was imagining those pancakes. He was being a friend. Helping out. She could handle that.

"All right." She hefted herself to her feet, then found an outfit for the day in her things. She dug to the bottom of her suitcase and double checked the pouch with her jewelry. Her reserve money remained in the hidden compartment in her largest suitcase. She started to relax and caught herself. She couldn't afford to trust anyone, not anymore. She couldn't afford to like him either. The end of the ride wouldn't be pretty. She couldn't afford to forget why she kept herself separate and guarded.

She wrapped everything up in a ball and tucked it under an arm, leaving for the showers. Her hand rose to the flap, and she paused. "Morgan?" He made a sound behind her. "Thank you."

"Any time," he murmured drowsily. She slipped through the flaps of the tent, the memory of the night before coming to her on the way.

How did he find her? How had he known she was in trouble? Did she call to him? Did she reach out for him? She remembered saying his name, right after she'd wasted her breath cursing her car for the umpteenth time. It had been her own fault for getting soaked to the skin, thinking she knew what she was doing and attempting to walk to the grounds when the car had slid off the road. She hadn't been as close as she'd hoped and had paid for it. All she'd managed for the attempt was a massive case of the shivers and being soaked like a rat on a sinking ship.

It was her problem to have found herself in this predicament. The rain had been horrible, unable to see past her bumper, if that far. There was little she could do with the rain pouring over everything in torrential sheets. But Brooke was right. The sun was coming up clear and bright.

She took a deep breath, smelling the clean-washed scent of earth and trees. Northern California was beautiful, and fall was nearly upon them. Which meant, after this show, she would have to start working her way south. If her car made it. She frowned, recalling even more of the night before. The hard slide down the embankment, the buck of the car when it stopped moving completely, settling in the mud like a fly on flypaper. How much was it going to cost this time to get the poor beast fixed? Even though she had run off the road, the engine should have still turned over. She let out a disgusted sigh. One thing at a time.

"Um, hey, N'Réa."

She stopped and glared at the young man as he jogged up to her. "Turner!"

He held up his hands. "No, it isn't what you think!" He gave her a lopsided grin. "Can I walk with you?"

"Isn't that what you said before?" She planted a hand on her hip. He stood several inches taller than her and while she wasn't intimidated, she wasn't going to let history repeat itself. He flushed from his neck up.

"Yeah, and I'm sorry." He peeked over his shoulder from the way she'd come, one hand stuffed into his pocket. With an anxious puppy-dog face, he said, "I'll walk. I promise, nothing else."

"O-kay," she said with a break in the word. They were almost to the showers anyway. If she screamed, someone was bound to hear her.

"I owe you an apology," he said in a repentant voice, both of his hands shoved into his jeans now, his toes dragging with each step. "I shouldn't have done that to you. Just because we're here, well, my mother didn't raise an ass."

She stopped. "You mean it, don't you?"

He avoided her, a red flush crawling up his neck. "Yes, I do. I forgot how to be a gentleman, as was pointed out to me."

She examined his face, then his body. Nothing was in a cast, and he wasn't favoring anything. "All right, who beat you up? 'Cause I'm not seeing it."

He jumped a step away and shook his head sharply. "No one!" His shoulders drooped. "I guess I let the whole knight thing go to my head. It won't happen again." If she hadn't thought he meant it, his pleading convinced her. "Forgiven? Friends?"

She relaxed. "Yeah, sure. To both."

"Thank you," he said on a relieved sigh, then he turned and scurried away. Her head was still shaking by the time she reached the women's showers.

On the return, she walked by her tent and wanted to cry. Her tent was flat. Morgan hadn't been exaggerating. Marie's voice reached her before the hand on her shoulder. "I'm sorry, honey. It happened before we could stop them. You're welcome to stay with Bailey and me. We have room in the camper."

She shook her head, blinking the swollen weight in her eyes away. "No, I'm fine. I'm staying with friends until I get my life in order. I've got problems with the car too."

Marie's mouth popped open in concern. "Oh, N'Réa! How awful."

A short, coughed harrumph slipped out. "Tell me about it. This whole trip has been one disaster after another." She shrugged at her friend. "And only one week has passed."

"Don't talk like that! It'll get better. It has to." Marie wrapped an arm around her and pulled her into her ample body.

N'Réa double checked her tent after Marie left her with hugs and promises of help with anything. Morgan, or whoever, seemed to have retrieved everything by the looks of the inside of the stripped tent. She stood up and called out to Marie. "I'll toss it later. I just showered."

"I'll get Bailey to do it," she shouted. "Don't get dirty. That's my favorite outfit!"

N'Réa ran a hand over the maroon and black outfit, the matching hair scarf in her other hand. "Thank you!" Marie waved in answer, and with her bundle of clothes in hand, N'Réa headed to Duncan's World, as his camp was commonly known.

She'd lost her tent, but she did have her clothes, her health, and a new batch of friends. Her car needed work, but she wasn't alone, and there were a few weekends left to get the money together to get the car fixed. She let the sun shine on her and let the rest of the bad thoughts be washed away in the flowing warmth.

Her optimism lasted until she reached camp. Morgan, Mitch, and Brooke stood huddled together outside their shared tent. Morgan was dashing in dark trousers and those black boots. The shirt he wore was a tucked-in, billowy linen. And, like a true knight, he wore his sword.

Sucked in or not, he was enjoying this.

N'Réa slowed when she caught their gloomy and worried expressions. Brooke started to speak, but she lifted a hand. "Let me drop this off. Safer if I don't have something to throw." She said it only half meaning it, but feared the news was not going to be good regardless. Brooke's disheartened expression smoothed into patient understanding. N'Réa ducked into the tent to put her things away, draping the robe on a hanger.

"All right, what's the bad news?" she asked, standing next to them outside.

"The car isn't worth fixing. You broke an axle sliding down the embankment. It looked like it had been cracked for a while," Mitch explained.

Her legs went loose. She was barely aware of Morgan's arm as he caught her to his side.

"What?" she said in a squeak. "It's broke? As in really, really broke? How much does an axle cost?" An axle? How was she going to fix *that*? A silent moan welled up, but she managed to bury it before it became real.

"Around eight hundred dollars, but you'll have to replace the joints too if you do it. It'll run you well over a grand with the repair costs," Mitch explained, extremely sorry to have to give her such bad news.

"Oh God!" She didn't notice it when she gripped on to Morgan's side in reflex. "I don't have that kind of money!" Desperation clawed at her. She dug into his shirt with numb fingers. "What am I going to do?

I'm stuck here. I can't buy a car! I don't have the money to fix it."

A cell phone rang. Mitch slid it from his pocket. He waited with an expectant expression. "It's the wrecker. Where do you want him to take it?"

"Trash it," Morgan said, his thumb rubbing her side in comfort. "Is there anything in the glovebox?"

She shook her head, numb and bordering on shock. "Maintenance records, napkins." *What should be in there?* Was she missing something? Her head snapped up as his words filtered into her jumbled brain. "Trash it? I can't! It's my only car!" He folded her into his length. "What a messed-up trip." She cursed into his chest.

"Trash it," Morgan repeated. "We take care of our own," he whispered into her ear, bent close.

She tore herself out of Morgan's one-arm hold. "I'm not a damn charity case. Don't you even think it." She glared at Mitch. "That is my car!"

"And its dying wish is to be shot and put out of its misery." Morgan consoled her, his calm nonchalance blindsiding her. "We'll work out something."

She clenched her hands, her voice low and vibrating with rage. "I won't sleep with you to get a car! I will work out nothing with you!" Morgan staggered, his face stricken at her savage attack, but she didn't care. No one was this kind for nothing. "Why are you being so damned helpful? What do you want from me?" Nothing was free. She'd learned that the hard way.

Morgan obliterated the gaping paces between them until he towered over her, his breathing harsh yet controlled. The stormy gray of his eyes erupted with turbulent sparks as he stood over her. "Have I ever said anything about sex?" he hissed. His entire being pulsed with his anger. N'Réa's stomach twisted and quaked under his backlash. "I want nothing from you. God forbid you be thankful for someone's *selfless* generosity!" His hands were tight fists, shaking at his sides. "Have I asked for one thing? Just one thing for what we've offered, what you know? I haven't even asked for your silence," he pointed out with a scathing sneer. "I trusted you. Now I know I can't."

The jab sliced inside her, choking as his words hit home. "That's not true!" But he was already halfway across the camp and out of earshot. "That's not true," she whimpered.

Brooke put an arm around her waist. "Come on. He'll cool off. He'll beat up something if he has to, but he'll be all right."

She leaned into the slight blonde holding her side. "You know I won't say anything? You know that, don't you?" N'Réa felt the pendulum swing as her desperation returned. What would they do to keep her silent?

Brooke blinked, holding her closer at her near terrified tone. "I know you won't, and you have nothing to fear that it won't be by your own choice. Our code is very strict. We do what we do by our own choice. If our choice is wrong, we cannot harm those who know about us for our own mistakes." She squeezed. "N'Réa, you aren't a mistake," she told her truthfully "I know you're not a mistake."

"I'm sorry," she murmured, looking at both of them and then at the ground. "I don't know how to handle this," she admitted. "I've been moving and alone for more than ten years."

"Don't worry about it," Mitch said, taking up her other side, having dispensed with the wrecker. "He's fighting it too hard."

"He always has," Brooke agreed.

"Fighting what?" N'Réa asked.

"Fate," Brooke responded. "Come on. I promised these people pancakes, and the morning's half gone."

N'Réa glanced over her shoulder once, but Morgan was gone. She numbly trudged after the other pair.

* * * *

N'Réa sat in her show tent late in the morning. She'd had a great morning, after ten or so when the gates opened. She didn't want to think too much about before then. She still felt ill over how she'd reacted to Morgan's offer of help. The flow through her tent was steady as her name carried far and wide among the vendors, sending her business. Her problems spread like wildfire, the car and the loss of her tent. The two guys who had drunkenly destroyed it came in sheepishly apologizing to her, sporting proof of their brawl on their jaws and eyes, giving her a hundred dollars apiece to pay for it.

She read cards and palms until she couldn't see straight. Several of the Faire folk came in to say hi and offer hugs, surprising her with their generosity. N'Réa felt two feet tall remembering what she'd said to Morgan that morning. It made her sick all over again thinking of the shock she'd put on his handsome face with her accusations.

He was right. They'd been nothing but kind, and she'd thrown it right back at them, accusing him of having ulterior motives. The man exuded honor. She hung her head weakly as she stood by the flaps of her tent, breathing in the warmth of the day after the heavy rains. He was a good man. Kind. Considerate, gentle, and caring toward her in ways no one could match. She thought of all the things he'd done for her, all the concerned actions he had taken. N'Réa had never felt so humbled in her life.

No, he didn't have motives. She hadn't recognized a good heart when she had first seen it. That was the largest detriment to keeping herself unattached from others: not allowing herself to be open to their real emotions. She hadn't recognized the reality of what Morgan was doing for her. Shame built inside her until her head hung with the weight of it.

"Want to watch the duels?" Bailey asked, splintering her misery. She lifted her head as his shadow fell over her, where she stood at the edge of the gaped opening of her tent.

She shook her head. "No, I need to stay here."

"I understand Morgan is fighting. He's a damned good fighter."

"Yes, I've seen him. I would like to." She cast a glance over her shoulder, wishing she could. "But I need the money too much at this point."

"I'm sorry about that." He gave her a chuckled grin. "At least you weren't in it asleep. You would be as flat."

She smiled at his attempt to lighten her spirits. "I hadn't thought of it that way." She peered up, taking in the giant of a man. "When are you going?"

"After lunch."

"Would you take something for me? Make sure it goes to Morgan?"

He shrugged. "Sure. Lady Brooke is his sister, right?"

She pulled the wound material from her hair. "Yes, she'll give it to him. A favor from me."

He folded it into his hands. "All right. I'll tell you how he does."

"Thanks." She couldn't help feeling lower than dirt and wouldn't be at all surprised if Morgan refused her offering. It would be no less than she deserved.

The afternoon dragged, though her business kept her busy. She ate a small lunch, falling deeper into her thoughts and how she'd behaved. She could hear the faint cheers of the crowd at the edge of the grounds where the arena and jousting lists were, wishing she could watch. Even if he didn't want her there, she would have cheered for him as loud as the next person. It was the least she could do in apology.

"Marie! You aren't going to believe this!" Bailey shouted as he plowed right past her tent. "Marie! Where are you?" N'Réa heard as he talked excitedly to his wife, and she shouted in amazed surprise.

N'Réa rocked her head back and forth. She had to know what this was about! She lowered the flaps and scurried over to their booth, an open walk-in armory. "What happened?" she called, getting their attention.

"Morgan took down Godfrey!" he exclaimed. "It was brilliant. Godfrey never saw it coming!"

"Godfrey? Lord De Brasse's Second Lieutenant? But he's a Master of Swords!" She lifted her hand to her heart and found its pounding rhythm in her chest.

"It was incredible!" Bailey was saying. "They fought like animals. No shields. Just chain shirts and helmets! That man fears nothing!"

"How? How did he do it?"

Bailey hefted a sword from the wall and went outside to demonstrate. Both women hurried after him to watch. "He took the first point by tripping him with the blade. He got behind him and locked up Godfrey's legs!" he said as he spiked the ground, bending a shoulder as if throwing his weight into his imaginary opponent, reciting the duel with excitement. "Second point was even better! They got nose to nose, and you know Godfrey is no little man. Morgan held him off and slid his blade until Godfrey was on the ground."

Bailey shook his head. "I don't know how he did it! It was poetry."

"Third point was the winner. They swung and met and the next thing I know, Godfrey's sword flew almost fifteen feet!"

N'Réa gasped as deeply as Marie. "Really? He unarmed him? Dirk isn't going to like this," his wife remarked in amazement.

"He fights like a warrior! Morgan is incredible to watch. I will never set blades against him," he said firmly, shaking his head in wonder. Bailey lifted his sword and returned it inside, giving it a loving caress with a cleaning cloth to restore any loss of shine to the blade.

N'Réa couldn't believe it. Morgan beat Godfrey! "But Godfrey is good." She had watched Morgan fight, but it was hard to wrap her mind around it. Godfrey wasn't a Second Lieutenant for nothing!

"N'Réa," Bailey said with the assurance of knowing what he'd witnessed. "Morgan is better. Where he learned, I don't know, but he may beat Dirk in the tournament. No one else out there has that man's fire."

"Won't Duncan fight Dirk?"

"The way things stand right now, Hugh would have. Morgan took his slot on the lists. The tournament is already shaping up. Duncan is slotted to fight Lord Abernathy, the camp with the crown and olive branch on their pennant."

"I know them! They were in Anaheim last year." She delved into her memory. "They did well, if I remember right."

"They usually do. They head one of the SCA chapters on the West coast. They teach and train. A swordsmith needs to know where his business is," he offered at her surprised reaction.

"Unbelievable," she whispered. She noticed Bailey peering over her head with intent interest. "What? Is someone coming this way?"

"I think Morgan has come for payment on the favor you sent to him," he said with an indulgent smile.

N'Réa spun sharply on a slippered heel, and there he was, marching up the aisle like he owned it. She stood frozen until he stopped before her, his chest rising with each breath. His shirt clung to him. She licked her lips as time stood still. His hair was soaked through, a testament to the exertion of his fight. His gaze was mysterious and heated and pulled at her in a way that scared and thrilled her at the same time. Her hair wrap was tied to the leathered grip of his sword hanging from his belt, a small banner. Seeing it there made her throat tighten.

He dropped to a knee in front of her. "I ask of thee, sweet maiden, of what privilege I may offer for the honor of thy blessed favor?" he asked in a respectable accent.

"I ask only for thy acceptance of my apology," she replied in a shaky voice, meaning it.

"Granted. And my boon?" He shot her a mischievous grin. "A kiss. I ask thee for a kiss," he said as his voice rumbled over her.

"Aye," she whispered and he rose before her. She could see nothing but the darkening of his gray irises as he wrapped a hand through her hair and set a finger to her chin. She closed her eyes and let it happen as he tilted her to meet him.

This kiss was nothing like the concerned touches he'd offered last night. The instant his mouth fit to hers her hands flew to grip his arms, the fire of his passion ripping over her as he controlled her with his mouth. He didn't demand more than the merest of chaste kisses, but the pulsing of his need in the few seconds he held her close rocked her. She had felt that! What was happening here? To her?

He lifted free with a single reluctant brush. Her heart started beating again. She remembered to breathe. Her eyes fluttered open and found him staring at her with intense, smoke-gray depths. "Aye, my fair maiden. In this, we have just begun," he whispered before he let her go, his breath skating over tingling lips. Her hands slid away from the strength of his biceps and he stepped back, bowed, then turned on a crisp heel and marched the way he had come.

Chapter Eight

The next morning, word spread like wildfire through the grounds when another woman was attacked in the wee hours of the morning. N'Réa had almost managed to put last weekend's assault completely out of her mind. There was someone out there stalking them, following them, and lying in wait for a chance.

"But why on one night?" Brooke asked as they sat around the circle drinking coffee and tea.

"It has to be someone who isn't staying on during the week," Duncan said. "Nothing happened at all from Sunday on."

"Someone who lives in the area, maybe? They don't have to camp," Mitch suggested. "Is the woman all right?"

"Yes," Cale said. "She's the wife of one of the squires on Lord De Brasse's team. I know them." He gazed into the morning fire with a troubled frown. "I don't like this."

There were murmurs of assent from around the circle. N'Réa didn't protest when Morgan put a supportive arm behind her, his body shielding her.

"Did they take anything from her?" Mitch asked, cradling Brooke on his lap, not at all shy about showing his affection for his wife.

"She wasn't carrying anything. Whoever it was took a chain from her neck and her rings," Cale explained. Tension ran through Morgan all along her back.

"Do you know where she was attacked?" Morgan asked.

"I do, near the front," Cale offered, downing the rest of his coffee in one swallow. "I don't know what she was doing up there."

"Can you show me? Before the gates open?"

Cale stood and brushed his hands off. "I'll take you now. I want to stop and see them."

Morgan stood with an easy grace. "Don't go anywhere," he said, breathing into her ear, the command subtle but there.

She shook her head as the pair walked away. "What can he do?" She turned to Brooke, wondering as they disappeared within the forest of camps.

"He's a tracker back home, aside from his ranger status with the forestry division. He's helped find hikers and lost pets. If there's anything to be found, he'll find it." Brooke sipped on her tea as their gazes met. There was more she wasn't saying. It was in the shadows of her dark eyes. N'Réa nodded anyway, leaving the questions unasked, and waited.

She was almost ready to go to her own tent for a day of cards when they returned. Morgan's expression was thoughtful.

"Did you find anything?" Brooke asked. He nodded, waiting for everyone to gather to discuss what he could share.

"I think Duncan might be right. I'm not convinced it's one of the attending role players or someone from one of the camps. I think it's as likely that it could be a trespasser, maybe a vagabond, but if he does something during the week when there's no more than twenty percent on the grounds, his chances of being caught are too high."

"Why do you think that?" Mitch asked.

"The shoe prints. They weren't a matched set, but the trail was too old to try to follow, especially with the gates about to open."

"So next weekend we set him up and catch him," Brooke said.

"I don't like that," Duncan stated. "I don't want to endanger anyone." They were bunched together, talking among themselves to not alarm anyone else in the camp.

"If the cops find him without evidence, he'll be back out on the street attacking again within hours," Mitch advised them. "If we catch him with evidence, he'll get help."

Again there were murmurs of agreement. "We can plan this during the week. Mitch and Morgan can do it. I can be the bait," Brooke explained.

"No way!" Mitch refused with a strong sweep of his hand. "You're pregnant! I'll risk a lot to catch this guy, but not that."

"Pregnant?" N'Réa asked, gaping at her petite friend. There wasn't a sign of it anywhere.

Brooke grinned with a new gleam lightening her features. "Two months."

"That still leaves you out of the running," Morgan said flatly. "But we don't have to do it this minute. Next weekend, us and Duncan," he said loud enough for them and Duncan to hear. "No one else in case I'm wrong. Don't want to give up our hand."

"Agreed," Duncan said soberly. "I'll pay attention, and we'll see if anything happens."

"Damn! I really wanted to go home this week." Morgan lifted a hand to rub his face.

"We can still go. Morgan, you can't protect everyone." Brooke rested a hand on his arm. N'Réa's nerves tingled as something silent passed between the two. Then Brooke looked right at her. "N'Réa, please come with us. No reason for you to stay here unless you have plans."

She shook her head from side to side. "No, no plans. No way to get anywhere anyway." She offered a half smile. "If I won't be a bother, I think I'd like the company for a change."

"You can stay with us. We have this huge house with nothing but floors and walls. You'll like it," Brooke said.

N'Réa's head snapped up. "Oh no! That was the gate call! I gotta get out there!"

"See you later!" she heard from behind her as she sprinted for the grounds.

* * * *

All day Sunday, she wondered why she'd accepted the invitation, her anxiety level rising with each passing hour. She would be staying with Brooke and Mitch, not Morgan. It wasn't enough to calm her. She could get her clothes washed and straighten out the mess with the car. Insurance wouldn't do anything except pay for the tow, which she needed to pay Mitch for. Even with those thoughts to keep her occupied, she was antsy about spending all week with his family.

She didn't know the last time she spent time with a family. She hoped she'd remember how.

N'Réa popped up from her dreaded thoughts when the gap of her tent opening darkened. She knew instantly who it was. He looked good enough to eat, wearing a red tunic with Duncan's coat of arms, belted at the waist with his sword. He'd even begun to queue his hair with a strip of leather. He was magnificent, dressed as a knight of the kingdom. "Still think you got sucked into something?" she teased him.

"Every day," he said without heat, an answering grin shadowing his sexy mouth. "You can't tell them, but..." He quickly peeked over his shoulder to make sure he was alone. "With the duels, I'm getting into it." The way his mouth lifted into a full smile with his admission sent her heart into a full-paced flutter. "I never thought I'd say this, but I like the fighting." He walked in and stood at the corner of her table. "But I absolutely refuse to wear tights. Not going to happen."

She dropped her gaze to hide her rising reaction to his nearness. "You've got the legs for 'em," she joked.

"Wench," he said in a low breath.

"Jackal." She tossed the words out in answer and laughed. "Want a reading? I think the world is out to lunch."

"No, I learned my lesson." He put a finger under her chin and urged her from her chair to stand with him. "I know I said I didn't want anything, but I can't get rid of this." He pulled her forward, his hands gentle yet firm until he stopped, a whisper from her lips. "Tell me no, and I'll walk away."

Her hands spread across hardened muscles and her lungs hitched as she tried to remember how to breathe. "This will only complicate things," she warned him unsteadily.

"I know," he murmured against her cheek. He groaned as he pressed his forehead to hers. "You have no idea how complicated it could get." Morgan's voice rasped over her ear. "But I've thought of your kiss all morning. Just tell me no," he pleaded with her. His gaze was almost haunted, something indefinable hidden in their darkening depths. A battle that had nothing to do with swords, something only he knew how to fight.

His thick, black lashes lowered, waiting.

She wet dry lips. "I can't."

Her words vanished into the air, not at all faded when his fingers suddenly speared into her hair and his mouth devoured hers. There was nothing chaste about this kiss as he moved against her, pulling her into the hard shape of his body. She gasped and whimpered as he kissed her, soared as he urged her reactions and multiplied them with his body and hands caressing her.

She melted into his hold, his tongue seeking out hidden secrets, his lips burning hers as she met him. The heat flush against her sent desire spiraling, coursing through her body, settling like a low-lying hum of need, a need he started, a need only Morgan could quench. Strong fingers in her hair and on her back held her steady, forming her like a living blanket to his hard angles, meeting her soft curves with exploratory newness. Hanging on was her only option because her legs shook too much to support her.

She was panting when he finally pulled away with sipping kisses and tender brushes on her sensitive skin. He cradled her into the solid curve of his shoulder.

"This will only complicate things," she repeated.

"N'Réa, it was complicated the first time I saw you," he rumbled under her ear.

She rubbed her cheek against his tunic, and his growing purr of pleasure sounded beneath her ear. Complicated was only the tip of the iceberg.

* * * *

"Are you sure no one will mess with our stuff?" N'Réa asked again as they neared Bend. She tried not to fidget on the seat, but there were some things she couldn't help. "I've never left it for so long."

"It'll be fine. Everything staying is in the tent, and Duncan will keep an eye on it." Morgan lounged next to her on the backseat, one arm thrown over her, keeping her close. She'd tucked up her legs, and at some point fell asleep to wake up resting against his thigh. Not that she minded. It shortened the trip and helped hide her nervousness.

Now, she was awake and ready to gnaw through a door to get away. *Would Mitch be terribly upset if she crashed out a window to escape?*

Morgan's hand threaded through her hair, his smile gentling, tugging her around to him. "Relax. You'll be fine." He pressed his forehead to hers in understanding.

"Glad you're an optimist," she whispered, swallowing down her anxiousness. A moment later, she noted where they were and that Mitch was slowing. "What a cute town!" She sat up straighter, looking around with interest.

"This is Bend. I'll point out the corner store I'm going to use."

"The Babbling Brooke?" N'Réa asked as they drove by, following Brooke's directions to the end of the block.

"Family joke." Brooke snickered under her breath. "Babs is my nickname."

N'Réa laughed. "I get it! That's great!"

"And that is the house we bought," Brooke said, pointing ahead a few blocks later.

"Wow!" she exclaimed. "It's huge. And gorgeous."

"Mitch wanted to be closer to town for his duty hours. We have plenty of room for you."

"And the rest of the camp," N'Réa agreed.

The Victorian-styled home stood three stories tall, painted a lovely cream yellow with white shutters and a wraparound porch. "Is that a balcony?" N'Réa asked, craning to see the whole exterior as they approached.

Brooke nodded. "There's one on the back of the house, too."

"Closer? Where do you live?" she asked Morgan.

"I have a ranch-style log house north of Bend. Selene and Bram have a smaller cabin west of town, and Roman and Del live east of Yellowstone. Beautiful up where they are," he mused, continuously running his fingers through the loose curls coating her shoulders.

She gave a brave smile, trying to hide the beat of her heart. "That's a lot of family."

"Don't worry. You won't meet everyone. Roman and Del returned from Japan not that long ago. They're beat. Selene will have us over Tuesday for dinner."

"Tuesday," she parroted weakly. "Okay."

Mitch pulled into the drive and hit the garage button. "Last stop, everyone out." The rear door of the SUV popped, and she had no choice but to move.

"I guess it's too late to claim the flu or something," she said with a nervous peek through her lashes at Morgan.

He kissed her on the temple, a simple, comforting gesture. "You'll be fine. We're loud and obnoxious, but totally tame," he said with a cajoling gleam.

"Tame. Yeah, I'm holding you to that, buddy," she stated as she slid from the vehicle, surprised that her knees held up considering how badly they shook.

N'Réa followed everyone in, with Morgan and Mitch doing the carrying. Brooke hit the lights and showed off the house as they went in. "Let's get you a space and then we'll figure out dinner. Personally, I could eat a whole cow myself."

N'Réa followed upstairs and gasped with surprise from the doorway. "I was thinking you hadn't done any decorating yet! This is lovely!"

"I set up one guest room, ours, and the kitchen. We'll do more this week while we're home, and Mitch will spend a couple of shift hours at the firehouse." She waved N'Réa in. "Go ahead, the shower's through there." She pointed to a second door to the side.

Her bags arrived, and there was no more time for excuses. She faced Brooke, putting on a brave smile. "Thank you."

"No problem. Come down whenever. The kid is hungry." And with an answering grin, she spun and left N'Réa to her own space.

The room was filled with soft, rust-color accents, with natural parquet flooring. The bed linens and comforter were matched in a creamed yellow to the curtains, and there were a few throw rugs on the floor. The furniture was a natural hardwood, and everything fit.

"I don't belong here," she whispered. "I can't do this."

She whirled to flee and found the door closed, Morgan leaning against it with his arms over his chest, watching her.

"Why can't you do this? You're a guest now. No expectations. Just eat and sleep and laugh. You do that sleeping on the ground. Why is it different here?"

She paced two steps and turned. "I'll mess it up somehow. I always do." The energy continued to build and crackle as she paced. Two steps, turn.

"If it'll make you feel better, I'll be sleeping in my own bed. At home."

His voice was calm, the want to soothe her frayed nerves in every syllable. It still had the capacity to rake over her, regardless. A hunger that had nothing to do with food claimed residence in her system. It only added to her confusion. She tugged a hand through her hair, trembling all over.

"You like Brooke, remember? And she adores you."

"Why? I've been trouble from the first minute we met. All my troubles." *Pace, turn.* She shot him a pensive look out of the corner of her eye. "I can't take something for nothing."

"So, do the dishes, wash the Toyota. She'll let you do it, too."

"But this is beautiful," she exclaimed, waving a hand around her. She was terrified of being in a house, of being with *family*. She didn't know how to do this!

"So? To you it is. The Queen of England wouldn't even walk in here."

She stopped pacing. "She was here?" she asked on an incredulous note.

Morgan laughed deep in his chest, his well-shaped body shaking in humor. "Not literally, vixen."

Her shoulders sagged. "Oh, I get it." Her head snapped up and her thoughts were right on her tongue, but he stopped her. He pressed a finger to her mouth and swayed her into his frame, making her his captive with the lightest of touches.

"Shh, N'Réa. You'll be fine, spoiled even if you let my sister have her way. She's the caretaker of the pack. You may think you're a project, but you're not. She genuinely likes you." He pressed his lips to where his finger's warmth had scalded her. "And so do I." It was a quiet admission, churning her insides harder with a growing lust that she couldn't fight and didn't know how to resist.

Standing wrapped within his arms, her world soon settled, the trembling and anxious fear bleeding away. "You're right. I'm an adult. I can act like one." She rested her head against his chest. "How did you know?" she asked on a tremulous breath.

"You started running the second we pulled onto the highway from the campgrounds. You didn't have any way out until we stopped moving."

"That obvious?" N'Réa couldn't meet his expression, shamed at how obvious she'd been.

Ashamed of her own misgivings. None of them had earned her distrust, yet it was hard to let go of the fear.

He tightened his arms around her. "Just to me." He slid down the door until she was on eye level with him. "No running. You will enjoy this." His finger traced her jaw with a delicate stroke, sending her pulse into a new gear. The heat of his gaze caressed her as he studied her, secrets and questions that caused a bone-deep shiver, creating ribbons of electricity to slide down her spine. "I'm still wondering myself about those complications, so there is no rush to do anything. My promise."

"Still not asking for anything?" she clarified.

He shook his head. "Just you as a friend. And when I can't bear it any longer, a kiss."

She shivered as his voice roughened, turning husky with need. Her entire body responded, heavy with desire. He was staring at her now like he was starved for one of her kisses.

"Would now be one of those times?" She licked her lips, and his groan vibrated under her splayed palms.

He lifted both hands into her hair, massaging, teasing. Goosebumps cascaded down her neck. "All you ever have to say is no. Say no," he prompted her, his warm breath bathing her lips, filling her with need, daring her to reject him.

"Yes," she whimpered, then fell into a well of heat as his lips claimed hers.

* * * *

Monday was spent doing laundry and grocery shopping for the week. Brooke squealed and danced when the living room furniture arrived. She was a constantly happy person, N'Réa soon discovered. She positioned the furniture where she needed it, offered the deliverymen fresh lemonade and a tip, then wished them a happy day as they left.

N'Réa followed their departure in amazement as they disappeared down the street. "You probably made their week."

"And did you see how easy it was to do?" Brooke replied happily. "A smile, a drink, and a tip for their efforts. They'll feel good for a few days at least." She plopped onto the overstuffed leather couch. "What do you think? Mitch was afraid it would be too dark."

"Dark? You're kidding!" she argued. The mahogany color of the leather complemented the subtle greens of the room with a natural blending that reminded N'Réa of a summer glade. "This is perfect." N'Réa sat down too and sighed, tucking herself into the plush corner. "Nice," she purred.

"Exactly," Brooke said, running her hand over the high back.

The leather was a buttery-soft sensation that N'Réa could easily envision being a good napping ground.

"Thanks for coming to stay with us." Brooke made herself comfortable at the other end.

N'Réa sat up. "Why?"

"Because I get lonely and bored when Mitch is at the firehouse. Selene is eight months pregnant and being careful, and Delilah lives too far away for a day trip."

"The whole family is close?" N'Réa asked.

"Very. Even Aunt Jerry who lives in Belgium and our parents in Minnesota. We're very close."

The walls were closing in on her. This wasn't her family. The fears from the night before dared to trample her again. "It must be nice," she said awkwardly.

Brooke's smile drooped, her usual glow shrinking. "Don't you have family?"

N'Réa cautiously opened up. Her thoughts and her heart. "I'm an orphan. I lived with foster families until I was sixteen. I moved out and moved on, took over my life then."

Brooke tucked herself up onto the couch facing N'Réa. The wash of warmth and acceptance coming from the blonde shook her to her core. Her throat closed automatically from the fear of discovery. "You know, don't you?" Brooke nodded without a single vibration of malice. N'Réa's stomach knotted in apprehension.

"I've known since I first held your injured arm," Brooke said without apology in the lyrical, soothing voice she was so well known for.

N'Réa caught her unperturbed gaze, her dark eyes staring back unblinkingly. "It doesn't bother you?"

Brooke laughed, glancing up to the ceiling. "N'Réa, look at who you're asking. I've never pried because like you respect privacy and anonymity, so do I."

"I imagine compared to you, I'm insignificant," N'Réa said. "You have power I could never imagine."

Brooke smiled again, a touch of wicked playfulness floating in her expression. "Well, actually, now you could." Brooke's teasing lightened N'Réa's spirit, pulling her away from the abyss of her fears, and the crying need to run, to escape. "I don't flaunt it, and if Morgan hadn't said anything, you would have never known a thing. I'm as good as you are in keeping my mind blocked. You have an incredibly strong mental ability to channel everything out."

"I've had to, out of necessity. I overloaded easily when I was young."

"That's something I could only imagine. You have this guarded nature," Brooke said thoughtfully. "With cause. Do you know what you are?"

N'Réa chewed her lip. "I don't, not really. I could just be a really intuitive woman for all the good it has done me."

"I can sense the pain behind that," Brooke said sympathetically, nodding in understanding. "What happened?"

N'Réa sucked in air, her fingers moving to her lap to twist together. "I foresaw a death when I was nine, which was what prompted my foster family bounce."

"And you've been hiding it, controlling your ability and yourself with an iron will," Brooke murmured without condemnation. "You're an only child."

N'Réa nodded, her head a dull weight on her neck. "I never knew anything about my parents, except that they died when I was very young. They weren't American, and I had no family here."

Brooke smiled warmly. "Well, that explains the Romanian blood. You're thick with gypsy influence."

N'Réa's eyebrows pulled together in confusion. "I don't understand."

"It's like having your personal nature imprinted on your thoughts, on your soul. I sensed it when I first touched you, but I couldn't tell anything else on the surface and if I had tried, you would have felt the intrusion."

"So everything I've done has been natural?" N'Réa asked, staring in stunned shock at Brooke. She'd never considered the possibility. After years of trying to find herself, N'Réa had simply fallen back on what she felt was right. It wasn't like she wanted to make a fortune or be a big shark in a large pond. All she'd ever wanted was to be happy and her nomad existence did that, leaving her free to do what she wanted, be where she wanted. There had been hard times, plenty of them to teach her resilience, but she'd never cried mercy to the unknown, either.

"More or less, for yourself. You knew what to do to make yourself happy when you were ready to take over your own future." Brooke offered unfettered understanding, laying a caring hand over hers. "Are you happy, N'Réa?"

She thought for several seconds, thought on it hard. Brooke was asking for honesty, and N'Réa felt they both were owed that much. "Most of the time. Except for my most recent problems. I don't know yet how to fix them." Even though she'd made back more than enough to cover the loss of her tent, her car presented a much larger problem.

Brooke waved a hand in dismissal. "Nothing to it. And don't argue," she said as N'Réa popped open her mouth. "We can figure out the details later."

"I still don't understand," N'Réa said, shaken at Brooke's easy acceptance. No one in her lifetime had offered N'Réa this depth of unconditional friendship and caring. She sagged backward against the couch. "How can you be so...?" She dug for a word, but found none as her fingers swept through the air.

"Nonjudgmental?" Brooke offered.

"Yes, that would work. I mean, I know what you are, and your family accepted you. This is a first for me." N'Réa was still aware of the unending comfort Brooke was sending to her, the understanding of what she was, and sharing in that secret, like a sister would. Two of the same, yet so different.

N'Réa couldn't recall one other person with talents on Brooke's level. There'd been no one like N'Réa either.

Taking a chance, believing in what was being shown to her, she said, "I've never opened up to anyone. Morgan doesn't even know." She couldn't say it, but she was also aware that he may have been the only other person she'd ever reached out for and had him respond. A shiver hit her shoulders and crawled down her back at the implication.

Brooke nodded sagely. "Your situation has made you strong, resourceful, and clearheaded about a lot of things." She slipped from her end of the couch, stretching, then said, "Just do me a favor. Don't shortchange Morgan because of what you are, what you know. He's a good man, stubborn, but good."

N'Réa blushed, dropping her chin as the heat of her shame blazed through her once more. "No, I knew I was wrong. It's hard to let the defenses down after so long. It's been years and years since I've been this close to another person, man or woman. I like him, but this makes things complicated. This is my dark, ugly secret."

Brooke laughed with a light humorous giggle, a sympathetic warmth in her words. "Morgan's secret is far worse, but it's his secret to tell. Our family defined complications." She motioned, and N'Réa stood. "Now then, let's put our heads together and see where the nursery is going."

Chapter Nine

Tuesday night at Selene's was warm and welcoming. Though buried with doubts and concerns, then spilling her guts to Brooke, N'Réa was comfortable surrounded by the rowdy group. She laughed like she hadn't laughed in years as the guys argued over baseball, Mitch and Bram being St. Louis Cardinals fans and Morgan rooting for the Mariners. N'Réa laughed at the rolled eyes and jabbed jokes, at stories from their childhoods, and of their parents.

They didn't poke and prod at her, didn't ask a lot of questions, didn't demand to know who she was. They sympathized over her problems, then shared their concern over her attack as they offered support in their solidarity.

Selene cleared the table when they finished their meal, the conversation flowing in lulls and bursts usually broken with raucous gales of laughter. N'Réa caught Brooke glancing toward the window. She shook her head, knowing that *dare the world* smile.

"Who wants a light show?"

"Me!" cried Selene.

"I do." Mitch added his two cents' worth with a nuzzle against Brooke, but she poked his shoulder playfully.

"You're biased," she accused.

N'Réa hid her shaking hands under the table. "I would," she told her, hoping she wasn't stepping over a line. Morgan's hand moved under the table and gave her knee a squeeze in comfort. She was an equal tonight. The urge to melt swiftly followed his touch.

Bram, Selene's husband and surprisingly also Mitch's older brother, smiled as he held open the door and led the procession to the porch.

N'Réa paused going out the door, her attention locking on the wall with the fireplace, which was filled with numerous paintings of wolves. "Those are beautiful." She couldn't help but stop and gawk at the collection.

"Dad did them," Morgan said from behind her shoulder, the warmth of his voice tickling her nerves. "We all have an assortment."

"Your father is incredibly talented. They're so lifelike," she whispered, standing before a large, black wolf with gray tips on his coat. Her hand began to rise to caress the beautiful animal, then fell. The thick coat gleamed in the moonlight, and the striking eyes... It pulled at her, tugged, and she wanted to fall into those soulful windows. She'd never been affected so deeply by a painting. "The moon is beautiful on this one, in its eyes," she murmured in honest admiration. There was the slow brush of Morgan's breath lifting her hair from where he stood. The heat of his chest lined her back, he stood so close.

"How do you feel when you look at him?" he whispered into her ear.

"Feel?" She studied the painting, seeing the many facets of the animal. The soulful gaze, its strength, its power. "He's a leader, proud, arrogant. Alpha, definitely," she mused. Envisioning the animal as a living, breathing wolf, she could almost hear the music of its howl, long and piercing into the darkness. "I see him as a protector."

"You're very perceptive," he murmured in a neutral tone. "Come on. Don't want to miss the entertainment." He draped an arm around her waist and led her outside.

N'Réa's feet stopped dead in the doorway. "Oh my! You weren't kidding. Those are really lights!" She scuttled forward when he prodded her. She heard the door close and his slide to the boards of the porch. He tugged on her jeans until she sat comfortably held between his spread thighs, leaning into the solid warmth of his chest.

"Just watch," he said and she shivered, his lips rasping over her with a featherlight stroke. He drew her closer, wrapping his arms around her waist, embracing her protectively. She reinforced the walls guarding her mind, unsure of what was going to happen next. She felt safe within the strength of his arms, but experience dictated she not let down all her barriers.

"Here's Selene's favorite," Brooke said with a toss of her hand.

"Polka dots!" Selene cried. "In red! My favorite color."

"Who can tell me what this is?" Brooke said as she moved her hands gracefully. The lights began to sway, and the nimbi of the lights formed a cohesive pattern in the darkness.

"A Celtic love knot," N'Réa blurted without thinking.

"Very good," Brooke said with a cheerful laugh. "Here's a harder one." She moved again, making the lights dance and move.

"Oh, I know it," N'Réa muttered. She studied the glowing design and tried to place it. "Heaven's, where did you find the pattern for a Scottish good-luck charm?"

"I have all kinds of stuff packed away between my ears. Years of training that stuck. But here's the question: Good luck for what?"

N'Réa bit her lip with concentration. The lights began to move and sway again in a ballet of movement.

"Do you know?" Morgan asked, his voice wrapping over crying nerves. She nodded in a cautious way. He brushed his cheek to her hair, sweeping it out of his way so his lips could caress a sparking trail down her neck before he said, "She's holding out on us. What's it for, N'Réa?"

N'Réa groaned at the sensation. "It's a true love charm," she said, distracted by the man behind her. Morgan stiffened.

"Are you serious?" he demanded over her shoulder. "Brooke? What are you doing?" His tension vibrated skin where she pressed into him. The urge to run clawed at her anew, her enjoyment obliterated by his anger.

"Oh, lighten up! I was playing," Brooke retorted. "I didn't know she would know those."

"Maybe she's gifted," Bram suggested, as though suggesting she liked ice cream. "No one knew Delilah was for the longest time."

"Because it was her secret," Morgan reminded everyone, stiffly. "She didn't want to announce it to the world."

"Let me try something here," Brooke said, and N'Réa knew she was going to do something that included N'Réa. She silently begged her not to do...whatever. Brooke left the lights in the sky and murmured a few words, uncurling her fingers to produce a stone in her palm.

"Catch!" she called. Brooke tossed N'Réa the stone from where she sat on the porch rail. N'Réa caught it in her hands. A long piece of blue quartz.

"What is it?" She held the smooth stone and waited for the worst.

"A divination stone."

"A divination stone," she echoed numbly. "Will it do anything?" She prayed not.

"Not until you ask it a question."

"Like the cards?" N'Réa said. She chewed on her bottom lip for a second. "And then?"

"If you're a diviner, it will tell you your answer. You said yourself you weren't sure."

N'Réa forced a hollow laugh and stretched out her hand. "I can answer without asking a stone. I'm not a diviner. I learned to read Tarot to pass the time and palms for a challenge." Why would Brooke do this? Why was she putting her on the line like this? N'Réa wasn't at all gifted, not like Brooke. She knew she shouldn't have shared so much! Too late to take it all back now.

Brooke didn't hold her hand out. Dropping hers, N'Réa swung around to encounter expectant expressions surrounding her. "You people are serious? You think I have that kind of ability?" They all looked at her with some level of genuine interest and belief. She shook her head. "I know I don't. Morgan?" she whispered over her shoulder. "Back me up here, friend."

"It is possible," Selene stated, her expression open and friendly. N'Réa wanted to scream and run. "All of our mates are gifted in some way."

Morgan growled low in his chest, surprising and startling N'Réa. Selene snapped around and covered her mouth.

"Oh God! I'm sorry!" she gushed, appalled and contrite.

"But you do come from gypsies, don't you?" Mitch asked.

"I guess I do," N'Réa replied with a stilted stutter, the blood seeping from her cheeks. Walls were crashing all around her. Years of protection and secrecy, obliterated by one afternoon conversation. How much had Brooke shared? The line between fear and friend was blurring. She bit back the fear, the crying need to escape. These people were friends, weren't they? Confusion added to her fear, no longer sure about anything. "I don't know my family. I never knew my parents. You can tell that too?" she asked weakly.

"I can sense things through Brooke," he offered in a calm tone. "I'm sorry. I didn't know it was so fresh." Mitch turned toward Brooke and then nodded in acceptance. "I'm sorry, N'Réa."

"You're right," Brooke said in an appeasing voice, but it didn't hide her disappointment. Disappointment for what? For proving she was a freak? For making her the center of attention to her family? N'Réa didn't understand what happened to the caring blonde she'd thought of as a friend.

"I'm sorry. It doesn't really matter." She snapped her fingers, and the floating lights extinguished with little bursts. "Didn't mean to scare you, N'Réa, or pressure you. It's your choice."

"My choice?" she croaked on a raw whisper, drifting to the glinting stone in her hand. "You're not saying that because of what you know, twisting my arm?" Her need to escape grew as Brooke hopped from the porch rail.

"Of course not. I don't twist arms," she replied, sharing a smile. Brooke waved away her outstretched hand, refusing the stone. "Keep it. Even if you don't use it, I can't do anything with it." She clasped hands with Mitch, saying, "We can go in a minute. I need to go inside."

"Yeah, sure," Morgan said as he pushed away from the door, helping N'Réa to her feet. "Let's walk." She saw the others go inside and suddenly felt isolated.

"I upset them, didn't I?" she asked when they walked away. She felt terrible and wasn't sure why, when just a moment before she'd been terrified and on the edge.

"No, disappointed them would be my guess." He pushed a finger through one of her belt loops and walked down the steps with her.

"But why? I'm not gifted," she argued in a convinced tone. Lying seemed to be the safest route of self-preservation. No one but Brooke knew, hopefully, if she hadn't told them what they'd talked about the previous afternoon. N'Réa no longer knew who she could trust or believe. Why would she do that?

"But you weren't even willing to try," he said. "You knew the charm."

"Not exactly a glowing endorsement of supernatural powers," she replied in annoyed exasperation. "I know them from reading the texts to help liven my readings." Her voice dropped. "I can't do anything with what I know, Morgan. And even if I could, I didn't want to be put on display!" she said defensively, an accidental slip.

N'Réa had hid herself for too long. None of what Brooke did naturally came to her as easily. Trusting, sharing, exposing herself and her talents. N'Réa couldn't do it, not even with these people, the ones she'd thought were her friends.

"You would never be treated like that!" He whirled her around to face him. "Whatever happens in this family stays in this family. We take care of our own, and that means all of us!" His gray gaze was slicing through the nighttime, nearly accusing as he stared at her, through her.

"Why do you keep saying that?" she demanded. She took a step back, shaking with his nearness, with the swarm of emotions emanating from him, unable to stop the onslaught as it careened into her senses. "And what did Selene mean by mates? I don't understand any of that one."

Morgan paced away a step and dragged a hand over his head. "That one is a bit complicated."

She snorted into the darkness. Why wasn't she surprised, she thought sarcastically. "Complications! I knew it. I warned you!" She threw her hands up in the air. "So what? Now that I like you, are you going to walk away?"

His mouth formed a harsh line. "Do you really think I would?"

"No, actually I figured you'd run! You would if you were smart," she advised scathingly.

He grabbed her by the arms. "Run? Not in this lifetime!" He snarled. "Do you want the truth? You'll be the one running if I told you everything. My whole family is different. We protect one another. Mitch and Bram and Delilah, they know the truth and have accepted it. They protect us, and we protect them, because they do know the truth." His lips tightened into another snarl, his teeth bright in the darkness. A predatory gleam. She fought off the shiver as pure fantasy.

"What?" she demanded. "A family of axe murderers? One is a witch. Are you all like that?"

"Of course not. Brooke is phenomenal. She's the rarity even with what we are." He pushed her away, raking his hands over his face. "I knew this was a mistake. I had no right to pull you into this." He muttered and cursed under his breath as he paced in front of her. "I don't care about the stupid dreams! This is wrong."

"I never believed in them either," she retorted. "Arrogant bastard."

"That's twice you've called me arrogant," he barked rudely. "And I meant my dreams."

"What?" she said in a squeak, staggering a step. "Your dreams?"

He prowled around her, the air seeming to crackle with electricity between them the way it had the day of their first meeting, as he stalked mere inches away from her. "Yes, I knew who you were almost two months ago. I had no idea when I got suckered into going to California that I would run into you there."

"Sorry, I'll be sure to leave the instant I get back," she announced caustically. "Oh, wait, I'm at your mercy there, aren't I?"

She leaped a step away from him at the fire of pure rage emanating from him. "Don't you dare use that against me!" He snarled viciously, bearing down on her until he stood over her. "If you want to refuse our help, that's fine. You have every right to, but never, ever accuse me of something I've never done to you."

If he had shouted it, she would have flinched less. "But I don't understand why you even appeared! Why are you helping me, Morgan? And don't tell me you don't want anything. I'm not stupid."

"Do you want to know?" He paused for several long seconds. "Really, honestly, want the truth of what brought us together?"

She curled her hands and stiffened her spine, meeting his seething anger. "Yes. Yes, I do." She refused to let him bully her, to dominate her. She deserved the truth, damn it!

His head reared back until he faced the sky and he growled once more, a pained sound she had never heard a man make. "Fine!" he snapped. "I don't know where the dreams came from or why they started, but

I know what they mean." He paced with a stiff stride in front of her. His frame tightened like a knot as he fought for his control. "The dreams brought us together because you are supposed to be my mate."

"What is a mate, damn it?"

He whipped around on her, eyes blazing fiercely in the darkness. "My love, my wife! But it can't be. I could never care for a coward. Or a deceiver." He spat out the words.

N'Réa's face drained worse than before with the stone, her chest bleeding with the blow of his words. "A coward? I'm not a coward! Or a deceiver!"

"Aren't you? My sister believed in you!" He shouted at her without an ounce of control, pointing to the house. "Don't you think you, of all people, could have shown the decency to test your own strength? Here, with friends? People who trust you, who trust you with our secrets? Whether you are or aren't, it doesn't matter. She thinks you can. Brooke thinks you are something special. If she was wrong it would have been her mistake, not yours, but you didn't see it that way, did you? Someone wanted to use you was what you thought, wasn't it?" He nodded roughly when her mouth opened, not giving her the chance to dispute him. "Make you do something that gave them power over you because you are capable, but we don't work that way! Hell, I knew you were the real thing by the time I walked out of your tent Saturday. I *knew*. I never doubted you. Until now," he said bitterly, his chest heaving with the force of his emotions. Through the numerous walls, he bared everything to her, each one crashing against her. With her eyes and ears, she understood more.

"All because I said no?" Was he telling her the truth? Could she trust them equally? Brooke had exposed herself to N'Réa with very little concern, taking Morgan's word that N'Réa was someone to be trusted. Was that belief equal? N'Réa's chest ached, unable to convince herself that what she was hearing and seeing wasn't a lie. Years of protecting herself, walls and barriers to protect her heart and the truth about her powers, were being rammed by his anger. Cracks were forming, but they hadn't fallen. She held them together with tenacious strength, kept them standing against his anger. Somehow. But they were wavering, and it frightened her.

He let out a long hiss of frustration. "No, N'Réa, not because you said no. Because you doubted yourself. And us." His gaze literally froze over, but she couldn't miss the heat of his anger. It swarmed around him. "After what you knew, how much I trusted you with our secrets, I had hoped I had earned some of your trust. I was wrong." He slid his hand through his hair, tousling the long length with agitated fingers. "I'm sorry. I'll try to break the connection, but it's difficult. I don't even know if it's possible."

"Connection?" she whispered over a dry tongue.

"Yes," he replied, sounding less ragged. "When one of us finds our mate, a bond develops. It's more of that supernatural stuff," he said with a cruel interjection, mimicking her earlier complaint.

"Like when I needed you and you found me?" she said almost inaudibly. She thought she'd done that one all by herself. *Nope, think again,* her voice snidely pointed out.

The expression meeting hers could have been cut from stone. "Yes, like that." He faced the house. "They're ready to leave. I'll let you know what I can do with the bond by Friday. Since I'm obligated in the tournament now, I have to go." His tone said he wished otherwise.

"I know." N'Réa could barely look at him. Sooner or later she'd grow larger than two feet tall! She had to.

"Fine," he said and stomped away. He didn't once look her way when he drove by in his own truck, the roar of the engine punctuating his mood.

She blinked back the tears filling her eyes. "All right, N'Réa. You're really screwing up this time," she scolded herself. The car ride to town with Brooke and Mitch was silent and cool. She could only pray she got the chance to fix this one.

Chapter Ten

N'Réa drew a steadying breath as she hit the bottom step the next morning. She found Brooke sitting at the table drinking tea, staring off into space. Her greeting was warm when she saw N'Réa.

"Hi! Sleep all right?"

N'Réa stumbled, but she recovered. "Yes, I did."

"There's tea or coffee if you want it," she said, waving toward the counter. N'Réa's hand shook as she poured. She steadied her hand and wondered whose planet she'd awakened on.

"Brooke, about last night," she began, twisting marginally to catch her out of the corner of her eye.

She waved a hand from her seat at the table. "History. Life's too short to let little things like that be a burden."

N'Réa's head plunked forward, dead weight. Her throat closed up. "I wish I could be like you." She blinked hard, but she couldn't stop the tears. Twin trails formed, burning her skin with her confusion and misery.

She faced the other woman when Brooke put a comforting hand on her. "You could be if you lost the chip on your shoulder," Brooke said honestly. "That thing is huge!" She smiled, trying to soften the candid blow. "But it takes time and until now, you've had no reason to try."

N'Réa leaned into the counter, wiping her cheeks with shaking hands. "No, I haven't." She gazed into

Brooke's eyes, seeing her empathy. "You've already walked this road, haven't you?"

"I didn't just walk it, N'Réa, I paved the damned thing!"

N'Réa laughed through the heartache in her chest. "So how do I fix the pothole I made? I need to apologize to Morgan, which is all I've done since we've met."

"Get your tea." Brooke sauntered to the table and sat. "He's not making it easy on you either. He's avoided and fought this since the beginning, but he's not unaffected. He fought like a madman when I gave him your head wrap. He had a reason to win. He wanted to win for you," she explained in quiet earnestness. "You do like him, don't you?"

N'Réa nodded carefully. She wasn't ready to examine the depths of those emotions. It was something for her to admit to them at all, especially after last night's fight. She steadied herself for what came next. "So, can I talk to him?"

"Today's not good. He needs to cool off. He went running."

N'Réa slouched in her chair with disappointment. "You're right. This weekend is soon enough." She rubbed at her eyes, wanting a clear answer, doubtful she'd find it. "God, I said so many things!"

"I'm sure he did too, but that's what I mean. He's always controlled. He keeps it inside because he's the oldest. Strong firstborn and all that nonsense." Brooke gave her a secret smile. "I think you're exactly what he needs to shake him up a little."

N'Réa cupped her hands around her tea. "I don't know if I'm ready to believe in fate and mates," she admitted in a quiet voice. "But I do like him." She gave Brooke a quick glance, remembering the night before with a punch to her stomach. "I hated hurting him."

Brooke patted her hand. "It will work out."

N'Réa flattened her hands on the table. "Help me?" she pleaded.

"Of course. We take care of our own." Brooke gave her a wink and sipped at her tea.

* * * *

Friday afternoon, they all piled into the Toyota with clean clothes and coolers of food. Morgan was distant, but N'Réa wasn't going to let it deter her.

She'd talked and managed a lot of thinking to clear her mind since her fight with Morgan. It was time to grow up. It was time to move on with purpose rather than simply move around aimlessly, letting life move her as it will.

Which included with Morgan. She had to meet him halfway, except by the way he was following the flow of the scenery instead of her, he was going in the other direction. She had a long road ahead.

She maintained her patience until they reached the campgrounds to have a private moment with Morgan, but it didn't start quite the way as she hoped.

Morgan and Mitch unloaded the Toyota while N'Réa helped Brooke straighten up after being gone all week when she heard Leslie's voice and Morgan's.

She walked as calmly as possible around the side of the tent and found Leslie wrapped all over him like a climbing weed.

"I don't have a place to stay." She pouted invitingly. "My friends won't be here until morning."

N'Réa wanted to tear the other woman apart but curled her hands instead, unsure of how to deal with this, while a possessive anger she'd never tasted before swam through her veins. Should she fight for him? Did he want her enough still? Did he want her at all?

"Could I bunk with you?" Leslie purred, running a finger over Morgan's chest. Red flashed over N'Réa's vision.

Morgan put his hands on Leslie's waist. "I don't mind. But it will be crowded." He lifted and smiled cruelly at N'Réa, his expression cold. "Unless N'Réa would mind finding someplace else to sleep." It was a taunt, a challenge, clear as day. Her pulse thundered, undecided.

"Fight for him," Brooke murmured as she walked behind her without stopping.

With the little nudge to prod her, N'Réa's power soared, feeling more like a woman worthy of her man's attention than ever before. And damn it! Morgan was her man!

Letting her anger flow around her, embracing it, she rushed the pair. She ripped Leslie's hands off Morgan. "I don't share!" She wouldn't have been surprised if she were throwing sparks, as furious as she was. Until otherwise stated, no one would take Morgan from her. Not until she'd lost every chance she had to apologize and win him back to her.

Leslie cried out. "He wants it!" She tossed her red braid spitefully. "And if he wanted you, he wouldn't have asked you to leave!"

N'Réa launched her right hook, sending Leslie windmilling backward until she landed in a strangled heap several feet away. "That is not your concern," N'Réa answered with biting scorn.

She faced Morgan bravely, letting him see her thoughts on her face for himself. "We take care of our own," she told him with strength behind it, lifting her chin. She stood before him, her chest heaving with emotion, scared but strong. He slid that icy gaze contemptuously over her to rise and rest on her face. His expression was blank but she could see the battle, and it made her bolder. She took the first step when he didn't tell her not to. He didn't turn away from her. She took another, then didn't stop until she was standing directly in front of him. "We take care of our own," she repeated with meaning. "And I don't share. Ever."

His hand plunged into her hair, snapping her gaze to his uncompromisingly. His nostrils flared as he yanked her closer, his eyes narrowing to heated storms of color. There was no warning for what came next. His mouth punished her as he kissed her. She let him, instinctively knowing he would recognize her surrender. He swept his other arm around her, pinning her to his length. Her hands lifted to curl over his arms, relishing the hard planes of him beneath her palms. His kiss was hard, brutal. She recognized what he was doing and refused to bow to it. He was trying to force her away.

Just as she began to fear she was wrong, that she'd lost everything, his kiss changed, gentled, and his entire body shuddered along hers where he captured her within his embrace. His hands began to caress her and he deepened the kiss until her head swam, her body yearning and filling with desire. His tongue melted her as he nipped with his teeth, soothing the harshness of his kiss on her lips.

Delving between her lips, she tasted him, dueled with him, and moaned with renewed sensations. Giving in, she showed him how sorry she was, how much she'd missed him. A low, growled groan rumbled in his chest, where she flattened a hand to his warmth, his strength. The beat of his heart pounded into her palm and she wanted. Craved. She pressed into him, inch by inch, and silently thrilled at his reactions. She hadn't lost him.

Morgan was breathing as hard as she was when he slid from her mouth to her ear. His voice raked over every nerve, sparking them with whips of electricity. "There's no way to break the connection," he told her.

She twisted and nipped at his neck. "Good." His entire length hardened against her, making her go limp with hot, demanding desire. She wrapped her arms around his neck and held on tight. Longing pooled in her stomach and lower. She knew what it was to feel desire, to want, but she'd never experienced anything as all-consuming as she did when in Morgan's arms.

"I'm sorry. For everything. I keep pushing back as a defense mechanism." She whispered against his skin, pleased when his hold tightened reflexively around her waist, his fingers kneading and caressing in intervals. "I don't want to lose this." She pressed her lips to his throat, dropping light kisses to his flushed skin.

"Ah, N'Réa." He brushed a cheek against her hair. "There's so much you don't know."

"One day at a time," she told him, more than willing to meet him halfway. Hungry, gray eyes met hers. She fanned her fingers across his chest, tracing the tumbled pounding of his heart beneath her seeking touch.

The corner of his sexy mouth arched. "Is this the same woman who told me off not once but twice?" he teased her. He lifted her hair with a tender hand. "She's here somewhere."

"She's still here. And a warning — if I ever catch you with your mitts on another woman, you're in trouble."

He curled his hand possessively around her neck, an *oh, really* taunt in his expression. "Is that a threat?" He neared and nibbled over her throat.

"Do it and find out," she replied with an angelic grin, batting her lashes at him.

"Big words for someone who didn't want to sleep with me," he whispered into her ear, keeping their earlier animosity, and the content behind it, private.

"I could say the same thing, but I'm willing to change my mind." His eyes darkened immediately to spike with an inner flame at her words, his breathing growing haggard. "Are you?" she asked, her heart pounding a ferocious rhythm in her ears.

The glistening gray glittered with suppressed desire for her. "You should be thankful I have control, and there's over twenty people here. Otherwise you'd be naked and being pleasured beyond your wildest dreams."

"Confident?" she teased him, running her hands over his chest and arms.

"Only with you." He dipped his head to hover over her lips, his voice so soft it flowed like a summer breeze on her skin. "All those dreams I had were of making love to you. I woke up every night craving you, smelling your heat, tasting your skin." She shivered in his hold, the delicious pictures he painted becoming an erotic enticement too strong to fight any longer. "I've been a walking hard-on since I met you," he told her in a gravelly voice.

She tapped the collar of his T-shirt, right where his pulse ticked like a single beat of time. "I might be able to do something about that."

He shook his head as his hands continued to hold and caress her, learning her all over again. "Not yet. But yes, it will happen."

Her wandering fingers rose to his face, finding the shadow of doubt flicker, clouding his thoughts. "Morgan, I trust you. I do!"

The warmth of his palm covered her hand, his lids sliding to half mast with a darker meaning hidden behind them. "I hope you do because when I share my secret with you, there's no going back." He stood straight, creating a minimal but meaningful gap between them. "This is important to me."

"You're important to me." Her heart tripped when he gave her his first genuine smile since Tuesday.

"Have you two made up yet?" Brooke asked from the other side of the tent. "Dinner's ready."

"Yes," Morgan called. "We made up." He shared a deliberate grin with N'Réa. An eyebrow arched. "Hungry?" The simple question was laden with innuendo.

"Starving," she answered, and he lowered to kiss her breathless all over again.

* * * *

N'Réa sat by the campfire with everyone after they'd eaten. They all listened as Hugh and William, with his guitar, sang bawdy songs about wenches and skirts. Hugh, unfortunately, was sporting a cast on his injured foot, which got him a lot of sympathy from around the camp. Leslie had disappeared since she'd been decked, and N'Réa refused to regret it. Probably off to find some other easy mark to bunk with for the night.

She noted when Turner showed up with a girl on his arm and introduced her as Kim to the camp. Turner grinned and winked in her direction, a mark of a passage between them. *Good, he'd found someone for himself.* He was a nice kid. He deserved a little affection.

N'Réa relaxed, feeling more like one of Duncan's World than she'd thought possible. Everyone was kind, welcoming. She dared to reach out briefly and found no animosity for her inclusion. That helped her conscience as well as her mind to relax.

She curled up against Morgan's chest, his arm wrapped around her supported on a raised knee boxing her in. Earlier, she'd changed into a light sweater after the sun set to ward off the nighttime chill of Northern California, the sweater teasing with a deep V-cut and buttons lining the front. She didn't have to guess when Morgan was inspecting her wardrobe. Every now and then he shifted behind her, reassuring that she was comfortable, then having to do it again in very short order. It wasn't because his butt was growing numb! It made her smile secretly.

She was feeling the same thing, the rush of excitement, the new heat of desire burning like a candle's flame with every touch, but respected that they needed to do this slow. What they shared wasn't a romp on the beach kind of relationship. This was different. Special.

May leaned over during a lull in the songs and conversation. "N'Réa, what is that?" she asked, pointing to her throat.

N'Réa pulled out a linked chain, the blue quartz rocking at the end. "It's a stone Brooke gave me." She'd wrapped it in gold wire and wore it on a long chain, where it now rested between her breasts. "Isn't it beautiful?"

"Very," May agreed.

"You kept it?" Morgan asked, curious.

"Yes."

After several seconds, he asked, "And?"

"I'll tell you later," she said, in no hurry to break the languid spell of being in his arms and at peace with the world surrounding her.

Unfortunately, she didn't get to enjoy it for longer after that answer.

He stood up. "Be back in a minute." Then he tugged her up on a whoosh of surprise.

Oh, not again! She prayed he wasn't going to blow a gasket over something now, not here. He cradled her hand in his as they walked deep into the campgrounds, out of earshot. He tugged her to face him, an intense expression set on his features. "And?" he repeated, dead serious. His hands held on to her shoulders.

She ducked her head. "You were right. The both of you. I had no idea how much ability I did have," she finished, embarrassed. "I don't use it. I've avoided it my entire life. I use illusion and flowery words to do my bits. I had no idea I was really telling people their futures!" Her head popped up as the fear resurfaced. "I just read the cards!"

He swept her into his chest, comforting her with his nearness. "Do you have any idea how exact my reading was?"

She shook her head, her arms holding on at his waist, afraid to let go. "I only knew I was involved somehow. I never know if I'm right or wrong."

"What did the stone tell you?"

"I asked the sex of Brooke's baby," she mumbled. "I hoped it was safe. She's having a boy."

"Did you ask anything else?" His voice cooled with caution, his stance stiff, waiting.

"No. Brooke was with me when I did it. I didn't want to try twice."

"You didn't ask about me?"

"No!" she answered, appalled he would think she would. "If there is something you want me to know, then you will tell me." She pressed into him, sensing his doubts in the way he held her, cautiously, uncertain. "I swear, Morgan. I wouldn't do that to you."

"You swear?" he asked in a disbelieving voice. "A swear among my family is a valid oath. It's as strong as any contract, as strong as blood. It is binding."

She didn't hesitate, didn't blink. In this, she could tell the absolute truth. "Yes, I swear I would never seek anything about you. You will tell me, or I will ask you."

He fought against something deep inside, his head turning as he swallowed several times. His entire frame vibrated within from some battle only he knew he waged. "N'Réa, I don't want a mate! I don't need one." His gaze was liquid smoke and fevered with sheer lust and desire when he captured her again. "But I do want you! There's so much about you." He pressed his head to hers, his arms shackled around her like chain links. The intensity in his eyes sent her entire being into a heated whirlpool of need.

Something inside him snapped. The final restraints containing him broke. He groaned thickly before his lips attacked hers. Hot. Passion. Possessive. Dominant. All were thoughts coursing through her shattered brain. Then even those stopped.

His hands. His lips. His tongue. His heart.

She writhed when his hands moved over her, then she shook forcefully when he cupped her breast in a palm. He groaned deep in his throat as he raked a thumb over a hardened tip. "N'Réa," he whispered in a desire-laden voice. "I want you."

He brushed hot sparks from her lips to her neck, biting and kissing until she was a quivering heap of endless nerves.

"Yes!" she cried against him, lost to the growing yearning that was swiftly turning into a wildfire of its own.

He lifted from her and licked his lips. "You're wet. So ready. So sweet." He shuddered violently as he inhaled. "Hot." He hissed through his teeth in sheer need, every muscle clenched with a control that amazed her so much that she wanted to crack. N'Réa couldn't remember the last time she'd wanted, hungered, like this. He shook his head hard as if coming out of a trance a moment later, the thunder of his heart loud under her hands. "If we do this, it is one step closer to no turning back."

Her voice was thick, charged as she tried to focus on his words, and failed. "No turning back. Right." She whimpered hungrily as she pushed her hands upward into his hair, dragging him down to her. She'd never known she was capable of this much want, of burning desire.

He gripped her wrists, halting her, resisting her insistent hands. "Listen to me. If I make love to you, we will be bound. The connection, the bond, will become stronger."

Her head was swimming, or floating. Something. It definitely didn't feel attached. "Stronger?" she asked weakly. She blinked. *Connection?* "Bound?"

He took a deep, deep breath. "Yes. Bound." He pulled her flush, though his touch gentled, his insistence cooling. "You need to know everything before I ask that of you. I need to show you my secret. I can't force you. You have to accept me, all of me, before I make love to you properly." Tender fingers brushed through the hair sheeting the side of her face, caressing her with heated fingertips with the pass.

Her world wasn't right. "Are you saying you don't want me now?"

"God no!" He growled fiercely, yanking her tight into his frame. "I want you! Hell, I want you so much, I'll be lucky to get any sleep at all next to you all weekend."

It took a few seconds for that answer to make sense, but when it did, the worried tension in her leaked away and she smiled at him. "Just so long as the excruciating torture goes both ways, I can suffer."

The rough sound of his chuckle tickled her ear where he nuzzled her. "I hope you still feel that way after you know."

*　*　*　*

The camp was settling down several hours later when she entered the shared tent and opened her largest suitcase. She slid out a bunch of her clothes and opened the secret compartment she'd added to protect her most precious possessions. She touched her money, making sure it was all there with a quick flick of her nail. Then she went to the bottom of the pile and carefully, with delicate fingers, slipped out the old, grainy black-and-white photo from the very bottom.

She'd been too distracted earlier to show Morgan. He drove her persistently over the edge, easily. He had a right to know how much she'd discovered about herself. Brooke was a remarkable woman, one of the truest friends N'Réa had ever found, and with her help they'd opened up N'Réa to find her inner capacity. It had frightened her at first, a lot, in all honesty. N'Réa had never known what she'd been carrying inside for so long. There was no way to tell if what they'd discovered over the last few days was everything, either. Brooke had mentioned the same thoughts absently after their last session to delve into N'Réa's mind.

Something was happening between Morgan and herself. He had his secrets and now, more than ever, so did she. He deserved to know everything. She refused to keep herself apart any longer. For the first time in her life she wanted to share all of herself with a man, not just her body.

Brooke knew, but out of the entire world, she was one woman no one would cross and N'Réa respected her and her ability to keep her secrets close. Morgan was becoming something more to her. She couldn't argue the truth any longer.

She couldn't deny the way Morgan made her ache, the raging burn he created with a touch, a word. The way he left her light-headed and more after one of his kisses. She sensed the amount of control he used whenever she touched him. She knew it was partially the awakened sense of her own ability, but there had to be some correlation to the bond he had mentioned. She had called his name, and he had answered. She'd never reached out before. She'd never had anyone hear her.

There was something going on here. Definitely. And he had a right to know everything. She heard a step outside. The tent flap moved behind her. "Morgan," she began, expecting him.

"Sorry, not Morgan."

Her head snapped around, and she found herself face-to-face with the wrong end of a gun.

Chapter Eleven

Friday night, Morgan and Brooke walked the Faire grounds doing a cursory check, hoping for anything to help them narrow possibilities. Once again, there had been an entire week of, thankfully, nothing happening while the grounds were empty. It grated on Morgan that he couldn't figure out who the nighttime stalker was after searching the grounds for any clues. He still wasn't willing to swear for sure that the attacker was a person at the Faire, but for a person stalking, they were being extremely cagey in their methods. He didn't like the pattern. If it had been a desperate act by a person, then they didn't get away with very much. It worried him that the easiness even for the paltry gains would be too tempting for whoever the person was, waiting for another chance. He'd examined the area of the previous week's attack, pinpointing where the attacker may have waited, or made his escape, but there was no way to know.

Duncan had been strict about keeping his camp constantly supervised. The women were always with someone. Even Dirk and Abernathy, that Morgan had heard, had taken this situation to heart. They were as adamant about finding the attacker as Morgan himself, but only Duncan and he were aware of the trap they were trying to lay out for the person behind it. It wasn't difficult, it wasn't even ingenious. It only required the man to attack again.

Morgan was confident it would happen. The nighttime attacker had been successful twice without discovery. Also, the tournament rounds started this weekend. The grounds would be packed and active all weekend. Not everyone would pay attention to common sense. Someone would stray, some woman would walk alone. Morgan hoped he was able to catch him before someone else got hurt.

He stopped outside their shared tent at the edge of Duncan's World, his hand on the flap. "All right, Brooke, I'm going to bed. I guess N'Réa already has."

"Be in after Mitch is done pulverizing William at hearts." She waved, walking over to William's tent, where anyone left awake watched the battle of poker-faced wills. He smiled, thinking how lucky Mitch was to have her undying support and belief.

He slipped inside their tent and started to pull off his shirt, but froze. "N'Réa?" He slid his shirt down slowly, instantly uneasy.

"Hi, handsome," Leslie purred. She was stretched out on his bedroll, the top buttons of her blouse undone as she rested on her elbows. "I hope your offer still stands." Wicked temptation was offered with every breath.

"Where's N'Réa?" he demanded, anger at her presence making his voice whiplike and sharp.

"Don't know, don't care." She shrugged in unconcern. Leslie's eyes glittered in the dimness, sweeping up to his face. "She deserves whatever she gets after hitting me."

"What did you do?" He cleared the space between them in two long strides.

"Me?" Leslie laughed with haughty mockery. "I haven't done a thing, but I could, to you." She ran a hand up his jean-clad leg. "You're magnificent, especially when you fight. Hard muscle and slick skin." She licked her lips.

He jerked away from her touch, instantly repulsed as anger filled him. "Where is N'Réa?" He clenched his fists, sickened by the woman splayed on the ground.

"That whore is gone! White trash is all she is." She rose to her knees. "I'm a much better woman in bed," she cooed, playing up her appeal, which left Morgan more than cold. Her presence froze him solid, a problem he helped create by using Leslie to make N'Réa jealous, to hurt her. Now he didn't know where N'Réa was.

Morgan reached and grabbed Leslie by the belt to drag her outside the tent. His growl was loud enough to echo. "Where the hell is N'Réa?" he shouted at her. He threw her to the ground in a shocked heap.

Leslie leaped to her feet, shaking with rage. "She's gone!" Morgan twisted to nod over his shoulder at Duncan. Two men moved in and flanked Leslie. "What! What are you doing?" She gaped around herself in a panic.

"You will tell me where N'Réa is and then you are being escorted off property. Permanently." He snarled, venom coating the sound. "You are not welcome here any longer by any man. Do I make myself clear?"

"Who are you to tell me I can't come back? I'll be right here first thing in the morning! I have friends!" She shrieked with rising fury. "I know people."

Duncan appeared to stand in front of her, glowering with disgust. "No, Leslie, you don't. Not anymore. You've demoralized yourself for long enough. Don't come back."

"Patrick?" She sputtered with disbelief. "You'd turn your back on me? On me!"

"Leslie, I've put up with you. I haven't cared one whit about you for more than three years. You stopped hurting me long ago. If you return to the Faire, I have given Donegan permission to have you escorted off property, by force, if necessary. He gave me permission long ago," he indifferently revealed, the meaning perfectly clear. Patrick had always had the power to get rid of her.

"You got permission from King Henry?" Her face paled. He nodded stiffly.

"Now, for the last time, do you know where N'Réa is?" Duncan demanded as he loomed over her.

"Like I said, don't know, and I really don't care!" she shouted, glaring at everyone in the group, blue eyes flashing, promising retribution. "You will all pay for this!"

"Take her out the rear gate, and make sure she leaves the property," Duncan said, before watching Leslie and her escorts disappear into the darkness. Duncan let her go, a man beaten too many times for too long to feel the pain any longer. "I never thought she'd get so bad. She's been out to hurt me for years."

"What happened?" Morgan asked.

Duncan spat, then wiped his mouth, as if removing a bad taste from his mouth. "I got a little fresh when I was drunk one night with a friend of hers. She played it up big with Leslie, said I had sex with her, the whole setup." He faced Morgan. "I haven't had a drink or a woman since."

"And Leslie believed her over you?" he asked, shocked for his friend. That wasn't the man Morgan knew.

He rolled thick shoulders. "It wasn't a stretch for her. She'd been cheating since the beginning. I was the last to find out." Duncan waited until the trio was gone and then in stark silence, he left to his own tent.

"Has anyone seen N'Réa?" Morgan asked those still around.

Everyone shook their heads. He cursed, and not quietly, worry gnawing at him. She wouldn't just take off without saying something. Even if she'd just wandered to the restroom, not with a stalker on the grounds. Whipping in every direction, he could see a lot of people, but not her.

"Morgan," Brooke called from the tent. "You need to see this."

He was beside her in a second flat. She crouched in front of N'Réa's suitcase, her clothes scattered on the floor.

"She never would have left this all out like this," Brooke stated worriedly.

He lowered his voice. "Where is she? She was here earlier; I can still smell her scent." It was there, beneath Leslie's cloying perfume, N'Réa's summer rain. He would never mistake it.

"I don't know," Brooke was saying when, with no warning, his skull felt ready to burst wide open. N'Réa's terrified voice filled his ears. His gut clenched at the fear and panic riding over him, drowning in the onslaught of pain.

He gripped his head, shouting out when it splintered his mind.

"Morgan!" Brooke cried. She jumped to her feet, grabbing his arms to hold him steady when he rocked on his heels as though he'd been punched with a cannonball. His head pounded as stars exploded.

"Hurts!" His jaw clenched, and his stomach roiled. He slipped to his knees. "N'Réa!" He gasped, taking deep breaths, waiting for his world to stop tilting. "She's close," he managed. He looked up at his sister, pleading her understanding. "There's only one way I can follow her trail."

"How can I explain a wolf?" she demanded sharply.

"We'll walk out, and I'll circle around until I can find her scent. Bring me Mitch. He's going with me."

"I'm going too," she corrected him.

He shook his head, breathing to quiet the thunderous pace of his heart. "No!" He ground out the words. "Stay here." Morgan shook his head. "Someone's going to pay." A flash of teeth, then he snarled at the far canvas wall as her pain sluiced over his nerves. "Hang on, N'Réa," he whispered, his eyes closing again, fighting the waves of nausea assaulting him, reaching out for her the only way he could.

* * * *

N'Réa felt Morgan's comfort pour over her and allowed her lids to stay closed. Stars circled her vision from the blow to her temple. Whoever said that was ineffective didn't know jack. Her hands were tied behind her where she sat, propped against a hardwood wall like a sack of bones. She couldn't remember much after she'd been escorted from the camp. The blow to her temple had given her short-term, momentary amnesia.

She positively didn't know the big guy who'd hid the gun in her shirt, pressing it into her ribs while they tromped out beyond the edge of the camp. Yet he was evidently known enough to walk in and act chummy with her, or at least talk to her acting like he knew her. No one even blinked when they left, if anyone had paid attention as late as it was. With their tent at the very edge of the camp, it had made it far too easy to walk in and walk out, unseen. Now she was gagged, so she couldn't even ask why he was doing this, or for who.

A cell phone rang, breaking the silence while the noise screeched across her skull.

"Yeah, I have her. They kicked you out! No, of course I'm not mocking you," he offered in a conciliatory tone. "So what do I do...?" He went silent for a moment, grunting, she assumed in some kind of answer. "Are you sure? She didn't do anything," he said. She swallowed, hearing him speak again. "Yeah, I can do it." She tried to crack an eye to see and flinched with pain. She let it drop closed once more, unable to take the agony to her senses. It was dark. That was the most she could discern. She heard the phone beep. End call.

"Well, I guess I better take you farther into the woods. Can't have them finding a body before the end of the Faire." He said it so nonchalantly, she quaked with fear.

Morgan! she shrieked inside.

Big and Stupid picked her up and threw her over a shoulder, unsympathetic to her pain. Her head swam, hanging upside down as he strode from the building they'd been hiding in. The caretaker's shed? She squinted into the night. That's what it looked like through the pounding of her temple and the agony of trying to see at all.

Who the hell *was* Big and Stupid? And who told him it was all right to knock her off, damn it! She started to squirm and he thwacked her on the butt, hard, with a flat hand.

"Stop it. You're turning me on. I don't want to add rape to this, but I will," he said with a gleeful sound. She froze like a statue. She bit her lip when his hand lifted to caress her butt, murmuring in appreciation. "I might do it anyway. I never knew how firm you were. You're not as cheap as she made you out."

Mooorrrrrgan! Her head hung limply, painfully dazed from the blow to her head as he went deeper through the trees, leaving everything and everyone behind. How long would it take them to discover she was missing? Would they realize she hadn't simply left, thinking she'd come right back? She was dead. It was hopeless.

Hold on, N'Réa, we're almost there! She heard Morgan's voice in her head and shivered hard, unprepared for the vibration of his voice. No one had ever done that!

The attack was silent. One second she was upside down, and the next she was on the ground in a heap as Big and Stupid howled in pain.

"Get it off'a me!" he screamed. She heard throaty growls and grunts, but it hurt too much to keep her eyes open to see what was happening. Hearing it was bad enough.

"Who are you?" *Mitch!* She sagged with relief into the leaves and who knew what else as he demanded an answer.

"Get it off'a me!" Big and Stupid repeated, terror making him sound like a prepubescent girl.

"I'm going to let him tear your throat out if you don't tell me who you are and who told you to take her!"

N'Réa heard Big and Stupid squeak, and she forced an eye to crack. They flew open in shock, ignoring the bite of agony. A wolf! A freaking huge one! And it controlled the man who had taken her by the throat.

"Curtis," he wheezed. "Leslie told me to hide her."

"Where were you going?" Mitch demanded tersely as the wolf threatened with a low and mean growl.

Big and Stupid, AKA Curtis, pinched his eyes shut. He yelped when the wolf moved. "Leslie wanted revenge! Please, make it let go." He babbled through tight lips.

"No," Mitch stated coldly. "I'm going to check on N'Réa." The wolf shifted, casting a pale glance in her direction, then returning its attention to the man between its jaws.

Mitch cradled her head, careful of her injured side, helping her sit. "You all right?" He untied the gag, and she spit it out. N'Réa sucked in air, grateful and thankful and relieved beyond measure.

Mitch whipped around in his crouch when the man yelped again. "Move and you're dead. You're going back to camp and telling the cops everything."

"No! I can't," he cried. Big and Stupid started to fall apart, blubbering incoherently before saying, "I can't go back to jail! Leslie will leave me for good!" The wolf hunched over him, pinning him to the ground, the meaning clear with the way he hunched over the sobbing man. He screamed. "Call him off! I won't move!"

"Turn a little bit," he told N'Réa. Mitch reached for her wrists, ignoring the whining of the captured man on the ground. "How's your head? Can you walk?"

"I think so. Is the wolf going to kill him?" It hurt to swallow and blink. God, her head hurt.

"Him, maybe. He deserves it." With a thoughtful inflection, he told her, "You never have a reason to fear the wolf." He bent over to finish unwinding the ties on her hands and helped her to her feet. "Lean on me."

Together, they stood over Curtis. "He's going to let you up now. If you run, he will kill you. If you stop moving, he will kill you. Do you understand?"

"He had a gun," she said around the ache in her head. She lifted a quaking hand to the pounding, sorry she'd said anything, but she couldn't risk anyone being shot.

Mitch loomed over Curtis. "Where is it?" Curtis blinked up, unmoving. The wolf put a paw on his chest and growled when he took too long.

"My pocket!" N'Réa saw the man's terrified gaze move to the animal holding his life. "Please, make it let go," he begged.

Mitch crouched at his side and pulled the short nose .38 from the man's pocket. He rolled open the chamber and palmed the bullets. "I have the gun. You can let him go now," he calmly told the wolf. "She's safe."

Mitch slapped a hand on Big and Stupid's chest once the wolf stepped clear. Its teeth were sharp and unbelievably white in the blackness of its fur as it kept up a low, vibrating snarl. "Remember what I said. One wrong move, and he will kill you."

Big and Stupid nodded weakly. Mitch lifted his hand. "Get up." Curtis rose to two shaking legs and led the procession through the trees. Mitch kept a supportive hand around N'Réa as the wolf took the other side of their captured kidnapper and would-be murderer.

Every now and then she heard a low growl pointing Curtis in the right direction. She stumbled, and Mitch swung her up into the cradle of his arms. "Mitch." She gasped in shock. "Put me down." Then she blinked when her vision doubled.

"No, Morgan would be very upset if anything happened to you," he replied evenly.

"Where is he?" she asked, her headache growing. "Mr. 'We take care of our own.' Yeah, right. Sent you and your trained pet." She waved a hand. "Where have you been hiding him, anyway? He's beautiful," she murmured, dizziness swooping in on her. She didn't feel as the blackness took over on the trek to their tent.

"N'Réa? Can you hear me?"

She lifted a limp hand to her aching head. "Yeah, unless I'm dead now, I can hear you," she answered Brooke. "God, my head hurts."

Brooke removed a damp towel from her forehead. "He hit you hard, but you're okay now. You're at camp, safe."

She groaned as her lids tried to crack open, just a little. "God, I need a real job, like Secret Service or something. At least I'd get paid for this crap," she muttered.

N'Réa heard Brooke's musical chuckle. "I know, but I think it's over. You helped capture the Saturday night bandit."

Her eyes popped open with that news. "I did? How?" She winced in the low lantern glow but kept them open.

"Curtis wore an orthopedic shoe. He's been casing women while he escorted Leslie around the grounds. When he knew a woman owned something he could pawn, he'd get them at night. He had a whole list of women. He only waited for one to leave somewhere and then would trail them."

"And he didn't think he'd go to jail!"

"Hey, I didn't say he was smart," she quipped.

"Big and Stupid was what I called him." N'Réa sighed. "This has been the weirdest damn trip I've ever had." She rolled her head to the side, trying to ease her headache, but noticed she was alone with Brooke. "Hey, where is it?"

"What?"

"The wolf? Mitch had a huge wolf with him."

"He took him back to where he lives," Brooke said, glancing down and avoiding her sweeping questions. "We can't keep him."

"I guess it makes sense. Wild animal laws, but how did Mitch get him to begin with? How was he trained? Where have you been hiding him?"

"Shh, rest. Eventually everything will be answered."

N'Réa began to get angry at the evasive answers, and there was no sign of Morgan. Still. "And where was Morgan? Why did he send Mitch and a wolf after me? I thought I heard him in my head," she said, annoyance making her voice sharp. Her temple didn't appreciate the pressure and began pounding with a new sledgehammer ring when her strained attempt at thinking increased. "But that's not possible, is it? I mean, I know I can project," she said, her confusion mixing with adrenaline and her anger. She reached for Brooke. "Was he going to let me die?"

Brooke seemed to startle at the idea. "Of course not! He knew where you were! He's the one who got Mitch to you. Remember? I told you, he can track. He was there; you probably didn't see him." Brooke folded the towel she lifted from N'Réa's head with steady hands.

N'Réa let her eyes drift closed, the dry pain getting to be too much to fight. "I did have double vision, and it was hard to see." She sighed, yielding to the pain in her head and relaxing clenched muscles. "You're right. I'm sure he was there. It happened so fast. I probably just didn't see him." Though she had her doubts.

Why would Mitch take care of her if Morgan was there? Where did the wolf come from? Mitch had spoken to the animal as though he knew it well and could trust it. Not in simple commands, but as a person. Was the wolf Morgan's? Was that where he was, helping to control the animal?

It was too confusing and too hard to concentrate with the train clacking with a hard rhythm in her head.

Brooke patted her arm. "I'll send him in a minute. I wanted to make sure you were conscious before anything else happened tonight. Before you ask, Big and Stupid is on his way to jail now. He caved and told them everything. Leslie isn't getting out of this either."

Brooke's touch was light. "He told the police what her intentions were and why he had taken you. We're all very glad you're safe with us."

Brooke lifted herself from N'Réa's side and vanished out the panels of the tent.

N'Réa listened to her soothing voice outside, glad she was safe too. Glad to be in the tent, glad to know her friends were close by. Exhausted and sore, she was grateful to simply be lying on a semisoft spot, not needing to do anything else but rest for a while.

N'Réa hurt, she was tired, and so help her if one more person did her bodily harm, she was going to snap!

A little while later, the nylon of the tent slid apart and she smelled tea. Brooke must have brought her something. She hoped it was for her head. Like a new one to replace the throbbing one.

"Hey, how are you feeling?" There was gentle concern in Morgan's voice, a tentative question. He sat close to her side, his heat flowing over her.

She soaked it up, sighing. "Like I've been trampled."

He swept her hair away with featherlight strokes. "Can you sit? This will help."

"I was hoping that was for me," she told him. He held a hand to her spine until she was sitting up and then folded her into his chest. She sipped gratefully as his body heat infused her. "Better," she said tiredly.

"I heard some of your questions," he said in a low tone, nuzzling her shoulder as she melted into his embrace. "I can answer a few, just not everything, but I was there."

"I thought the first time this happened it was odd, but you surprised me again."

He brushed kisses over her head, finding the shell of her ear with his lips. "You're stronger than you think. Telepathy," he mused.

"I was going to tell you tonight when we had a few minutes alone what I had found out about myself," she admitted. "But I got distracted when someone kissed me senseless. You're not the only one who has avoided certain issues." She released a pent-up breath, his nod of understanding brushing behind her. "I've kept myself walled up and locked away for a long time. I never had a reason or opportunity to find out what I was capable of. Brooke isn't even sure of my depths. I don't know if I'm ready for it either," she whispered with a trace of uncertainty. The silence cocooned them within the tent walls. She felt warm and cherished in his hold. There was no hurry now as she sipped at her tea in the calm.

Slowly, the air inside the tent seemed to begin to crackle and become charged as his thoughts gathered momentum. Deep breaths rocked her from behind, intense but controlled.

"I never would have let Mitch go after you alone. You are mine," he said without remorse, with a distinct firmness, a possessiveness that didn't frighten her any longer. "It's been a hard fact to accept, but I can't ignore it anymore."

"Yours?" she murmured. "*Does that have anything to do with this?*"

"*I think so. That bond I warned you about.*" It was a quiet, chuckled caress.

"*This is normal? I know I can read thoughts and feelings if I open myself up, but this is weird even for me.*"

"*It's because of you that we can.*" He dropped a kiss on her shoulder. "*Mitch has absolutely no ability but because of Brooke, he can sense things through her. Like the night at Selene's."* Morgan switched back to speaking. "When he mentioned what he felt through her, what he sensed she knew, he didn't realize he was backing you into a corner. No one did. He didn't mean any harm," he whispered, continuously sending shocks through her system as his breath wove over her ear.

"So you knew when I was in trouble?" she asked with a hard swallow, a wondering question. Was that even possible?

His arms circled her loosely, but there was no denying the tension radiating from his taut muscles. He dropped his forehead to her shoulder, his voice rough, thick when he spoke. "I saw red when he hit you. All I could think of was making him pay for hurting you, for touching you. I had to find you."

"You felt that?" she asked, shock rifling her, pausing her cup at her lips.

"All of it. I almost blacked out." He didn't move from his place behind her, rather pressed closer, as though needing the contact, needing to know she was safe snuggling her within his arms.

"Got you beat. I did," she teased him. "Had the double vision for proof."

Pride and affection coated his words, making them silken on her ear. "You're a strong woman, vixen. That blow could have killed someone else."

"Head like a rock." She sipped at her tea, letting his comfort blanket her.

He pulled her hair away from her injured side with gentle fingers, and he let out an angry hiss. "That's going to be a real charmer come tomorrow."

"I guess too many people saw or know about it to have the magic touch." She sighed forlornly.

His chest thickened as he chuckled, pressing tender touches to her neck with lips that warmed and comforted at the same time. "Afraid so, but the tea will put you to sleep, and I'm going to hold you all night."

"Sounds lovely," she murmured. And it was.

Chapter Twelve

Morgan awoke with N'Réa cushioned on his shoulder, his arm around her waist. Her length curved along his in repose. Closing his eyes, he relished the nearness, her weight and body heat forming her tighter against his side. She'd slept well through the night, the tea Brooke had made the night before soothing and relaxing her into a dreamless state. He wished he could have done the same. His dreams, instead of being about N'Réa, had been vicious and angry. Even deep in sleep, he wanted to destroy the man who'd harmed her.

It was easy to recall the pulse of Curtis's life between his teeth, a snap away from death. There was little doubt he would have if Mitch hadn't been there. Anger and possessive rage had ripped through him when they'd finally found N'Réa being hauled like a corpse into the trees. He'd wanted to tear the man apart when he overheard his confession that Leslie had told him to kill her, and he was willing to do it. Even in his dreams, he wanted to make him pay. At least he'd serve his time in jail for it. Curtis and Leslie should both pray they never meet again. Morgan would never forget last night.

Calming himself to not tense and disturb her rest, Morgan lay partially beneath N'Réa, listening to her breathe. Her hair was scooped behind her, making it impossible to miss the garish bruise on her temple. He wanted to soothe her but refrained from touching her, not wanting to wake her. Even bruised, she was the most beautiful woman he had ever met.

Time stood still as his thoughts became clearer. He'd fought it for what seemed like forever, this needing a mate. A friend he could trust, though he still needed to show her, needed to let her make the choice before he claimed her completely. Morgan would keep his word. He wouldn't touch her until she came to him. Until she knew the truth. A deep breath was the only indication of his anxiety.

She murmured in her sleep and pulled herself closer. Wrapping his arm tightly around her, he craved her openly now. Acceptance had lifted a jagged weight from his shoulders. She was strong in spirit, tough out of need. What he saw now was the softer side of his vixen, relaxed, with no barriers.

Her skin was smooth and flawless, framed by her thick midnight hair, and he would always think of the flash of her green eyes with wonder. Dark and smoky with her secret passions or bright and bottomless with the fire of life. N'Réa was beautiful to him as she'd been in his many dreams, even more so now. Morgan could feel her now under his palms, could breathe in her own sweet scent, could hold her. There wasn't a woman anywhere who could compare. Sometimes giving in was more satisfying than winning the battle. In this case, having N'Réa made succumbing to the demand of Fate a much more delicious surrender.

She shifted again. The sun was breaking the horizon and the tent was growing warm. Or was it just him? He smiled easily for her when her eyes drifted open. "Morning."

"Hi." Her voice held the rasped edge of sleep. The husky tone made his body thrum.

"How do you feel?"

"Still flat and trampled." Her lips curled, relaxed.

Skin to skin, he yearned for more. He let his hand roam over her tenderly, keeping his wants locked up tight behind a wall of control.

"You don't feel flat to me," he said, flashing a wicked grin. She giggled, burying herself into his shoulder.

"You animal," she accused good-naturedly.

"That's me." He took a few minutes to enjoy her in his embrace. After a few deep breaths to keep his burgeoning needs from getting the better of him, he eased her up above his chest to study her now that he could examine her injury.

"Are you well enough to spend all day at your booth? I don't want you to overdo it."

She twitched her shoulders and pressed into him when she flexed her hip and legs. "Headachy, a little stiff from being tossed to the ground." She looked at him, then let her gaze roam down his chest. "I also feel warm and relaxed and," she peeked under the blanket, "can commiserate."

"Wench." His breathing and heartbeat doubled. "I could make you pay for that," he warned her, nipping at her neck. "You're really going to push my buttons, aren't you?"

"Depends. Buttons, levers, or gears? I'm sure I could find a few," she said with an innocent toss of her chin, a devilish glint sparking in her emerald depths. She reached for his earlobe and caught it between her teeth. His entire length went rock hard in an instant.

His blood surged with a volcanic heat. "N'Réa, it's too soon. You need to know..." He released an earthy groan when her tongue created a wet trail, caressing his neck.

"I know I'm tired of fighting this," she murmured, the vibration sending a shock of wanting down his spine. She laved another trail across the pulse of his neck, and he shuddered all the way to his toes. "How bad can your secret be?"

He moaned when she lifted herself above him. "N'Réa, please." He could barely think as his body did what it had been wanting to do for so many long weeks — react to her.

"I plan to," she teased throatily.

"I don't have any condoms," he blurted. He needed to stop her! But he didn't want to. Her touch, her caresses, were too good, too wanted. He'd craved her for so long. He'd fought himself and her. He lifted his hands to her shoulders, except they curved over the seductive warmth of her skin instead of pushing her away.

"Morgan." N'Réa hovered over him, a sincere, potent desire for him, and it made him hunger more. "I'm clean, no sex in more than three years, and I've been very careful with my life."

"Not quite that long," he admitted with a gentle kiss to her chin. "And I know how careful I've been. But I can't. You could get pregnant," he pointed out. He pinched his eyes shut. Cold shower, cold shower, *cold, cold* shower. "I won't do this to you. You need to know!" *Damn it!* He moaned with a sharp hunger when her fingers discovered sleep-warmed skin. He rolled his head to the side, praying for salvation. They were alone. Why did Brooke have to be such an early riser?

"Tell me," she beseeched him, dropping sizzling little kisses across his bare chest. Her fingers raked over his thigh, and he couldn't control the groan.

"I didn't want to do it like this," he managed hoarsely when she nipped at his stomach. "God!" He would have to dress in a parka to sleep next to her again!

"Tell me. I want you," N'Réa murmured above his ribs.

"Stop!" he ordered thickly. He was panting and so ready, he ached with the need to be with her. He sucked in air. "Stop, and I will tell you." He knew she wouldn't want to continue when he was done explaining. He could only pray she met him halfway.

N'Réa pressed herself up on her palms, her sweet body inches from his. "Tell me."

His heart pounded, the need to be with her tearing through him. He swallowed, forcing air into his lungs, fighting to think over his lust. "I didn't want to do it like this." He brought his hands up to cup her face, pulling her close for one lingering kiss. "I would never hurt you. Please, just remember that. I swear, I would never hurt you," he told her firmly. "Yes, I swear," he repeated, seeing the shock on her face. "This is important." He let her go, steeling himself for what was about to happen, allowing his hands to fall to his sides. "Last night, there was a wolf," he began to explain very, *very* cautiously.

"So you were there! You saw it!" she said in a relieved voice, speaking as quietly, as secretly.

"I didn't see it, N'Réa. I didn't have to," he told her. A small hole seemed to dig into his chest. It was where all his fear drilled into him.

She pulled away and sat up. "What are you talking about?"

"The wolf is a coal black with gray shades. Where have you seen that wolf, N'Réa?"

"I've never seen it," she said in a whisper of confused astonishment.

"You have. At Selene's."

She snapped her fingers. "The painting! But how did it get here?"

"He's been here all along." He forced himself to relax completely for the next step, a long exhaled breath of fear and trust. The tension was so thick, he waited to hear it snap. "N'Réa, that was me."

She fell silent for a long moment. "But that's impossible!" she yelped, then brought herself closer to keep her voice lowered.

"So is having a witch in the family," he agreed. "But we do. I didn't want to do it this way. There are too many people here."

She placed a hand on his chest, and his eyes jumped to hers. "You're trying to tell me you're a werewolf?" she said with incredulity.

"No!" He raked a hand down his face. He knew he'd screw this up. It wasn't something he was forced to explain every day. In fact, like never. He continued with, "Werewolves are a myth. I'm a shape-shifter; we all are. That is the secret we all share."

She peered at him doubtfully. "How?"

A flicker of hope lit his soul. "You're not scared? Shocked?"

"I don't know," she admitted, staying close to keep her voice private between them. "How?"

"A mutation in our DNA and a little magic from somewhere. Dad has never been sure. As far as we know, we are the last line of an ancient race. There once were shifters of all types of ability, but now, we stay quiet and to ourselves. If there are others, we don't know."

"Shape-shifter?" It was hard for her to breathe.

She rocked back and fell silent, her gaze becoming unfocused and almost glassy. *Not good.*

"You don't believe me," he confirmed a minute later. "I don't blame you. I didn't think you would. I didn't want to do it like this. You deserve the full truth, and I can't do it here."

He sat up, unable to remain lying flat while the unbelievable circled her thoughts.

"This is your big secret?" she asked in a stunned voice.

"Yes, and I'm sharing it with you. I need to know I can trust you with it," he told her questioningly. "I need to know I'm not wrong."

"How would you show me?" She tilted her chin, daring him.

He bowed his head. "I can't do it here." Nerves twitched. What could he do? Morgan had to show her, let her see the truth, or she'd never believe him. There was no way around it. He owed her that much because he was determined now to win her. He was done pushing her away, done fighting how much he wanted her. Maybe there was a way...

"Will you walk with me?" When she hesitated, he put a finger under her chin. "N'Réa, do you trust me? Really, deep down, trust me?"

She licked her lips. He noticed the way her pulse pounded and knew she was battling with the impossible. He thought he would forget to breathe when she finally whispered, "Yes."

Maybe he could make it easier for her. He helped her play connect the dots. "What did Mitch tell you last night about the wolf?" he asked her tenderly, his thumb caressing her, creating a path of warmth between them.

"That I would never have a reason to fear it. It would never hurt me." All he could find was a blank gaze, studying him, as he waited for any signs to her thoughts.

"Do you believe him?"

"I think so." She returned his stare, realization darkening the pools to the richest green. "Because he knows, doesn't he?"

"Yes, he is Brooke's mate in every sense of the word and my pack brother. Now, I ask you, can you trust me to walk with me? Can I trust you to show you this?"

Time slowed. The sun beat on the tent as it crested the horizon, the first sounds of movement and life reaching them where they sat, sequestered in their privacy, away from the world.

"Yes."

He stood, offering her a hand. She changed quickly into jeans and a T-shirt while he pulled a shirt over his head. A few minutes later, they stepped out and he reached for her hand, holding her close. As close as he'd ever dared.

They managed to sneak away without anyone noticing their leaving as he led her away from the sleepy camp until he found a spot to enter the woods. He picked his path carefully. He needed to be far away from curiosity and interruptions.

The trees stayed thick for several long minutes. They started to thin, and he slowed his pace when the ground opened up. He took a lungful of air and smelled nothing but the fresh green of the trees and the damp earth, cool with morning dew. There were no cars, no voices, no sounds of the grounds. Nothing to threaten intrusion on them. Private. It wasn't perfect, but it would do.

He turned and reached for her hands. Then he pinned her with his gaze, willing her to understand. "Whatever happens, know you are important to me, and I swear to you on my life, I would never hurt you. If you can't accept me, all I can ask is that you keep my secret."

"Brooke told me the rules." Those dark green eyes of hers bored into his. "You have to abide by those, don't you?" She wanted nothing less than the truth, and it was what he wanted to give her.

"Yes, we do. I'm doing this of my own free will. My choice. I can't harm you if I make the mistake. Am I making a mistake, N'Réa?" he asked with a tremor in his voice, swallowing, not wanting to acknowledge it. Not wanting the uncertainty to freeze him solid. "You will be the only one I've ever shown."

She cupped a tender hand on his cheek. "No, Morgan. No mistake. Your secret is mine." He let his eyes slide shut. She was in a state of disbelief. Humoring him now that a little time had passed after his explanation. She'd begun to dissuade herself from the possibility. That wouldn't last for long.

Morgan stepped back, her hands sliding free of his, and he almost changed his mind. If Morgan could have walked away from her, he would have, but he knew it was too late. This woman was his mate, if she accepted. Somewhere in the last twenty-four hours, he'd realized the cold, hard truth. This was all that was left between them.

He stripped his shirt and laid it across a branch, toeing his sneakers off. His socks went in those, and he slid out of his sweats until he stood completely naked before her. He didn't think about turning around until he caught the blush on her cheeks but by then, it was too late. Modesty missed the train. He whispered her name with his heart beating heavily. A light sweat formed on his brow. She followed his every breath.

He closed his eyes and sought the inner fire, the heat that changed his heart, which made his blood run wild. He felt the hair as it grew along his back, welcomed the transition from being on two feet to four. He focused on the beat of his heart, hearing it thunder in his ears until he was wolf.

When he shifted his gaze to find her, he flinched. Her face had paled, white as snow, and her mouth hung open. He didn't move a muscle. *Please,* he thought. *Don't let me be wrong.*

"You're a f–freaking wolf!" N'Réa stammered. She shook her head, trembling wildly. When she focused on him, she fell to her knees. "That was you!" She gaped at him with shock-widened eyes.

He dared not move an inch. He wanted to change to human, to talk to her, to calm her, but he needed her to accept him. His heartbeat ticked off time. Patience was his enemy as he waited for a sign, any sign, from her.

With hope in his chest, Morgan moved a paw, tentatively. She didn't blink. He stepped forward. The warmth of the sun arced through the canopy overhead falling on his coat and her thunderstruck gaze swept over him, taking in his form. A faint pink was coloring her cheeks. "You're so beautiful," she declared in quiet awe.

He wanted to jump in an ecstatic circle, but managed to keep it inside, praying every second until he stood frozen inches before her. He dropped his head within reach, encouraging her to accept. His heart squeezed and withered like a leaf in the desert heat when she didn't move. He picked up his head and met her glistening stare.

"Your eyes. Oh my God! The dream. The wolf. I always saw your eyes in the dream! It really is you."

She lifted a hand toward him. Morgan's heart raced with pure bliss as her fingers slid over him. "You feel incredible." She laughed when he wagged his tail.

N'Réa ran a trembling hand over his cheek, furrowing the thickness of his coat. He moved a step closer when her hand became surer, when the disbelief turned to wonder, and he released a sigh of gratitude for the woman she was. Acceptance was never guaranteed.

She straightened a moment later and said soberly, "All right. I believe you. I think you better change before they miss us."

Morgan arched his spine, prancing a step or two. He was animal, after all, and enticing his mate was natural. His wolf enjoyed the chance to show off.

Calling for the heat, feeling the race of his blood, within a moment, Morgan knelt on the ground before her.

Morgan locked on her, seeing so many questions and wonders flying through her expression. "N'Réa?" Her name was the barest entreaty to know her thoughts.

He wasn't prepared for the impact when she launched herself at him. He caught her within his arms, pinning her to his chest. "N'Réa!" he cried, half laughing, half gasping, tumbling under the force onto the forest floor. "I guess this means you're okay with my secret?"

"So many things make sense now!" she said, her eyes sparkling in the early morning sunlight. She pushed him into the leaves. She started dropping sizzling kisses onto his bare chest, making his world spin.

"N'Réa!" he managed to say, the sound of her name sliding into a groan. "Oh God!" He dug his fingers into her hair. "N'Réa, no doubts. I want you!" He sighed with rippling pleasure when her fingers traveled from his throat to his navel.

"No doubts," she repeated.

"No condoms." He gasped when she curled a hand over his length. "I respect you, damn it!" His entire frame shook in her hold. He was going to explode with the merest touch.

"My choice, my mistake. Not a good time to make babies," she mumbled over his skin as she continued to drop hot, needy kisses across his body.

He yanked her up to his chest. "You are never a mistake!" Her vixen green eyes were as hot and passion filled as he felt. His head snapped on his neck, and he cried out when she moved her hand over his flesh. "Please, N'Réa, you're killing me!"

His fingers slid free from her hair as she moved all over him. His world was spinning, and he knew he was sunk. He couldn't stop her, and he gave up trying. Her mouth singed him everywhere as she worked a hand over him, keeping him hostage.

Her fingers taunted and tormented him as her tongue traced designs over his stomach. She moved lower and lower over his abdomen until he felt a warm puff of air flow over his erection.

"You're beautiful." She breathed slowly as her hand moved lower to cup him. He took a deep breath that left him in a shout of bliss when she took him into her mouth.

He groaned like a wild thing as she slid over him, her mouth and tongue. Hot. Wet. He was going to lose it. His last shred of control exploded when she caressed his sac. He lifted his hips, hearing and feeling the swell of her answering moans as he gave her what she wanted.

His heart was pounding like a sledgehammer behind his ribs when she finally lifted with a satisfied smile. He reached for her T-shirt and yanked it over her head, her full breasts coming free to his touch, and did he want to touch. Her head tipped with a sigh and a moan when he found one hard nipple with his tongue, caressing her as mercilessly as she had just done to him, but he needed to be inside her as his desire grew. He unsnapped her jeans and worked them over her legs, pushing them off with a toe.

"Sorry, vixen. Playtime is over," he said hoarsely as he rolled her over onto the leaves. He buried his nose in her neck and inhaled. "God!" He breathed her in as her scent continued to drive him.

"Yes!" She moaned against him. "I need you!"

He didn't wait. He slid her legs open and pressed at her core. He hissed through his teeth. "So wet!" He shuddered hard, delirious with the sensation of her hot skin when he entered her.

She cried out as he filled her with long, thrusting strokes, and his world exploded into a brilliant fall of light as he moved over her, inside her, enveloped by her. Her hips moved with him, urging him, and he answered, pushing further, deeper, until he couldn't control it, until he needed to feel her completion, until she screamed in ecstasy. He lifted himself onto his palms and thrust deep, meeting her, joining her as they fell off the world.

* * * *

Morgan held on tight to the luscious woman in his arms, both breathing hard, his heart beating like a caged animal behind the bars of his ribs.

"I've died," he barely managed to say when he could talk at all.

"You're too hot to be dead," she replied, purring. Her fingers stroked his side, and he melted into her.

"Marry me," he murmured into her ear. Her stroking fingers stopped. Disappointment hit him. It was the next logical step, but too late he realized his mistake. "Too soon?"

He heard her hesitation, her questions. "No, not really. I wasn't expecting it."

Morgan rose over her. "Why not? I want to be with you. I thought you felt the same."

She started stroking again with wandering, enticing fingers. "I do," she said carefully. "It's just, fast, maybe," she said with a nervous uncertainty in the explanation.

"What you really want to know is why," he said, seeing the doubts fly across her face. He slid his fingers into her hair, holding himself above her on his elbows. "Because I want you. I can't get enough of you. I hate being away from you." His voice dropped, and he gave her a tender kiss. "I want you for my mate."

"Do you love me?" she asked tentatively.

Hesitation was unavoidable. He hadn't been expecting that one. That one question packed a hell of a wallop.

"I believe in honesty," he told her with a meaning-filled sigh, not avoiding her. "I don't know. I'm making this up as I go along, but I know after last night," he dropped another kiss on her throat, "and this, I can't walk away. Not now. I will protect you to my last breath. I will take care of you. You will be my mate, a part of our pack and family, if you say yes."

Chapter Thirteen

N'Réa studied his earnest expression. He was serious. His gray eyes were calm, like the calm after a storm, and she did feel like she had weathered one.

"I've given you everything I have to offer of myself," he said in a solemn tone. "I know enough about you to know I want you. I'm asking you, N'Réa, will you marry me?"

"What about the Faire and my stuff?" she asked with a budding fear. "You're not a control freak, are you?"

His rich laughter filled the quiet as he rolled from her and maneuvered her to his shoulder, the sunlight dappling his sweat-slicked skin. "No, I'm not a control freak, except maybe with myself. As for the rest, I'm here until I win or get knocked out of the lists."

She rose on an elbow and spotted his pleased smile. Her heart flipped in her chest as his hand lifted to her face. He was tender around the bruise, his caress light, aware of how much she hurt.

"I would die for you," he said, his eyes glowing with sincere emotion.

Her head sank to rest on his chest, over his heart, hearing the steady rhythm in her ear. He let his hand float across her back in easy sweeps as he let her think, but she knew what she was going to say. No matter how much he drove her insane, what she knew about him, she knew in her heart her answer.

He might not love her, but she refused to lie to herself. It was happening slowly, a little at a time after each battle, after each tender, caring thing he'd done for her. She trusted him. He had protected her since the first moment they'd met. She knew that was the one thing he would never fail her on. She did care for him. It was a start, and time could make it stronger for the both of them.

She lifted herself to meet his cloud-gray eyes, then pressed a gentle kiss to his mouth. "Yes, Morgan. I will marry you."

His gaze warmed like the sunlight, and he smiled broadly. "Never a regret, no mistakes."

"No," she replied. "We take care of our own. You are now mine."

"Gladly," he whispered as he pulled her closer for a kiss.

When he let her up a few minutes later, it took a moment to gather her wandering senses. "You better watch those. They could be considered a lethal weapon."

He gave her a huge grin. "Come on, we need to get back. I have duels today and sooner or later, someone's going to realize we're not there." He stood and offered her a hand. She squealed when he tickled more than brushed her off but eventually they were dressed and, hand in hand, walking in the direction of camp.

"Are you going to work today?" he asked with a note of concern, glancing toward her temple as they neared camp. "Do you still feel headachy?"

She shook her head. "No. I had a good shot of drugs to take care of it." He squeezed her hand, and she winked at him. "I really need to. I still have to replace my car and make some money."

He murmured a contemplative sound. "How about this? Make the money, keep it for whatever, your next show, and let me worry about the car. You will have to get used to someone else being there for you now." He pressed a finger to her mouth when she wanted to talk. "And before you start yelling, I adore your independent streak, but we are a team now, and I will take care of you."

She ran her tongue up his finger and saw the way his eyes grew heated with desire. "I was going to say thank you. Just remember, it goes both ways."

"Wench!" He breathed slowly as his eyes slid to half mast, following the sweep of her tongue.

"Jackal!" She retorted with little fear and started laughing when he tugged her into his chest.

"There they are!" someone cried. "Brooke has been going nuts!"

"Sorry, Natalie," Morgan answered, his arm curled around N'Réa. "Wanted to see the sunrise."

"Through the trees?" Someone snorted.

"Easy if you're on your back!" another voice crowed. It didn't take long before the whole camp was laughing, rifling bawdy jokes to each other. A normal morning.

"All right, you miscreants," Morgan warned loudly. "You've had your fun. Where's my sister, anyway?" N'Réa saw him search in all directions with a small frown. Usually Brooke was somewhere in camp until the gates opened.

"I'm here!" she called, coming from the far side of the camp. She was dressed in her blue dress, the cape N'Réa had given her clasped at her throat with the hood loose behind her. "It's late! The gates open in less than half an hour! And you missed breakfast!" She glared at the pair of them, her hands on her hips.

"Ah, therein lies her ire. We didn't get fed," he teased his sister. Brooke stuck her tongue out at him.

"Sorry, Brooke. We had a few things to talk about," he explained with quiet meaning.

"And?" Brooke waited, a breathless anticipation spinning in the air.

"She's fine with it, and she said yes," he said with a devilish grin, looking at N'Réa with so much devotion, she felt her cheeks warm.

Brooke threw herself at N'Réa. "You said yes!"

"What?" came a feminine cry. "Yes to what?"

"I can't believe it!" Brooke cried. She clasped N'Réa's hands. "I'm so happy. For the both of you."

"What? Who said what?" Duncan asked, drawn from his tent by the commotion and the growing throng, strapping his sword on.

Morgan moved behind N'Réa to wrap his arms around her waist. "I asked her to marry me," he announced to everyone with more than a hint of pride in his voice.

A loud cheer went up from the camp. "Woohoo! Party at Duncan's World!" someone shouted.

Brooke clasped N'Réa's hands, catching her attention. "No regrets?" she asked with an undercurrent of mutual understanding.

N'Réa shook her head. "No, I understand my part." She leaned over to whisper into Brooke's ear. "I know how to keep a secret."

Brooke clasped N'Réa's hands. "I had a good feeling about you from the get-go." Brooke stepped away, letting her hands slide free. "You've got to get dressed! Are you working today? You know you don't have to. Donegan was told first thing this morning about what happened last night. He would understand."

N'Réa smiled at her sincere concern. It warmed her and proved again that she hadn't been wrong in trusting Brooke. "No, I'm fine. I'll wear a scarf to cover the worst of it." She peeked over her shoulder with a wide grin. "But I will be closed to watch my knight knock the hell out of whoever."

"You can sit with us!" Brooke replied in invitation. "Can you believe he already has his own fan section?"

Morgan groaned, his frame shaking as he tried not to laugh. "Morgan's Mares. Who came up with that, anyway?"

"I did," someone called. "Because you're such a stud!"

"Natalie!" He groaned behind N'Réa's shoulder, trying to hide the gruff sound. "William needs to put you in the stocks!"

"He's not bad enough!" she boasted, then she looked around sharply. "He's not here, is he?"

N'Réa laughed until she couldn't breathe. Thank God Morgan held her upright until she could.

"Go dress, vixen. I have to dress too, and you naked is too much temptation." His promising, silky voice curled over her ears, and getting dressed suddenly became the very last thing she wanted to do.

She spun in his arms, purposely pressing into his chest and warming his thighs with hers. "I'll have to remember that," she teased him.

He made a growled sound low in his throat. "You better go, or I won't be held responsible."

She nipped his chin, and his breath caught. "Come and see me," she said.

"Like I could stay away. Now go!"

She shot him a teasing smile and slipped from his hold, seeing the fire in his eyes. She could get drunk on that alone.

Her feel-good aura followed her everywhere. Her readings were optimistic; everyone received a smile. N'Réa was on top of the world. She felt ready to burst with happy energy, her last customer at least ten minutes gone.

She'd spoken to Bailey and Marie earlier, finding herself amazed again at how explosive the grapevine was at the Faire. Not only were her adventures from the night before out there, but her engagement also. People stopped her to congratulate her, to empathize over her kidnapping. Everyone knew of her by then. It should have scared her into a bunny hole, but it didn't. She should have felt cornered and watched, but she didn't. Morgan was with her constantly. In her thoughts, on her lips. She felt safe.

It had been a long time since she'd allowed herself the luxury.

She wore her most flamboyant outfit, her favorite. A bright mixture of colors flooded the skirt with the matching blouse and hair scarf, but she also threaded colorful sequined hanging scarves from her waist so they would drift and sway while she moved. She wore her bangles and rings along with a harem bracelet and anklets with bells. She tinkled and rang with each movement.

She couldn't sit there another second! She ran next door.

"Marie! I want to dance!"

Marie jumped from her chair, startled out of her quiet reverie. "You do? You haven't danced in forever!"

"Time to change that," N'Réa cried as she spun on the grass, her smile full, as full as she felt, and she wanted to share it. She skipped from the front of the armorer's booth, tapping her tambourine on the heel of her palm. The sound grabbed the attention of passersby as she began to spin and skip. Marie brought out the skin drum they owned and began to keep a tempo for her.

She danced like a reed, bending and swaying with the varying tempos. The tambourine jangled and rang and the crowd clapped to keep her rhythm for her. Her skirt flew and the scarves fluttered, a rainbow of color as she moved. Her hair billowed and draped, and she felt alive. She felt free.

* * * *

Morgan walked up the aisle holding a bag of sandwiches for lunch when he noticed the crowd ahead. As he got closer, he could hear the tambourine, the whistles of the crowd, the passing echo of a drum. He ducked his head into N'Réa's tent, but he didn't find her there. He set the food on the table and searched outside.

He listened to the music for a minute, trying to see who the source of the entertainment was. The Faire maintained an entire employee roster to help keep the patrons in the mindset of the time. Morgan nudged his way forward through the circle of onlookers, and his jaw dropped when he saw the oranges and reds of the skirt.

N'Réa! And she was dancing like a magical nymph. She was beautiful, her smile lighting the whole day as she swirled. People swayed and called as she moved, encouraging her. N'Réa reached up and untied the scarf from her hair to let all her gorgeous hair with its inner fire glisten. She skirted the crowd, swaying and teasing until she reached him. Her eyes widened, surprised, but in the next instant, soft and seductive as she wrapped the scarf around his sword, the innuendo all too apparent to him, hoping no one else knew the secret message. Then she danced for him.

The crowd cheered her on as she swayed and braced against him, including him in her antics as though he were part of the dance. It was a good thing he was wearing his tunic as she moved and spun in front of him, unable to hide his physical reaction to her teasing. Her color, her eyes, her scent, it all reached him, seduced him.

She spun away and, nearing the middle of the group, smiled with a nod at the woman on the drum. In the next instant, the world fell silent.

It didn't last a heartbeat before the applause erupted. The whistles and cheers filled him with pride. This was his woman. His fiery, green-eyed vixen. He whistled as loudly as any of them.

She bowed and blew kisses, saying thank you for their attention. "Enjoy thy day in the Kingdom!" she called out, laughing, breathless. When the crowd began to disperse, she offered the woman on the drum a big hug, then turned and looped an arm through his to walk to her tent. She stopped him when he reached for the scarf to return it.

"My favor, for my knight in shining armor," she said, teasing laughter and devilish desire woven through her voice.

"But I thought you were using it to hide the bruise." He turned her into the light to inspect the injury. "Brooke doctored it, didn't she?" He frowned a little as he continued to examine the damage, his fingers stroking the side of her face, eliciting shivers as he brushed over her skin and through her hair.

"Only a little," she confessed. "So I wouldn't look like an abused woman. It would make it uncomfortable for my clients and for me. She didn't remove much."

He frowned, not thrilled, but accepting. "Well, if Brooke thought it was all right."

"I put makeup on it too. That helps."

Relief loosened his muscles. "That's why it looks so good. You did a great job of hiding it." He took her inside her tent and tucked her into a corner, hidden from everyone. "Now, thy punishment for being a wanton wench, vixen," he threatened with a low mock-menacing sound. "Dancing on the street." He shook his head at her, admonishing her.

She lowered her eyes, but not before he caught their lighthearted gleam. "What shall be my punishment, my lord?"

"This," he whispered just before he captured her mouth. She shivered in his hold, and she wound her arms around his neck. He groaned as need flashed through him. He wanted her now. He would always want this woman.

He pulled away with a regretful sigh. "I can't stay. I need to get back to the lists. I brought you lunch."

"Thank you. For the lunch, too," she whispered with a grin.

"Ah, wench," he said breathily, leaning his forehead to hers.

"Jackal," she teased him. "When are you scheduled?"

"The duels start at one. The fighters are becoming more determined with the end in sight." He straightened, then lifted her hand to his lips and kissed her fingers slowly, sheer decadence in every caress. "I will see you there?" he asked in a seductive tone.

She sounded breathless when he let her hand go. "I'll be there."

He bowed low. "Then, I bid thee a good day, good mistress." And he slipped out before he kissed her again and didn't stop.

* * * *

They were calling the first fight when N'Réa was finally able to get to the arena. Brooke waved to her where she'd saved a space for her with Natalie, May, and several others from Duncan's camp to watch and cheer their men on. She laughed outright at poor Hugh and his cast. He'd enlisted one of the artists to paint a dragon on it, also with a broken leg.

"Lay on!" the announcer called, drawing her attention to the field. The crowd cheered as the knights fought back and forth, the ring of steel echoing over the stands. The clashes of broadsword to shield were bone jarring as one opponent, then another, succumbed to their challenger or were unarmed.

"Ladies and gentlemen of the Kingdom! We call Sir Morgan Aiza and Lord Dirk De Brasse! First call!"

The roar was deafening as both men entered and saluted the royal court. Morgan turned, wearing a belted red tunic of Duncan's knights over the shirt of chain mail he wore and a combat helmet. He saluted to his Mares and then brought the scarf tied to his sword grip to his lips. Her blood ran hot at the innocent gesture.

N'Réa blew him a kiss, and he dropped his chin in acceptance. "Go get him!" she yelled at the top of her lungs, and his cheering section rallied.

"Lay on!" This was the official cry for their battle, and she tensed as they started pacing each other.

Dirk was as tall and a little broader at the shoulder than Morgan, but he also had years of experience. She held her breath when the first swings sliced the air. Morgan swung up and deflected, the ring of steel making her set her jaw. Neither used a shield to help deflect or take cover under. Morgan gave Dirk a hard shove and came around right, swinging across with an arced sweep. Dirk recovered, spinning out of the way on one foot.

Morgan didn't give him an inch to escape, slashing across his path and pacing him until Dirk either had to go down completely or run. Morgan didn't give him the choice.

She cheered as Dirk crashed, rolling to his back. "That's my knight!" she shouted, jumping up and down in her seat. "Come on, baby!" The crowd yelled, cheering them on.

Dirk raged on the offensive and took Morgan to the ground in a matter of seconds. The gasp was collective through the stands, every person growing quieter until Morgan rocked up on his heels and stood. The crowd ripped open with noise as the swords started clashing louder than ever.

"Pound him into the ground!" N'Réa yelled, feeling each blow in her head as the sting of steel sliced the air.

"One point apiece," Brooke murmured from beside her, her attention as focused on the two men in the arena.

"Oh!" N'Réa cried, leaping up to see better at the next hit. Her heart fell to her feet as Morgan's sword flew through the air, his head snapping hard on a back swing follow-through, catching the chin of his helmet. He landed on his back, not moving.

"Morgan!"

Brooke's tight hand was on her arm in an instant. "He's fine," she said. "Look, he's getting up."

Her blood ran like ice water until she witnessed him moving for herself. He rolled to a knee, popping his helmet off with a jerky movement, shaking his head.

"He's hurt!" N'Réa shouted, trying to yank free.

"Give him a second, N'Réa," Brooke said. "He's stronger than he looks."

N'Réa chewed on her bottom lip. Her fingers were tightly balled into her skirt. Morgan shook his head, gingerly pushing to his feet. The crowd leaped up and cheered him on. She could barely breathe.

His shoulders rolled as he reached for his helmet at his feet, then bowing to the court, he retrieved his sword and walked out.

"He lost!" she said with slow realization. "Oh, my God. He lost!" She sank to her spot on the bleached wood planks.

"Sooner or later he would have," Brooke said. "He's a big boy; he'll survive."

"But where will this place him?"

"He'll drop to the next bracket," Brooke replied as the next duel was called. "He's going to be fine, N'Réa, honest."

N'Réa sat through the remaining two fights even though she desperately wanted to make sure Morgan was all right. She knew he could lose or win, but to see it, to watch his loss, tore her apart, and he had been hurt. She knew it as sure as the sun shined overhead. She sincerely doubted that the follow-up hit was legal, making his loss that much more tragic. Damn Dirk!

A head shot after he'd lost his weapon! She clutched her skirt tightly, waiting as patiently as she could, until she was able to walk with Brooke to the camp. She fought the urge to run, this time to him, to make sure he was all right. He sat on one of the camp chairs, stripped to the waist, his head held in his hands as he leaned over his elbows.

He straightened up as she neared. "The stud was a gelding today," he remarked with wry grin.

"No, you weren't!" She dropped to her knees next to him. "You fought a great fight." She searched his face, her fingers flitting over the tension lines along his mouth. "Are you all right?"

"Yeah, my head was ringing for a while. Nothing but a normal headache," he replied without a hint of discomfort. He lifted a hand and brushed a thumb across her bottom lip. "I wanted to win that one, too."

His eyes darkened to a stormy gray at the warmth of him pressing to her lip.

"You're not out of the tournament," she reminded him.

He shook his head. "No," he agreed. "I wanted to win because it was the first time you had watched me."

She felt the blush surge under his stare. "For me?" No one had ever done anything like that for her before.

He nodded. "Sorry I didn't win."

"Don't be sorry! You were kicking his ass!" She clasped his head tenderly between her hands. "You can beat any man here! I know you can. However you figured it out, came to be here, wound up in the arena today, isn't important. The only reason Dirk won was because he slipped your sword. Then there was that backhand, which I don't even think was legal!"

"She's right," Hugh said. "About the backhand. It wasn't necessary once your sword was loose." He limped up on his walking stick, May by his side.

"Well, he did win by unarming me," Morgan commented. He sat up and stretched out his legs. N'Réa snuggled closer when he dropped a hand to her hair naturally, comforted by his nearness. "He was playing up his role of the evil knight. I'll be more careful next time." Morgan smiled down at her where she rested against his thigh. "Next time, I will win for you."

"And I'll be there to scream my heart out."

"Yeah, I thought I heard you," he said with a teasing wink. He searched the growing throng as people returned from the arena. "Has anyone seen Mitch? I don't think I've seen him most of the day."

"He went to town to get supplies for the party tonight. Food, booze, the usual," May said. "An engagement is big news."

He looked down at N'Réa, a glimmering, beckoning heat in his eyes. "Yeah, pretty big news."

She couldn't help herself, melting a little more for her knight. She sighed as his hand sifted through her hair where she sat, resting against his muscled thigh.

Chapter Fourteen

"I'm never drinking trash can punch again as long as I live," N'Réa vowed, unable to move her head. She lifted a leaden hand to the aching portion of her body. "Can someone turn down the sun? I'll beg." She cracked an eye and snapped it shut when her brain screamed in agony. For the second time that weekend. "Oh, Lord. Kill me now."

"I warned you," Morgan said into her ear.

"You did? When? Before or after I was drunk?"

"Before and after." She heard him move right before he scooped her hair away. "After, then I gave up. Damage done."

"How can you sound so normal?" She regretted talking so forcefully.

"Because I'm moving slowly," he admitted. "And I've already been awake a good hour." His voice purred in her ear as he brushed a lingering kiss on her brow.

"Was I embarrassing?" She cringed when all she could remember was one huge blank from the night before.

"Between you and Natalie, it was a great night. I love to watch you dance," he said breathily into her ear. "Although she beat you. She streaked."

N'Réa gasped, a groan immediately following as pain lanced her head. "She didn't?" she said weakly. "Oh God, what did I do? I don't remember anything."

"Don't worry about it. I doubt anyone will remember a thing from sundown on. I pulled you away from everyone when they broke out the chocolate syrup."

"Chocolate syrup?" The possibilities running through her mind caused the words to squeak.

He chuckled. "Don't ask." He slid an arm under her shoulders to pull her onto his chest. "Brooke has a great morning-after brew. It's bitter and as strong as four-day-old coffee, but it works."

"I'll take two," she immediately said. N'Réa felt like hell and probably looked it, but she wasn't ready to move. Not yet. If she couldn't move, what was five more minutes in the grand scheme of her day? "How can Brooke be up so early?" she mused, noting the other half, the empty half, of the tent. "I swear she doesn't ever sleep."

"They didn't partake of the evening's evil. She couldn't anyway, being pregnant," he offered. She heard his heart beating under her cheek, solid, warm, steady. "She's got a delicate system to start with. She can't even handle coffee. Neither of the girls can."

"Is that strange?" N'Réa asked curiously. It still amazed her on levels she'd never considered knowing what he was, what they all were. She'd never suspected anything, never knew such people existed. She had a hard enough time dealing with her own quirks; expecting or anticipating others had been beyond her scope. But not anymore.

"Mom has certain things she can't handle, either. I always guessed it had to do with being a woman. Dad is the shifter, not Mom, but she has certain things, other abilities, in her family also." His fingers trailed leisurely over her, haphazard sweeps that tingled and teased without demanding. She stretched and warmed under his hand like an ember until she glowed. There was a slow burn beginning to spread beneath his touch and radiating outward, through her, licking her with a flame of desire. He made a growled sound in his throat when he drew a breath next to her skin. "Ah, vixen," he whispered as his touch became more insistent. "I can smell your heat."

"And?" she asked on a tentative moan. The slide of his skin next to hers was sending shocks to every nerve.

Morgan rolled her over until he hovered above her. His gaze was hot, searing when he found hers. "It drives me insane," he said, nearing to nip at her collarbone. "I can't believe how much I want you, to feel you, to taste you." His tongue traveled over her, creating a path of sensation, and she shook in his hold. His fingers lowered to the ebony curls of her center, and he made a purely possessive sound when he found her ready. "I want you, vixen," he whispered against her neck.

"But they will hear!" she argued. Her hands urged him closer, stroking his chest and shoulders. It was only a halfhearted attempt to stop him and deep down, she knew he knew it.

He lowered his lips to hers. "I will keep you safe, always. You still have the right to tell me no."

"I do?" she asked, surprised. Searching his face, the proof was there.

"Always," he said with a tender caress of his lips on hers. "But it won't stop me from wanting you." He pressed his fingers into the dampness of her core to show he meant it.

She whimpered once more and arched into the pressure.

He reached for the blanket covering them, pulling it higher. "N'Réa," he purred against her throat as he moved above her, his hands tender, seeking, pleasing. "Do you want me?"

"Yes." She sighed through quaking lips.

He rose above her and entered her slowly, tenderly, his fingers embedded in the rich wealth of her hair. "You are my mate, N'Réa. I will protect you until my last breath," he said, licking lightly at the curve of her ear.

She spiraled with heat as he moved above her, inside her, until she couldn't separate anything beyond the two of them, no outside world, nothing but Morgan and her.

N'Réa didn't mean to do it, she didn't even know she could, but she wanted him to feel what she did, to feel him and everything she was experiencing. She opened her mind, seeking his.

Morgan froze, his eyes widening above her. Terrified of what she'd done, she instantly threw up the walls, protecting herself the only way she knew how. Her chest burned as fear stole her air. "I'm sorry!"

He blinked. "That was you?"

N'Réa turned her face, biting her lip. She nodded, closing her eyes and her heart from him. She should have known better. Taking a chance like that was dangerous, even if it was with this man, especially not knowing her own strengths or limits. Wanting to or not, she shouldn't have.

He released his hold on her hair, cradling her face in his caring palms. "N'Réa? Look at me." She fought the gentle pressure of his fingers, but he persisted. "Look at me," he pleaded tenderly.

Gray and stormy, there was understanding and desire in his gaze. "I'm sorry, Morgan. I had no idea. I've never — "

He silenced her with his mouth. The fire between them raged wilder in an instant. He stroked her with his fingers, his lips.

"Do it again," he said. "I want to feel you." His lips hovered over hers, teasing her with their sweeping heat.

Focusing, N'Réa wove herself into Morgan's consciousness, cautiously, as he rocked over her. She felt his heartbeat pound in her ears, felt the depth of his emotions, his possession. She melted from the inside out as he urged her on every level, physical and mental. Electricity, sparks of heat and passion, rose between them.

"Oh man," he said breathily. He lowered his mouth to her shoulder, grasping tender flesh between his teeth, gentling before the sharpness of pain became unbearable. He soothed the spot with his tongue, treating her like a delicacy.

"Vixen," he moaned, the sound awe-filled as shudders rifled down his frame. "I can feel everything."

"Yes!" She pulled at him, burying herself beneath his rock-hard chest. She answered the need, the will to be one. *"I am yours."*

The tendons in his neck tightened as he brought them closer to the edge of bliss. The strength of his will encased them, his desire to completely possess her, needing her. Needing her to need him as deeply, as strongly.

She gave herself over to him completely, stroking hot skin with hungry hands, kissing and caressing with demanding lips. His movements grew urgent, propelling her, bombarding her with sensation after sensation. She felt the world fall away as his nature took over, the need to possess, to dominate, to protect, to mate filled him, then filled her.

Her world exploded before her as the force of her climax ripped over her, roaring down her body with massive flames of energy.

There was no stopping it. The world heard the detonation.

* * * *

"Please tell me that wasn't applause," she lamented some time later.

"All right, I won't tell you."

She thumped his shoulder with a closed fist. "And don't sound so damn smug!"

"Not me. Want to shake the showers?" he asked with a wicked grin, wiggling sexy eyebrows at her.

"How can I even walk out there?" she asked, glowering at him as she lifted to an elbow. "I'll be the talk of the town."

Gentle lips soothed her, their warmth on her cheek. "Never," he said. "Besides, you're as good as married to me. No one will think less of you, unless someone besides me happened to walk out of here with you." He gave her a meaningful stare. "We both know that will never happen."

"No, of course not," she said, lifting her forehead to his. "I can't even imagine another man."

His posture lightened, making her aware that her answer had mattered. He played with a swirl of her hair. Tension reappeared when he found the bruise once more. Without makeup, she was sure it was still very noticeable in her hairline.

Pain dampened his gaze. "I'm sorry that ever happened."

She pressed a single fingertip to his mouth. "Don't. You have held up your offer. I'm the most protected woman on the grounds, with the exception of Brooke."

Sounds of the camp outside were growing, but she couldn't find the strength yet to move. Or to leave him.

He continued to caress her with strands of hair sifting over curious fingers. "Come home with me tonight."

Hesitation within his tone made her pause. "You say it like you think I might say no."

He shrugged, his gaze following the path of his hand. "I'm still getting used to this. I told you I will never own you. You are mine, but not in ownership."

"You don't know what to do with me!" A giggle was hard to resist, amazed at his bluntness. Was he growing to trust her more? Insecurity was one thing she never expected from Morgan, especially not over her.

His fingers continued to comb through her hair. "No, I don't. I've never held a lasting relationship," he admitted, avoiding her stares. "But you are my mate; I can't walk away, I can't leave you. I was born to protect you, to be with you. No other."

His words, the way he said them, the complete absence of emotion, as though he'd never had a choice in this, chilled her heart, destroying her previous hopes. It wasn't insecurity. He wanted to find a way out. Pain knifed her chest, but she swallowed, pushing through the onslaught.

"If you could, would you walk away? Do you want to?" She clenched her hands, forcing the rising tremors to cease.

Like bricks tumbling from a wall, her heart shattered into chunks when he took several tense minutes to answer her. He tipped and tilted, then swallowed once, as though considering the question, when it should have had a quick and simple answer. Only one answer, yet he didn't say it. The silence stretched between them, laughter and shouts beyond the cocoon of the tent seeming to be amplified because of it. "Well?" she snapped. "Would you, of your own free will, walk away?"

"N'Réa, you don't really want me to answer that," he replied cautiously.

She shoved herself away from him, unable to bear his touch a second longer, her entire body, her heart, frozen. "You just did."

She escaped the tent, blindly racing for the showers, unseeing of any person on the way as tears blurred every step. Now she stood under the tepid spray, cursing him, herself, and anyone else she could think of. Damn him! How could he be like this? Didn't this mean anything to him? Did he feel nothing at all? She'd completely opened up to him. Heart, mind, body, and soul, and he refused to allow himself to do the same, holding everything to himself more tightly than a chest under lock and key.

Controlled.

She slammed a fist into the slick wall in front of her, shaking in her misery. She'd known from the start that this was a mistake. Why did she keep trying? Why did it matter? She'd made the mistake of opening up, the mistake of allowing herself to care when she knew the risks. It just sucked that she'd been proven right yet again. Caring for another person brought her nothing but pain. When would she learn?

She turned off the water and wrapped herself into a towel, rubbing her hair vigorously, trying to spend some of her anger. Now what could she do? She was stranded, sharing a tent with him and his family. Why did he ask her to marry him if he didn't want to be with her? All that talk about fate and mates and crap. She barked a cruel laugh aimed at herself. N'Réa had begun to believe in it! Faced with his family's and Brooke's undying loyalty, she'd actually begun to think she would finally find someone who could love her and not fear her. Joke's on her, she guessed. Running the towel over the thick fall of her hair, she continued to wallow in her pain.

Morgan didn't love her and probably never would. Fury made her strokes short and sharp. Her eyes widened as the cold, hard truth hit her. She was a duty to him! She bowed her head, fighting hot tears of shame. A duty! And she knew she was falling for the asshole, hook, line, and sinker.

"You're not a duty, vixen," he said from directly behind her.

She whirled, startled by his voice, dropping the towel to cover her front.

N'Réa glared at him, seething hotter at his invasion and interruption. "Stay out of my mind!" She hadn't felt him! At all. Nor had she heard him walk into the showers, so buried in her own miserable thoughts. Yet even furious with him, she craved to be held in his arms.

She stepped back, unwilling to bend to that want, deliberately keeping space between them. She clutched her towel closer, her damp hair swinging with her agitation. "And what are you doing in here anyway? This is the women's shower," she pointed out with scathing brittleness.

"I needed to take a shower too," he said, reaching around her to turn the water on. She squealed and jumped when the spray splashed her calves. The move brought her within an inch of Morgan.

"Damn it, Morgan! Just let it go. I won't be a duty." She closed her eyes, fighting the roiling heat in her stomach. Bile soured her throat. "I won't keep you to your offer. I will keep your secret safe." Her voice cracked, but she had to say it. She refused to make him pay for something he had no choice in, namely finding her. "You can walk away," she told him, even though it split her heart right dead center to let him go.

Tender fingers flitted over her cheek, sweeping and tingling. "No, I can't walk away, vixen." With a crooked finger, he lifted her face, meeting his searching gaze, and her heart tripped. The energy in those enigmatic, gray depths pierced her. "I can't walk away. You are one half of a whole. Apart, now that I've found you, I would cease to live."

"You would die?" Her mouth rounded at the seriousness of his tone. Was it possible? She didn't want to hurt him.

"Not physically, but we are bound."

Instead of relief, she felt dejected. "So you're trapped," she said through numb lips, her one whisper of hope destroyed. "And I put you there."

His hand fell away, leaving a light heat in his wake so he could strip in front of her. He eased the towel out of her hands while he blocked her escape at the same time. He coaxed her backward into the shower's spray. "I'm not trapped," he told her. His voice rumbled over her, stroking her nerves. "I never wanted a mate, but I do want you." He teased her neck with his tongue, reaching behind her for the soap.

N'Réa shivered under the water, unable to ignore the spark he created. "And that's supposed to make this all better? You want me, but I happen to be your mate. You will eventually hate me for putting you in this position."

He shook his head. "Sarcasm doesn't look good on you, vixen. When I said there were complications, I tried to walk away then. Tried to leave you alone." He ran his lathered hands over her in long, slow passes. "I couldn't." Heat soared up her arms where he swirled lather over her, her stomach tightening with desire as his fingers roamed. "I don't love you, but I do need you. I need you to complete me."

Her head fell back on a weak neck when his hands found her breasts, urging moans she couldn't fight. His palms were delicious, rubbing over her nipples as they grew taut for the attention. "You don't play fair."

She heard the male smile in his voice. "I never said I did."

N'Réa gripped on to his shoulders as his fingers washed her thoroughly, tenderly. "I don't think this will work," she said breathily even as her body opened for him. She went boneless when his fingers reached between her legs. "I won't be a duty to you," she managed to say in spite of his brain-numbing bathing skills.

He sucked on her bottom lip, tempting her with the tip of his tongue. "You aren't a duty, N'Réa," he said, nibbling at her. "You are my mate, and before you say it, there is a difference." His hands cupped her at her waist, lifting her, wrapping her legs around his hips. He plunged into her in one swift, commanding stroke, guiding her until she was captured, pinned between his body and the shower wall. Her cries rose until she couldn't think beyond the man who held her and the solid thickness that filled her. His arms were bands around her as he thrust into her with powerful motions.

Morgan stroked his teeth over the sensitive skin of her pouting lip and she burst apart, clutching him. He held N'Réa steady, in unrelenting arms, as she rocked with the power of her climax, his own shout of pleasure quickly following.

His quiet words gradually filtered into her mind. "N'Réa," he murmured as he set her on her own feet, his hands still tenderly washing her skin as though he'd never stopped to give her the best few minutes of sensual bliss of her life. "You are my mate. You accepted me, and I have claimed you. For me, there can be no other. That is why I had to let you choose."

She leaned into him, weak and sated as he turned off the water, and began to dry her once more with the towel he'd discarded moments before. Her mind was mush. If he kept doing things like that to her, she'd never be able to think straight! How could she care so much for him when he didn't want to love her? How could he not feel something, anything? Why did it matter if she was his mate if he refused to love her?

"Love isn't necessary," he pointed out, sounding far more reasonable about it than she thought he should.

N'Réa groaned inside, slamming up walls to protect her inner complaining. It appeared that paying better attention would be a necessity if he could walk in and hear her whenever.

"Would you quit it? I can't tell when you're in there, too." She glared at him icily.

"You think loudly when you're upset," he told her with a sincere, musing chuckle. "I don't intentionally do it." He urged her to turn the other way, and he began to dry her hair for her.

"What do you mean, it isn't necessary? Don't the others love?" N'Réa knew that Brooke and Mitch were as sunk as a battleship for each other. She was positive that Selene and Bram were the same. The four were inseparable between their spouses. The absolute love and devotion was written plain as day in their expressions and actions for one another.

He swept her hair through the towel, drawing out the excess water, then began to brush it out for her. "You have the most incredible hair. I think I would bleed if you cut it."

She planted a fist on a hip. "Morgan, don't evade."

His sigh washed over damp skin. "Yes, N'Réa, they all have loving relationships. I've never seen a bond like Mitch has with Brooke in my life, but she melded with him by blood."

"Melded?"

"A bonding spell. Long story," he said as he continued to work through the length of her hair.

Her head fell forward, tugging the hair from his fingers causing her to wince, though she barely acknowledged the pain. It was minuscule compared to the pain inside, surrounding her heart. She felt absolutely awful. Her voice wobbled weakly and she knew as she said the words, they had to be true. The facts made it glaringly obvious. The pain within tightened more around her heart. "Then it's me. There's something wrong with me that repulses you, that you don't want to love me."

He spun her so fast, she fell right into his damp chest. Morgan wouldn't let her fall, but the move made her gasp; she wasn't ready for it. His eyes glittered with an inner fire, like embers beneath the smoke gray, as he captured her attention. "Not even close," he informed her sharply. "And if you look down, you will see I am in no way repulsed by anything about you."

"That's all this is, then, is lust," she snapped, shoving out of his arms, getting angrier by the second. "This is confusing, Morgan!" She started dressing, determined to put space between them. "How is this supposed to work? What am I to you?" She noticed he remained naked, and Lord help her, she wanted him and his passionate kisses and anything else he was willing to give her!

She had to get away from him. N'Réa couldn't think or formulate a cohesive anything with him standing there absolutely unconcerned about his modesty.

"And if you say I am your mate one more time, I will give you my right hook!"

She stomped away, gathered her things, and twisted everything up into a ball to carry to camp. She could find his warm, male scent lingering in the moist air and fought to respond to it. She closed her eyes briefly, searching for the strength to face him.

"Look, Morgan. I like you, a damn lot. I care for you, but if you can't reciprocate in some manner other than sex, regardless of how unbelievable it is, then we will not make it. And if that is the only reason behind your marriage proposal, then I will have to change my mind." She managed not to choke on the words, barely.

Anger flickered to life, darkening the gray of his eyes, black lashes framing the spark of impatience and maybe something more. "You would change your mind?" His stance tightened as she tried to move past him, but he shot out a hand stopping her. She lowered her gaze to his hand. He loosened his grip but didn't release her.

"I have the prerogative. I won't lie to you or to me, regardless of this bond we share."

He stepped closer, so close she could feel the heat of his skin flowing over her in waves. "I told you when I asked you to marry me I didn't love you, and you accepted. I offered myself in every way I know how. My life, my protection, my support." She felt his temper flare stronger underneath the surface. She met his stare, unafraid. "I care enough to give all of those things to you, when I never have for any other person," he said, a coarse depth to his voice that ran like quicksilver down her spine. Morgan didn't like having to explain himself. *Tough*. She had far too much to lose in this and for the first time was willing to fight for it, even if he wasn't. And it terrified her because she knew what losing would cost her.

"And I gave the same, because yesterday, I had the faint hope you could love me. That you could someday give your heart to me, not just your mind, your body, or your protection. But if you refuse, won't by choice, then what is the point to any of this? Lust dies. Fates and mates can do nothing to help us if you hold yourself apart from me." She widened a hand to cover his heart, his skin quivering beneath her palm. "I care for you, more with each breath, but I won't live a lie. If I marry you, there will have to be something besides lust involved."

"You are my mate!" He ground out the words through a tight jaw, as if that would end the argument.

She pleaded with him. "What difference does it honestly make, Morgan?" Daring his wrath she delved into him, searched him, and could only find the tight spring that was Morgan, his emotions held together with a will of iron.

She slipped out of his hold with no resistance from Morgan. "Brooke was right. You are way too controlled."

His voice stopped her before she could take more than two steps to leave him alone. "Do you love me?"

She spun with considerable slowness, crying inside but refusing to let it show. The pain she felt could be cured. She knew it, but Morgan was the only one who could fix this. N'Réa was willing and capable of meeting him halfway on this journey. The rest was up to Morgan. It didn't terrify her half as much as it did in the beginning, knowing that this man held so much of her in his hands. The knowledge that she was right gave her the strength to challenge him.

N'Réa forced her voice to remain calm to answer his question, not letting the destruction inside be visible anywhere. "I'm halfway there, Morgan. That's why this scares me so much. I can't force you to love me, but if you out and out refuse, then why?" She gave him a quiet moment to answer and when he didn't, she left him alone in the showers.

Chapter Fifteen

Morgan glared across the few feet between him and Lord De Brasse. The dirt under their feet puffed up in small dust clouds as they circled each other in the arena, all signs of the rainstorm long gone. Chain and plate armor scratched and jangled as they paced around each other. De Brasse lost to Abernathy in the last round the day before, which put him in the same bracket as Morgan, and neither man was happy about their situation, facing each other again.

The tournament was tightening up, narrowing in options as men and teams fought for the positions that would put them in the money at the end of the next weekend. As things stood, fighters from Duncan's World were making a good-sized dent in those slots, if Morgan could defeat Dirk this time. Morgan sliced Dirk a cold stare, knowing without a doubt that the back hand at their last meeting had been deliberate. Dirk's brown gaze taunted him to make a mistake from behind the grill of his helmet.

"Swine maggot," Dirk jeered at him. Morgan focused, deaf to the verbal abuse. He deflected a swing, his grip secure on his sword as he danced out and beyond the wrath of Dirk's blade.

"Words," he said, snarling. "Words from a wench harm me more."

Dirk's foul expression intensified, his swing arching overhead to drop his blade with steel-biting precision. Morgan caught him, sliding steel on steel until their swords and guards locked together. He shoved with a vicious scowl, watching with satisfaction when Dirk stumbled. Morgan took a perfunctory swing at his off-balanced side, and Dirk hit the dirt.

"A weak wench at that," Morgan said, mocking the man on the ground. Dirk hefted himself to his feet, both men oblivious to the cheers and cries of the crowd. Morgan centered his weight, knowing Dirk would go on the offensive. His aggression after a fall was well-known among the fighters. Morgan planned on making that information useful. He wasn't going to lose this duel. N'Réa was watching him from the stands, and he would not lose twice.

"Thee will pay!" Dirk shouted as he launched another attack. Morgan's blade was quick, precise, dropping and rising to meet Dirk's swings and chops.

"Not this day!" Morgan roared, finding his opening as Dirk swung his blade across his front. He crashed the edge of his blade into Dirk's, then pushed and dipped at the same time with all of his weight. When the first tremor vibrated between them, Morgan yanked, ripping his blade straight upward. Dirk bellowed in rage and disbelief as his heavy blade was torn from his gauntlet-covered grasp, flying in a swift arc into the dirt.

Morgan stepped back, breathing heavily, his chest rasping from the combined heat of the layered armor, dust, and overhead sun. He could hear Dirk cursing to bury him, but he didn't care. He was doing what he'd promised, nothing more, nothing less. And winning for N'Réa.

He swept the hot helmet from his head and took his knee in front of Donegan, ignoring the drip of sweat on his temples. From what Morgan knew of the King, he was a decent guy, knew how to run the Faire while making a profit, and kept the patrons and participants happy. When Morgan rose, he caught a pleased smile on Donegan's, or in court, King Henry's face, receiving a head nod of recognition for his battle. Donegan knew how hard it was to unarm Dirk. He'd witnessed hundreds of duels under his current reign with the Faire Kingdom.

Morgan aimed for the awning, slowing to find N'Réa in the crowd, sitting with Brooke and Mitch in the bleachers. She clasped her hands and waved them in a winner's cheer for him, and he smiled. There was at least one more duel that afternoon depending on who won between Lord Abernathy's camp and Sir Roger Avante, who was from one of the other competing camps. The list was practically endless, with the number of men fighting for money and honor of the court.

Morgan had been surprised at first when they made their initial entrance before the court to even find her at all in the stands with Brooke. N'Réa had left for her own tent by the time he'd dressed and returned to camp to start his day. Yet, as he had pledged to her, he knew she wouldn't take her pledge lightly. He trusted her completely. She knew him now as no other did.

"Then why are you scared to love?"

He shook his head as a gentle smile lifted the corners of his mouth. *"You're impossible, vixen."* He walked to the edge of the stands where he could see into the crowds, finding her vibrant outfit with ease. The staging area was off limits to anyone other than the fighters. The rear area could get crowded as men geared up, and often when the jousters were preparing, it got plain messy. Morgan had never regretted the duels being before the jousters.

He searched the sea of faces until he found her, her expression impassive but she was there in his thoughts, a finger light touch that was only N'Réa. He saw her arch a dark, sensuously curved eyebrow at him when she knew she had his undivided attention.

"Odd, I really thought I was very possible."

The remark vibrated through him with a playful tease. He stifled the chuckle as she gave him a slow wink. He ignored the duel behind his shoulder as he leaned against the stand frame to stare out into crowds.

He lost her for a moment as the crowd surged at a development during the duel. *"Are you still upset about this?"*

He felt her restrained disapproval, as though she were pursing her lips and fighting to not lose her temper. *"I'm trying not to think about it right now. My knight is kicking ass, and I want him to win."* Playfulness welled up in her, pouring into her words. *"When you see him, could you let him know?"*

"Wench," he replied, cursing her, laughing lightly under his breath.

"Jackal," she responded immediately.

Morgan heard her sharp cry of surprise inside his ear and the immediate silence following as her walls slammed up between them, a barrier that blocked her from everything he sent her. He frowned as she shrank into a crouch next to Brooke. The instinct to flee was strong, no matter how hard she tried to hide it from him.

He reached out to her and caught her shock and a tendril of fear hovering within her thoughts as well. Morgan stood straight, his hand on the hilt of his sword. He didn't question why his hand went to his weapon. It had become as natural as breathing to wear it. Somehow, it felt right. Inside, the want to challenge whatever was hurting her was strong, much stronger than he would have ever expected. But he didn't have the time to study that want, either.

N'Réa's gaze was rounded when she finally faced him at his prodding.

"What is it? What's wrong?" he demanded.

She shook her head. She refused to open to him.

"Come here." He sent it as a firm order, one he knew she would hear. His heart lurched, noting the pale white of her face over the distance as he pushed the words to her. She nodded almost imperceptibly, as if worried someone would notice what they were doing. Then she said a few quick words to Brooke, who held N'Réa's hand in a firm grip. Brooke followed her progress as intently as he did when she stood from her place and rushed through the masses in the stands. He set his helmet on the wide wooden rail separating the grounds from the rear staging where the fighters prepped, waiting for her.

Morgan didn't take a single relaxed breath until she stood safely in front of him. Regardless of the fence between them, he desperately wanted to wrap his arms around her and calm her fears, wanted to keep her safe, no matter what. Her hands trembled in his when he reached for her, rubbing them lightly to warm them. Even in the heat of the day, they were chilled to the touch. He leaned closer to ask, "What happened?"

N'Réa licked her lips. Her cheeks continued to be too pale, and his stomach knotted in answer. Someone was threatening N'Réa, and right that moment, there wasn't much he could do about it.

"Someone reached out to me."

He splayed a hand through her hair, massaging her in comfort, his thumbs caressing sun-warmed skin. Gradually, a more natural pink and tan hue filled her features. He didn't say anything for a moment or two until she ceased to shiver.

"How?"

N'Réa rubbed her fingers across her forehead. "It felt like a question, like who are you. There was force behind it." Her smile was weak. "I wasn't expecting it."

He pulled her as close as the fence would allow, resting his cheek to her head. Perusing the crowds, it would be impossible to pick out someone in the hundreds who filled the bleachers and stands. "Did it feel threatening?"

"I don't know. I think they were as surprised as I was. I'm not exactly normal."

He buried his chuckle into her hair. "Vixen, you're looking at not exactly normal." He lifted his head as a surge in the crowd erupted with a fresh wave of roars. He held her chin with a tender strength, traveling with a searching gaze over her delicate features. "Can you tell if someone is probing?"

"I could, if I let the walls down enough."

He frowned. "You've been very open with me. Maybe we should try to keep it above ground until we leave tonight." He grazed her eyelids with his lips. "You are still coming, aren't you?"

Her whole expression lightened, her smile lifting from worry to pleasure in a heartbeat, and he felt the reaction like a punch to his gut. All she had to do was smile, and it made him want to tear her clothes off and love her for hours.

"Try to keep me away." Her voice lowered to sheer seduction, matching the beckoning heat in her eyes. A fire he could understand, wanting to comply with it immediately. Parts of him were aching, and it was all her fault.

He leaned over to whisper in her ear. "It's a good thing I'm not an exhibitionist because I want to kiss you until you can't breathe right now." She sighed against his neck, and his blood boiled. He ran his tongue over the pink shell of her ear and her immediate response filled his nostrils, her arousal as clean and clear as any scent he'd ever encountered. Exotic and sweet, perfectly blended with the summer rain of her skin and hair. Needing it more than he wanted to admit, Morgan drew her close just to have that scent in his senses, on his lips, in his lungs.

N'Réa trembled in his hands with want as her arousal soared. He hated to send her back, wanting to continue, but he had no choice.

"Stay with Brooke until the duels are over. Don't leave her side. I want you with her or with me."

She stretched on her heels to look stiffly up at him. "Morgan, I can take care of myself."

He brushed a thumb across her sweet, pouting lip. "I'm going to make sure you stay safe."

"More of that 'I'm your mate' stuff?" she demanded, her eyes flashing green fire, a warning.

"No, more of 'I want to take care of you and you enjoy making it hard on me'," he teased her, but only half joking. "Please, N'Réa, stay with Brooke. I don't like this." Morgan lifted from her, searching once more. "There's no telling who, from where, or what they want."

She calmed under his reasoning. "You're right." Her hand gripped his damp hair without asking, without apology. "Kiss me anyway. For luck," she softly ordered as she tugged him to her.

"Your wish is my command," he replied as his lips met hers, and the fire he'd been skating around leaped to life. He kept his kiss gentle even as he began to burn inside with the kindling of his desire for the vixen in his arms. Morgan tasted the sweetness of her luscious mouth and discovered her willingness, found the scent of her desire between one breath and the next growing headier by the second. He released her reluctantly.

"Down, girl. I still have to win this thing," he pointed out on a harsh growl.

"Then win the damn thing so we can go home!" She stamped her foot but couldn't stop giggling. It ruined the effort of being impatient.

Laughter rumbled from his chest. N'Réa's joy in life was too wild to have a little thing like this frighten her for long. The unknown interruption worried Morgan, but he hoped it was only a chance encounter, a mistake of some sort. Maybe their mutual surprise would be enough to disenchant the person who had touched on N'Réa. He could hope.

Morgan released her hair, sweeping it behind her ear, the silken texture sliding through his fingers. It was no secret. He loved her hair, the feel, the length. Even the hidden fire that he would sometimes find lost in the dark strands. It was all N'Réa. He relinquished her reluctantly.

"Go sit with Brooke, vixen. I'll keep watch until you're there."

She rose up on her toes and delivered a quick kiss to his cheek, then turned and made her way to her seat, much more at ease if the sway of her walk was any indication. Brooke smiled back at him over the heads in the bleachers, saying with a nod she knew and nothing would happen. He was grateful for his sister when he couldn't be right next to her where he should be. For a mate who had sworn his protection, he wasn't doing all that well, he mused in a brooding way while waiting for her to find her place. He really shouldn't watch her walk anywhere. Apparently the motion caused his mind to cease to function coherently.

"She's quite the handful," Dirk said from his side. "I heard you plan to wed. Congratulations."

Morgan continued to follow that swaying skirt until she was sitting once more, only paying half of any attention to Dirk's interruption. "Thanks. Was there something you wanted?"

"Don't have to be bullish, Morgan," the other man retorted.

Morgan took stock of the blond man.

"I wanted to say good fight. You were impressive at the exhibitions and if I didn't know any better, I'd say you have improved."

Morgan rolled his shoulder, keeping one eye on the seats where Brooke, N'Réa, and the others of the camp and Morgan's Mares sat. "I had room to improve."

"So you're sticking to your story that you've never fought?" Dirk asked, his hand resting with its own comfortable arrogance on the hilt of his sword, his helmet tucked beneath an arm. There was still a sense of disbelief in his question. What he thought mattered little to Morgan.

"No story." A bored expression filled Morgan's features. It mattered absolutely zilch what anyone thought of him or his fighting skills. "This is the first Renaissance Faire I've ever attended."

Dirk's doubting gaze narrowed. "You've unarmed both me and Duncan."

Morgan shrugged. "You leave yourself vulnerable."

"You can tell? Just in the few fights we've had?" Dirk's mouth popped open, aghast at the possibility.

"What do you want, Dirk?" Morgan rotated now with N'Réa safe in the stands with friends and family to protect her.

Dirk lost his feigned hauteur. "Teach me how you do it. I never felt it coming."

Morgan grinned in spite of himself. "Seriously? You want me to show you?"

Dirk peered over his shoulders both ways and then stepped closer, an anxious energy apparent now. "Are you planning on staying on, joining the circuit?"

"I hadn't considered it. This whole thing came about as one big joke by Brooke." Morgan returned his attention to the arena as the fight between Sir Roger Avante and Sir McClellan of Abernathy's camp trotted out to cross swords. This was the one he needed to follow and hopefully learn something from.

"And yet you are such a natural, relentless fighter."

"That didn't sound like it was meant as a compliment," Morgan pointed out without any real anger as the call for the duel echoed through the loudspeakers.

"All right, so I don't really like you, but Hell's gate, even I know a good fighter when I see one."

"I respect that, Dirk. Believe me, it's mutual."

The two seasoned warriors in the arena paced and swung at each other. Morgan concentrated, feeling out the way they circled and held each other, following their motions and maneuvers and committing it to memory. He noted as each man made the approach, the attack, and the eventual defense. He knew either man would be a challenge, but he sensed a weakness in Roger he knew he could take advantage of. McClellan would be harder, but not impossible.

"Would you be interested?"

"After the matches, no sooner." He gave Dirk an unassuming show of teeth, more of a shark's grin. "Unless you were hoping I'd give up secrets to help you win?"

Dirk gave him an equal smirk. "Would it have hurt to believe, maybe, yes?"

Relaxed beneath their show of bravado and bantering, he huffed a chuckle or two. "To believe, no." He shot Dirk a warning stare. "But it won't happen."

Dirk accepted his decision with a gracious, sweeping bow. "You are a true knight of honor. Duncan is a lucky man to have found you." He pivoted on a heel, satisfied with Morgan's offer, to disappear with his own band of ruffians.

Morgan shouted after Dirk's retreating shape. "Hey, Dirk! I'm thinking about joining after all." Just to see his reaction.

"And I await the day to kick thine ass again, Sir Morgan!" He shouted clearly with an honest laugh. Morgan capitulated with an equal bow of respect.

"Thinking of changing camps?" Duncan asked with a confused brow at their banter as Roger fell for the third time to McClellan. Morgan had about forty minutes before he would have to face McClellan.

Morgan let out a disgusted sound at even the idea. "Not in this lifetime. I think we hit a mutual understanding of respect and dislike for each other." He let his attention sweep to the stands, seeking and finding N'Réa sitting with Brooke. Their heads were together talking calmly, so he focused on Duncan.

"Yes, Dirk has been around for a long time. He's seen a few fights." The arena emptied of the two warriors as the next combatants were called to prepare and enter. "Are you thinking about staying on? I heard that taunt. His look was priceless, by the way."

"I don't know. I threw it out there to make him sweat," Morgan said as he grabbed his helmet close.

"If you decide you do want to continue, I would like to offer you a permanent place. I know you haven't fought before and you haven't served your time, but it isn't engraved in stone as a law that you must squire first. And as far as the tests go, I doubt a man on the council would say you aren't a worthy, safe, and honorable fighter. I have noticed you exercise a great amount of caution and control in your duels. I'm glad my first assessment of you wasn't correct."

Morgan rested his chin on the top of his helmet. "Are you trying to convince me to stay?" For some reason, the idea appealed to him. As weird as this month had been, why not? Morgan was really beginning to feel a kinship with Duncan and the others of the camp, valuing their friendship and knowledge. He might have started this as a lark, determined to grind fate beneath his heel, but even a glacier can change course given enough time.

"I am, with the camp's full support. Brooke and Mitch are as welcome, and not because of her unbelievable generosity. She has been an uplifting addition to the group. You three are all welcome, four if N'Réa is crazy enough to stay with you." There was a hint of amusement in the last part.

"All of us?" Morgan was astounded. "Just like that?" All of them had been strangers only weeks before, now they were being offered a place among them. Comrades and equals.

Duncan coughed, using a fist to hide his laughter. "Actually, we took a vote. It was unanimous."

Searching the stands to keep an eye on her, he found N'Réa, who was watching William's current duel beside Natalie screaming at the top of her lungs, cheering for her own knight in shining armor. Brooke and N'Réa were right there with her, jumping up and down and yelling for all they were worth.

"I need to talk to them about it. Put it out there for them," he allowed himself to say. "But somehow, I think I know how they will answer."

"And you, Morgan? What say you?"

"I've never experienced anything like Duncan's World." He faced the arena in time to see William defeat his opponent, the large, round shield useless against William's attack. He whistled his support when William hefted his sword to claim his cheers. When William knelt in front of the King, Morgan said, "But I think I could really get into this."

"Hugh will be able to fight by the spring without a problem. There's a Christmas Faire we attend, but it is more for the holiday cheer than the fighting and it's only one weekend. I can give you the schedule, and you and the others can see if you can work your way into it."

Morgan nodded as the crowd calmed to a mere buzz before the next called duel. "Just how much do you guys win doing this?"

"Well, there's the tournament champion, then there's placements beneath it, going to tenth place. There's money for the highest pointed camp also. That's where you really want to make the most points; that amount gets split equally, at least in my camp. Not all the Faires pay like this one does, some are higher or lower depending on a few different things, and we take care of those who don't fight, like Cale and Turner. Turner will probably be ready next year. Cale doesn't like to fight, so he squires."

Morgan's head threatened to spin. "No wonder you guys fight like you do. Where does the money come from?"

"We pay entrance fees for the tournaments, and the Faire pays the remainder. The Faire does well, we do well. We work to fill the seats."

"Like any sport. You can't get paid if no one watches." Duncan nodded his agreement. Morgan stood straight, searching for N'Réa again, needing to touch on her every few minutes to soothe his nerves. Morgan discovered he hated being so far away from her when he should have been right there with her. Thankfully, she appeared relaxed and seemed as pleased as Natalie when William won. She shifted in her seat and the sun hit her hair, the inner fire of her shining through. Morgan was beginning to think it was the fire of her soul, the way it shined and flickered in the sunlight. He knew how strong-willed she was. He licked dry lips at the sight of her.

"But I never paid," he said to Duncan, trying to remember what they'd been discussing.

"You were covered when you took over Hugh's slot. Nothing to it. Think about it." Duncan clapped him on the back and walked away.

He leaned a hip to the wood rail, following the crowd, considering it. Really considering it. It would be fun; that went without saying. He pictured a soft smile on N'Réa and knew she would welcome it. Her life circled around these shows and Faires. Morgan didn't want to strip that from her. He didn't even have to consider Brooke's enthusiasm. So long as Mitch wasn't on duty, they could attend as well.

His hand fell to the hilt of his sword, wondering why it felt right. The weight of it, the feel of the leather-wrapped hilt in his palm, almost as though he'd always known the steel blade. How was he able to fight at all? How did he know how to judge a turn, a change of weight? There were infinitesimal cues during a fight, and one by one he was discovering them and putting them away for another day, another fight. Morgan remembered the first fights, the training duel and then the first with Duncan, and could see an improvement in himself and in his skills. Yet somehow he had the knowledge to fight to begin with. He couldn't remember dueling with sticks as a child. He probably had with Roman, but he couldn't remember.

Was it something he had done when he was a kid? Had he fought and forgotten? Had he pretended to be a pirate or a knight and not remembered? He wished he knew, if only to solve the mystery. There was no vanity in the fact that he was doing as well as he was. Determination, yes; ego, no. Morgan understood he wasn't a top-caliber swordsman. Except for the slip that Duncan hadn't anticipated, he could and had kicked Morgan's ass more than he'd won against Duncan.

As the fight in front of him came to a crowd-roaring end, he went to the water table and mentally prepared for his fight with McClellan.

This was his first chance to fight Steve McClellan so anything was possible, but he had examined the man's fighting style with Avante and knew he tended to favor one side. He was a solid fighter, aggressive and seasoned. If Morgan won this one, it would not only be by a stroke of sheer luck, he would be placed in the top five.

Gulping the cold water, he then flipped the cup into the trash. There wasn't going to be an if in this fight. He would win the duel.

Considering Duncan's offer, Morgan admitted he was enjoying Duncan's World. He prepared for the duels with a taste of anticipation, which had surprised him in the first few days. The weight of the armor, plate, and gauntlets didn't feel uncomfortable any longer as he'd grown accustomed to wearing all of it for any length of time as he waited for his turn behind the scenes. It was even fun to walk the grounds as a troop and play the gallant to the guests. More than one woman had flirted with him, and as a knight, he took it in stride. It was a far different reaction than that first morning. And he wasn't being paid for any of it. Not that the money mattered. For him, like many of the camp, this was all for the fun of it. To play, sweat, and fight where it was not only allowed, but encouraged.

He shook his head once. Brooke and Selene had been right. This was enough to shake him up. Add N'Réa to the mixing bowl, and his life would never be the same. He was looking forward to the next week, five days of her company to try to figure out how this would work between them. Would she be happy at his home? Would she be restless? Adjustments were expected from both of them. Whether she knew it or not, Morgan cared enough to want to try to make this work, not just because he was meant to, but because he wanted her, N'Réa.

He leaned around the edge of the canvas, searching the opposite bleachers for her blue outfit. He let out a relieved sound to see her with Brooke, both watching the duels with interest. She was the one woman he had been made for, to protect and cherish.

Morgan secured the combat helmet over his head as his fight was called. He would win against McClellan and any challenger for her. He would prove he was more than enough to honor his pledge to her, to be all the man she needed. Even if he couldn't love her, he would be everything else. That became his silent vow as he strode into the arena.

Chapter Sixteen

N'Réa clutched at Brooke's hand when the attack shattered the awed silence. The clash of steel on tempered steel pounded through the arena as cheers erupted all around her. Morgan was magnificent, a graceful, unrelenting fighting machine deflecting McClellan. Their grunts and curses were muted, but it wasn't difficult to hear as she made out several. "His swearing has improved," she mentioned to Brooke out of the corner of her mouth.

Brooke giggled. "Mitch and Duncan have been helping him."

"Mitch?" she asked, surprised. N'Réa had never heard Mitch utter one foul thing in the time she'd been in the group.

Brooke lifted an eyebrow in humor. "He's eloquent, trust me on that."

N'Réa bit her lip as Morgan overcompensated and whirled to fall with the aid of an outstretched leg. She cheered and stomped her feet when Morgan rolled easily to his feet. "Come on, baby!" she yelled at the top of her lungs.

"Do you still feel all right?" Brooke asked as the knights circled one another in the dust hanging in the air.

"Yes. I don't know where it came from." She cast a furtive glance around the arena, but it was hopeless. So many faces, so many people. The voice was no one she recognized, and there was no one other than

Morgan who had ever reached her like that. The shaking had finally subsided, but the chilled edge of fear remained.

Brooke squeezed her hand. "Don't worry too much. It probably came as a surprise to them as much as to yourself."

"I hope so. I don't like that kind of attention. I've guarded myself too closely and for too long to not take this seriously."

Brooke gave her an understanding pat on the arm. "I know that, too."

"Brooke, if I ever had a sister, I would have wanted you."

"I have one, but I'd take you in a heartbeat." N'Réa's heart squeezed at the absolute openness in Brooke's gaze. Brooke didn't lie. She made N'Réa feel like family.

N'Réa's attention swept ahead, jerked forward by the sound of clashing metal. Morgan was in excellent form as he forced McClellan to pace backward or lose something vital. Morgan took him down three steps later. "That's my man," she crowed with pride.

Morgan took his opponent to a full three fall, unable to unarm him as he was quickly becoming known for, but N'Réa didn't care how he won. She jumped up and down in her place like an eleven-year-old, cheering and whooping along with the others in the group.

"All right, girls! You ready?" A cheer went up around her as Natalie stood and lifted a hand. Slicing through the air, she shouted, "Now!" And at least eight women brayed long whinnies for their champion knight. Morgan whirled on a boot heel as he removed his helmet, a huge grin breaking out on his face, with N'Réa joining in on the fun. He went to take his knee, his head shaking as hard as his shoulders as the women collapsed on each other in cackling glee.

"Natalie!" Brooke gasped through peals of laughter. "Oh, that was priceless!"

Natalie situated herself on William's lap, his duels done for the day. Looping her arms around his thick shoulders, she squirmed on his lap, getting comfortable. "It's easy to rock his boat," she said with a shrug and dimples. "And he's a damn good sport."

N'Réa sat with her and the others, adjusting her skirt. "And William's not jealous?" she asked, giving a teasing poke to the man who gave Viking a new meaning with a long red braid and thick russet beard, holding Natalie snuggled up on his thigh.

She tugged on William's twisted braid. "Nope. I'm absolutely devoted to this guy," she said, smacking a loud kiss on his bearded cheek, which reddened under the attention. "He works hard and plays hard. We both do. This is stress relief for us."

"What do you do?" N'Réa asked.

"We're high school teachers," she explained, her chestnut-brown hair bobbing as she talked. "He's history, and I'm biology and chemistry."

N'Réa shared her surprise with Brooke. "Never saw it coming," she remarked, confounded.

Natalie leaned over. "I know. It blows your mind, don't it?" she retorted with a wink. "That's why we aren't usually around during the week, and I'm stuck at the tent when we are. Grading papers and junk." She snapped around to face the court when the horns sounded. "Hallelujah! The duels are done for today."

"Who's thirsty?" Brooke asked. A resounding chorus of 'me's said it all.

They caroused on the way, rowdy and loud with the energy of Morgan's last fight boosting them, singing and dancing from the arena to Duncan's

World. Guests and participants alike joined in the energy until they were in the vicinity of the camp. N'Réa headed for their tent in time to meet Morgan exiting sans armor, his hair tied away from his face with a leather strip. She launched herself at him and he caught her, his hands wrapping her legs around his waist, pinning her solidly within his arms.

"Now that's a welcome," he purred with heated meaning. He kissed her as the cheers rolled around them, both oblivious to the energetic throng. He let her slide from his hold until her feet were on the ground, but he kept a steadying hand on her waist, tucking her close into his side.

With her feet on the ground, N'Réa moved to let others congratulate the fighters and Morgan on their wins and his placement in the tournament. William and Beuchard were in the running to place, though Duncan was the highest ranked in the camp with Morgan next. Somehow, he'd ferociously held Hugh's standing in the lists. Pride for his wins filled her.

Duncan lifted his hands for silence. "We have all worked hard this year for our placements." Several shouts of boisterous agreement broke from the crowd. "Next weekend is the finals of this tournament, and we will work to do our best. Take this week to rest and regain your strength from this weekend," he advised with wry smirks for the guilty surrounding him. There had been several with hangovers early in the morning, himself included for the first time in years. "Meet here with confidence on Friday night, and we will celebrate our victories together!"

The cheer was overwhelming as more than twenty voices echoed his sentiments. N'Réa was glad and not as surprised as she would have been two weeks ago to see the silent hunger for the battle in Morgan. Her knight had discovered himself, and she knew she wasn't ready to give up on him.

As the fighters began to discuss strategy for their upcoming duels, N'Réa slipped out of camp for her tent for the last two working hours the grounds would be open. Most already knew who they would be fighting the coming weekend. It would be a mental and physical challenge to win.

N'Réa wound her way through the vendor booths, waving to Marie as she untied her tent panels. She rolled the side edge up, retying the strings, then ducked inside.

The biting chill hit her when she was almost to the table. She froze, unprepared for the sensation, clutching her hands together to halt their immediate reaction to tremble. Turning in a slow circle, there was no one else in the tent with her, yet someone had stood where she stood, had invaded when she had been away watching the duels. She could swear to it if she had to. Cautious steps carried her to her table and she laid a hand on the cloth, her fingers testing the material cautiously.

Yes, someone had been there. Their malevolence still billowed like a lingering fog over her table. But who? And just as much, why? She'd spent the last two hours at the arena, her money in a wrist tie reticule on her arm so she couldn't be robbed. Scooting behind the table, nothing appeared to have been moved. Her cards were safe in their case where she had left them, tucked under the material covering the table, out of sight.

So why did it feel like she had been invaded? Why did her personal space feel like it had been invaded? The whole situation made her nervous and jumpy.

"N'Réa!" came Morgan's concerned call.

Her head snapped up. *"I'm fine."*

"You're scared," he replied. *"Put up your walls; I'll be right there."*

She frowned at his imperious order, noting the impatient edge of his anger.

Opening her mind to tell him what he could do with his attitude, her legs weakened as another voice entered her ears. The urge to collapse completely swept over her with a terrifying force.

"Please don't," it purred. *"I enjoy listening to your spats."* The male voice laughed with ill humor before she slammed up the walls, making them as thick as she could possibly think of: steel, iron, stone.

Painfully, white fingers clutched at the edge of the table as her head fell forward, panting as dots swam before her. What was happening? What was that? Who was that! She'd never had that happen. She'd never heard that voice, either!

"N'Réa?" Morgan's calming voice washed over her and she lifted her head, finding him just inside the open gap of her tent. He opened his arms, and she flung herself into his embrace. He wrapped strong arms around her, pinning her securely to his solid chest. The steady beat of his heart was detectable under his linen shirt, comforting with the faint scent of his skin enveloping her.

"I told you to stay close," he reminded her.

"I'm sorry," she allowed herself to say as he ran a caressing hand over her spine. "I thought I'd be all right here. This is my tent." Shaken by the voice, it was hard to speak.

"I know, vixen." He held her until she could breathe, then he carefully held her in front of him, studying her. "Have you been alone?"

She nodded. "I heard it again," she told him, her fingers tying themselves into his shirt. "I don't think they're nice." She was positive of it.

Morgan nuzzled her with his lips, sharing his warmth with her. Releasing her, he then walked to the tent entrance and ran the fabric through his fingers. Kneeling on the ground, he picked out blades of grass to hold to his nose as he sniffed. "Someone was here while you were out," he said simply. "Male." She saw him recoil a little. "And no, he's not nice," he informed her. A scowl hovered over his features as he continued to examine the tent.

"Who?" Her voice was weak. "What do they want?" He didn't face her as he brushed his hands off, the muscles under his shirt flexing with his movements and thoughts. "Morgan? What is it?" she asked, growing concerned with his continued silence. "Do you know who it is?"

"I don't know who it is, but I know evil when I find it."

N'Réa felt a new shiver climb her spine at the ominous reply.

"Has anyone tried to reach you before this? Have you felt someone searching?"

She shook her head, wringing her hands. "No. I'm sure I would remember it. It feels like someone is tearing at my mind when my walls are up."

He paced to one side of the enclosed space. "But you've been very relaxed with me." Following his every step, N'Réa heard something in his voice she refused to accept.

"Don't you dare blame yourself if something is going on, Morgan Aiza!" She crossed her arms and faced him, any hint of her fear completely evaporating. "I made my choice, same as you. I chose to let you know, to let you in."

"But what if someone happened to come in while you were open, would you know?"

"I would know if someone was poking around, yes. If they were sitting there like vultures, enjoying a day of voyeurism, maybe not," she conceded. "I've never had this problem before."

More agitated with her explanation, he began to pace once more, to and fro, devouring the inner space of her tent with his muscled stride. His hands clenched and unclenched. She followed his hand when he lifted it once to the hilt of his sword, wanting to take his frustration out on her unseen enemy. His spine was stiff as he searched out the answer.

She chewed her bottom lip for a second as the situation became clearer. The reasoning behind his growing agitation, and if she wasn't wrong, Morgan's worry.

"You think whoever this is could know all of our secrets, don't you?"

His pacing never faltered. "Yes." A flat answer.

This time, the impulse to collapse was inescapable. Another shiver rocked her as the blood drained from her cheeks, and she hit her knees. "Oh God, Morgan! I'm so sorry. I had no idea!" This time, it really was possible she might be sick.

Morgan lifted her in an instant, his arms crushing her close. "This isn't your fault, N'Réa." His voice was rough but caring. "You didn't do this."

"But I did. Like I always do. Somehow I screw things up. No matter how hard I try to protect myself, something happens." She paused. *"And I have to run."*

He gripped her by the shoulders and shook her firmly, snapping her attention to him, before the brewing panic she felt was released in a wailing storm of hysteria. "No one is running! What has happened before that you would have to run? Have you been threatened?"

N'Réa nodded. She licked her bottom lip, her voice shaking as she remembered years into her history. "Twice. I had two exact readings that foretold a death. One, I learned, was a murder. I gave the reading and didn't think anything about it. But when the police came..." She burrowed into his welcoming heat, shivering as the memory returned. The questions, the irate family. "The brother came to see me when it happened. He had visited me, trying to rationalize his brother-in-law's behavior. He said if I didn't tell the police everything about how I knew she was going to die, he would come back and make me talk. I didn't stick around."

"And the other?" While the rough timbre of his voice did little to hide his restraint, his comfort was twofold. He didn't loosen his embrace and every few seconds, he would tease her temple with his lips, offering his support.

"It's hard to remember." She rubbed her forehead as she leaned away, her gaze squinting as she tried to focus on the memory. "There was a man, older. I don't think he was expecting the reading to go in that direction. I can't even remember what he asked. All I can remember was it told of a death also. He was angry, very, very angry. He said some things to me then, and I never saw him again." Why couldn't she remember that one clearly? Even if after so many visitors, a reading like that, like the first, should have been easy to recall. This one was as a grainy as a sixty-year-old, black-and-white photo. She'd been young, maybe twenty. That was as close as she could get to the memory.

"You haven't had any trouble from either of them since?" Morgan wrapped his fingers through her hair. She let her head sag into his chest, not wanting to remember, not wanting to be scared.

Thankfully, she'd never encountered a reading like either of those again. "No. I'm low-key. I don't make waves. I never talk to anyone. I've known Bailey and Marie for years, among a few others, but otherwise no one knows I'm around."

"I sure the hell did."

N'Réa managed to relax a little beneath his teasing, but his next caution couldn't be ignored.

"We need to be careful. Someone out there knows about you, and you have changed, become stronger in the last few weeks. You've tapped into your ability. At least some of them."

"There's only one weekend left." She wasn't ready to acknowledge just what those gifts, or curses for that matter, may be. N'Réa couldn't deny them, but if that was why someone had discovered her, she was ready to leave. Five minutes ago.

He soothed her anxiety, absently rubbing his fingers along her back, letting his thoughts fall free. "Maybe we can do a few things this week to strengthen your walls without all the commotion here to disrupt you. I have a few questions myself, if you're willing, but I don't want to mention them here. There isn't a point in talking about it until we are safe at home."

She let out a wondering sigh. "Home," she whispered. "A real home."

"Yes, vixen. A real home, with a real man. And no, I won't tell him when I see him," he joked, reminiscent of her earlier teasing. He lifted her chin. "Are you going to be all right? I don't like the idea of leaving you alone, but I have to get ready for the last parade."

The strain of leaving her behind was on his face, etched into the firm sides of his mouth. She traced a finger over his lips, urging him to calm down. "I'll ask Bailey to help keep an eye on things. He won't question. With all the bad luck I had this trip, he's been exceptionally gallant. Even Marie says so."

Some of the tension eased from his sun-drenched features. "I trust you, N'Réa," he said, a meaningful caress in his words. "You are not to blame if someone is picking at your head, but please keep yourself safe." He lifted his hands to cup her face, cradling her as he drew her closer, teasing his lips over hers. "I could have killed Curtis; I wanted to. I don't want you taking any risks or taking that beautiful head of yours outside of the tent for anything until I come for you after the parade. Promise me," he added.

"I promise. I'll wait for you."

All the pent-up worry and concern he carried leaked out of his frame. "Thank you, vixen." He gathered her into his chest, kissing her hard. His gaze swirled like thunderheads when he lifted from her, his voice rich and husky. "I'll be here." He sipped one more kiss from her. "Thank God tomorrow is Monday," he said with a humoring drawl. He turned with a sweep of his red tunic and left her standing there next to her table.

"Damn, I love that man," she whispered.

She blinked when a woman poked her head through the tent. "Are you open?"

N'Réa waved her in. "Very," she said. She moved behind her table to do what she did best.

When her customer had paid and left, N'Réa slouched into her chair. What was going on? This trip had been weird from the first day.

Maybe this unknown person was only curious about who she was, curious about what she could do, since whoever it was seemed to be as capable on some level. No, she couldn't fool herself. The voice, link, whatever it was that made it possible for them to talk to her mentally, had a bad feeling to it. She needed to be careful, needed to pay attention to what was going on around her. She really wished, and not for the first time, that she knew more about her parents, more about who and what she was. For years, most of her life, she'd hidden everything about herself, not wanting to take a chance to examine any of it and cause herself more problems by bringing whatever her talents were out into the open again. After what happened to her as a child, it was too great a risk.

Brooke had recognized her immediately as a kindred spirit. The other woman was undeniably the most talented woman N'Réa had ever met. If Brooke could sense more in N'Réa, just what was she? She'd never touched minds with anyone either, yet she could with Morgan. What did it mean? What kind of gifts or power did she really have? Were they dangerous? Was she? She didn't believe so. She'd never tried to use them or her skills for nefarious reasons.

She hid a near-snort behind a hand. Being bad wasn't the way to stay unnoticed either. She knew her seeing skills were real; she had true talents as a diviner. A small knot dropped like a stone into her stomach. What else was she? N'Réa's fingers tapped over the cloth-covered table as her thoughts swirled, unanswered.

N'Réa tilted her head in thought, flipping all of what had happened during the last few weeks over in her mind. She'd never wanted to share before, either. Not of herself, more than just her physical body. N'Réa could claim very few relationships; her nomadic lifestyle made them near impossible to maintain. Yet between her and Morgan, they shared an incredible attraction, not merely the physical, but a mental attraction for each other. Something deeper. She didn't understand it completely, but felt she was beginning to. Like whenever she needed him, called for him, or was in pain, he was there for her, he knew. *Her protector*. Those words left a lump in her chest. She wanted more than a protector.

She wanted him. All of him.

It was late in the afternoon when a shadow crossed her doorway, causing a chill to walk up her arms in trepidation while her next customer stood outside. "Can I help you?" she asked. The man, she guessed by his size, nodded. He was dressed in a black costume, a long cloak, and a cowl covering his features. There was a strong sense of foreboding seeing him, but she sought to dismiss it. It was simply because her thoughts had been more tangled than a ball of yarn.

"I need your services."

Narrowing her eyes, she hesitated. The voice felt, *familiar*, slightly accented. Did she know this man?

"I am available," she replied, dismissing the niggle of warning. She had to be wrong. The person who had surprised her with his mental invasion wouldn't know where she was, would he? Wouldn't know who she was, right? She hoped not. "Please, come in and ask your question." She realized her mistake the instant he was inside. Evil radiated from him in serpentine waves. Her luck had run out. She forced herself to stay calm, exuding a nonchalant serenity she was nowhere near feeling.

He slid the cowl away from his face with large hands, staring at her maliciously. He was tall hidden beneath the cloak. His black hair, with only a slight show of gray, lay thick above bottomless midnight eyes.

He gave her a small mock bow while his lips curled in derision. "Thank you for being so kind. You didn't know your friend placed a ward on the doorway, did you? You have powerful friends, N'Réa Gordon."

Blindsided, she reached for the table with numb fingers. Her tongue refused to work right. "How — how do you know my name?"

Hidden power made his eyes glitter within her tent in the absence of sunlight. "Why wouldn't I know it?" he scoffed, as though she were insignificant, as though she should be thankful to be in his presence. "You don't recognize me?" He took another step toward her, taunting her, caging her into a corner.

"Who are you?" she demanded, launching from her chair, not caring for the submission he was demanding from her by towering over her.

"You are the image of your mother, beautiful, radiant," he replied instead of answering, a compliment that was anything but kind. He loomed forward, a pace at a time. She refused to bend to him as she reinforced her thoughts. "You didn't recognize me the last time I came to see you. I wanted to introduce myself, but I was sidetracked." She detected a hint of sadness in his voice, but he quickly moved past it, the harsh grate of his voice filling the tent once more. "I lost track of you for more than six years after that. I can't believe my own luck to find you here. I've been watching you, waiting for the right time," he told her, and she shuddered at the implications.

She planted her palms on the table. Why would he watch her? What did he want? Either way, he didn't sound half sane. All she had to do was scream, and help would be there. "I have to ask you to leave. I don't know you, and I am positive I don't want to."

The stranger didn't move, but the lowered growl of his voice seemed to echo inside her ears, filling her head, then her chest and further before she could grasp a single breath to block him. "Oh, but you do know me, child."

N'Réa had no warning and no protection against it. A sharp cry escaped her throat as her head crashed to her chest like a dead weight, as if a two-ton hammer slammed into her thoughts, rattling her skull until she couldn't hold the weight. Her mind erupted with excruciating pain. Bright bursts and thunderous explosions rapped across her ears and blinded her vision. She collapsed to her chair, neither her arms nor legs able to support her violently shaking form. She bit her lip, fighting to keep him out, fighting the pressure he created to break her walls. She locked the urge to scream in shocked agony behind a determined jaw.

"Leave me alone!" She was positive her head would split wide open at any second. Sparks and pain attacked her from every direction, drilling into her mind without surcease. N'Réa's stomach curdled as her enemy renewed his attack, pummeling her thoughts with deeper force, a higher pitch, stronger battering. Anything to make her crumble before him. The burn of scalding tears tracked her cheeks with the effort of keeping her mind closed to his assault.

"You will obey me," he ordered her, a clenched fist raised as though he held the strength to crush her in his hand. She feared he did. "I am more powerful than your friend and you combined."

N'Réa sobbed repeatedly when the pain receded even a fraction, finally able to breathe in short, strangled gasps.

"Who are you? What do you want from me?" she croaked, her voice hoarse, her body wrung out.

He laughed, a malevolent sound that rattled her ears. "I want what I should've already had. I want power! Your mother died before she would give it to me. She refused me! She hid you from me when you were a baby, to protect you. How wrong she was! How ironic, don't you think, that you foresaw your own mother's death?" He flexed against her mental protections, and she whimpered. She couldn't take much more. "You don't even know what you are," he taunted cruelly. "But you will, and I want it! I demand it!"

N'Réa lifted her head in defiance, every inch pounding with the weight of his thoughts bombarding her will, screaming at her to give up. "No! I will not." She spit at his feet with the last of her strength.

The humorless laugh that filled her tent was evil, edging on maniacal. "Yes, you will, but I must go. Your hound is on his way, once again too late to truly help you." A crude bark seemed to punctuate his opinion. "You should find a better class of friends," he paused, biting out one last word like a curse over his shoulder as he slipped outside, replacing his cowl and striding away, dissolving into the crowds as though he'd never been. Her head thudded to the table onto trembling arms, her frame weak and shaken beyond anything she could ever remember, his one flung word haunting her. With a sickening feeling, she realized who her tormentor was.

She forced her stomach to stop its planned rebellious upheaval by sheer willpower. N'Réa shuddered uncontrollably as she fought to regain her equilibrium, worried at any second she'd lose the battle. Each breath was a torment in and out of her lungs. Everything ached, burned, or felt like it was bleeding. It felt like she'd been pulled apart on the rack and then hung to dry in an iron maiden. Never in her life had she endured or suffered this much pain, this much agony. There was almost no sense of the world around her, she was so buried beneath the onslaught of his attack.

N'Réa bawled brokenly as strong arms lifted and rocked her. Morgan's hand caressed her everywhere he could, lovingly holding her next to his body.

She tried to draw a slower breath and nearly fainted from the pain exploding between her ears. "I didn't leave!" she tried to tell them, yet it was no stronger than a whimper against his shoulder. She clutched at him, the terror washing over her in waves as each attack replayed on a constant loop. Even when he wasn't there, he was able to hurt her. "He came in."

"Shh," Morgan murmured. She couldn't think, she couldn't hold her eyes open enough to see. Bright bursts blinded her, making it impossible to focus. Shivers rocked her where she lay huddled into his chest. Weak as a kitten, all she could do was stay there in his embrace.

There was a tender sweep of cool fingers to her forehead, and immediate relief enveloped her. The aching, crunching feeling of being crushed between steel walls vanished. Within moments, her lungs were working normally without straining for every gasp of oxygen. It was more than she could've hoped for after all that pain.

N'Réa was exhausted. She'd never encountered anyone so powerful, so evil, so intent to harm. She shivered in reaction, to the reality, that he could have killed her if he'd wanted to.

Morgan cradled her on his lap, rocking her. She blinked after several minutes and noticed her tent panels were layered for privacy to keep out the world once more. Brooke stood close to Morgan's shoulder, which meant Mitch was standing guard outside. She felt the tears well up again. She'd put them all in danger.

"I should have mentioned the ward," Brooke was saying. She tapped her fingers to her upper arms, where she held them crossed over her body. "He walked right through it. He knew."

"You didn't even know she would need it," Morgan told her, but N'Réa felt every one of his muscles as it grew taut and became strung like wire beneath her. He was furious, and she was so very, very sorry.

"Don't!" he snapped, glaring at her. She shrank, wanting to vanish, still feeling ravaged and hurting. He relented immediately, his head rising to stare at the roof of the tent as he growled in frustration through his teeth, holding her tighter. "I'm sorry. I'm angry, but not with you, vixen. Never with you," he assured her. His voice was a soothing balm after the encounter.

He continued to hold her until she could separate her fingers from his tunic, the tips white from her punishing grip.

"I didn't mean to do anything," N'Réa explained.

"Quit it! This is not your fault." He took a long, deep breath, letting it out very slowly as he searched for calm somewhere. He shifted her weight to allow her to sit more comfortably, not quite ready to let her go, his hands curving around her waist, keeping her tucked into his chest. "Can you tell me what happened?"

She nodded, haltingly giving the short interlude between her and the stranger.

He shook his head like a dog. "It reeks in here of him now!" He cursed savagely.

The restraint Morgan had was noticeable. With his frame locked, it felt as though he held himself in tight chains to not find the man who had attacked her, wanting nothing more than to punish her tormentor.

She clutched at him, terrified he might try. "You can't! Not alone, he's powerful, Morgan!"

"She's right," Brooke agreed. She shivered delicately. "I have never felt this, and I've seen a few."

Morgan bowed his head over her, his voice hoarse with worry, rough with anger. "Why, N'Réa? Who is this guy? What does he want?"

Tears began to fall in earnest, hopeless, painful tears. "My father."

The stunned silence lay thick between the three.

"Your father?" he barked in shock. He soothed his hold when she squeaked in protest. "Sorry." He gave her an apologetic kiss. He closed his eyes and took another breath. He shook his head, frowning in distaste as he found the powerful scent filling the tent. "Let me try again. I thought you were an orphan."

Her heart fluttered painfully in her chest. "I am! I didn't lie to you. I was in homes until I was sixteen."

Brooke held a nail between her teeth. "If that is your dad, no wonder you're so capable." She paced with methodical steps, her brow furrowed in thought. "What does he want?"

N'Réa sat up, leaning against Morgan with her strength returning instead of lying across his lap like a child. "He said something about the power I have that my mother wouldn't give him." She made a raw sound. "If he wants more, he'll find me lacking. I thought I was going to pass out, keeping him on this side of my skull."

"There must be something we don't know, then," Brooke stated firmly. She stopped her pacing, giving N'Réa as calming a look as she could. "Is there anything you can remember about your parents, either heard of them or that you know?"

N'Réa shook her head very carefully. "Nothing. All my records are locked up. I only knew I had been placed because my parents had died." She shivered against Morgan's arm. "He said my mother had hidden me, kept me from him."

"Smart woman," Morgan muttered. His head turned as the sound of a horn reached them. "That's gate call. Let's get the hell out of here. I need to feel home before one more thing happens this weekend." He helped her stand, leaving one hand on her to keep her steady. She smiled weakly but couldn't argue. She still felt awful, teetering on her own two feet.

They tied down her tent, ensuring they had anything important to take with them, and headed for Duncan's World. Morgan wound an arm around her and held her close. "I'm getting really tired of people picking on you," he mumbled under his breath.

"You? What about me?" She pointed a thumb at herself. "I feel like a pin cushion. An overused one at that."

She felt the squeeze of his hand at her waist as he smiled down at her. "We'll take care of that. I promise you." His brows drew together. "We need to work out a plan, but we don't know our enemy."

"Before we go much further," Brooke cut in, "I want to talk to Aunt Jerry. She needs to meet N'Réa."

"Who's Aunt Jerry?"

Mitch smiled warmly. "The best aunt on the planet."

"If Mitch didn't love me, he'd date her," Brooke said, teasing the man she held on to.

"I would not!" he cried, playing offended.

"Why?" Morgan asked.

"Why wouldn't I date her?" Mitch asked with apparent confusion on his face, brow lifted in surprise.

Morgan laughed. "No, why Aunt Jerry? Last time I checked, she caused your problems with the amulet."

Brooke waved a hand. "Forgiven. Besides, she owes me big for getting rid of the demon."

N'Réa stumbled. "Demon?"

"Long story," three voices responded at once, followed by laughter. It helped to relieve the tension in the man who held her, and she let her own shoulders relax in answer.

"I think I want to hear it."

"We'll tell it on the way home," Mitch offered. "It's got a great ending." He pulled Brooke up to his side and dropped a kiss on her mouth. "A really great ending," he repeated.

N'Réa wrapped an arm around Morgan and let him lead her home.

Chapter Seventeen

N'Réa held Morgan's hand tightly as they walked up to the Victorian house the next morning to meet with Brooke, Mitch, and Aunt Jerry. She had spent the night with Morgan at his cabin and had never experienced so much tenderness for her well-being in her life.

He had washed every inch of her and her hair with caring hands, had fed her, and had held her all night. She'd slept without a single dream, a deep sleep with his arms braced around her. She hadn't realized how exhausting her weekend had been until she cuddled up against his warmth under the sheets of his bed. It had been wonderful to completely fall asleep with the night sounds of the woods floating in through the open windows of his room.

Waking up in his arms had been more sensual and invigorating than any morning she'd ever had. His hands had caressed her into wakefulness with slow, deliberate movements to bring her body awake, his lips and touch warm on her skin. She could still feel the strength of his body taking hers, the power of his passion as he tenderly loved her.

She glanced up when he squeezed her hand, and her sweeping gaze was captured by the undeniable heat in his gray eyes. She blushed deeply when she realized he knew exactly what it was she had been thinking about.

He laughed, a purely masculine sound as he swept her into his hold at the bottom step of the house, kissing her with an unmatched heat, her heart beating within her body wanting to feel him again. Her hands wound around his neck and held on fiercely.

He lifted gradually, his voice rich when he spoke. "Soon, vixen. I could stay with you all day and all night and still want you."

"We're being watched," she warned him.

He was instantly alert, his body hard in anticipation of a confrontation, his head up as he scanned the drive and the street surrounding them.

"From the house, Morgan." She gave him a sheepish smile. "They know we're here."

He grinned at himself, tension seeping from his frame. "Oh." He let his hands slide to her waist. "Let's go." He clasped her hand in his and led her up the porch. The door opened before he could knock.

"They're in the kitchen," N'Réa said evenly, the door closing silently behind them. She refused to let the door faze her. She was beginning to understand a little more about Brooke and instinctively knew Aunt Jerry would be much stronger if she had been Brooke's teacher.

Sunlight streamed in bright paths through the windows surrounding them as they found Brooke, Mitch, and another woman with beautiful, knee-length black hair.

"Morgan!" cried the woman cheerfully as they entered the kitchen. She was wearing a red shift and sheer gauze tunic overlay with silver bangles and bracelets sliding to make chiming sounds on her wrists as she lifted her hands to reach for his.

"Aunt Jerry," he said with a reserved smile and easy kisses on her cheeks.

She accepted them and then leaned back, giving him a critical stare. "You know, Roman has forgiven me. Why can't you?"

N'Réa actually saw his nostrils flare, his gaze falling flat. "You endangered Brooke and everyone else."

Aunt Jerry didn't so much as flinch. "And you have never made a mistake?" she asked, not censuring, only curious.

He looked for Brooke and N'Réa saw the genuine smile she offered her brother. "It is time, Morgan. I have forgiven her. She is family, and we need her help. Like it or not. N'Réa is in danger."

Those last words acted like a catalyst for Morgan. N'Réa witnessed the true depth of his bond for his family as he let his anger go. He looked down at his aunt. "You are right. We all make mistakes."

Aunt Jerry still held his strong hands in hers. "Morgan, you are the protector of the pack and I know you and Roman felt it was your responsibility to do what you could, but it was her destiny to fulfill. It is now time for yours."

N'Réa swallowed when she found Aunt Jerry's gaze settling on her, a silver gray that was startling in their sharp purity of color. "N'Réa, I am Aunt Jerry." She offered a slim hand and felt herself become wrapped in the other woman's warmth, a surge of power making her skin tingle.

Aunt Jerry held her hand in a peaceful clasp as her other hand rose, cupping them.

"I know you," N'Réa whispered, feeling the heat of their joined hands form and whip through her. Confused green eyes met silver gray and locked. "How do I know you?" Her mouth felt dry as she tried to remember.

"Open your mind, love." Her voice was sweet and melodious as N'Réa did as she asked. Images flooded her, too young to remember on her own. Images of a beautiful woman, of a strong man. Her parents. The pictures swirled, a ceremony, a priestess, candles, incense. Words, old words, chanting. A sense of agelessness. Her attention had been focused on the woman holding her and the one chanting.

A woman in red.

N'Réa's eyes widened. "You!" She cried as shock filtered through her, but the pictures kept coming. Of light, sound, peacefulness. Of belonging.

N'Réa began to sag and Morgan's strength was there to support her as he held her close, not letting her fall as the truth of her birth bombarded her. She felt a whisper of him in her mind, comforting in her confusion. Aunt Jerry's gaze never wavered, and neither blinked as their thoughts melded.

She inhaled sharply at the surge of power when her mind opened completely without warning, quaked as the floor seemed to shift, feeling as everything within became weightless. She had power, incredible power but had never known it, had never known how to confront it, to test it, to challenge herself with the knowledge of her own ability. She had stayed away from it, kept silent, fearing discovery, fearing for others because of her ability, because she didn't know how to control it or herself.

It was like a sudden exhalation, a breeze running through the kitchen as she focused again to find Aunt Jerry smiling warmly back at her. "Bun venit casă, fiică de la cerc." *Welcome home, daughter of the circle.*

"Jeralynna." She choked out the name, crumbling to her knees, holding her forehead to their clutched hands. She began to sob uncontrollably.

"What did you do?" Morgan demanded brusquely, reaching with tender hands to bring her back to her feet. N'Réa lifted a shaky hand to his arm, stilling his anger with a touch. His darkening gaze sought hers. "You have the worst effect on women, Aunt Jerry." His hands shook as he cradled her. "Are you all right?" he asked N'Réa, still shooting sparks at his aunt over her shoulder.

N'Réa nodded, absorbing what she had learned, had always known and never faced. Years of walls, piled upon walls, finally fell free. "I need tea," she managed to say through dry lips. Aunt Jerry waved her hand and there were mugs for everyone, as chairs pulled from the table.

"Please, sit," she said in a calm voice. "You've had a shock, love."

N'Réa made an inelegant sound, her throat sore and her gaze still watery. "If that was a shock, keep your epiphanies to yourself." But she didn't argue when Morgan sat and pulled her onto his lap rather than let her sit alone. Mitch and Brooke sat side by side and Aunt Jerry took a chair for herself, settling herself gracefully.

It was silent for several minutes as she sipped at her tea, Morgan's touch comforting as her realizations began to make sense, could be rationalized and accepted.

She set her cup down with a careful hand, a hand that amazingly didn't shake. "Wow," she finally said, breaking the silence. She looked up at the expectant faces surrounding her. She took a deep breath, knowing she had only one choice in her future. She sat straight, knowing she was protected, with family and friends, and felt their strength surrounding her. She felt doubly blessed never having known those emotions with such honest and open hearts before.

Evidently the day she and Brooke had *found* her ability and unleashed her inner knowledge had been the tip of a whole different iceberg, had only been the beginning to a depth she'd never even had a hint of. The very idea of what Jeralynna had brought to light stole the breath from her lungs, but the thought that came back to her was the loss she had felt, the caring woman of her memories, who had been absent from her life for too long.

"What really happened to my mother?" N'Réa asked. Her hand cupped the mug, a tactile sensation to prove to her disbelieving mind that this was reality, her reality. Morgan set his chin on her shoulder, his embrace warm and snug around her waist.

"She protected you by sending you away. As your father aged, he became distorted with his own power. Never doubt that he loved her. I knew them both for a long time," Aunt Jerry said, her voice warm and sincere as she spoke, filling the kitchen with the soft sound. "She began to fear for you when you were a baby. She loved your father, but she loved you more. Knowing what you were to become, she had to protect you from what he didn't see in their future. He never believed what he wanted for her to share with him would ultimately kill her. She did."

"That's why he felt so angry and sad at the same time," N'Réa said. "But if he caused her death, what does he think he will do to me?"

Aunt Jerry's expression turned thoughtful. "I believe he wants to control you, thinks he can save his soul through you."

"I won't let him hurt her again," Morgan stated coldly. "He's already done more than I should have allowed. He attacked her in broad daylight."

"She can't do this alone," Aunt Jerry told them. "She's untrained. He will use her confusion against her."

N'Réa swallowed, clearing a suddenly dry throat. "So...what exactly am I?"

"You are the daughter of a priestess, N'Réa. You are the daughter of a goddess's chosen one."

Brooke inhaled sharply. "Oh, my! No wonder I felt so connected to you from the beginning."

"A priestess?" she said weakly. Her anxious gaze circled the table. "Uh, what does that mean?"

"It means you have ancient magic, ancient history," Aunt Jerry explained. "You are one of the last of a strong line of women. Myself, Brooke, and now you amount to some of the strongest casters. I had no idea you were still even alive. When your parents left, I lost several connections because of my own problems." She let out a regretful sigh. "I should have kept in touch. You would have had the training you will need for this challenge in your path."

"There is nothing to regret, Jeralynna," N'Réa assured her.

"Why do family fear her name, and we don't?" Mitch whispered to Brooke, who laughed, stopping before she had choked on her tea completely.

Aunt Jerry gave them all a humorless smile. "Because during a rash moment, I turned their father into an ass for a day. I felt if he wanted to act like one, he should look like it too. I doubt he ever forgave me for it," she said with a slight twinkle in her eye. "Their mother thought it was hysterically funny, of course. Pompous male that he was, but that took some of the starch out of him."

"I thought it was just a family story," Morgan said.

"A lot of them are true," Aunt Jerry said with an unrepentant air. "I was a wild child for decades." She took a long sip of her tea, giving everyone time to assimilate everything that had transpired so far.

"So what do I do about my father?" N'Réa asked cautiously. "I don't want to hurt anyone."

"I know you don't, child." Aunt Jerry ran a hesitant finger over her cup. "But you've had no training. You're a telepath, an empathic, a diviner, and Goddess only knows what else. I barely touched you to find your truth, and even I felt the power you own. He must have always had some sense of what you are."

N'Réa flicked out a tongue to dry lips. "He had said he had been following me, looking for me for a long time. He can link with me," she said, frightened, her eyes shifting as she remembered that.

Brooke set a steadying hand on her. "He can't follow you here. I cloaked our departure. The farther you are from him, the harder it will be for him to link with you. It is exhausting to share strength that way, over a large distance."

"How long before you are expected back in California?" Aunt Jerry asked as she sipped again at her still steaming cup.

"Saturday morning at the latest, but we're not going back if it will put her at risk," Morgan stated firmly. "I won't endanger her."

"But they are counting on you!" N'Réa cried, her hands reaching for his at her waist. "All of them!"

"You are more important than some duel. I still don't know how I got mixed up in that."

She wanted to pinch him for his scoffing tone.

One of Jeralynna's finely shaped dark eyebrows shot up. "You haven't figured it out yet, Morgan? Men can be so dense," she groused with a twinkle in her shining eyes. Brooke and N'Réa giggled, then fought for innocent looks between them.

"Why do I suddenly feel outnumbered?" he muttered. "All right, Aunt Jerry. Explain yourself."

Mitch's expression became enlightened, answering for her. "I think I get it. You explained it when we first met. In our lives, our mates are our equal in every way. If she has ancestry beyond time, then Morgan would have some ancient connection as well."

"I applaud you, Mitch. I knew you would be worthy of Brooke," Aunt Jerry said, smiling at them all. "Yes, that is true. Morgan's soul is as ancient as N'Réa's. If she looks deeply enough, she could even find the true nature of his heart. He is a fighter, a protector. He is a man of honor and strength, compassion and loyalty."

"I'm still in the room," Morgan retorted.

N'Réa pressed her head into his. "Oh, quit it. I knew you've been wanting to know yourself, so stop acting so surprised."

He looked up at her, his gaze bottomless. "You knew?"

"Yeah; it has to do with being mates," she said with an unaffected, careless shrug, hiding her voice behind the actions. "Remember? You kept throwing it at me all weekend." She tried to keep it light, tried to express it smoothly so he understood. She could tell by the heat in his gaze that he did. "Just remember, I don't take orders well, and I don't fight fair."

He cleared his throat and shifted beneath her, his adamant arousal pressing against her, showing his possessive wants at her declaration. "I do remember," he replied, his voice neutral even as his gaze fired at her in primal possession.

She blinked to break the spell and took a deep breath. She turned her attention to Aunt Jerry. "So, what do I do? I don't think I could hurt him. I don't want to kill anyone."

"Maybe you won't have to hurt him at all," Brooke said. "Could she use compulsion on him?"

Aunt Jerry shook her head, a frown forming on her brow. "No, I don't think so." She looked over at N'Réa. "Did he feel truly evil? Did you sense any good in him at all?"

"I felt compassion when he mentioned my mother, but that was it. I didn't feel anything kind about him.

It wasn't exactly an experience I had any control over."
N'Réa snuggled a little closer to Morgan's comforting
warmth, trying not to think about the fact that this was
her father they were discussing.

Aunt Jerry's gaze turned shrewd. "I wonder," she
mumbled. She tapped a thoughtful finger to her
mouth. "Maybe we can do this without harming
anyone." She looked directly at N'Réa. "Call him here,
on the condition he has to forfeit his powers and accept
our hospitality, in the name of the goddess. If he
refuses, we have the right to defend ourselves."

Morgan's hand slapped the table with a
resounding boom, making her jump in his lap. "No!"
He glared at the other women. "He wants to hurt her!
He has already been in her mind and knows all of our
secrets. I won't let her be harmed again!"

N'Réa ignored him. "Do you think he'll do it?
Come here unprotected?"

"It will be a show of faith on both sides. The man
I used to know was strong, dominant, and powerful. I
think he is wounded and sees you as his salvation."
Aunt Jerry stared down at the cup between her pale,
slim hands.

N'Réa felt a low sound emanating from Morgan's
body. She shifted to see him better. "Please, Morgan?
If we can do this without hurting anyone..." She
wanted to hold him close, but he was tight, angry, and
fighting his urge to protect her, to keep her safe.

His teeth ground together as he fought against his
own nature. "Fine!" He glowered at them all. "But I am
against this. I saw her after his attack. I felt it!" he
nearly shouted. His jaw clenched, going white. "I will
not stand by and let him hurt her."

"No one will let her be harmed," Brooke said
evenly. "She is not alone in this."

"It goes against everything I am to stand aside and let this happen," Morgan said, thunderheads brewing in his gaze.

"For me?" N'Réa asked. She turned toward him, her hand on his jaw, soothing his torment. "I don't want to hurt him. I'm not capable of it, for one. I don't have any idea what to do with what I learned today."

"But he attacked you!"

"I'm aware of what he did," she said. "But if there's a way…"

His gaze was ominous. "I will warn you, all of you, if he harms you in any way, I will do something about it."

"I wouldn't expect less from you, Morgan," Aunt Jerry said in agreement. "But I used to know the man he was. I hope he can still be reasoned with."

N'Réa felt the immense tension in Morgan's body everywhere they touched, from shoulder to shin. She could taste on her tongue his adamant distrust of openly confronting the man who had hurt her, of inviting him like a guest to share their home. He didn't trust the other man to not try something.

"Please, Morgan. I can't hurt someone." She sought his turbulent gaze, pleading.

He let his forehead fall to her shoulder, cradling her into his chest, his breathing harsh and deep. *"I trust you, N'Réa, but you are my life. I can't lose you."*

"You won't. I have family for the first time in my life. A real family and their absolute support. I have you. Feel what you mean to me." Her eyes grew damp as she let her heart pour forth for him. She knew the instant he found her secret as everything about him reacted, finding the feelings she had been keeping hidden from him. His gaze swept to hers, glassy with wonder and awe. *"You are my air, my heart, my life. I wouldn't do this if I didn't think it couldn't be done.*

I believe Aunt Jerry knows something about him that could keep this from getting out of hand. I will fight if I have to, but you have to understand, I have no training! I'm helpless beyond my own experiences."

He didn't move at all from where he faced N'Réa, his insistent gaze never wavering from the woman in his hold. "Aunt Jerry, I want your promise right now, when this is over and we have found out what her father wants, that you will train this woman to within an inch of her life. I will not have her defenseless again." It was spoken as a request, but the command was easily heard.

"Happily." Aunt Jerry breathed as if a great hurdle had been crossed. "All right, child," she told N'Réa. "Call to him and give the invitation. You can mention me if you like. He probably doesn't realize whose toes he's stepped on by messing with you." Those words bloomed with warmth throughout her — complete acceptance.

She gave Aunt Jerry a grateful, if weak, smile. "Thank you. I hope I can do this," she muttered even as Morgan held her tighter. She enfolded his hands in hers and bowed her head to concentrate.

Chapter Eighteen

Morgan watched and waited as she stilled. Even her breathing slowed as she concentrated, her brows pulling together. She took a sharp breath, paling, and his hold tightened automatically, her heart racing beneath the curve of his arm, but she smiled in the next instant and released an exaggerated grunt shortly after.

Her head lifted, green eyes flashing with wonder and a touch of amusement. "He'll be here within the hour. He agrees to the conditions and was surprised to know you were still around."

"Did he send you any ill will?" Aunt Jerry asked.

"I woke him up." She snorted. "He wasn't happy about it, and I think he believed I was going to walk on over and let him do what he wants, but I set him straight right up front. He laughed. I get the feeling he's a very sly, old fox."

Aunt Jerry laughed to herself over her tea. "You could say that."

"So why did he attack her so strongly?" Morgan asked.

"He was testing her," Aunt Jerry said. "He's a very dominant male, likes to make demands and order people around."

"Gee, who does that remind me of?" N'Réa laughed.

She shrieked, then giggled when Morgan pinched her bottom.

"Did you feel threatened this time?" he asked, his fingers already caressing where he had punished her.

"No, actually I didn't. It wasn't exactly friendly, but he was amicable. I hope he wasn't bluffing," she said, a little touch of worry coloring her tone.

"We'll know soon enough. He won't be able to enter the house if he holds any ill feelings. I have my own protections," Brooke said. "Unless he's invited in directly, he won't be able to walk in the door at all."

"Oh!" N'Réa gasped, then ducked her head.

"What is it?" he asked her curiously.

"I invited him into the tent," she said, guilt coloring every syllable.

He rubbed his head against hers, still feeling the shot of wonder at what he had discovered in her thoughts minutes before. "You didn't know who he was. And you have a business to run. How could you have known?" He inhaled the scent beneath her ear, enjoying the silk of her hair and the warmth of her skin as he held her close.

"Well, if we have some time, I'm starving. Who's ready for breakfast?" Brooke said, standing to gather together ingredients at the stove.

"I have to get to the station. If you need me, though, let me know," Mitch said, standing also. "I'll eat when I'm out of the shower." He dropped a quick kiss on Brooke and headed upstairs.

"So do you want to know?" she whispered into his ear, a sexy, breathy touch that had his blood singing again. His fingers dug into her jean-clad thighs.

"About who I may have been?" Morgan cleared his throat and his thoughts at the same time when Aunt Jerry shot him a smirk. So he was obvious; he didn't care. "I guess it isn't as important now, but it does make sense." He turned to catch his aunt's stare. "So we are all equal to each other in capacity. Is that why Mitch was able to blood bond and Del could wrap Roman and his temper around her finger?"

"He'll never admit it," she said with an airy laugh. "But yes. Bram is equal to Selene's compassion. Two halves that make the one whole."

"Could you tell me about my mother?" N'Réa asked with a wistful note.

Aunt Jerry nodded with a light of memory in her eyes. "She was a graceful, energetic, compassionate woman of the arts. She had incredible ability. She was a priestess and a chosen one. The goddess blessed her with you. I never knew, even as close as we were, how deep her abilities were. It looks like you have acquired from both of your parents. Not easily done."

"What will happen to me?" N'Réa twisted in his lap, and he sucked air through his teeth. She gave him an apologetic smile, but he refused to give her freedom when she tried to stand.

"After this, I imagine Morgan is right. You will need training. Although Brooke is as trained as myself now, and you wouldn't have to spend too long in Belgium away from home."

"I couldn't ask — " She started to protest, but Brooke waved her hand in dismissal.

"Done; no arguments allowed."

Morgan smiled and ducked his head, seeing her want to argue rising quickly. "Get used to it," he told her, chuckling against her shoulder. "The whole family is like that." His laughter warmed when all she could do was shake her head in bewilderment.

He remained by her side as they talked, not wanting to let her stray too far. He didn't trust her father or his intentions. He had really hurt her the day before when he had confronted her, and Morgan refused to allow anyone to harm her again. N'Réa was filled with compassion and tenderness. The fact that this was her flesh-and-blood father only made it harder for her.

Morgan, however, had no such qualms. He'd felt her fear when she'd been touched at the arena and her pain when he'd tried to open her mind. The man had an agenda. He wanted something from N'Réa, and Morgan was not going to let him take it, but he had to be patient. Aunt Jerry did know something, of that he was certain. She never gave everything up front.

He bit off the disgusted sound before it erupted, remembering in the recent months how that very fact had affected Brooke and had changed her life forever. How much would this change N'Réa? Was she strong enough if it came down to having to fight?

He couldn't help but worry for her. She was a slight woman, strong in spirit and mind, but so much had happened to her in the weeks since they'd met.

"I'm fine," she whispered into his thoughts. He felt the sensual caress of her fingers against his skin, and his gaze shot up. Her hands were on the table as she talked with quiet energy, with Brooke standing at the counter next to Aunt Jerry. She hadn't moved at all, yet he had felt her touch as real and warm as flesh to his skin.

He patted her shoulder, then stood to talk to Brooke, letting N'Réa take over the chair. "Could you do me a favor?" he asked at her shoulder as she scrambled eggs. The sizzle of bacon made his mouth water.

"Sure," she said, snapping her fingers to make the bacon flip over. She put down sausage and poured the eggs into another pan.

"You remember the ring Mom said I could have?"

Brooke's dark eyes widened. *"The* ring?"

He nodded. "It's at their house. Could you bring it here?"

Brooke smiled knowingly, her face glowing as she realized what he was asking. "Of course. I knew you meant it, but I didn't think you would want to use the ring, Morgan. You never were the one to pay attention to our heritage."

He shrugged. "I changed my mind. It's in the safe on the second floor. She told me she would leave it there for whenever I wanted it."

Brooke shot a look over her shoulder, glancing at N'Réa. "You know, it almost feels appropriate that it would be going to someone like N'Réa. That ring is very special."

"Mom told me the story." He leaned against the counter and grabbed a piece of cooling bacon as she moved more to drain on a plate. "I think that is why I want to do it. She deserves something like the ring. She's something else," he said.

"You're in love with her," she stated easily. "You want her to have the best you can give."

"In love?" His hand froze before him. His stomach clenched. "I don't think so. I don't need love. I found my mate, I made my vow. The rest isn't necessary." He shoved the bacon into his mouth, not wanting to expound on more.

"Then you have no reason to give her the ring," she informed him, turning to her cooking with an impatient glance. "That ring is to be passed on, by you, to your mate, who I shouldn't have to remind you, you should be in love with. If you don't love her, then the ring will lose its significance and most of its power. Even the pendant Roman gave Del has energy, but you are the firstborn. You have a right to pass down the ring."

"That's why I can't love her," he said deliberately. "I am the firstborn. I won't turn my back on the pack for anyone."

"And you are a living, breathing idiot." She scowled at him, her sparking gaze narrowing at him in disappointed anger. "You are hiding behind that self-made title."

"I am not!" He stood straight and glared down at her. "She loves me. That is enough."

"For how long? Really? For how long can she live knowing you refuse to care, when you hold her apart from you?" She dished food onto a platter with short, jerky strokes.

"I will honor my vow. I will do as I have promised."

"It means nothing if you refuse to love her," she said. It was in her gaze, the utter disappointment in him, the stark knowledge that he was not playing fair. That he was hiding behind his responsibility to the pack and to the family. "I will not get the ring until you care enough to love her, Morgan. It will be pointless and become useless. That ring is our heritage, a birthright. You do not have the right to disregard it." She moved stiffly to the dining table and slammed the platter down, silencing the talking pair to storm away from him.

"Tea?" Aunt Jerry's voice broke the taut silence a moment later.

"Later." Morgan stalked from the room in the opposite direction. He stopped to stare out the large windows to the front yard, breathing heavily, feeling her condemnation still. Brooke was wrong! He didn't need to love. He hadn't even wanted a mate, for what that was worth, but now he had N'Réa and a responsibility to her, to protect and cherish and keep her happy.

He had never asked for this, damn it! He raked an agitated hand through his hair. He heard as Mitch came downstairs and sat with the women to eat. He should too; he was starving. But he couldn't make his legs move. How could he face N'Réa when she had given herself so freely, so beautifully to him? She hadn't spoken the words, but he had found the true feelings in her thoughts. She had accepted him completely. He had found the warmth she carried for him inside of her. She had given him permission to search, to find it, to comfort him when he couldn't trust her father or their plan.

His gaze followed Mitch when he walked out a few minutes later, waving as he left for the station in his car. Brooke would be alone for three days while he was gone. For the first time, he realized how much that bothered him. None of them should be alone, least of all the girls. They should always be protected.

Her scent reached him before her arms encircled his waist.

"You are a stubborn man. Don't fight with Brooke. She means well and loves you." She pressed her cheek against his shoulder. "I, most of all, know how much it affects you to feel challenged, to feel helpless. I've been there, with you." Her touch was enveloping as she held him close to her. He heard the beating of her heart, the pulse of her body against his. "I love you, and I'm not giving up on you."

He was torn between crushing her into his embrace and needing to push her away to prove to himself that he didn't need what she was so easily giving. "How can you say that? You heard every word. This isn't any large surprise."

She wound herself around him until she stood in front of him, still holding him, pushing against him, against the ridge of his erection. No one could make him respond like she could. His breathing was sharp and ragged by the time she stopped moving. Her gaze was intense, a luscious green of wrenching emotion. His hands lifted to her trim waist without effort and he pulled her tighter still, wanting to be buried deep inside of her and feel whole.

"That's why I'm not giving up," she said, pressing hot kisses to the side of his jaw, feeling her signature touch on his thoughts. "I told you, lust dies, but at least I have a chance so long as we have this." He smiled when she purred, rubbing against his chest, her nipples hard beneath her shirt. "And believe me, I am very willing to wait you out if I get this regularly." Her voice was hot, sultry, seductive. He obeyed when she wrapped her hands through his hair and pulled her down to him. *"And I'm not above using it either,"* she telepathized, taunting him.

Her lips met his with a possessive force, making his world spin. Her tongue traced his mouth, and his arms encircled her. She teased him, made him ache with need, made him want. His tongue met hers and returned the wonderfully sweet torture. *"Would you ever leave me?"*

He could sense her hesitation, and she pulled away from him. "You once told me you would die. I think I understand it better now. I don't want to live without you, but if you remain apart, I will die anyway," she said sadly. "I don't want to think about it right now." She stepped back, her touch gone, and he felt absurdly alone, bereft. Her eyes drifted closed to snap open with an expectant look. "He's here." And without any great surprise, a knock sounded on the door a few seconds later.

"N'Réa, if anything happens, don't put yourself in danger," he warned her, pulling her gaze to his. "Let Brooke and Aunt Jerry handle him. I don't trust him."

She nodded, her emotions and thoughts evident in her pensive expression. He crossed the room to open the door and stood face-to-face with her father.

"Hello," the older man said easily, his gaze sweeping over Morgan's head to the room behind him. There was a chilled aura about the man, a swirling coolness that reminded Morgan of yesterday in the tent.

Morgan held the door open, aware N'Réa and Aunt Jerry were watching.

"André!" Aunt Jerry said warmly. She walked forward with her hands out, stopping to let him come forward. He walked right through the door, and Morgan felt the quiet sigh of relief brush his skin as N'Réa let it slip past her lips. Morgan closed the door as André clasped his aunt's hands.

"Jeralynna!" His dark gaze traveled over her in appreciation. "What a welcome surprise." Morgan moved with a sliding, stealthy step to stand with N'Réa, his hand possessively and protectively on her hip. He wanted to push her behind him, to make her run but knew she wouldn't leave.

Brooke descended the stairs at a regal pace, dressed the same as Aunt Jerry in a crimson shift and gauze tunic. A united front. Morgan met her gaze. She would fight with him if it came down to it. He nodded once in acceptance but focused on the stranger in their midst, every muscle tensed.

"So, tell me," Aunt Jerry was saying. "What are you trying to do to the poor girl, André? You've scared her and angered me."

André released her hands. "You never were one to wade through pleasantries," he said in a lightly mocking tone. He finally turned and faced N'Réa fully for the first time. Morgan felt her reaction. A mixture of fear, apprehension, and hope.

"I thought you were dead," N'Réa said cautiously. "Why did you hurt me?" Her voice was small, a child's heartbroken query.

André's expression changed little. "I needed to know if your ability was as strong as I need."

Morgan tightened his hold. "For?"

André's smile was stiff, while his forbidding, cold gaze raked over Morgan. "You have no reason to trust me. You are right to keep her at your side." He shrugged, an elegant movement. "But I came as she asked. I am unprotected."

Morgan shot a look at Aunt Jerry. "He's telling the truth. He's dismissed his powers to be here," she informed them all. Brooke had moved to stand next to Aunt Jerry, a serene, calm expression on her features.

"What do you want with me?" N'Réa asked in a firm voice that betrayed nothing more.

"I made a grave mistake with your mother," André admitted. "I need her to come back to me, and you are capable."

Aunt Jerry's fists tightened even as her face remained impassive. "You would sacrifice your daughter for your folly, André? You were once a better man."

His laugh was low and unkind. "No longer. I have suffered for my mistake!" he snapped. N'Réa gasped as a flash of icy wind swarmed the room. Morgan wrapped her completely into his embrace, soothing. "I would sacrifice the world to bring her back," he told them, his eyes blazing.

"You need healing," Brooke said calmly. "She will not return to you. You are not the man she loved."

"How dare you!" he shouted, challenging Brooke.

"I dare because I am who I am," she said simply. "You have let your guilt and your anger turn your soul black. You have harmed the one thing she ever felt you could threaten. You are obsessive. You have done many things, André, but you never meant to hurt Gloria. I know it, she knows it." Her face was still expressionless, breathlessly pure. "She is with me," she informed them in a quiet tone. "She has brought you here, given you one last chance to make amends, to be healed. If you cannot find it in your heart, then she will remain forever in the land you sent her to in your greed for more. You must acknowledge your limits."

Morgan followed this interchange with bated breath. He couldn't even begin to understand how Brooke knew what to say.

"I will take her. I don't need healing!" André shouted and reached to pull N'Réa to him. "She is my flesh and blood. She will do as I bid her!"

Aunt Jerry threw out a hand, and Morgan felt the heat of a shield surround them. "Do that again, André, and you will feel it," she warned him, her tone deathly calm. "If Brooke says Gloria is with her, then do not tempt me to send you to her!"

"You are nothing!" André swore at her. "N'Réa is mine. She will do this."

Morgan was stunned as Aunt Jerry began to laugh, an unworried, humorous sound. "André, André. You always were the arrogant one," she teased him. "How did Gloria put up with that ego of yours?" She walked forward. "Either let us heal you, or you will be banished and N'Réa will never know her father. Consider your answer carefully," she told him on a silken threat, silver-gray eyes flashing in warning. "There is more involved than your desire to be reunited. It is never as simple as that," she reminded him.

"And you never tell everything until you feel it is right," he returned, his bottomless gaze still blazing in fury. "I have no reason to trust you."

"Yes, you do," N'Réa said. "Because I do, implicitly. And you did once when you stood before her and made my blessing at the altar of faith." She closed her eyes, dipped her head, and Morgan felt the air leave her body.

Chapter Nineteen

N'Réa reached out to her father again, felt his shock at the ease in which she could enshroud his thoughts, his mind. With each stretch of her mind, it became easier. Like a dam had opened, she felt the surge of her own possibility within. She shared her found memories with him, the love she had felt held in her mother's arms, the joy she had experienced. She felt the supporting touch of Morgan and his strength as she joined minds with André. She didn't let the bleak despair of his soul frighten her. She ignored the anger in his thoughts, delving deeper until she found the spark of the man that was still good, a faint glow that had been his only allowance to even meet with them. He would have never agreed to come unprotected if he had truly turned, if his soul had been corrupted beyond repair.

She breathed life into him and again felt her father's sharp indrawn breath. She felt a gentle breeze flutter across her skin, a warmth of encouragement. Her family still stood with her.

"You need healing," she said simply, her head still bowed as she searched through him. "I can see the light of your soul and can feel your pain. I can help you, but not by decree."

"You saw your own mother's death," he sneered, fighting her on both fronts, within and without.

"It was a warning, and you know it. I am no more to blame than I was for my foster uncle's death. You had the opportunity to change the card's will. Instead, you embraced it and lay the blame elsewhere. You are tainted." She released a breath and raised her head, leaning into the solid heat of Morgan's shoulder. She found André's intense eyes and held him, embraced him as she had held his thoughts. "You must accept your own failures. You cannot force me. You made a bargain with a devil and found the payment was too high. He still holds you in his grip. It is he who does not wish the healing. You have become a puppet but are too strong to allow him to rule you completely."

She saw the benevolent smile on Aunt Jerry's face and knew without asking that she had passed a large test. She had discovered the force behind André's behavior.

André bowed his head, seeming to age before them in his grief. "I did, and I have paid the price. I still do not have Gloria."

She offered an understanding smile. "And you think trading me after you have gotten what you want from me will suffice?" Morgan's arms tightened fractionally, but she kept her touch light on his arms where he held her. She no longer felt threatened by the man before her. He gradually relaxed as she pressed the truth into Morgan's thoughts. "I can guarantee you will not win in the bargain. Ask Brooke how deals with demons work," she remarked, remembering the tale she had heard on their way back to Oregon.

She urged her father to look at her, to see her compassion for the man he had once been, could be again, if he took the step. "It is up to you, but I will not allow you to hurt any of my family."

"You couldn't stop me if you wanted to, N'Réa. You don't have a mean bone in your body," André jeered.

She concentrated on a sunbeam streaming through the window. It shimmered in the room, elongating, strengthening until it was a rope of heat and energy. She wrapped it snugly around his body, surprising even herself as the sunbeam continued to surround him. André followed its movement, a flicker of acknowledgment in his gaze as she stretched her boundaries. She couldn't hurt him, but she could find other ways to hinder or restrain him.

"I think I just did," she pointed out. "But you're right. I don't want to hurt you, and nothing good would come out of a conflict. So that leaves only one choice. You let us help you." His expression tightened. "I've seen the darkness on your soul, and I know we can bring back the man who loved not only my mother, but me, before his quest for power grew to be insatiable."

The silence hung in the room as the ribbon of light gradually fell away from him, his gaze never leaving hers, never flickering to the other women in the room. "You know I can help you. Turning me over is not your only option," she told him, meaning every word. "I would like to know my father and my mother."

She released her hold on Morgan and stood straight, still feeling his apprehension like a band around her. His arms fell away when the shield protecting them disappeared.

"You can't save me," he whispered thickly. "My soul is chained." His dark eyes became haunted. "I made the bargain, and I lost."

N'Réa shook her head. "Why did you name me as you did?" she countered with a confidence she barely felt. Sheer bravado, but it sounded believable. "No one messes with what is mine. Tell me you want to try, and we will. Tell me you still love my mother, and she will help. Tell me you still have a shred of the man within who held me as a babe with a tenderness only a father would recognize, and we will destroy the chain."

She felt Morgan's hands on her waist again as André grimaced, his mouth pulling into a fine white line, fighting an urge that had controlled him for far too long.

"You could die!" André breathed slowly, shaking his head, his inner torment evident.

"I won't," she assured him. "I've learned a lot from my family; they protect their own. I made my vow to Morgan, and he accepted me as I have accepted him." Her gaze flashed at him in warning. "But never discount that I will strike if you speak of their secrets. I know you have seen. He is mine and mine to protect as I am his."

André met her steely stare. "Your mother would be very proud of you, N'Réa." His voice softened, and he turned subtly toward Aunt Jerry. "Is there a way? Can it be done? Can the order be broken?" He asked it almost inaudibly, as if he were unsure if he could be overheard.

"Do you truly wish it, André? It can't be half desired. You must want it regardless if Gloria can or cannot be returned." Aunt Jerry waved a hand, and the curtains closed to give them privacy. "You know he will fight, and you will pay the price. You've been under his influence for a long time, and even you will fight it."

"I may die," he said simply. "But even that would be preferable to feeling this emptiness I was left with when he promised me more for Gloria. She was too easy on me." He looked deeply at N'Réa. "She knew what I was asking, and I failed her. When it was over, I was chained and she was gone. I lost thrice on that bargain."

N'Réa nodded and walked forward, her gaze compassionate to his dilemma. She held out her hand.

"Show me," she simply said and waited until he rested his hand in hers.

She opened her mind and instantly was flooded with pain and anger, disbelief and guilt. Pictures of her mother bled into her. Dark, mysterious, and breathtakingly beautiful. Her lids slid closed as a hurricane of information filled her mind. Years and years of inability to correct a wrong, deceived and influenced because of the trade he had made, unknowing of the consequences. Nightmares of deeds done under the influence of the chain holding him. Sorrow at his loss, remorse at his own actions, a need that no longer made sense for the reasoning behind it. A greed that no longer made sense.

She wet dry lips, speaking in a faraway voice. "You were not entirely guilty for your mistake. You were deceived into making the decision. I can feel the trail on your memories. Someone guided you into this, suggested using her to obtain the power you thought she could give you, that you think I can give you. I can't feel the weight of the spirit that binds you, but you did not do this on your own."

She weaved a little and immediately felt Morgan's secure arms. She dropped André's hand and let Morgan hold her. She swallowed down the sick feeling the stain on his soul had created on her tongue. "They really think I would follow as easily." She laughed at the assumption. "They don't know me," she said, feeling a little breathless from her efforts. "I don't follow anyone."

She felt Morgan's silent chuckle in her thoughts. "And that's the truth," he said for everyone else's benefit.

N'Réa faced the other two women. "He can be released. For some reason, the hold isn't very strong right now."

André told them, "After this morning, I let him believe you were willing. He is biding his time."

"Who are we working against, then?" Brooke asked, still holding a calm and serene expression. "Belphagor wouldn't dare, not after the last battle. You would think it would have learned to pass the message that you can't mess with this family and expect to get away with it."

Aunt Jerry smiled ruefully. "You would think so."

André shook his head. "I don't know a name for him."

"Well, that does complicate things a little," Aunt Jerry said. "N'Réa, search him again and find the end of the chain. Find the one who holds his soul."

She nodded, saying, "Let's sit down for this." She glided to the overstuffed couch she had admired during her last stay and let André sit beside her. Brooke began to gather herbs and scents and candles, placing them throughout the room.

"Will this work?" he asked, for the first time sounding apprehensive and a touch hopeful. "I don't deserve this."

"No, you don't, but it isn't in me to judge you." N'Réa reached for his hands again. She glanced up and found Morgan's gray, watchful gaze completely attuned to her. "I've grown past that part of my life." She sent a wave of warmth over Morgan and saw his irises react, a smile softening his otherwise harsh and concerned mouth. N'Réa bowed her head and emptied her mind one more time. "Don't resist me," she warned him. "I'm still winging this."

"I'll do my best," he offered and squeezed her hands.

* * * *

A thick feeling of apprehension and dread poured over Morgan's heart, tightening his lungs with the harshness of a clawed fist. The last search had been very draining on her, and that had no purpose. This time she was deliberately looking for the one who held her father enchained and enthralled. Brooke started to light the candles scattered around the room, soft scents wafting around them, relaxing him as the flames rose and wavered in the small drafts of the old house.

He watched the entire scene unfold and couldn't help but wonder about André's purpose. Was he testing her again, wanting to know how much she was capable of? Was he purposely draining her, making her complacent?

He felt the bitter metallic taste of fear on his tongue but forced himself to remain composed and relaxed as she continued to sit motionless, her head bowed with her flowing hair covering her body and shoulders, her father's hand in hers in a tender hold. It amazed him that she had released her fear of him. Morgan still wanted retribution for the pain he had caused N'Réa.

He stiffened when she moaned and paled, her hands cradling André's larger one in hers, but Morgan didn't dare move. Brooke and Aunt Jerry were both watching with a keen interest to what was transpiring between the two. André paled a little and a grimace formed on his face, N'Réa barely breathing for several heartbeats. Her head moved slowly from one side to the other, her brows pulling down in concentration.

He saw her strain, the drain of her strength as she remained in her searching state. He barely dared to breathe himself.

Suddenly, the room seemed to dim and chilled with an icy rush. He heard the distant crash of thunder as a storm began to move in. He reached a hand to peek out a window, sensing the utter stillness before the storm, the malevolent feeling pushing forward. The black and gray clouds roiled and billowed with a fierce wind that didn't touch anything on the ground. Lightning crisscrossed the dark mass. It was not a usual cold front storm.

A fine sweat broke out on his skin, and he knew what was coming in that storm with clarity. "N'Réa! Stop!" he shouted.

He leaped across the room, yanking her from André's hold. A crack of thunder sounded directly over the house when her fingers slid free. Lightning struck right outside, and the windows shook with the force of the energy wave as it rolled over the house. Morgan landed on the floor, her body cradled protectively against his chest. André was breathing heavily, slumped against the couch as a torrent of rain slammed into the house.

Aunt Jerry and Brooke shared a speculative look. N'Réa began to shake in reaction and exhaustion, and he held her tighter. No one spoke for several minutes until the storm began to abate and eventually drift away.

Mugs of tea appeared instantly around the room. Morgan stood on shaking legs and carried N'Réa to a large chair, falling weakly onto it with her on his lap to rest in his embrace. Her face was still pale, and she was breathing in a shaking pattern. He ran a soothing hand over her hair, willing her to relax.

Brooke touched a hand against her forehead. N'Réa's breathing evened out, and her cheeks drew color again. She did the same for André, who seemed as weak. A few minutes later, he opened his eyes and found Morgan's hate-filled gaze without hesitation.

"I didn't do that!"

"I know you didn't," Aunt Jerry said in a consoling tone. She and Brooke settled themselves into chairs of their own. Morgan wished he could share in her confidence.

He felt the chaotic hurl of her thoughts, her heart still pounding beneath his hold. He formed himself around her, for the first time feeling completely out of his element.

"Give her a minute, Morgan," Brooke said, a calm inflection to her words to help alleviate his concerns. "She pushed harder than she realized."

"She's exhausted." Morgan's hand shook as he stroked her body. "What happened?" he finally asked, unable to sit still and not know, not to have a crime to pin on the other man.

"She drew his attention," André said in a shaky, deep voice. "I had no idea how much she could do." He visibly paled again, shaking his head with hard movements. "I can't do what he wants. She shielded me for as long as she could. She didn't have to," he said humbly, taking the tea Aunt Jerry handed to him. "I can take his punishments. She kept him from sensing what she was doing, covering my own thoughts with hers."

"You were draining her," Morgan bit out, his gaze narrowing.

"I wasn't," he argued back. "He found her through me." He shook his head once, letting it fall back tiredly. "I'm so sorry," he whispered to everyone and no one.

"Who?" Morgan forced his palms out of their clenched hold, his only concern keeping the woman on his lap safe and whole.

N'Réa's voice was a whispery sound, soft and magical on his skin. "Not a who," she said, her eyes still closed, her hands grasping him in comfort. "A what."

"Can you drink some of this?" Morgan held the steaming cup up for her and let her take shallow sips. Her entire body rippled as delayed exhaustion ravaged her in its hold. She whimpered once and fell asleep between one breath and the next. He took a quick drink himself, then set the cup down, his chin resting on the top of her head.

"So now what?" He still kept an eye on André, but he looked as worn out as N'Réa.

"We release the hold on André," Brooke said simply. "He's proven he's still in possession of some portion of his soul, or the attack would have been instantaneous. He would have called immediately for whoever has the bond on him."

"I never called for him," he repeated. His head still rested on the comfort of the leather couch, his eyes closed. "But it wouldn't have been hard to feel the energy she possesses through me. I tasted it yesterday and felt driven to have it. Like I did with Gloria," he said with bitterness. "But I am powerless here except for a few simple protections. I knew with you and her, I wouldn't be hurt. I never lost my faith in you, Jeralynna." It was a solemn statement, and Morgan could hear the sincerity in his words.

"She needs to rest. She's not used to being used like this," Morgan said firmly. "She had a very trying weekend. And forgive me for being unkind, but you didn't help any."

André gave Morgan a ruefully sad smile. "No, I'm sure I didn't. I scared the hell out of her. Please," he said, lifting up to meet Morgan's gaze. "Accept my apology for harming her. Without the need to possess her magic drilling against my conscience, I can acknowledge the poor manner of judgment I made."

"Greed?" Brooke asked. She shot a furtive glance to Aunt Jerry. "It couldn't be Belphagor again, could it?"

"If it is, then this was done many long years before, and it couldn't have known the two families would be tied together this far in the future." Aunt Jerry tapped a finger to her mouth in thought. "When she's awake and rested, we will try to find out what is going on." She gave André a stern look. "Until then, you best stay here. I'm sure you've really ticked off your holder by not delivering when you had the chance. You won't be safe outside."

"I couldn't move even if I wanted to. I'm worn out. Age is not pretty," he joked tiredly.

"Speak for yourself," Aunt Jerry said with a twinkle in her eyes. "You're only a few years older than me."

Brooke gasped. "But he can't be! N'Réa isn't even thirty. She's human and so are you, Aunt Jerry."

"Being human has nothing to do with it," she replied. "It has to do with what we are."

Brooke blanched white as a sheet. "You mean I'm going to outlive everyone?" She pulled her legs up to her chin, the tunic falling to surround her in red color.

"No, love. André and I come from an old cut of cloth. Gloria was too, but she lived a human's life. N'Réa will too. I fear this will have a very strong adverse effect on André once he is free. You do know that?" she asked, her words no less meaningful.

He nodded. "If I am free, dead or otherwise, then so be it. If I can spend my eternity with Gloria and beg a thousand mercies from her, it would never be enough. And no less than I deserve." His haunted gaze slid closed as his thoughts turned inward.

"You're incredibly humble when you leave everything on the other side of the door," Morgan pointed out drily.

"N'Réa has a kind heart and more faith in me than I have in myself. I can still feel her," he whispered. "She is so much like Gloria." His voice cracked. "Saying I was wrong isn't strong enough."

Morgan clasped her still sleeping form to his body. "I'm taking her upstairs. Let me know if anything changes." And without another word and one last passing glance at her father, he rose and took her to the room she had used the previous weekend.

He eased her tenderly to the bed, removing her shoes and his to stretch out beside her on top of the coverlet. Her breathing was deep and regular, and her color had returned to normal. He held her close to his heart, letting her feel his warmth and his affection in his hold. Her exhaustion was complete. He inhaled sharply when he realized what she had done.

"You crazy woman. You tried to do it by yourself. The training you need is in self-control," he warned her. "No wonder the holder felt you. You shook the whole cage when you did that." He wondered if André was even aware to what extent she had pushed herself. Maybe that was why he was in such a friendlier mood. Maybe she'd had some success, and it had angered the other end of the leash.

He pulled the cover from the end of the bed over them and held her close, her sighing breath flowing over his skin. He marveled at the woman she was, unselfishly trying to help a man she had never known in her life, a man who had hurt her intentionally and deeply the day before. Maybe she had found more in him than any of them could have ever considered.

He began to wonder who and what N'Réa was, from what he had heard that morning to everything he had experienced because of her, had tasted, had felt. It was all happening so fast. In just a few short weeks he'd met her and made her his mate, his own vows of restraint useless against her vulnerability and her strength. He felt a wisp of a caress, a lingering touch of warmth spreading through him, and knew he was in her thoughts even in her sleep.

He brushed a tender kiss against her warm skin and held her tighter yet. He would do whatever he could to keep her safe. And maybe she would never find a reason to feel she would need to leave him after all.

Chapter Twenty

N'Réa sighed, stretching her arms, legs, and toes. All her limbs fell to the bed with a thump. She opened her eyes and focused on the ceiling. Morgan rested next to her, his arm thrown with a caging weight across her stomach. Not like she was in a hurry to get out of bed. There was a lot to do that night. And she knew it.

Her father was still alive, and he could be saved. The stain on his soul was horrible and debilitating, but destroyable. She swallowed, still tasting the faint bitterness of it on her tongue. She hadn't meant to do so much, but once she found a path, an avenue to follow, she'd kept moving forward. She'd felt the presence, the anger at her invasion, but she'd felt no fear. Aunt Jerry was calling this destiny, a test of life. She was as ready as she'd ever be. Brooke had four days to prepare for her destiny.

N'Réa's was a-learn-as-she-goes kind of day.

It made her smile. She felt the ebb and flow of her ability, a glow of energy she had never dared explore. She had kept her mind walled off, away from others, but had also managed to keep some of her own life secret from even herself. *Now that is a trick*, she thought with a touch of humor. Purposely avoiding one's self. Even Brooke hadn't known, she'd kept it so well hidden. Jeralynna had pulled it forward, had brought it into focus.

Good Lord, I'm a witch too! Her smile grew, and she started to laugh, cutting it off when Morgan moved and tightened his hold. Hysteria? Not this late in the day. Well past that point, but when she had a minute, she was going to laugh herself silly. She knew it.

Real magic. Real ability. Jeralynna knew she was empathic, and yet she didn't feel overwhelmed at all by any of their family. Mitch had never touched her, but Brooke did constantly and even Morgan, but she never felt overwhelmed by emotions or voices. Was it her or them? Was she controlling the impulses, or were they holding back? Was she stronger than she had ever guessed? She realized she was more than she could have ever known.

A real witch! She fought the urge to laugh again.

Her eyes fluttered down on a sigh when his hot tongue moved across sleep-warmed skin. *"You think too loudly,"* he chided.

N'Réa smiled again, broadly. "Sorry," she said.

"Forgiven," he mumbled as he kissed her neck. He slowed and stopped, his lips resting against her pulse, his arms tight around her, purposely keeping her close to him. "You scared me for a while there, vixen. You did too much."

"I know." She lifted her hands to rest on him, to touch. "I couldn't stop. I wanted to help, and I did, I think."

She felt the curve of his mouth on her skin. "You did. He even apologized for yesterday. Whatever you did took away some of the darkness I felt."

"The holder won't be happy that he's lost some of his edge. How long until sundown?" she asked, shifting gears.

Morgan lifted his head, looking at a wall clock. "Around an hour, I guess. It's after six."

She gasped. "No! I slept the day away." She pushed on his arm, but he didn't let her move.

"You needed it, stubborn woman. You passed out in my arms." He moved until he was positioned over her, one leg pinning her to the bed. He dropped little kisses on her jaw. "I don't want you taking that kind of a chance again, N'Réa. I don't want you to get hurt."

She shivered at the rough depth of his words. She arched with a heated moan when his hands cupped her breasts beneath her shirt. "I can't argue when you do that to me," she gasped, a mewled panting sound that made him laugh in a deep tone.

"Then I guess I will have to keep you in bed," he warned her. His lips burned a trail of fire to her collarbone, her insides melting into a molten rush of heat.

She cried out when he grasped a nipple between his teeth, her fingers spearing into the rich length of his dark hair. "Morgan, we don't have time," she groaned heavily. She tugged at him, feeling his resistance.

"I can't keep you in bed to keep you safe, can I?" Her heart ached at his tone. He sounded helpless to help her. He settled his head against her chest instead, smoothing her clothing back into place. "I don't want to lose you," he told her thickly. "Brooke was gone for three months. We all thought she had died. In a way, she had. No one knew what had happened to her. She was just...gone." He held himself above her, staring into her eyes with a wrenching intensity. "I couldn't live through that."

"I'm not doing this alone," she reminded him, her fingers tracking lightly on his face. "I won't die, and I won't be cast into a dimension. I love you. That's all the reason I need to not let anything bad happen."

"You are too good for me," he said, still holding her tight. "I'm going to lock you up and throw away the key after this." He moved from her, cool air touching her where his body's heat had been.

"You are a control freak," she teased him. He shrugged, then held out his hand.

"Come on, they've been patient." His words were once more gruff and definitely male in command.

She stopped him when he reached for the door. "Morgan, I do love you. Never doubt that. I hope someday you will understand and feel the same way." She leaned forward and brushed her lips against his. He swept her against him in response, a primal sound in his chest as he devoured her.

She took a deep breath when she was finally free. His gaze was hot and turbulent when he placed her on her feet. "I know, vixen," he murmured, brushing against her one last time.

"Let's go," she said, leading him downstairs to meet up with everyone else.

People were all over the house. Her feet dragged, taken by surprise. She felt Morgan's relief as he squeezed her hand in support and led her forward.

"Roman, Del," he said as he received and offered hugs of welcome. "Where's Adrian?"

The woman he had called Del, a tall woman with raven-black hair and piercing blue eyes said, "He's asleep in the spare, but he won't be for long. He's getting too curious to let something like sleep slow him down."

N'Réa hesitated, her hold on Morgan tightening.

"Don't worry, vixen. They're family and won't bite."

"Glad to know it," she managed in answer. She worked up a smile and shook hands. "Hi."

"Glad to meet you," Del said as she reached for her hand. N'Réa's eyes shot open as she held her hand warmly.

"You too?" She released the taller woman's hand quickly, unsure of what to do.

"Afraid so," she replied without heat, a glinting humor lighting her eyes. "The only sane person in the whole pack is Bram. Mitch couldn't even escape, and he's as white bread as his brother."

"Mitch is a sweetheart," Brooke shouted from the kitchen.

"Of course he is," Del called out soothingly. "She's very territorial for a she-wolf," she said, her tone amused.

"I heard that." A laughing shout came from the kitchen.

"When did I walk into the twilight zone?" N'Réa muttered.

Her head turned as a knock on the door floated to them. She heard as Selene and Bram came in. "Everyone?" she squeaked.

"Everyone," Morgan repeated. "There's strength in numbers."

"Not Mom and Dad," rumbled Roman's deep bass voice. "They send their love, though."

She craned her neck to stare up at the giant of a man who made Del look normal. "I feel so short," she muttered.

"Join the rest of us," Selene chuckled warmly. She reached for N'Réa and gave her a hug. "Welcome to the family," she said.

"Thank you," she said breathily. *Morgan, what is going on? Where is my father?*

He gave her a *that's a good question* glance. "I'll ask." He sauntered off to the kitchen to find out what was going on. He returned a few minutes later with Aunt Jerry and André in tow.

"Sorry, love. We didn't want to disturb you while you were resting." Aunt Jerry smiled at everyone as they gathered by the dining table. "It's too bad Mitch can't be here. Every little bit helps." Aunt Jerry cast a long look over everyone, a warning. "This is N'Réa's father and an old friend of mine," she began as introduction. "He's been chained, and I called everyone together because we need the women, and I know you males wouldn't stand to wait at home."

Roman crossed his arms. "Why do these things always involve you, Aunt Jerry?"

"Because I'm an old witch, and this is my only fun," she retorted drily. She clapped her hands together. "Ladies, we must prepare a circle of healing." Brooke walked up from behind and reached for one of N'Réa's hands.

"It'll be all right," she assured her in a quiet voice. "This will be a cakewalk compared to what I had to do."

"Men, you can wait in the kitchen. Brooke has cooked; just leave us something," she asked them with a saccharine-sweet smile. "Now then." She waved her hand. Dozens of candles lit up the living room. "André, are you ready? You remember everything we've discussed?"

He nodded. N'Réa's breath froze when he moved to stand in front of her, feeling Morgan's body tense. André's gaze was sad, and yet, somehow held faith in her. He kissed her on the forehead. "For all the years I threw away and all the pain I caused, I am deeply sorry." He turned and moved to the circle Selene was creating with several long, carved poles, no thicker than a finger.

She turned and found Morgan's intent gaze on her. "Save him," he whispered. "He needs you." He kissed her once, deeply, passionately, uncaring of the crowd of family gathered. Her lips quaked when he finally released her, holding her tenderly. "I believe in you."

Bram's quiet voice filtered into her thoughts, speaking from somewhere next to her. "The baby won't be affected, will it? She's nearly term."

Aunt Jerry's calm but decisive voice held all their attention. "No, Selene and her child are safe. We need her energy. Brooke, N'Réa, and myself will be handling the binds of the holder."

"I can help," Del offered. "I know I'm not as strong, but I can help."

"Then we will accept your help," Aunt Jerry said. "Everyone take your places. The sun has nearly set. André, face east; N'Réa, face your father." She did as told and sat cross-legged on the floor where more candles had been set and lit, their flickering glow beginning to fill the dimming room. Aunt Jerry waved a hand, and all the curtains closed. "Ladies," she beckoned, reaching for hands.

N'Réa instantly felt a rush of warmth. She smiled at her father, blocking out the concern she couldn't deny coming from the men standing on the edge of their circle, on the edge of her thoughts.

N'Réa heard the soft chant begin, never losing her visual contact with her father. She heard the first clap of thunder and knew the holder was aware. A solid warmth filled her, the energy of the women held in each other's hold. Brooke was a healer, Aunt Jerry was a powerful caster, Del was sentient. She felt all of their powers. Even Selene held a magnitude of compassion and healing, but no magical influence.

André's gaze slid closed as another crack of thunder shook the house. They opened again, slowly with a dark malevolence, piercing N'Réa with a glacial coldness and evil. She only smiled, refusing to accept the holder, to believe they would fail.

The chanting words grew in volume, their melody filling the room as she and her father battled. Except, it wasn't her father. It was the being who held her father's soul chained, and he was not happy. Voices rose and fell with ageless rhythm. She joined her voice as the chant began to make words in her mind, as the age-old spell unwound the evil that had scarred her father.

"Now, N'Réa!" Aunt Jerry's voice reached her. "Find your father and pull him to us."

N'Réa's head fell like a dead weight as another clap of thunder shook the windows, but to her it sounded like an echo, through walls and fabric, so faint when her mind opened up and searched for the light of her father's soul.

She gasped as a cold, clutching strength wrapped her up, began to strangle her, but she refused to give in. She fought with warmth and love and heard a hissing cry of pain as the sensation receded. She delved through layers of pain and guilt, forced her way into the darkest alcoves of his thoughts, and faced her father's tormentor. She shuddered as pure hatred rained down on her.

"Is that the best you have?" she taunted it. *"I will not fail."*

Suddenly pictures of her mother, bleeding and crying and in pain, tore through her thoughts, begging her to stop, to let her die in peace. She felt her resolve weaken, made her want to pull away. She couldn't hurt her to save him. She couldn't save him and let her die. She wanted to cry as indecision racked her.

"It's a trick, vixen. N'Réa, you are stronger than him. I am with you."

She felt warm arms encircle her waist, Morgan's strong thighs bringing her into the safety of his chest. She lifted her head and found the fiery, triumphant gaze of the beast holding the chain to her father's soul. Her eyes narrowed as she went forward again. She felt the support of the ones in the circle surge through her as she kept moving forward, deeper and deeper into his thoughts, searching for the light of his soul.

The cold of the holder's thoughts slapped against her, making her recoil, but she refused to give in. She knew her strength was lagging. She heard Morgan's voice but concentrated on the empty gaze before her. The voices of the women filled her, and she found the will to keep moving.

"You will leave him and never return," she told it confidently. *"You cannot win in this or take him from me!"* She forced her way past the vile energy holding her father enthralled and surrounded the light of her father's soul with peace, love, and acceptance.

A shriek of powerful rage split her mind, and she cried out as sharp talons ripped through her thoughts. André's head listed as his mouth fell open and a slimy gaseous substance began to rise from him.

Brooke's voice echoed in a sharp command and a band of light began to wrap around the vapors, taking shape over André's head. A high, angry scream filled the room as the light bound the small creature. André slumped to the floor, breathing raggedly as the women concentrated on the band of light until it was squeezed tight into a long, oblong shape. Nothing of the darkness could be seen through the shell.

N'Réa's gaze was fixed on the creature as Aunt Jerry slid her hands from hers and stood before the hovering globe. Her voice was strong and carried many promises of retribution if ever the demons who had cast the spell on her father decided to want to test their family again. She waved her hand in the air and a glass ball formed, and between her words and a motion of her hand, she pushed the creature into the glass ball. She tossed the glowing ball into the air, and it disappeared.

N'Réa collapsed into Morgan's hold and her eyes slid closed in relief.

"Foolish woman," she heard mumbled somewhere over her head. "You're going to have your hands full if she never follows orders. That's twice now." She could make out the admonishing words, filled with tender concern. "I tell her to find her father, and she battles the holder instead! I tell her to find out who has the chain, and she tries to heal him herself!" There was a disgusted sound as a towel was draped over her forehead.

"Love you too," she managed to say through a dry throat, then coughed when it hurt to breathe. She sipped at the warm tea at her lips, letting her head stay cradled against Morgan's shoulder.

"Training?" The voice spoke again. "She needs to be taught control, and self-preservation would be nice." N'Réa smiled at Aunt Jerry's ramblings.

"Will she be all right?" The voice was deep and held a touch of an accent. André had survived.

Warm kisses touched her skin. "She's too stubborn to die," muttered Morgan.

N'Réa's gaze flickered open, finding several sets of eyes watching her in return. One set of very wounded eyes were filled with deep concern.

"She can't be saved," she said simply. "She is gone."

André's head sagged weakly. "I know." He lifted it again. "Rest. We'll talk when you're able." He stood and left her alone with Morgan, the rest of the family fussing over her and the other girls. She felt spoiled. Morgan's arms cradled her tenderly.

"Promise me, no more. I can't take it," he said in a shaking voice. "I thought I lost you when you screamed."

"I did?" She shook her head slowly. "I don't remember that."

"I heard it; that was more than enough for me," he replied. He brushed a hand against her, touching her constantly. "You were incredible."

"I had help," she said demurringly, her lips lifting at his tone. "A lot of help." She turned her head and found Del resting on her husband's lap. Brooke was stretched out on the couch. "Where's Selene? She's all right, isn't she?" She pushed hard to sit up, washed with panic.

"She's fine. Bram is guarding her at the bathroom." Morgan chuckled. "I think she's ready to have her baby."

"I'm sure," she agreed.

"I'm not in the least bit worried about her, or anyone else. Just you," he told her very tenderly right into her ear. He rocked her in his strong arms for a while longer before he let her out of his reach.

"I'm ready to get up," she informed him. "I'm not feeling as bad or as tired as I did the first time." He nodded and helped her with a steadying hand to her feet. The living room was clean once more, no sign of candles or of the healing circle. "I think I'm going to hire your aunt's services for spring cleaning," she joked as he wrapped an arm around her waist. She walked over to Brooke and settled a hand on hers.

Brooke's liquid gaze was tired but pleased. "You did good," she said. N'Réa suffused her with warmth and felt a flow in response. Brooke sat up and laughed. "Damn, but you're a fast learner."

"It helps when I have good teachers." She moved to kneel in front of Del and did the same, lending strength and warmth.

"Welcome to the family," Del said, with Roman's arms holding her tight.

"Thank you for your help." Both women looked up smiling when a squeaky call came from upstairs.

"That would be the prince." She took a deep breath and eased from Roman's hold. Roman's unblinking gaze never left her as she disappeared upstairs. He focused on N'Réa.

"You energized her." His words were even and a touch thankful. "She's very cautious about letting others know."

"I understand," N'Réa said. "It was the least I could do. I have the blood tie. It was my battle. She's a wealth of understanding and acceptance."

Roman's smile grew, lightening his stern features. "I know it too. She's been a handful since the first meeting, and it hasn't changed." N'Réa felt Morgan's laughter as he tugged her up to stand at his side.

"Sounds like someone I could name," he said, glancing her way. She studied both brothers and realized how much they looked alike. Roman was tall and broad, Morgan almost as thick, with the same dark hair. They were cut from the same stone, no doubt about it.

"Worse," he murmured as he led her into the kitchen for a fresh cup of tea. "We're quads."

She almost stumbled. "Are you kidding? Quadruplets? But you're so different."

"Thank Mother for that," Brooke said, joining them. "Could you imagine me eight feet tall or Roman with blond hair? It just doesn't work." Her expression lit up with her laughter as she popped an olive into her mouth. "Man, I hate cravings. Can't eat anything normal. Last week I wanted sauerkraut. Nothing else, just sauerkraut."

Selene's laughter filled the kitchen as she and Bram joined them. "Wait for the ice cream to hit. I wanted, what was it, pistachio and cinnamon?" She shivered delicately. "It sounds awful and looked worse, but the kid liked it." Bram chuckled as his arms looped around her waist.

"Christmas colors was what I called it," he informed them.

N'Réa looked around. "Where are Aunt Jerry and André?" she asked.

Brooke's tone dropped. "They stepped outside to talk about things. He's having a hard time realizing he was misled into believing Gloria would be coming back. She wanted to, but she knew it was one or the other once the battle began. It was another ploy. If he had succeeded with you, he still would be in the same position he is now."

"So the images I saw were real?" N'Réa felt faint. "I killed my mother to save him?" A sick, weak feeling filled her.

"No," Brooke replied, stretching out a steadying hand. "The holder had her images ingrained into the enchantment. She's been gone for a long time. Saving him was her last effort."

She rubbed her forehead. "I'm never going to get used to this."

"Sure you will. Remember my tale?" Brooke laughed and hugged N'Réa, even though Morgan refused to let her go. "It's part of being in the pack. We all have trials and our own paths, but we all meet back to be family. That doesn't go away." N'Réa shared the hug, then leaned into Morgan's strength. She would need to talk to her father soon.

"Delilah was an undercover agent when she met Roman," Morgan said. "Bram and Selene have a connection that started years before they even met. You will fall right into the circus that is us, I promise you."

"It doesn't pay to talk about me behind my back," Del warned, carrying a healthy and excited Adrian. "I'm mean and bitchy; just ask the giant."

"She's also a damn good shot," he joked as he wrapped his arms around her waist and dropped a kiss on her shoulder, then started to play peek-a-boo with the baby.

"Would you like to hold him? He's met all his aunts and uncles already."

N'Réa reached out for the giggling little ball of energy. "He's heavy!" She gasped. Adrian weighed like an anchor in her hold.

"Built to sink," Roman said with a touch of pride. "He's going to be huge."

"I never would have guessed," she replied, dropping little kisses on his smooth skin.

She felt Morgan's penetrating, watchful gaze on her and didn't even have to reach out to know what he was thinking. She felt it too. Adrian was a dark-haired devil of an angel, and she knew instinctively how she looked holding him on her shoulder. His solid weight and baby warmth filled her. Then, she felt Morgan's desires flowing over her like a silken caress. *And he calls me stubborn*, she thought, tender amusement filling her. She sighed as she breathed kisses on Adrian's smiling face. "He's beautiful, but when he's old enough he'll be handsome too." Roman's grin went from corner to corner.

"Now that's a woman who understands. Men are not beautiful."

"No, you're stubborn, whiny — " groused Del.

"Just stop!" Selene cried, fighting back the laugh. "This house is too small for that much testosterone."

"Damn, I thought I did good with this one," Brooke said with a look of playful consternation.

"N'Réa?" She stopped laughing at the quiet call, nodding when she caught Aunt Jerry's gaze.

"Be right back," she said and slipped from Morgan's hold, offering Adrian to his parents. He caught her by the wrist, his fingers wrapping her possessively. Her entire body tingled in his hold. "I'll be all right. I feel fine," she said. He let her go, and she thought she heard a sigh escape from him. It made her heart flip.

Chapter Twenty-One

Drowsy fingers drifted up and down N'Rea's body, bringing out a soft purr of pleasure as she lay in the warm cocoon of Morgan's arms. The windows were open to his room, and the distant sounds of a night owl in the trees reached her. It was late but she couldn't find the impulse to fall asleep as the moon rose above, sending shafts of light across the bed and various naked body parts.

"You're still worried for your dad, aren't you?" His breath fanned against her throat as his fingers continued their random traveling up and down her body.

"Yes, I guess I am. He feels so disillusioned, so drained and used. He took the reality of those first minutes very hard after he woke up." She couldn't hide the strain of her concern from her voice or her thoughts. "I guess I'm glad Aunt Jerry offered to give him help to work this out."

"Don't let the fact that he left with her worry you. She's very good at what she does and can help him through this. Remember how she refused to tell everything?" She nodded as he nuzzled her throat, bringing out a sensual smile for his efforts. "That there was more to his decision to be healed than his own wishes?"

"How could I forget. Your aunt is the queen of drama." She shivered when his tongue traced her ear. He could melt her entire body with a look, make her want with a touch. It was almost scary, except she knew he reacted the same way.

"She knew the reality would make him change his mind because of the influence of the spell. She knew he was going to be shattered when he faced it. He had to believe in the healing for himself first."

"And she can help heal his mind and his soul. I thank her for doing that," N'Réa said sincerely. She lay still for several long minutes, letting the tender swish of his fingers and the warm feeling of his breathing cascade over her. "Your family is truly remarkable. I've never felt so much acceptance in my life. Even from Delilah, since I hadn't met her yet. She was made for Roman."

"And you were made for me, vixen."

She followed the movement of his lazy fingers with her eyes. "So, now that I've been accepted as one of the pack and you won't have to keep me or yourself separate, do you think you could say it?"

"What?" His fingers stilled while tension rode up and down his body, but she refused to back down. *Stubborn is as stubborn does.*

"I love you, Morgan." She lifted a hand to wrap fingers through his hair. "And personally, I would really hate to have our child come into this world knowing you can't admit to loving me."

She felt his thoughts jump and run like wild rabbits. She bit the inside of her cheek to not laugh out loud at him.

"A child? But you said it wasn't a good time."

"Don't try to blame me, buster. That was over a week ago, and you never mentioned condoms again. I love you and I'm willing to suffer under your thumb, keep your ego from getting too inflated. But," she rolled to the side to find his shocked gaze, "honey, that's what happens when you make love to me. We make babies. At least one."

His breathing shortened as his irises dilated. "You mean…" He stopped talking. He started shaking under her hand.

"Yes, Morgan. Tonight, without a doubt." She brushed a soft kiss across his mouth, feeling the waves of shock clearly as they rode over him. "So, for the sake of our son, could you admit it?" She didn't want to out and out demand it, but she could twist his arm a little.

"A son?" Shock tripled on his expression. "You're sure?"

She nodded, a calm feeling settling over her. "I love you, for everything you are, for everything you have given me. Don't make me pull out the big guns," she warned, her voice dropping to a silky purr.

He moved to rise over her. "Big guns?" he prompted with a wicked grin, his voice and his gaze losing its shocked quality. "Just what might that be?" He trailed his hand over her again.

"I can't tell everything, but I can guarantee you will love and hate it," she threatened with a taunting smile. Her hand moved to curl over his erection, and he tossed his head back as a hiss of pleasure escaped from him. He looked completely torn when her touch disappeared.

"Tease," he accused.

"Bingo." She laughed at the twist of his mouth.

"Hand me my jeans," he said. He added a please when she arched an eyebrow at the order. "I didn't want to do it tonight. I knew how tired and worried you were." He caressed the side of her neck with a tempting swirl of his tongue as she reached beyond the bed and his jeans floated to her. "You are going to be so useful."

"Only if you behave yourself," she laughed, but handed him his jeans. She waited in confusion as he pulled something from the pocket, then tossed them onto the floor. He rose to sit silently on the bed facing her, unashamed of his nakedness.

His gaze was hot, tender, adoring when he rose to find hers. "When Mom got this, it came from her side. It's older than most of the pieces in the family. It's rumored to even predate the amulet Brooke has control of. It was once given in love and can only be passed on in love, or it loses its significance in our family. Mom has no ability, but her grandmother did and was able to see certain things. She was the one who decided which son would pass down what piece. It seemed strange even back then, so many years ago, because she knew there would be four of us when a multiple birth had never happened in our history, in our family."

His words flowed over her, warm and inviting as she listened to the history of the ring. It glistened between his fingers, seeming to draw the light of the moon into its swirling mysteries. She scooted up on the bed, resting against the headboard as he continued.

"This ring was given through our mother's line for centuries until this generation, when we were given the right to pass down our heritage. I never considered the meaning of it until I met you." He stopped and seemed to gather courage for his next words. "It's been said that the wearer of this ring, when it comes to pass, will be a person of like ability to ourselves to help bring our line longevity and reunite those who have long since been lost to us. I don't know how much of it is truth and how much is just fanciful storytelling, but I always wondered why we were the last of the line." His gaze was intense as he thought inward and she felt her heart trip, seeming to find his rhythm with hers.

He stood from the bed and sank to the floor to kneel, his hands holding hers as he slipped the ring on her finger. "I witnessed your unending faith in not only yourself but your family. I witnessed your unbelievable strength to not give in when every bone in your body cried for it." His words were thickening as he split his soul wide open for her. "I have felt every ounce of love and affection you have for me and my pack, seeing it in your gaze, feeling it in your touch, and hearing it in your words. Even when you were exhausted, you saw to their comforts first. You are as unselfish as you are stubborn, and I would gladly claim you as my mate and my wife." He slowly lifted his face into the moonlight, a liquid shimmer in his gaze as he swallowed.

"N'Réa, I love you so much it scares me sometimes. Seeing what you did today, how much you gave, I have never felt fear like that and I don't want to ever again. I will stand as your protector until I can no longer breathe. I will stand over you and our son until the last sunset of our lives."

He lifted her hand, sliding the ring to its proper place on her.

"It's beautiful," she said, choking out the words. "You're beautiful, perfect." She caressed his hair, curling to hold the weight of him in her palm. "You give me that strength, Morgan. Don't you know that? You give me the courage to face the impossible, to know who and what I am, because I know I will always wake up in your arms, cherished at your side, and held in your thoughts." Tears ran unhindered down her cheeks as she fell into the softened gray depths of his soul and found his staring back at her. "You found me when I was too scared to breathe, too cautious to hope. When I feared the very dreams sending you to me. Your faith is mine," she said simply. "I couldn't have turned away, and believe me, I tried, wall after wall, but your strength called to me. I need you in my life. I love you. That will never go away."

His hands shook when he lifted them to touch her reverently. His lips quivered against hers as his heart tripped in a heavy tattoo against her ribs.

Her voice was raspy when she spoke again sometime later, his body half covering hers, sprawled in the moonlight. "Morgan, what was in your dreams?"

He sighed a pure sound of blissful contentment with his arms wrapped around her, his chin on her shoulder. "I would have the most incredible dreams about a woman with the deepest eyes of green and hair that held flame in its darkness."

"You're very eloquent for a man who usually doesn't say much."

She giggled when he tickled a rib. "I had a long time to endure these particular dreams. Every night, my vixen came to me." He stretched with a languorous sound. "And now she's here to stay. Why? I can feel your questions."

She licked her bottom lip. "I never mentioned mine in detail. I just knew that the day you walked in, I was in trouble." She played with the weight of the gemstone on her finger. "I didn't make the connection because I was so careful with everything about myself. I didn't even know where to look for answers." His fingers massaged, offering comfort in his touch.

"And?"

"Now, it makes more sense." She took a long deep breath, then blurted, "I think she was right."

"Who, vixen?" he asked drowsily.

"Your great-grandmother."

"You're talking in circles, sweetheart." She smiled briefly at his use of the endearment. "What do you mean?"

"My dream. I never feared the wolf in my dream."

"Because it was me," he pointed out with a nip at an ear.

"But there were two."

That got his attention. He lifted off his shoulder, his eyes sharp in the muted darkness. "Two?" he asked cautiously. He wrapped a hand through her hair, and she knew his need was to know she was there, that she was real. "Tell me your dream, vixen."

"It always went the same way," she began carefully. "I would be outside and it would change from day to night, like a movie scene." She resisted the urge to fidget, determined to stay calm. "There were trees, then a meadow, and out of the trees a huge black wolf came into view. As it came closer, I could see the eyes. They were gray — yours. It was like I was watching from outside the scene, watching as it came into the clearing, and it howled. Just a short sound, like a name. Or a calling."

She stopped talking suddenly, playing with the ring nervously. "Never mind, I'm sure it's just me being over stressed from my day to think this is possible."

Morgan was quick to shake his head. "Finish it," he said, a hoarseness in his words.

"I'm certifiable. I know," she told him, but continued when his intensity never changed. "I could see and hear and smell things like I was there, watching from nearby. Then another body came from the trees. Another black wolf, but when they met, it was me, at least, I think it was me. It felt like it was supposed to be me, you know, when you're dreaming, when it feels like you? Being held in arms, seeing your eyes again. No face, no body. Just a sense of peace and safety. I never saw anything about the wolf to say it was me, exactly," she said. "But there was always a sense of rightness about it."

"How often did you have these dreams?" he asked, a compelling sound in the room.

"Every night, like yours. I know it's crazy." She reached around him to pull him closer, but he didn't comply.

His silence was lengthening, and she began to feel even more foolish. "I told you, this isn't a big deal. I let my imagination run amok."

"But it is possible." He breathed slowly, speaking in barely more than a whisper. "The will said no one but me was allowed to pass down the ring."

"Coincidence," she told him. "I'm as out there as Brooke and Aunt Jerry. There isn't any way I could be part of a lost line of shape-shifters too. Someone would have figured it out by now."

"When was the last time you were sick?" he asked her. Excitement arced from his body with electric color.

She shrugged. "I don't know. Fifteen years at least, more than that I guess. Why?"

"Your blood. After puberty the changes are evident, but if you've never taken shape, then only half the mutation is complete."

"I haven't given blood or needed it." She lifted herself up on elbows. "You believe this? I'm telling you, Morgan. It was just a dream that brought us together."

"No, there's more to it. I can feel it." He jumped from the bed and threw open the windows fully. He took a deep breath. "Tell me, is there something out there?"

She rolled her eyes but joined him and inhaled. "Trees and dirt." She shook her head. "Morgan," she tried to say. His eyes glowed. He must have been a heartbreaker when he was younger. He was sinfully gorgeous to her now.

"No, wait. Your senses haven't developed because you haven't ever changed. You're still mostly human.

It's why your arm didn't heal at all before Brooke helped you. You haven't finished your transitions." He reached for her hands, pleading with her. "Let me help you. Now I know why certain things have bothered me since the beginning. I've always had a picture in my mind, but it was never one of us. A wolf, a black wolf that did and didn't belong to us. No one else knows about it. The few times I've mentioned it, I always got a blank answer. I guessed it was my imagination, but it's possible. We've never known any others of the lineage."

"And now you think I'm it?" She fought to not laugh. "Morgan, this is insane. I'm tired, and so are you."

"I couldn't sleep if I wanted to, wondering about this." He kissed her lovingly. "Please, N'Réa. I won't let anything happen to you. If it isn't to be, then I won't love you any less."

He said it with such an aching tenderness. She let her shoulders loosen as she relented. "All right, but you better be prepared for it to not be anything."

"And I think you should be prepared in case I'm right about this. Agreed?" He squeezed her fingers once.

"Agreed." She smiled for him. "All right, what do I need to do?"

"I'm thinking to when we started training for it. We began before puberty so when the changes came we wouldn't be overwhelmed. You won't have that luxury if this happens the way I'm thinking it will." Worry crossed his gaze for the first time. "It will be an overload. Sounds and smells and things you've never encountered. Everything will become more intense. You will have urges, but you have to remember you are wolf with a human brain. You can rationalize and think like a person, even though your body will be animal."

"All right. I'll stay close to you. I promise."

"Your faith humbles me some days," he admitted, his hands caressing hers in his hold. Then a grin split his face once more. "Okay, I'm going to help because it's going to feel different at first. It isn't painful, but you may experience vertigo." He captured her gaze and wondered for the first time if maybe he might be right, he was so sure. "Look deep into yourself, find the beat of your heart, feel the rush of your blood throughout your body. Feel the sensations become a part of you; a warmth will grow, will build on itself. Can you feel it?"

She nodded, feeling herself become swept up in the energy of his words, her eyes sliding closed to enjoy this, for better or worse.

"Let the heat build, let it flow with your blood, it will have its own beat, its own rhythm. It will pulse against your ears, grow louder." She leaned in a little as his voice changed in volume, deepened. "Picture the wolf, see yourself as a strong beast, pure and earthy." His hands drifted from hers, and she missed his warmth. "Your body will feel the difference the first time," he was saying, "but it shouldn't fight it. It's a spell woven through time, a part of each of us."

She felt the surge of her blood, could find the heat as it built and grew, deepened into its own force. There was an odd sensation on her skin, then of falling, and she instinctively reached out, then felt balanced again.

She let out a breath and opened her eyes. *"All right, I warned you. Why are you all the way up there?"*

Crickets sang on the night air, and a frog leaped on the ground beneath the window. An owl hooted in the distance. Strong scents of pine filled the room on a meandering, gusted breeze. She shook her head, trying to clear the overwhelming overload of information.

"Would you like a mirror? I don't know what to do when a wolf goes into cardiac arrest from shock," he said through an excited laugh. His smile was huge, and she could hear his heart beating like a caged bird in wonder. He smelled like Morgan and sex and all male. She wondered when that had ever happened.

"What are you talking about?" She blinked. *"I'm not talking, am I?"* Unexpected nails clicked on wood when she inadvertently stepped back.

He fell to his knees, his eyes filling with concern as her shock grew. "Don't panic. You are perfectly safe. I swear to you."

"Oh God! I didn't, I mean I did, but what...I mean how...I think I'm going to faint." And she sprawled out on the wooden floor at his feet. *Is that my nose*, she whispered to herself, flinging what should have been a hand over her face. *Paws?* Her gaze shot up in panic. *"This is temporary, right?"* Please let it be.

"Completely. You control it. And no, you're not werewolf," he said, tossing out the answer to her next question. "You are the most incredible, unbelievable woman. I can't believe you are mine." He said it respectfully. "Mom and Dad are going to fall over when I tell them."

"Um, could we keep this between us, just for a while." She lifted herself to her feet again, more than a little shaken up. *"It's been a busy month, if you know what I mean."*

"Of course, vixen." He shot her a grin. "I may need to find you another nickname."

"I like vixen just fine," she informed him with a haughty tone to her thoughts. She took a deep breath and found what he had outside their window. There were two does in his yard.

She could find scents and odors easily, could hear like nothing she'd ever experienced. She was glad she was still inside. Even the wood scent of the room was strong.

"Would you mind if I held you for a minute?" he asked cautiously. "You don't have to, but I — "

He fell silent when she moved forward and pushed into his chest. "*I need it too.*" She gathered her dazed thoughts as his learning touch roamed over her new shape, gave her dimension to what she couldn't quite comprehend. "*Is the baby safe?*"

"He's fine," he reassured her, his voice as loving as his touch. "You can't go picking fights and have to watch what you eat, but if anything, he's going to be strong and healthy and more than ready to join us when his time comes." She felt as he pressed his cheek into her shoulder, his emotions right on the surface for her to find, to comfort her. "Are you ready to change back?"

"*Yeah, I think this is enough excitement for one night.*"

He gave her an understanding look. "We'll run some other time. And I better warn you, things are going to be different now, but I'm right here with you. Your other half, and occasionally, your better half." He laughed when she nipped at his arm. "I thought you might say something like that."

She felt the laughter herself as he helped her find the strength of her heartbeat to bring herself to standing on two feet. She collapsed right into his open arms.

"I can't believe it," she said breathily as he swept her up to set her down on the bed, filled with awe. "And I can do that whenever?"

"Well, use common sense," he said, stroking her body with his free hand. "I wouldn't recommend shopping malls or the dog pound." She thumped his shoulder, making him laugh harder.

"No wonder you all live out of town and far apart. Territory issues, huh?" she teased him.

"It was known to happen growing up, but we've settled down and can even behave in a group."

"You're formidable in a group. You should probably know that." She snuggled up against him. Her brain almost fried on her next thought.

"What is it?" he asked, instantly concerned when her body stiffened and her breathing became ragged.

Her eyes glazed over with fear, blurring the room. "Do you realize I'm like some really huge freak? Magic and shifter, and good Lord, who knows what else?" Panic welled up in her. Her hand lifted to her throat. "What if someone finds out? What if I'm seen, or someone gets a clue? I could endanger the entire family!"

"Don't go hysterical on me," he said, soothing her with a touch and his voice. "You're fine. You haven't been found out for anything before now, and you still need training from Brooke. You said before you hadn't felt anyone's curiosity before me. Believe me, you learn to live peacefully." He pulled her close, pulling up the covers to finally fall asleep. Rays of light were beginning to turn the sky gray. "I'll keep you safe and remind you when you get out of hand."

His fingers burrowed into her hair, holding her next to the warmth of his skin. His thumb brushed in relaxing circles across her temple, and she fought to even her breathing. "You're right. I'm glad I don't have to be anywhere for a few days. I need to digest this."

"You are perfectly safe here," he whispered to her. "And I will be here when you wake up."

She curved into his body. "That's good. I definitely need sleep." His lips brushed against hers several times until she felt herself fade into a calm nothing.

Epilogue

"Knock him on his ass!" N'Réa yelled into the arena, and Morgan bowed in answer. "He owes Dirk for that last rude comment," she muttered under her breath. "That man has no dignity."

"He's not so bad when he's not in character," Brooke said over a laugh.

She shot Brooke a wry glance, knowing perfectly well she was trying to be fair. Dirk had a reputation, and it was well earned. The clash of swords began again, and N'Réa focused on the men in the dust bowl of the arena. Since the storm at the beginning of the event, there hadn't been a single hint of rain.

The tournament was nearly over, and Morgan was putting his stake in with every other man on the team. Brooke reached for her hand when Morgan went down hard. "Breathe, baby, breathe," she murmured, feeling the pain leave her chest when he sucked in air.

He stood, shaking his head, acknowledging a good knockdown to Dirk, but he raised his sword and took the offensive again. It wasn't even a minute later when Dirk's broadsword made a spectacular arc in the sunlight to land with a sound thump in the dirt.

She jumped up to her feet, screaming for Morgan along with every other voice in the arena. He took his knee in front of King Henry, slipping his helmet free and shaking his length of black hair. He winked at her as he walked from the arena.

"He took third place!" N'Réa managed around an excited squeal. "He really did it! I knew he could do it!"

She practically jumped over heads and people to get out of the stands while the next fight was being called. She ran, skirts hiked up around her knees, until she reached the pavilion and awning for the staging area. She raced through the gate, uncaring that it was off limits, and found him accepting congratulations from other fighters. When he saw her, he stopped talking to everyone and strode straight up to her.

He was the most handsome, incredible, strong—

His voice filled her mind, and her heart thudded against her ribs in happiness.

"You keep that up, and I'll never fit inside another helmet ever again."

Her laughter carried far and wide under the awning. He held his arms out to her and she leaped into them. "I knew you could do it," she said, dropping kiss after kiss on his stubble rough jaw. He backed her up until she was pressed between him and the wall. He settled his helmet to balance on the rail and unclasped his gauntlets to drop inside it.

"Armor was never conducive to romance; I don't care how good Ivanhoe is on TV." His eyes sparkled at her light laughter, their gray depths capturing her and captivating her at the same time. His mouth was hot and demanding when he claimed his prize from her.

Her hands flew up to twine into the damp fullness of his hair, holding him as close as his shirt of chain would allow. His heat, his need, filled her until she was practically wrapped around him. The want spread until she was a wiggling mass, a damp heat, an aching only he could cure.

"Now that's a compliment," he whispered for her ears alone, a wicked smile on his lips as he inhaled deeply. He licked his lips in appreciation, then touched his tongue to her mouth in a sensual tasting of her sensitive skin and she went up like a flame with a muffled cry. "Oh man," he said against her mouth. "I will never, ever get enough of that."

He held her close, hiding her from passersby and curious stares until her breathing evened out. She couldn't help it if he drove her completely out of her mind. She lived for it.

"You better behave. There are kids around, you know," she said, her voice still husky and slightly breathless.

"And thankfully not allowed back here. I forget everything when I'm around you." He nipped at her chin as his hands loosened but didn't let her go completely. "Have you talked to Duncan about the next event?"

She smiled at his valiant attempt to distract the both of them. "We're set. He's going to be so surprised."

"Do you think he knows?"

She smiled when she found that devilish gleam in his eyes. She shook her head, her smile growing. "Not a clue," she said, still resting against the walls, feeling very pliant. "How much is the placement?"

"Around seven, I think. That should take care of this event for the team, for my costs and Cale. He deserves more for all the labor he puts into everything." He shot a look out into the stands, looking for his sister. "I wish Brooke would tell me how much she spent so I could pay her back. If I'm going to do this for the hell of it regularly, I should pay her back."

"She wants to have her purpose too," N'Réa explained, running a hand across the red tunic, following the trim down his shoulder. "She doesn't see it the way you do. This is her contribution."

He tapped the tip of her nose and stepped back. "I know." He looked up as the horns signaled the end of the duels for the afternoon. "You ready to go back to camp?"

"Anywhere," she said breathily as she reached for his chiseled lips. His eyes darkened, and she heard his breath catch. Her eyes slid closed as the flame hit her again, his arm sweeping around her and pulling her tight to his body.

"Keep it up, wench. I'll carry you the whole way to camp over my shoulder," he threatened against her lips in a voice that promised much.

She twirled playfully from Morgan's embrace with a tempting, taunting wickedness. "Catch me, and we'll talk." Then she took off at a skipped run, her hair flying like an onyx banner as tendrils danced across her cheeks, her skirt clutched high and his rich laughter following behind.

About the Author

With more than fifty e-books currently to her credit and several books in print, Diana Castilleja has kept busy since she started writing professionally in late 2004.

Diana currently resides in central Texas with her husband and son. When not focusing her energy on her family and her writing, she loves to travel and haunt bookstores. She's lived in several states across the south and midwest, as well as traveling to Mexico. With moving every year or changing schools since the fourth grade to her sophomore year, she learned that reading was a fast escape. The freedom to read about anything and everything has fueled her adult imagination. She also enjoys romance, horses, and yes, still loves to read.

Visit her online at www.DianaCastilleja.com

PURPLE SWORD PUBLICATIONS, LLC
www.purplesword.com